FORTY ONE

Lesia Daria

Matador
9 Priory Business Park
Kibworth Beauchamp
Leicestershire LE8 0RX, UK
Tel: (+44) 116 279 2299
Fax: (+44) 116 279 2277
Email: books@troubador.co.uk
Web: www.troubador.co.uk/matador

ISBN 978 1784624 125

British Library Cataloguing in Publication Data.
A catalogue record for this book is available from the British Library.

Printed and bound by CPI Group (UK) Ltd, Croydon, CR0 4YY
Typeset in Minion Pro by Troubador Publishing Ltd

Matador is an imprint of Troubador Publishing Ltd

MIX
Paper from
responsible sources
FSC® C013604

To C. for seeing through me,
and M. for seeing me through

ACKNOWLEDGEMENTS

L ike many books, *Forty One* began in solitude, a short burst of creativity that grew into a bigger project. But without outside opinion, cooperation and camaraderie, I doubt I would have lasted the six years it took to complete the work. Family members, friends and colleagues, and sometimes complete strangers, seemed happy to give time, advice and sympathy, which eased the journey of writing and editing. Later I found this help was indispensible: others seemed to know better than I did when to turn a blind eye to perceptions of fault, or errors to be dealt with later, and when mistakes needed immediate correction.

I'd like to thank those who helped in the order of how the book came to be, so my earliest readers first: Sonia Franco and May Chien Busch, who, in casting their lovely eyes on something more stream-of-consciousness than novel, weren't overly critical. Their comments propelled me to improve the story rather than shelve it and give up. Next the Writers' Workshop, run by Harry Bingham, introduced me to a wider world of agents and publishers, setting me on the course for eventual publication. Workshop novelists-turned-editors Emma Darwin and Debi Alper provided constructive, encouraging feedback at a dangerous time, the middle of the process, when rejections and re-writing seemed a never-ending, perilous traverse. Joanna Moult's editing services gave me another positive push.

Coming across Richard Beard and the National Academy of Writing at the Free Word Centre in London was a game changing event. Just as rejections and self-doubt threatened to overwhelm,

Richard's intense but uplifting writing course tested my resolve and commitment to perfection, as well as ideas and style. Without Richard and fellow-writers Eamon Somers, Sally Hodgkinson, Sue Blundell, Laura Ashton and Mike Aylwin, the book wouldn't have progressed to a publishable version. They merit the highest praise for their good humour and persistence; Mike in particular deserves some kind of superhuman award for picking apart existential crises at Waterloo.

Next I'd like to thank The Literary Consultancy and the wonderful editor Alan Mahar, who helped me critically rethink the pacing at the end of the story, asking all the tough and right questions. The last rewrite made the book what it is. Thanks also go to volunteer readers who reviewed part or all of *Forty One* in its final stages: Sarah Maynard, Fiona Hinton and Jane Ince. Clive Ince and Arnon Woolfson steered me away from copyright trouble, for which I am deeply grateful.

Close friends Adrianna Oleksiyenko-Stech and Victoria Pillay provided native-fluent language assistance in Polish and French, respectively, while Laurent Lhermitte good-naturedly put up with all sorts of queries and visits, as did Andrzej and Nadia Kręciproch.

It was an absolute joy to work with Steve Varman, my photographer and book cover and website designer, as well as a moment of enlightenment to feel part of a creative team. I am also indebted to my proofreader Helen Baggott for her sharp eye and professionalism over the course of three proofreads. At Matador, Rosie Grindrod, Naomi Green and Alice Graham helped me through the process of publishing, printing, distribution and marketing. The team at Matador not only turned *Forty One* into a physical reality and flawless e-book but launched me into the world of internet and bookshop sales. The Alliance of Independent Authors and the Women Writers, Women's Books group on Facebook kept my spirits up as I waded through the swift-running waters of self-publishing.

No amount of thank-yous can really repay family and friends who put up with the strains of a writer's life, but I would like to mention especially Rowena Poulter, who pioneered for me the way to balance home life and a creative career. The women of Wey-Fit boot camp also never failed to cheer, reminding me that writing a book is an accomplishment, whatever happens next.

Most of all, for sheer staying power and vast help in editing, I want to thank Christopher Jackson. Christopher readily agreed to read and comment on *Forty One*, not realising until too late that he'd embarked on a very long trip. Perhaps he thought (and I too) that it would take a few days. But weeks and months later, Christopher was still determinedly on the case. A year on, without complaint, Christopher continued to comment and query, antagonise and dismiss, cheer and support, answer hopeless emails and unfailingly stand by me as a writer and *Forty One* as a work worth all that effort. He understood and believed in what I was trying to achieve. So more than any beta-reader I might have found and certainly beyond the call of duty of any friend, Christopher deserves a lifetime of credit and gratitude.

Finally I want to thank the person who made it possible from beginning to end: my husband Mike Scholey. Without his unwavering belief and financial support, there would not have been the time, energy or resources necessary to create *Forty One*. He literally provided what Virginia Woolf advised so long ago: money and a room of one's own. He also responded with reasoned calm whether I was in the depths of doubt and despair or the peaks of euphoria. He always came out positive, and for that, Mike, I am eternally grateful.

PART ONE

'She always harboured my criticism:
it was only praise that slid from her like the snow.'

Graham Greene, *The End of the Affair*

From across the room, she sizes them up, the new enemy – or more accurately, a former ally that's betrayed a confidence. Of course it's preposterous to view curtains this way – hard to fathom how it even happened – but in the rare glare of morning sun, the damage is unmistakeable. Silently and stealthily the sun, not life giver but destroyer, obliterating sections of the fine fabric. Now hanging threads exposed the thin lining underneath; possibly the whole thing would need repair.

She sighs, eyes her text. Always that same feeling. Sent, gone, irretrievable. Setting down the mobile, she knows what he might say but hopes he'll give her what she wants: simple guidance.

The home phone begins its tone-deaf ring. She hurries to the kitchen to pick up.

'Hi, got your message.' Harry's faraway voice instantly recedes to another conversation. 'Better wait on that.'

She returns to the family room, waits automatically.

'Sorry, I don't understand.'

He's probably talking to her now, so she begins.

'Me neither. But the curtains are frayed. We have to get them repaired before they fall apart. I sent you the quote.'

'What?' Disappearing again, he mutters something, returns. 'Are you serious? Four hundred pounds? A few years after spending a bloody fortune?'

The first battle line drawn. She doesn't answer.

'They were supposed to last a long time, Eva, forever. Things were on their fourth generation when I left home. Why the hell is it so much to fix them?'

'I don't know,' she says flatly. 'But frankly, all soft furnishings are a form of extortion – in this country anyway – and physically it is a big thing. No choice on cost.'

'No choice,' he repeats, as if she'd uttered some dreaded phrase. 'We *did* have a choice and you chose them. Obviously a costly mistake.'

Memories percolate to anger: true, the curtains had been expensive, but not the material, which she'd cleverly procured from a discontinued bolt reduced for sale. The problem was sheer size, the nature and magnitude of the project. Though he might have taken the view – oh well, torn curtains, small thing in the scheme of life.

'Eva?'

'Maybe they haven't worn well, but practicalities aren't the only things that matter, Harry. No one can foresee every potential problem.'

'Not every problem, but major ones. You should have known.'

She ignores the supposition, improbable as ever.

'I'm sorry too that they're damaged, but everything disintegrates eventually. Maybe I focused too much on aesthetics, but colour, texture, tone do make a difference. Curtains don't just shut out the world; they're integral to a room, a whole wall to look at, especially when the spotlights are on. I wanted them to radiate warmth as well as provide privacy.'

'Function first,' he interjects. 'No use if it doesn't *work*.'

She feels her whole body tensing.

'Actually I got in touch so you could help find a solution. But you want to lay blame? Fine, who told me where to go in the first place? Wasn't it your idea – *buy locally*? As I recall, that was the sole advice you gave years ago,' she stops, recalling the rush to move in, both of them balancing renovations with a newborn and his new job.

That way you can always go back if you have trouble.

More stale words, some other popular wisdom that didn't reflect reality – another thing he got wrong.

He says nothing. Maybe he's no longer listening.

'If you remember,' she continues, 'I was new to England, first house. That upholstery shop didn't advise me properly. They didn't take into account the south-facing window.'

Yes, she had been the novice, a foreigner at their mercy.

4

'Then why don't you go back and take it up with them?'

'Because it's closed.'

'Closed as in shut down?'

'Yes, so although we're in trouble now, there is no going back.' She says it emphatically but doubts he'll remember.

'What did I tell you, the recession's coming – banks in meltdown, small shops going under – these are just the early victims. Wait and see, we'll have much bigger failures later on.'

Focusing on doom he's still failed to appreciate her ingenuity, finding anyone to patch them. As if it were so easy to fix an old mess rather than begin anew.

'You might give me some credit, Harry. How hard I try to keep things running smoothly. I'm doing my best, but when I ask for help, I get criticism. At least you get satisfaction from a job well done – pay, promotions – whereas here, it's the same day after day, like being trapped in some kind of prison...'

'Wait, Eva, *prison*? That's what you call our house?'

'No, I...'

'I'm out here working like mad, you interrupt me for *this*, don't take any responsibility, then say what I'm providing is some kind of incarceration?'

'No, that's *not* what I'm saying.' But she knows it's too late.

'I have to go.' He hangs up.

Too late. She hadn't landed on the right word. *Le mot juste*, like she'd been taught. That exact word you could spend weeks searching for as if it might perfect a text, but which could never be found in time to enlighten a conversation. Why focus on phrasing when it was the idea that mattered? She'd been trying to raise a deeper issue – admittedly a digression from the much less difficult problem they'd been trying to address. But the deterioration wasn't her fault either, she'd been the one let down. And apart from big breakages like boilers – things that whirred, had moving parts – Harry had never expressed an opinion on interiors, as if only externalities merited a man's attention.

She throws the phone at the sofa, turns away, searches outside the window as if the solution might be there, in that external thing called the world. Maybe it was normal for a husband and wife in their situation, verbal exchanges unravelling. Or maybe danger lay in what seemed a minor pull. Sometimes a wayward thread couldn't be stopped. Life could slip away until you were left with nothing at all. Instinctively she turns around to the bookcase, books always a solace, but especially now with him gone all the time. Her eyes wander over well worn Tolstoys – it was Ivan Ilych, wasn't it? That hapless character who looked back in disbelief? Yes, how utterly stupid. In the future that might be her, muttering too late: *it could have begun with anything, but it began with, of all things, the curtains.*

Yet in this middle of life, which was really another beginning, like every day is the start of the rest of your days, how could one know what was worth saving, what was not? Turning back to the window, she spies her own reflection, the worst of all critics: a once self-assured Eva lost to the backdrop of a ransacked family room. Meanwhile the folds shimmer in the morning sun. Mesmerising, beckoning – that was the essence of how it began – being sucked in by this feeling of being able to touch something greater, infinite. Wasn't that worth pursuing?

She reaches out, fingers a few panels, stopping short of the tattered bits. This silk of an indescribable iridescence, a creamy peach, sometimes silvery, sometimes gold, itself a fleeting sunrise, how could she have chosen differently? Diffusing outside light on to the gilded frames of the paintings, brightening the worn wood floors and faded leather sofas, it was exactly right for the room. Or it *had* been right. Though maybe that too had been just hope, the room now devoid of it, even as she scans it, for hope or confirmation of what she was looking for. She knows she won't find it, not here in the chaos, so where can it be, that essence of what she wanted? She's not even sure what *it* was or is, only that the attempt had been so important. It had been the reason for bothering at all.

Probably for Harry's sake she should have separated inner angst from more mundane frustrations. *Come on, get on with it, you can't describe yourself as condemned if you're lucky enough to live like this* – a reproach from some possible distant observer but also conscience offering up another self-styled mantra. A mantra born of guilt, yet somehow intended to make you better. Why hadn't she questioned it before? Yes, why hadn't she questioned and explained it better to Harry? Looking at the mess of the room, even if words fell short, surely she was right: any place, any lifestyle, could be a prison if you couldn't escape. Existence itself was a kind of life sentence, a series of sentences maybe, at times purposeful, at times pointless, meandering. But whatever freedom you possessed, you were still encapsulated by this entirety, the finiteness of it all. No wonder it could be stifling. No wonder anyone might want to break free.

Arching her back, she straightens, again catching sight of herself as someone else: slim figure obscured by baggy clothes, auburn hair that once fell freely now dull in a hastily pulled back ponytail. For appearances there's often a solution – and she ought to do something before Harry returns – but for everything else? Anger mounts as a thousand past injustices refuse to go quietly. Why pick on the damned curtains? Picking them apart was the last thing they needed, a sore point and an eyesore. Whose fault was it they'd moved to a pricey Surrey suburb where things were as expensive as London? Who'd chosen the large Edwardian beleaguered by previous rentals? Hadn't they both taken it on for better, for worse? Floors torn up, electrics, new carpeting, dust clouds so thick she couldn't bring little Katya into the house. For richer, for poorer. And they hadn't been so careful, those electricians. The old curtains would have been a casualty in the war of refurbishment even if she'd been attached to them, which she had not. In sickness, in health. Yes, she *had* done her best, but even if her best wasn't good enough, did he have to adopt that tone of voice? As if the sum total of her work these years had cumulated in this singular failure?

As if in their fleeting phone conversations, curtains should have even come up. Harry in Budapest again for meetings, undoubtedly busy and tired, they could have written it off to past oversight or the strain of long hours, their separation sparking the argument. No, those fuelled it. Money was mere kindling; the spark had been the word *prison*. But she hadn't meant the house, only the emptiness, the dark nights, his absence. His absence and missing him, gone so many weeks.

She sighs, body softening, fury almost spent. Flickering rays of mid-morning sun illuminate the trees outside. The world is rich in autumn colour, fiery red and brilliant burnt orange. The curtains are glowing gold. He's missing all this, just by being away. These moments of authentic beauty, that's why he doesn't understand. How life is sometimes a vibrant explosion, sometimes only delicate shades, silhouettes. Then even as you watch, wishing for it to be like this forever, menacing clouds move in overhead, extinguish the light. The curtains reflect the change, take on a flatter colour, putty. It's a misty rain at first, then heavy pellets hit the gravel driveway, reverberating. An assault on the senses like hammering.

The phone starts to ring, chiming in with the cacophony. She looks at the sofa but the phone's not there. It's ringing, ringing, from somewhere but not where she threw it, not where it should be in its cradle, a bleating child who won't be quiet or still. She scurries to locate it though she might be burying it further in the debris, tossing cushions, toppling magazine stacks, shoving slippers aside, undoing what little order she'd established earlier. Wanting not so much to talk to anyone as break free of the noise. But then the ringing halts, just as the rain abates, and suddenly there's only the absence of sound, expanding to deafening silence. It might have been Harry.

Just as well she didn't catch the call then. Not ready to make peace, any exchange is potentially the same fight restarted.

Sadness wells up in the place left by anger. She begins straightening up, though really there is no relief in sight. Not since the beginning of the Plan, those signs of togetherness – stacks of unwatched films, holiday brochures, glasses emptied of wine – all the things they might have enjoyed when the children were in bed. But those had stopped appearing when he went away. Now there were only toys, broken bits, the vestiges of play halted abruptly.

The Plan. That awful straightjacket of an idea, though she was responsible for part of it, for having agreed. In the same way she was responsible for this mess, having stayed up late reading – she, Katya and Christophe – in the rush to bed leaving stuff scattered. But even applying reason, resentment persists, twists its way in, morphs to melancholy. Invades like a toxin: life beyond a simple tidy-up.

She bends down, tosses bits into the basket with more force than necessary. It had been difficult enough creating and balancing life as some kind of single parent with his sudden returns. And it hadn't been so long ago, those dark baby years, the ones that were supposed to be so fulfilling but which ended in near collapse. Post-partum, they said later – oh hindsight, ever clear! – but he'd abandoned her then too for his work, the career-building to benefit them both. She'd soldiered on mostly alone in this place. So he never knew the dark nights of nursing babies, the endless hours of playtime, the dreary rainy afternoons a mere countdown to bed. The ceaseless demands of children and house, how they usurped every last breathing space.

Now the children were settling in school, mornings unfolding into a day she might call her own – but not fully, not yet. Christophe's home by lunch, she perpetually has to remind Harry. That's barely three hours to wash up, run errands, do whatever else needs doing. And so the tedious tasks that await form mental images: shirts that should be on hangers, overflowing laundry, dropped socks and mouldy mugs still

9

hiding from when Harry was around. No, there's no doubt about it: through the years, she's become a maid in her own home.

A soft toy on the floor, its small leg protruding from behind the sofa, she reaches over. It's Pookie, which is surprising because Christophe rarely sleeps without him. But recently other bears had begun to find favour, and Pookie must have fallen, unnoticed. A different kind of sadness, placing him gently in the basket.

The kitchen phone's there too, starting to ring as she lifts it. 'Hello?'

'Mrs Holden? Mountmore School,' the woman launches in, then pauses. 'But it's nothing terrible.' Another pause.

'Oh?' Breathing relief, because it's the way they always begin – if you're lucky. If it's not a dire emergency, they say, *nothing terrible*, a phrase undoubtedly meant to stem parental heart attacks.

'Although Christophe *did* complain about a stomach ache after he was dropped off. I'm afraid after his morning snack he's been sick. I did try ringing earlier. You'd probably like to come and fetch him now. He's here with me in the office.'

For a moment, it's the conditional wording that's arresting – *you'd probably like to*. Yes, I probably would, but obviously you're asking me – no, telling me – I must. I would anyway, it's my child, who else would? But it's the way these English speak, indirectly, inviting doubt, asking but really ordering you. Simple goodbyes turned into a question, voice hesitant, going up, when really the matter's been decided, case closed.

'Yes, of course, I'll be right there. Thank you.'

The secretary doesn't reply, then thinks better of it. 'While I have you on the phone, Mrs Holden, our records show the voluntary contribution unpaid for this term.'

'Oh, right, sorry, I'll rectify that too.'

'Right then,' the secretary says with finality but not approval. The phone clicks. A gaping silence left by the absence of civility, though good manners and a sense of propriety were what she so admired and expected when she first came to Britain.

Don't feel guilty, no way of knowing, conscience kicking in to console. But you might as well feel bad, because it was there, in the disapproving tone. Another forgetful mother, another mother sending her sick child off to school so she can get on with her life. She's never done it, though apparently it is a common tactic. Except Christophe hadn't shown signs of illness, he'd gone to school as usual, sailing forth on his scooter, spindly knees pumping his skinny body up and down. How could she have known?

But then, wasn't that always the supposition these days?

You should have known.

∞

'Mama?'

Christophe, in the doorway in pyjamas, his head a tangle of matted curls.

'Mama, my tummy hurts.'

'Oh love, come here.' She leaves the dishwasher half unloaded, goes to feel his forehead. 'Your fever's gone. The day off school probably helped, and you slept all night, but you haven't eaten since yesterday morning. Maybe you're hungry? I could make you breakfast.'

His eyes light up. 'That would be good. Scrambled eggs!'

'Hmm, toast first, to see if you can keep it down.'

'But I can, I'm starving.'

Her laugh escapes. He's always starving, her boy.

'Okay, but we'll start with toast.'

Showing no signs of sluggishness Christophe starts hopping and chattering, the latter a trait that coincided with the start of school, spurting daily like a weed. Suddenly there's so much to say but the order isn't important, only that you get it out as quick as possible before someone stops you.

'Here's some toast and apple juice, they're okay for your stomach.' She sets down his cup and plate, watches him dive in.

'Why?' he says, already with a full mouth.

'Why? I don't know. They say that – bananas, rice, apples and toast, if your tummy's upset.' The BRAT diet, an American mother informed her, though she never found that acronym pleasing. Surely you could be strict without resorting to insults.

'Who's they?'

'They?'

'They who said it.'

'Oh, it's an expression, *they* means people in general, a saying, common sense.' Advice from other people, who are presumably like you, though they never are. She considers switching to Polish, but lately Christophe's had a hard time understanding and she has to repeat it all again in English anyway.

'Are *they* always right?'

'No, it means something's true in general. But you have to watch for particular cases.'

It would be good to add that nothing works universally, not all the time. That most people follow popular wisdom because they like having set rules to live by. Unfortunately in her experience that hasn't resulted in much success.

'Why?'

'Why what?'

'Why aren't they always right?'

'About what?'

'About sick, Mama,' Christophe lets out an exasperated sigh.

'Oh, because most times you don't get sick after bread. Unless you have a very severe tummy bug, then nothing will settle. But seeing how fast you've eaten, that's probably not the case.'

'So can I have eggs now?'

'Sure,' she smiles. Christophe's as good as Harry at getting what he wants.

Christophe starts rambling on about various schemes, something involving Jenny's boy James and catching snails. Her concentration's already on the scrambling, background words like *zoo* and *cages* reminding her that their elderly neighbour Miss Miriam is trapped indoors with a chest cold, they ought to pop over with cake for tea. A good idea anyway, she sets the kettle to boil. That great symbol of British life, she's even taken to drinking tea with milk and sugar instead of lemon and honey. But then you might get used to anything. In France it'd been harder to adapt, and in the end she'd given up. But England had a steadfastness about it, like its flat grey skies. A steadfastness exemplified by men like Harry.

But he hasn't rung, their quarrel still a live wire, his presence required to earth it. So best push him away and reach for Assam, pouring into that mug painted brightly by Katya at one of those expensive pottery parties where children are given crockery to make over. Another thing to get used to – spending hard-earned money to keep kids entertained – so different from her upbringing in Poland. But maybe it was different for people in England too, lives changing irrevocably because without thinking everyone went with the flow. Like the tea and milk swirling into a lovely dark caramel colour, Christophe humming, chomping, pretending to feed Pookie, while outside the rain turns to a steady fine drizzle. Leaves, grass, bark, all drenched in their compact triangular garden, though it's only compact compared with the house, unlike Miss Miriam's down the road. She'd thought their triangle was a consequence of being on a corner, until Harry pointed out the previous owner had lopped off land and sold it to developers. That's what made the house too big for its plot. From the back the proportions were all wrong, though you couldn't tell from the front, which, like everyone else's, was overlooked, given over to gravel in large parts. At least towering trees had been kept at the borders, because as ever it's the back of the house that really matters to a family. That's where the kids play and her vegetables grow, in a plot extending round slightly to the side of the house. You couldn't compare it with her parents' expansive beds in full sun, but she'd dug it herself, and as different as gardens are, in their essence they are the same: a spot of serenity in an otherwise manic world. Now the plot was mostly dug over, but other points of interest had emerged: the old oak's leaves gone yellow, ochre and rusty brown, and smaller chestnuts covered in bright green spiky balls concealing conkers. Their single quince tree, as ever, producing an abundant ripening crop, its branches heavy with gold pear-shaped fruit despite a recent big harvest. Soon they'd have to do something with all that fruit.

'Mama?'

'Yes?' She looks over. Christophe's no longer at the table but on the floor playing with some piece of plastic. 'You're finished, sorry. I was busy thinking.'

'That's alright, Mama. You think. I'm fine here.'

'No, we should do something,' she smiles. 'Let's read a story. Then if you're up to it, we'll go see Miss Miriam. Or if you're too tired, you can have another nap before Katya gets home.'

'Oh, I'm not tired, I have enough energies to bike with Daddeeeeee!' He jumps up into a jig. 'But for now,' he stops, tilts his head, 'a story will do.'

She laughs. Hard not to when he speaks, at times so adult-like, mimicking phrases he hears, the English so proper and constructed, so carefully fitted to emit the right emotion as it conveys meaning. Will she ever feel truly comfortable with it? Certainly Conrad managed, but Miłosz continued in Polish, didn't he? It must depend on a variety of factors. How well you fit in.

'Go on ahead, I'll be up in a minute.'

Sensing her distraction he doesn't hesitate, runs off upstairs, leaving her to sip the last of her tea. Really it's time to follow, perform motherly duties. Time to do something – action, activity, what everyone wants and demands. And in this way another morning shall pass, a slice of life drift by. It should be a positive thing, having Christophe, his quick recovery, having all this – house, garden, view – she *is* lucky. Harry back in a few days and hopefully rapprochement: an evening by the fire once the kids are in bed, maybe even satisfying sex, that ephemeral thing. It *had* been brilliant before, even with interruptions for the children. But then his long absences, her inconvenient periods, the fatigue and recriminations, and lovemaking became a precious commodity, tender and wistful. Where was the light-heartedness of it all? The lack of seriousness? The stripping away of inhibitions? Maybe this void was a consequence of youth slipping away. But equally Harry's returns were another responsibility, an obligation to reconnect. And sex couldn't be free or innocent if there's a risk of trying hard and missing the mark. That always made her inclined to withdraw further. So when he's not around – which sadly now is most of the time – a good cuppa does seem more satisfying than a rousing fantasy. Even hot water bottles weren't so curious any more. Maybe she was becoming English after all.

'Mama!' he calls from upstairs. 'Story time!'

'I'm coming!' She sets down the mug.

Not her time, not yet. But when it comes, what does one do with time?

Now or never. Anyway she's been meaning to do it: tidy up the study closet with those box files and photos, all those bits of paper relating to the past. A job promised for when Harry was away, when he wouldn't be around to interfere. Truthfully it's mostly for her own satisfaction. Harry's imminent arrival only makes it urgent because she promised to file the bills. But financial records haven't got a glance, or any other correspondence. She's been stuck on one letter in particular.

Dearest Eva,

I can't imagine everything you're going through right now, but I assure you I am here. I can buy you a ticket to come out, help with visa, anything. Don't feel abandoned. Because I can help. I am here for you, always. All you need to do is get in touch. Just say the word.

Yours,

Xavier

This message imprinted on an old *aeropostale*, flimsy as tissue paper, fragile as butterfly wings. Miraculously the paper hadn't disintegrated, the scrawl still firm, insistent. Postmark faded, a date barely legible but stamped in her mind: October 1993. Sixteen years gone. They'd been in touch since then of course, the last time maybe as late as five years ago. But this date, the letter, had formed the critical moment. His voice now obscured, but the words ringing as convincingly as if he'd offered them up hours before.

Don't feel abandoned. Because I can help.

A distant promise, seductive. Surely you only fell for such promises once. Or was it excusable human desire, wanting to be hooked, propelled forward with ease? Because at the time of writing, not she or even he, understood the implications – that you didn't necessarily control what came later even if your own hand was in it. Xavier, always holding his cards close, but maybe he never planned what was to come. Maybe it had all come as a shock to him too.

Heart racing, she stops from reliving the sequence of fateful afternoons, months after the letter: her arrival at his door. And months after that: he carrying her to the bedroom. Where it all began again: Paris, another life.

I am here for you, always.

Words unearthed were dead unless you breathed new life into them, but what would be the point of reviving memories now? For years Xavier had been erased completely; she still wasn't sure where he was. Sudden stoppage of the clock, dead end, no new information – only this – a testimonial, then scrutiny of what lay on the page. Because the emotions behind the words were so potentially dangerous she'd had to seal them away.

Sitting still for so long her legs ache, she finally stretches them, relieving the cramp from her cross-legged position on the floor. This letter, which she could never really forget, only forget for a while, on purpose. Yes, this letter's very existence presented a challenge. She had made other choices, another life with Harry, and for so long that had been satisfying. Surely the challenge was recovering that. Why trawl through the contents of a black box? What clues might be there to aid understanding? It was a reminder not only of old heartbreak but that previous catastrophe with Adam. Only questions could remain about what might have been, and she'd not really gone looking for this letter so much as her hand had been drawn, as if by guiding force. The appearance of a blessing. Touching it alone spoke volumes but she couldn't decide what to feel.

I assure you I am here.

Maybe feeling susceptible was an aspect of middle age, a cliché even. The heavy tug of marriage, children – but never with him. One could say it was better *that* hadn't happened, but she couldn't really allow herself that judgement. It was only a fact: something that never happened. A life not lived, piecing one together with Harry instead. Secret flights of fancy were only a way to fill an aching gap. Or were they something else?

I can't imagine everything you're going through right now.

No, he couldn't. But the saving grace of Xavier had always been his infinite compassion, hidden though it was behind a wall of arrogance. That, and his focus. He always got what he wanted. And at that time, it had been her.

She lifts the letter gingerly like a sacred object, folding it along

17

its well worn lines, placing it back in the box. This cardboard container of her muddled past – unrevised poems, letters unsorted – but no photos of him. They'd been so busy living freely, their future some assured expanse before them, they'd hardly taken any. Too late to seek them out now, the few images that did exist, stuck somewhere in weighty albums wedged on the back shelf, pages practically glued together. Perhaps better not to go there at all, to visualise. Because reminders of good times only made you feel more deeply the dissatisfaction of a dirty sink.

No, better to push down emotions, ghosts, as if they didn't take up any room. As if the world might remain safe so long as the lid stays shut. Setting the box back on the shelf, she shuts the closet door. She's lost the time she meant to allocate to various duties, these snatches of time to oneself an illicit pleasure anyway. Soon Christophe will be done for the day, she has to move on. But the words are in her head, rebellion in her heart.

Just say the word.

∞

The silence of a sleeping house so easily shattered by ringing, she grabs the phone. 'Hello?'

Harry clears his throat.

'Hi, it's me.'

Book tumbling, she fumbles to retrieve the right page, gives up. 'Hi.'

'So how are things?' he pauses. 'How's Christophe?'

She draws the duvet higher, sighs. So he got the email.

'Not great, but his fever's gone so he went to school. I told him to save his energies for the weekend. He and James are so excited for your cycling trip.'

Harry coughs, as if he's about to say something about it. She waits.

'Look,' he begins tentatively. 'I want to say sorry – about the other day. I didn't mean to be hard on you about the curtains. I only wanted to make sure you got them repaired properly. We can't spend money on new ones, what with other expenses laid out this year and next.'

'Okay,' but she bristles. Always about the money, when did that begin?

'But I trust you to do it,' he sounds uncertain.

'Fine, I'll go with the quote I got.'

'Eva, about the weekend,' he starts, then stops. 'Never mind, any news at your end?'

'No, but I've had it with the secretary at school.'

'What now?'

'You know, Mountmore's voluntary contribution scheme. I was castigated for an unpaid ten pounds. My English isn't perfect, Harry, but I always thought voluntary meant optional.'

'Your English is fine, just the state squeezing more from the middle classes,' he quips.

'I don't mind paying, Harry, not in principle or the amount, if it helps. But it's ridiculous, the school wasting time drawing up lists of offenders, policing and admonishing parents.'

'The state's short of funds, love. Head teachers have to turn entrepreneur. I don't mind donating to Mountmore either, but frankly, I don't see how it helps. Because the problem isn't them being short of a few books or computers. The whole school's overcrowded, kids packed in like sardines. Stupid badgering for a tenner isn't going to solve that. But that's why I'm here, getting us out of it.'

She sighs, knows what's coming.

'I don't *want* to opt out, Eva, I feel forced. I'm not for this in theory or practice. The Plan,' but he interrupts himself, 'nearly two hundred thousand pounds to put two kids through private secondary school, never mind primary if we have to go down that route sooner. After all we've paid in taxes anyway, tens of thousands, hundreds of thousands over the years.'

'Harry, sorry, I've never understood this – how can we pay so much tax and still not have anywhere to send our children to school?'

'The system's broken,' he pauses, lets out a deep breath. 'In the past there were options – more or less academically-oriented secondary schools. But then in the name of equality, everything was smashed, everyone lumped together whether they care to achieve or not. Of course religious schools kept state funding but they're allowed to discriminate on the basis of religion, so we have no good academic schools in our area, only the Catholic one, and we're not allowed in. The only other state option is deadbeat Fryers Point, where at best they keep kids out of trouble.'

'But we should fight the system. We can't let this kind of injustice prevail.'

'Eva, I'm one man, and not even in the country most of the time. The system's so entrenched people don't even *see* the problem. They think Church of England schools, state comprehensives, fine, everyone gets in, fair chance for all. But if you want excellence, high-performing schools, in our area the choice is going private or being a hypocrite – working the system like so many others, baptising kids and pretending to be devout. You'd have to un-lapse from your Catholicism, Eva. Start attending Mass piously every week. But that's repulsive, dishonest, and I'm not going to ask you to do it.'

'Thanks.'

'So the only alternative is saving up. The Plan.'

She's about to interject but he continues.

'You know I'm torn, love. Private education was once aspirational, now it's practically a liability, privilege and all that. Even my parents were sensitised, and they weren't snobs. Idealists, rebels, giving money away while we went to state schools, but those were selective schools, another time, another place. When we moved from London I imagined cosy villages like where I grew up, teachers who lived in the community, focus on academics, sport, music. Now everyone's shoved into a single mould, bureaucrats fiddling with policy to make it easier for them to tick boxes...'

'But maybe it'll work out, Mountmore's up for academy status, it might get better.'

Somewhere far away Harry heaves another heavy sigh.

'Eva, education is in perpetual disarray from a cascade of reforms. What makes you think rebranding Mountmore overnight as some kind of independent academy, with no oversight or redress for complaints, will make the situation better? Fake opportunity, fake equality. We can ride it out, the kids are young. But we'll still need somewhere for secondary school, the years before university. Maybe we settled in the wrong area, I don't know. Maybe we should look again at moving.'

She sighs too but he's right about Mountmore at least – parents frantically tutoring in private while the school claims credit for results; teachers veering chaotically from zealous enforcement of rules to complete disinterest in individual cases. For a year no one even noticed Katya couldn't hear properly, put her down for lazy. Then in a fit of punishment, someone seated her in front of the thirty other pupils, whereupon Katya finally diagnosed her own problem.

'Well,' she reminds, 'at least now you won't be paying taxes for what you won't get.'

'Thanks to the Plan,' he agrees grimly. 'We were just in time, mark my words. Whoever wins the elections next year, the government's going to change rules on domicile and tax. They'll make it impossible to accrue income this way: no more working abroad and coming home for carefully counted breaks. Only for a very short time is this in our hands – our future, our sacrifice, our Plan.'

But the way he says it reminds her of childhood, remnants of the disastrous Soviet five-year plans, the unforeseen and unintended consequences.

'Don't forget,' he takes her silence as a cue to continue, 'we're only capitalising on an existing situation. I was travelling so much last year I was gone most of the time already. It's not as if the Plan is some arbitrarily concocted idea. I was practically living in Eastern Europe anyway. If we didn't count days, I'd just be throwing money away.'

'I know,' she says, not needing the reminder.

'And bigger threats lie on the horizon,' his voice turns serious. 'University fees rising, and the new killer: fifty per cent top tax rate. That's regardless of which political party wins. All the politicians are pandering to popular sentiment, jumping on a bandwagon to find scapegoats for economic trouble. As if it was any one person's fault – national stagnation, debt – and waving a wand in one direction would erase it. I don't know how they plan to plug a deficit or debt the size of Britain's, but they can't do it on the backs of individuals. Not me anyway. We're not swimming in income, I'm working to death to save. Half of what I earn? You must be kidding. If that happens, they'll drive us out permanently. Or we'll need another Plan after this one.'

Another Plan? God forbid.

'But by next spring we'll be ready. We'll have saved enough for education and a slice of retirement so whatever insanity they lob at us for the privilege of living in the UK, we'll manage.'

With this he's reminded her to hold on, in the way all their recent conversations have become contorted, an exchange of reinforcements to stay the course.

'And the remains of old Holden debt will be cleared too,' she offers in consolation, though he doesn't like to be reminded of the financial hole left by his parents. 'Anyway,' she adds, 'you have to put in more time abroad if you want to make partner.'

'Exactly,' he exhales, as if she finally understood. 'It's a question of career too, really that's the critical issue. Unlike my parents, I'm going to have to work bloody hard just to stand still. And until there's more certainty, we have to,' he pauses, looking for an acceptable phrase, 'keep calm and carry on, I suppose. I know it's banal, and difficult, for all of us.'

But that ubiquitous phrase airbrushes everything, and it isn't wartime, she'd like to say, only class warfare, a peculiarly British sport whereby the haves try to hold on to personal gains while the have-nots see how fast they can take from them. Harry, always arguing that under slogans of equality and fairness, redistribution tips into slow descent, snowballing, turning into an avalanche, until like the Soviet system, eventually everyone's stripped and anything can be taken from you. She was never sure the comparison was precise but she agreed with one thing: there was nothing fair about taking from one and giving to another. She'd seen enough of that. Because who decides who's deserving? What's the basis of measure? You could try to level a playing field but it would never stay level for long. There was no way to regulate or abolish personal ambition, and why should anyone want to?

'Well, I better get some sleep,' Harry says.

'Me too,' she yawns. 'In case it's not over with Christophe yet.'

'Goodnight then, sleep well,' he pauses. 'Oh, and on the curtains, love, see if you can find another quote. Seems a high price to pay for a stitch-up job. That shop closing, it's a sign. Things are going to get worse before they get better.'

∞

Peeking in on Christophe she breathes quietly, he's still dozing. Having hardly eaten dinner the evening before but sick again, a rough night for them both. The relapse – she could almost blame herself, for thinking it was possible to move on quickly, for being optimistic. Though what was the alternative? Because if you didn't believe things would get better, there'd be no point in being patient or carrying on. She looks for clues as to how the illness might progress, but even with close study it's indeterminate. He's fast asleep. And not the phlegmatic sleep of a sick adult, coughing and moaning, sweating, tossing and turning, but the settled angelic slumber of a child who's barely running a fever, who ate his apple slices this morning, who might be miraculously better when he rises. Well, that's the hope, as they say, only time will tell. At least one can be grateful for friends like Jenny, taking Katya to school and back, she won't have to disturb Christophe at all.

Clicking the door shut, she heads downstairs: to begin again. To prepare for Harry's arrival, the countdown of days. This whittling away of hours, a life comprised of so much waiting, time itself must be filled with piecemeal action: predetermined duties, useful jobs, infinite minutiae to tackle. She takes a soft, yellow cloth and wax polish from under the sink. The study with its vortex of a black box already poses too much distraction, so better to start with the family room. Even if that task risks never nearing completion, dusting: a losing battle, silent war of attrition, like curtains versus sun. She sprays the coffee table legs and surface, wiping until they gleam. Of course it's a temporary victory, because no matter how many times you attack dust you can only push it around. Isn't grasping at discrete particulars meaningless without some overarching purpose and continuity? Where are they all going, why bother? But it's a part of existence, must be done if you're to be viewed as a person who does things properly. So you carry on. As any good English person would.

She lifts the frames on the top shelf of the bookcase to wipe underneath: old family photographs with Piotr when he was small enough to qualify as a baby brother, and Magdalena, the oldest, always older looking even then: sullen, preoccupied. Maybe that's why she stopped having photos taken altogether, or because later she didn't have anyone to take them with. More recent shots show Piotr and his brood, and Mamcia and Tato smiling outside their rabbit-warren of a house, her parents ageless despite their years. Why didn't they find it so tedious? Home never seemed a form of enslavement when they were growing up and there were many more people around then. In fact every household in Poland in the 1970s was overflowing with relatives, every corner crammed with monstrous furniture, the Soviet standard having been weight, not functionality, quality or aesthetics. Yet work was done and no one seemed overwhelmed or grumpy about it. Maybe a different character yielded a different result. Or in the past little else was expected. Maybe they ignored dust, deriving satisfaction from the labours of daily life and large family gatherings, the preparations all the merrier when someone managed to procure a good cut of meat or, so rarely, exotic fruit like bananas. Though it might have only seemed so merry because they were all squashed together, no privacy whatsoever. Perhaps the dust just never had a chance to settle.

The spray of aerosol in the air glistens momentarily, then vanishes. But it's still there somewhere, like the dust in the universe, invisible specks to be eradicated that cannot be eradicated, only flicked someplace else. No, it's not an absence of application or a lack of enthusiasm marring her experience of domesticity. But something *is* missing. She's never been able to summon up Mamcia's simple happiness or the excessive joy exhibited by other mothers at school. Even Harry acknowledged child-rearing and housekeeping had taken their toll on her. But they simply hadn't known what to do about it.

She stops. Certainly there didn't appear to be an ultimate solution. From the beginning, only tactical manoeuvres to take chunks out of the void. *Get a cleaner*, Harry advised, but she refused because others didn't have one, and if Jenny could manage so could she. Besides she hadn't grown up like that, with help, not like him. Later the rebuttal was for different reasons, checkmate in an argument: *aren't we trying to save money, Harry, isn't that the point of the Plan? Cleaning is one of those duties of a stay-home mum – keeping house tidy, cooking meals, caring for sick ones – part of the overall picture and in every detail. Might as well embrace life, what you are.* That was indisputable because throwing money at a problem was not a resolution, even if at times one could regret standing on principle. But she'd meant it ironically too, sarcasm eroding belief in teleology, that everything might be determined by its ultimate purpose. No, whatever its design, the success of the Plan simply rested with Harry. Her role was to wait it out.

Moving to lower shelves, pulling out books one by one, Harry's, hers, side by side since their first integration. Her scattering of literature and philosophy, his honed acquisition of business and law, which somehow complemented each other in breadth and scope until they coalesced into a single collection. But when his work began to take him away it became harder to feel something communal was at stake. He didn't seem to understand that. That this inability to embrace shared duties was like being frozen in hurt. Nothing to snap the chain of sadness, prevent bleak memories from snowballing. Being alone, life rolled back so easily to those early baby years: the fragility, exhaustion, feeling illogical but helpless to stop it, breaking down at the dishwasher, that symbol of mindless repetition. Then she'd remember how lucky she was not to have to wash up by hand. So always the guilt, this terrible guilt, weighing heavily on the dissatisfaction, erupting into terrible rows: *you don't understand, Harry, I have university degrees too, I was successful in my career though it didn't pay well, I was someone at the journal, now*

plunged into this world of chores and crying and endless nappies.
She didn't ever remember saying *hideous dependency* but other
big words had been thrown about, like *complacency* and
selfishness and *frivolous spending.*

A puff of a sigh escapes, almost inaudible, dissipating like the
particles crinkling in a fleeting sunbeam. Eventually she *had*
resurfaced. To what the English call a better place. It was hard to
assimilate such a metaphorical way of speaking, the phrase
making it sound as if you could actually arrive somewhere quite
trouble free. But you couldn't – not in real life. Even if
occasionally you might banish cobwebs, let in light, the
underlying situation often remained the same, and sometimes it
looked worse for being illuminated. Godless universe of dust,
where was she in it? Maybe the only solution was to look for
justifications: in the future, there might be other options. In a
few months, Christophe would be in school full-time like Katya,
and next year, Harry back for good. Maybe instead of desperation
some renewed purpose and satisfaction would spontaneously
spring up. Or perhaps it would take this long slow toil. In the
meantime, though, as Jenny said, having evenings to yourself
wasn't such a bad thing, less work at any rate.

Piles of books lying on the floor, a mess made trying to make
things better. Work that might be at cross purposes anyway,
because the barrage of being either in incessant demand or on
permanent stand-by would eventually turn into the ennui of an
empty house: everyone gone all day. So in the future she'd be
another mother cast adrift, but what *would* her options be? Jenny,
a talented cook, now steadily launching a catering business, but
how to resume a career if for years you've been doing just this,
picking up the pieces of everyone else's day? Harry, ever the
provider, another decision taken long ago when they agreed to
split duties, all those responsibilities that had to fall on someone.
Then his work and travel expanding to fill time and space until

it became logical for her to stay home – permanently. *Just the nature of the legal profession*, his oft-used excuse. *Life's growing more expensive in every direction you look.* And then the big one: *it's an uncertain world, Eva, we have to look after ourselves.*

So that's how the Plan was hatched. The Plan that snatched him away completely. Working abroad for a year or more he'd save on tax, double his salary, find that security, safety, even as banks teetered on the brink of collapse. *Of course I'll miss you, Eva, but the only worrying thing is something happening to us. Marriages can break up after episodes like these, separate lives. Remember Tilly and Steve.*

Tilly and Nathan now: a buffed, rebuffed and re-re-buffed Tilly, bearing no resemblance to her younger self, the natural beauty that was Harry's little sister. And another much older photo, she and Harry, rugged, clinging to a mountain they'd scaled. A previous era, before kids and promises. But of course every challenge was easier before you made a promise to succeed.

No, we won't fall apart, she told him, counting on her own devotion. *You'll keep healthy, work hard, make your name and earn your rightful place in the firm. We'll count the days until your visits and when this separation is over we'll both really live. Remember when we used to do that? Go out together? And more time with the children, simplicity. I didn't have any of this stuff when I was young but I turned out all right.*

She starts brushing off the books each in turn, stacking them one by one.

Yes, yes, but where should I live between visits home? Paris, Berlin, Vienna, Warsaw?

That's how it always went, the conversation drifting further and further from its starting point, until finally they settled on Warsaw, a small flat by one of the company's new offices. Pressured by the firm but also a compromise to have him closer to her parents. Not that it was that close to Warsaw – Przemyśl, the hilly old Polish town on the border with Ukraine where she'd been born and raised – a six-hour train ride from the capital, more hours on the road. But at least it was Poland, a place she once belonged, and perhaps their curious little English children, with their funny accents and broken Polish grammar, could be got out of their strict schools to visit their only grandparents and garden of fruit trees. What English people called an orchard whereas in Poland it was a garden like any other: Mamcia patting Katya, her plaited straight hair the colour of wheat burnished by a long summer, though now it had darkened, and Christophe, always darker curls, sitting next to a basket of apples by Mamcia's feet, mischievous look in his eye. Returning to Mamcia and Tato meant going back to a time of wonderment, the simple life she had somehow never managed to build here.

Ach, Eva, it's silly, you staying in England while Harry comes to Poland, Tato said. *Ironic verging on absurd*, Harry mused, and for a while they wondered if it was worth uprooting them all. Surrey life could be a gilded cage: houses, schools, pressures to maintain lifestyle. Elsewhere people were struggling to make ends meet but here the rationale for work largely had been displaced by pursuit of glamour. A new end goal, which seemed equivalent to happiness but wasn't, at least not for her. But maybe it was too late. That insidious line of thinking having wrapped up Harry inadvertently, then purposefully as it took hold of Surrey, England, the world. An imperative of need turned to tentacles of greed.

But they hadn't discussed that, the premise of the Plan. Or that morally it might be dubious, even if they don't intend to rely on state schools or the health service. Because it's easy to gloss over all that when a scheme is legal and possible. *Rich people do it all the time*, Harry said, as if *that* ought to be the ultimate sanction, the arbiter of what should be done. Understandably legality featured foremost for a legal mind like his, and technically he wasn't doing anything wrong, just working the system in a different way from parents who suddenly found God. He certainly wasn't breaking laws like those cheats milking state benefits with false declarations. He had paid in plenty before and he wasn't taking what wasn't his. He was preserving what he earned now – and at quite some cost to them.

Paris, Berlin, Vienna, Warsaw and *The Reprieve*. She fingers its soft cover, brittle with time, the back cover cautioning: *Europe mobilizing, commentary on moral paralysis, counterfeit heroism, betrayal, shame*. One of the Sartres that she and Xavier had argued over repeatedly, the Second World War having been a different experience for Poles and French. Recently she'd had to admit to herself the lessons contained there might still be valid – it might be mad to discard that book before she learned how to cope with the countdown of days. She hadn't kept many of the other works they'd debated so hotly though, because in the end, like this one, they'd left her feeling empty. Back then, in their student days, Xavier had taken existentialism to heart, even as she tried to introduce him to her world – Lem, Mrożek, Schulz. And Szymborska: the countless beauty of poetry that did touch some essence. But like most of his classmates, Xavier was unmoveable, romanticising the foreign while clinging fiercely to French superiority. Of course, like many committed existentialists Xavier later became an uber-materialist, a consummate consumer, a trader, as if the idea of nothingness had swung the door wide open to pure excess. Now nothingness prevailed, even as modernity claimed to have largely discarded Sartrean ideas. In fact, it seemed more like nothingness had been bought into fully: God's dead, life's pointless, might as well shop. Hedonism, just a form of pointless existence, but non-believers, atheists and religious alike nowadays could be seen carrying on building their little lives as if their petty concerns mattered. Well, she'd never believed in non-belief anyway. Everyone believed something. Like Tato with his physics and religion, God might be gone only because you couldn't find him, hadn't looked hard enough. Lately Tato was going on and on about singularity, that infinite but tiny density inside black holes. She didn't understand whether he thought symmetry was a workable proposition or whether he hoped God might be found there, where nothing made sense and infinities stacked up. He'd never subscribed to the theory of intelligent design, said the argument for God didn't lie in the observable universe anyway. Even multiverses didn't negate God because by nature God is something nothing can negate. She mostly wasn't sure, didn't feel too much in this regard. But nothingness certainly wasn't workable, had to be fought off. Because even if life seemed pointless, it still functioned in rational, repetitive ways. Even science with its great divide between order and chaos often revealed randomness as a false cover. That underneath it all, you could subscribe to beauty and simplicity, in one form or another. That the quest itself was important: the search for order and truth if not compulsion, then duty, ritual.

Continuing to stack more briskly, she returns books to categories proven to work. Like the start of the Plan, which was no different – a way of enshrining reason and practicality. No different to how most people managed their lives. When decision time came the Holdens dealt mostly with logistics, repackaging their residual emotions like weights on a scale. They'd considered how moving to Warsaw would mean upheaval after only just settling into Corner House. How there'd be no guarantee of return to this good English life, so carefully crafted. How they'd lose hard won places at Mountmore, a worry so paramount when the school's excellent reputation hadn't yet been tarnished by closer examination. How they'd lose friends like David and Jenny, their whole community – until she herself conceded, because actually who *would* look in on frail Miss Miriam? Besides, Harry was right. He'd be on the road – Vienna, Paris,

31

Berlin – not Warsaw most of the time, and a year wasn't long; afterwards things would be different. So many reasons she'd left Poland in the first place, if they moved there how would she fit in after so many years abroad? She no longer resembled women back home any more than these nubile twenty-year-olds working in local cafes, young girls recently arrived in Britain from a distant part of the EU, brimming with excitement and the prospect of foreign adventure. No, Slavic features, high cheekbones, a penchant for red hair, might be all she shared with them now. All that was left of that young Eva displaced long ago. Now she and the children were becoming English. You couldn't disrupt that, not for a matter of a few months.

Job done. She shoves in the last book, stands back to survey the old order of things. Well, slightly revised. Because of course in private Tato had asked whether her marriage was strong enough to withstand the separation, and she'd told him not to worry, because you could never doubt Harry. But as weeks turned to months one could see how inadequate self-styled mottos were – *rise to meet the challenge, battle to overcome* – her early version of *keep calm and carry on*. But the worry now was that sometimes you couldn't. You couldn't carry on. Sometimes you failed. She had failed before. And this experiment, like any other, was based not only on wisdom from past mistakes but hope. Yes, hope, pure hope, and the belief that one had chosen wisely. That the sacrifices had been and would be worthwhile. And it relied on faith, the kind of belief you gave blindly, when you weren't sure at all.

'Mama?'

She turns around, suddenly surprised by the existence of another. Christophe, clutching Pookie, his pyjamas showing a damp spot.

'Mama, my tummy doesn't hurt any more.'

'Are you sure?'

'Oh yes, I'm much better. All the sick's come out.'

'Good,' then suddenly it registers. 'What?'

'The sick's come out, Mama,' he looks at her sheepishly. 'But I missed the bucket.'

∞

'So how's everything today?' Harry's voice but curiously devoid of inquiry.

'Actually, I'm exhausted,' she drops the sponge into the sink, dries her hands. 'Christophe's back at school, some kind of new skills assessment he couldn't miss. Recovered, but that's only a guess after a week of ups and downs. I seem to be a failure at predicting.'

She sits down at the kitchen table, noticing only then how much her back aches.

'I was going to take him to the walk-in clinic but you know how they are, unforthcoming, disinterested. Sending you home saying it's a bug that'll run its course. Okay, who knows, maybe it has. Or maybe he's come round just because you're coming home tomorrow.'

He coughs. 'First of all, you're not a failure. And if you need to, make an appointment with the doctor. And if you're not getting answers, go private. That's what the insurance is there for.'

'Thanks for that,' she says, sarcasm levelled out.

Harry breathes out heavily.

'Eva, I didn't want to tell you this earlier, because I wasn't sure, I was hoping otherwise and you had enough on your plate, but,' he hesitates, 'I can't make it home this weekend. We won't be finished here until the middle of next week, earliest. Then we head straight to Vienna for the audit.'

It takes a moment to sink in.

'No, Harry,' she stands up automatically. Pressure mounting like a dam about to break, suddenly it gushes. 'No, you promised. Never mind me, what about the kids? Christophe, what am I supposed to tell him, or Katya? We made plans, remember? Lunch at the Old Stag with Jenny and David and their kids, what am I supposed to tell them all?'

'Eva, this isn't choice, it's work – and relatively small as disappointments go,' his voice hardens. 'It's not as if I don't *want* to come home or go out and enjoy myself. I'm working for us, our family. And I don't control my own schedule, the firm does. You know that.'

'Sure, I know. You barely find time to speak to the children any more.'

It's retaliation but he hasn't really made up for previous slights before launching this direct hit. Small disappointment?

'It's hard to catch them, Eva,' he maintains composure. 'They're asleep when I start the day, and I'm in meetings whole afternoons. Often they're in bed by the time I get free.'

'Then get free, Harry,' she starts pacing. 'Life's passing by. It's not asking much, the odd phone call, weekend home, time for friends and family. You've got time saved.'

'Thanks, Eva. Thanks for that, I really hoped you'd be more understanding.'

'Understanding about what?' Her voice almost breaks. She stops pacing, braces herself. 'I do understand, Harry. It's not like logic is beyond me. I know the Plan, the demands on you. But it doesn't change how I feel, how we all feel. We miss you,' she's pleading now, 'because you're away, it makes the times you come back that much more important. The kids haven't seen you since summer.'

Weeks of sun return as clipped images, a reel moving too fast: Christophe and Katya mucking about in the orchard, Mamcia's pork cutlets and *rossil* chicken soup, cucumber salads and cherry tarts. Driving up the Bieszczady hills to hidden streams, catching fish with makeshift nets and buckets found in old Pan Stasiek's barn.

'I came out for a few weekends,' he reminds.

'That was August, Harry. It's practically October now.'

A whole summer of sticks and stones and no broken bones though they climbed dangerously high in the trees as plums came pummelling down. All that sun, so quickly giving way to endless English grey, the back-to-school rush.

'So you're giving me a guilt trip,' his voice is tense now.

'It's your own guilt trip if you have one, mine's borne of frustration. You said we could manage this, but it's not easy being on your own with young children. Especially when they're sick, and weekends are the worst, everyone doing stuff in families…'

'I know,' he interrupts. 'I'm the one who's alone weeks without end. Working straight through weekends because it doesn't infringe on sacred family time. At least you have that.'

He's right, she breathes out, trying to let anger dissolve. Better find a different tactic. She sits down again, as if trying to plant herself firm.

'Harry,' her voice now level, 'I know you're grinding away. But that's why it would have been good for us, a break from routine. It's been crazy here too, even without added troubles like illness. Uniforms procured, instantly lost, three school runs a day – nine, noon and three – a myriad of forms and dispensations, websites to consult, parent evenings to attend. Never mind a national curriculum for children barely able to wipe their bottoms. I can't keep up, it's so complicated, almost designed to wear you down.'

'That's why I'm out here,' Harry starts.

She cuts him off. 'Being away means you *don't* know what it's like. This has nothing to do with deficiencies of state funding or hard earned money that might bail us out.' She presses on. 'I'm not complaining about specifics but that there's no relief in general – especially when they're ill at night and I'm on my own. Suddenly everything grinds to a halt, days wear on forever. *Nothing's happening*, Harry, don't you see? It's like treading water. Then snap, back to senseless running around, pool, football, this activity, that – but all of it – it's so, so *empty*.'

She stops then because actually children aren't the problem and a laundry list of offenses doesn't make for a more accurate portrayal of the whole. Will he even see the thing she's trying to point out?

'Eva,' he adopts a conciliatory tone, 'I can't do anything about the kids falling ill. But for the rest of it, minimise activities. Pick a few things and do them well. Don't try to compete. They're only little for such a short time.'

So easy for him to say because he isn't here to do the work. Anyway he's missed the point.

'Eva?'

'What?'

'Forget swimming. It's another modern day absurdity. Toddlers don't need to learn to swim.'

'They're not toddlers any more, Harry.'

'Christophe's four, Katya's six, you're telling me it can't wait? Especially if scheduling and circular driving only add to the mayhem?'

As always he's focussing on tangibles. What he can fix. So that's where the argument fixates. True, the drowning noise of sport, silent boredom of other poolside mothers, Baby Ballet, Kids Karate, SoccaTots, do all threaten sanity. But you can't keep yourself or children happy by locking them in the house for an entire afternoon, never mind an entire year. It's only because he's gone that they're so busy in the first place. There *is* no relief at the end of the day. You have to wear yourself out. Maybe the argument, the whole pattern of life is circular, but who can break the chain?

'Look, Eva, I have to go. I'm cranking out documents for tomorrow. I'm sorry it's tough, but we knew it might be like this. We just have to persevere. And I'm sorry if there are stretches that are boring, and I'm sorry I can't be home this weekend. But I'll make it up another time. You're coming to Warsaw for the kids' half-term break anyway. A few more weeks, okay?'

No reply, because what can she say? This isn't about boredom, or even his absence, and having made it clear she needs him, his answer is always, cope on your own. Hang in there. Just hang.

'Eva, okay?' he repeats the question.

'Okay.'

Her voice is an echo, but not an echo of him. His is the satisfactory triumph of reason over emotion; hers, fractured hope. Is there really nothing or no one who can help her find what she seeks?

∞

There's no immediate answer.

Ring the doorbell, once, sometimes twice, Miss Miriam can take up to five minutes to come even if she's on the same floor. It's been that way a while. Some days the radio's blaring so she can't hear, other times Miss Miriam's heading for the door but veers off to do something else, forgets. The health visitor's confided: they need to keep an eye on her.

Stomping in place to keep off the cold, the kitchen mitts and dish warming her hands, but the chicken's probably cooling rapidly even under the foil. A cold front's coming in. And she's got to hurry – only ten minutes to the midday dash to school.

'Coming,' a gentle voice suddenly sings over clattering keys and locks. No other warning, no faint footsteps even, a woman so light she barely makes a sound at all.

The door opens a crack. 'Eva! Do come in.' Miss Miriam opens the door wide and turns, prepared to be followed.

'I brought some lunch but can't stay long this time, Christophe will be out soon.' A brief flash of guilt – she should have come earlier – it's not fair to drop and run on someone fragile, living alone.

'Oh yes,' Miss Miriam turns around. 'Now aren't you a dear? I forgot it's Wednesday, and look at this, a whole chicken,' she smiles. 'Whom do you expect to eat all this?' She turns again, continues her slow progress into the kitchen.

'You should.'

'Never in a million years,' Miss Miriam waves her hand dismissively. 'But I do thank you, it's ever so kind, Eva. Come, set it down over there, it looks terribly heavy.'

Miss Miriam always says that, every time she brings lunch, though a small chicken isn't heavy lifting. But maybe if you're in your eighties, a cooked bird is a big contribution, becomes a formidable weight, along with so many other things.

'So how are you feeling today?'

'Today? As good a day as any other. Now where is that teapot?' She bustles around the kitchen trying to find it. This too is part of their routine, and Miss Miriam doesn't deviate. Or maybe she hasn't registered what's been said.

'I thought I'd washed it and set it over here.'

'No, that's okay, Miss Miriam, I need to get going now, no time for tea, I'm later than usual, for Christophe,' she repeats it gently. 'I have to feed him lunch as well.'

'Oh,' Miss Miriam looks crestfallen, then brightens. 'Well, why don't you bring him here? He can help me with some of this chicken. The Lord knows I won't make inroads into it myself and that skinny boy needs fat.'

She laughs. Miss Miriam could use the fat herself. Though it's serious too, dangerous when old people get too thin, nothing to protect them in winter months. Like her own grandmother, Baba Kasia, whom Miss Miriam increasingly resembles in stubborn gentility, a stubbornness too easily overpowered as the body weakens.

'Alright, if you insist. He does like chicken. And coming to see you.'

'I do, I do, I insist.' Miss Miriam's blue eyes gleam, icy pools of resolve. 'Two old birds then,' she laughs out loud, 'though I'm sure your roast is the younger of the two. While you're off, I'll find that box of biscuits. I seem to recall it was here somewhere…' Her voice trails off as she sticks her head in one of the cupboards.

'I'll let myself out, be right back.'

'Oh, you do that,' Miss Miriam waves, not turning around. 'Now where did I put them?'

Perched precariously on a stool, arms reaching high above her head, in the fraction of an instant no one's looking – the crash. The box of biscuits falls to the floor, scattering its contents.

'Dear me,' Miss Miriam says, stepping down carefully.

'Let me help,' she rushes to gather broken pieces from the floor, a beautiful Victorian pattern of black and red tiles that could really use a wash. The biscuits will have to be binned.

'I'll sweep up.'

'Dear, dear me,' Miss Miriam repeats despondently. 'I think those were my last biscuits.'

'Never mind, Christophe won't know,' she says cheerfully.

'Charlie,' Miss Miriam retorts accusatorily, scowling. 'I told him to pick up more biscuits from the shops but he forgot. Now whatever will we serve with tea?' She looks panicked. 'So many people coming, and the table's not even set.'

Charlie, her long dead husband? So many coming? This kind of mental lapse hasn't happened for some time, best wait to see if it'll pass.

'Oh, do be a dear, Lucile, perhaps you can think of something?'

'Miss Miriam, it's Eva, your neighbour.'

Miss Miriam stares at the dustpan and brush, a crooked embarrassed smile creeping over her face.

'Of course, Eva, I was thinking of something else, at this moment,' she snaps around trying to find something else to latch on to. 'And here, this chicken.' She contemplates it for a minute. 'It looks nice, smells lovely.' But she seems perplexed as to how it got there.

'I'll be back in a few moments with Christophe,' she coaxes gently. 'We'll lunch together.'

'Don't worry, I'll be fine,' Miss Miriam says quickly. 'No need to bother.'

Maybe she doesn't realise she's dismissing the plan, or does she want privacy?

'Are you sure? I can come back, no problem.'

'No, no, that'll do, Eva, so generous with your time already. Go and take care of your own.'

The statement, direct but wistful, as if she's aware it's not her own family coming around. Poor woman: two children, six grandchildren, but weeks and weeks between visits. Now it's past noon, Christophe will be waiting. She picks up the mitts, makes her way to the door.

'If you're really sure there's nothing else, Miss Miriam,' she turns around one last time though it's not English to insist. 'I can come back…'

'No, you go on,' Miss Miriam says, still looking flustered. 'No need to bring me lunch today. I'll be fine with this chicken.'

∞

Try not to be judgemental, but how can one not judge? Doesn't everyone? Shouldn't Miss Miriam's family be around to help? She surveys her own kitchen too tired to contemplate the various projects she's set herself. But maybe that's the way of advanced capitalism, finding yourself alone, everyone working longer, for higher, safer pensions and a social net wider and stronger than Poland's, so instead of relying on family to provide in later years – or church if you're all but morally destitute – people rely on the state. Though Harry says that too is disappearing – *pensions are drying up, people are fooling themselves thinking the state will be there. Miriam's generation is the last, a dying breed. We have to look after ourselves.* Try not judging that rigorous rationality, or that so far, his promises have been broken.

Forbearance. That's what's needed to fight off recrimination, a recurring wave that'll drown everything if you let it. For now, only one way to hold back the tide: this mountain of quince on the worktop. The house is silent, the children asleep; outside it's pitch black, cold. Quince is the antidote. Sunny fruits that must be peeled before they spot and brown irrevocably. Something she has to do but soothing too, embarking on a useful project that defies solitude, ordering a small part of this unruly universe. Some fruits will be preserved as jam, some pureed into paste, then pressed into a mould they call quince cheese. And chutney for the rest. A task with multiple outcomes – using up fruit, consoling the soul. Because of all the mindless things that home life demands, cooking and gardening can be great comforts, creative expressions of self.

She searches in the drawer for a peeler, begins on the first fruit, forcing back the skin slowly. In some places the fruit's too far gone; whole chunks will require amputation. Quinces, hard as rocks, always tough work, and so many of them and other produce too: squashes and the last courgettes turning to stony marrows, potatoes and parsnips still buried in the soil. There will be work well into winter, digging out lost vegetables, turning over soil in anticipation of spring. But until then there's this – preserving – a reminder of the past, her parents' plum, apple and cherry trees, whose entire harvest had to be converted into a steady supply of desserts and jams for the year. Preserving, always a moment of ending and beginning, more than remembering or a mere lifting of spirits, because it harbours a deep satisfaction of labour, saving and presenting to loved ones the product of your hands. It's a natural extension of gardening: planting seeds in the depths of winter, propping plants in the spring, bringing something fresh to the table in summer. Then in autumn, saving what's left. A cycle completed, of birth, death and regeneration.

Sometimes it has seemed that the very coming of seasons might depend on this work, that the months might stop rolling by if she were to neglect these tasks. Certainly when she first came to England that's how it appeared: everyone gardened, especially outside London, where famously tended topiaries weren't to be touched and lawns weren't meant to be traversed. Entire parks like Wisley, devoted to showing off the skill of bending nature to man's will. Except the grass, of course, which mustn't be bent: *mind the grass*. Meanwhile on television and radio, celebrity gardeners shared their secrets, then chefs moved in on the game, extolling virtues of a home patch. So it was natural when she and Harry moved to Surrey that she attacked their plot with gusto, mindful not only of Mamcia's efforts but these new English surroundings. She'd been prepared to fit in.

But, except for Jenny, she learned she was the odd one out. Other mothers found her efforts strange. Even now, they say *wow, you do that really? I hate cooking, I can't believe you actually make your own jam. My garden's just a bunch of weeds, I can't be bothered, the kids just ruin it anyway.* Then she struggles to explain why it's a critical part of living, why it might be for anyone if you're home anyway with small children. What could be more important for the family? But she doesn't say that, only *maybe I'll make a business of it*. Because that gets you respect in England, if it's work, not fun. *But where do you find the time?* they ask and she wonders, where do I really? Making time, *I make time*, another form of creation, because it's hard to imagine what kind of emergencies and more urgent jobs fill the other mothers' time that she has the time to do this. Is she missing something or are they? Because the truth is she couldn't stop even if she wanted to, you can't waste what the garden's given, the hours put in. This is the soothing part after all the hard digging and planting, being battered by the elements. And life should be slow and rolling sometimes, not all hurry up, get on with the next thing. Yes, life should be pleasing, and not just work.

Setting down the peeler, she fills a pot with water, puts empty jars to boil. Reaching for a heavier knife to start chopping and coring, she studies the lot. Some quinces are past their best and spots have spread into deep patches of rot within. But enough is salvageable that a good batch should come of it. It'll just take more time. You have to move carefully to excise certain bits, not gouge and waste the good while forcefully eliminating the bad. The effort's worth it although she'd be the first to admit it's strange to revert to such old fashioned pursuits after an emancipated youth. Because except at harvest time, she'd never been much help to her mother. And her mother hadn't cooked that much either, only weekends or late at night like this because she worked long hours as a schoolteacher. Really it had been Baba Kasia, Tato's mother, the Ukrainian grandmother for whom Katya had been named, who spent hours in the kitchen. Practically until her dying day, defying arthritis as if it were merely a case of gnarled hands, Baba Kasia moulded pastry into jam crescents called *rogaliki* and sealed dough into potato dumplings she insisted were *varenyky* though Poles called them *pierogies*. Baba had never been afraid to do things her own way and from this a younger Eva had drawn

43

inspiration. Much later too when Katya was born, she had figured Baba Kasia wouldn't mind if she altered her name to suit England. Kasia in Polish was a little too foreign, like Krzysztof for Christophe, but the name Kateryna could be shortened to Katya, its Ukrainian form, also closer to the popular English Kate.

Yes, independence and strong will, that's what got you through. Though for a family that shared few traits even those were exhibited quite differently. In her case, the will to escape was perhaps also the dreaded middle child syndrome. Because as the years rolled by that young Eva spent more time away from home than in it; when not in serious study, a whirlwind of demanding social engagements overtook. She'd sworn from an early age she wanted excitement, not security. She never wanted to be like either of her siblings: Magda, the homely girl who took solitude and study to extremes, now an esteemed doctor but still single in her mid-forties; or Piotr, who'd taken everything lightly, rarely leaving their hometown, marrying before he took his degree and now content teaching at the school they'd all finished at fourteen. No, by everyone's account, it was Eva who went on to lead the most hazardous, peripatetic life: study in Krakow, then Paris, then Krakow again, where that entanglement with Adam began.

Wincing at the effort, she pulls at the knife wedged deep in hard fruit. Stuck. She probably should have used a cleaver for this; now all she can do is apply full body weight, both hands, and press forward. A grunt escapes as the knife hits the board, slicing clean through. All this fruit left, so much more effort, the thought of giving up flashes through. If only she hadn't been lured by the prospect of turning quince to jam: hard to soft, revealing goodness, malleability. Like with Adam, seeing some endpoint to his moodiness, his propensity to think below the surface, which initially had been a welcome relief from Magda's silences, Tato's lapses into theorising, the family's chatter about *pierogies*. Adam had been someone of substance, deep thought, and perhaps more importantly, her first protector. And for that she had felt she owed him deeply, maybe forever. By the time she realised she did not, things had gone too far.

She jumps at the prick, blade almost in. She'd reached for the end clumsily, before she was ready. Inspecting the wound, it's only a surface nick, a small spot of blood, though she did come awfully close to coring her whole palm. Grabbing a plaster and stretching it across, she makes a fist. She'll be able to continue. But with a bigger knife – and not where life almost snapped in half. After Adam: the return to Paris, the resurgent affair with Xavier. Though that too exacted a greater toll than anyone knew. She sighs, keeps chopping. So on to London and landing in that sprawling city of possibility, but also after so many sorrows and defeats that even she thought she might have traded too much for excitement. And finally falling into Harry's arms, on the very eve of the millennium. It seemed ever so lucky. And so the house and the making of jam.

The making of jam: tossing chopped fruit into a second pot, measuring out sugar; adding a splash of water, mixing it all through. After the age of forty, one often marched in-step, looking backwards as much as forwards. Until recently she'd felt it had been something to be proud of – not only the point where she'd arrived, but the trajectory taken – the overcoming of it all. Leaving behind measured Polishness, staunch Catholicism, old habits, and carving out a life of one's own. Yet remnants of the old life kept stubbornly creeping in. Like the making of jam, or Mamcia, who'd taken over Baba Kasia's role in the kitchen, perhaps she too was preparing for that future when time slows again. Maybe fate had handed her that fortuitous meeting with Harry, the meeting which began the process of slowing. The meeting that landed her in a place, which if it didn't quite represent her hopes and dreams, was close enough.

Close enough, yes, but good enough? Corner House never seemed like a final resting place, though not because it wasn't

45

good enough or because, from time to time, Harry had other ideas. It was because she never had any preconceived notion of where she should go. Temporary or permanent, it was a good life. As good as any other, as Miss Miriam would say. So in that respect, yes, good enough. Like Mamcia and Tato, she too felt relieved when she'd finally settled down – a husband, child, home, another child – as if all that was conventional made good the affair with Adam. Of course, they'd known nothing of the lost baby. The persistence of Xavier.

She stops, then starts again, stirring quickly. The mixture heating up, precisely the moment you have to pay attention, just before bubbling point. The lost baby, for so long buried safely in the recesses of her mind, but really an uneasy peace, like Xavier's persistence. That too had dissolved into a stalemate when they finally separated. No, more like a permanent checkpoint: two sides staring at each other warily, not so much distrusting one another as knowing intimately what the other might do. With so little communication since then, was it still fair to call it a mutual obsession? Her hidden letter a prelude to an affair as intoxicating as Paris itself – passionate, churning, steady in a hot simmer – then suddenly buffeted by external forces. It had finally boiled over, for her anyway. She had to conjure up the determination to move on then. It was the second time around with him already and she'd passed that awful milestone, turning thirty. In the back of her mind the escape route was ready: in the face of adversity you can always leave. A pattern begun in childhood, reinforced by Adam when things went horribly wrong – *don't be afraid to cut the cord and run* – a corollary to that motto of meeting challenges and hurdling over them.

Maybe it would always remain a mystery between her and Xavier now, but then she must have known something. She had steeled herself to the outcome, leaving Paris for a new start, London, where she soon met the honourable Mr Holden. Her parents, instantly forgiving their daughter her many sins, like not coming home and tying herself to a Pole. They didn't speak English, didn't get the joke, never knew about the clubs, the dancing with Poles around poles. They'd never suspected Adam's deficiencies, so closely knotted to her own. Xavier had only been a figment of their imagination, and she'd never had the heart to explain it all to them.

Stirring slowly, determinedly, breaking up the bigger bits, the obvious catch had been Harry. Even with recent arguments she couldn't deny her admiration or their love. Harry was caring and hard-working and handsome and well-spoken. And like her parents she'd fallen easily for the cultivated old worldliness that the new post-Soviet Poland could never match, the reliability and steadiness that France could never muster. Unlike most men, Harry didn't flatter, he thought before speaking, which made most of his pronouncements irrefutable rather than a topic for discussion. Of course over the years she'd come to realise that trait was better suited to a lawyer than a husband, but it was easy to concede as an irrevocable product of his sad past. Because while she'd been living dangerously with Adam on the edge of a world collapsing, Harry had been battered by tougher realities: parents dying while he was at university. His whole world had come undone then. The threatened loss of family home, scurrying to hold on to it, in the end exhausting every alternative and still losing. It must have extinguished whatever youthful naiveté he may have possessed.

Sugar coagulating, time to scrape the sides, remove excess froth – if you don't work quickly there's a risk of losing the setting point. She skims the foam, steadies the heat, keeps on stirring. She'd always thought having a chance to prepare for death made it more bearable, as oddly enough Xavier too had lost both parents, his father much earlier and his mother after many years ailing. But for Harry, coming so suddenly and so close together, and at such a trying age for him and Tilly, it couldn't have been but total devastation. Like an asteroid smashing a giant crater, death displaced brother and sister, launching them forcefully in opposite directions. From there they simply continued to steer down separate paths: Tilly, craving security, pounced early into marriage with money-obsessed Steve, two children, divorce, and another try with Nathan producing two more. Their lives were now a chaotic balancing act of exes and in-laws, competing grandparents and split holidays. By comparison, they made her life with Harry seem an exercise in meditation. Industrious but indulgent, somewhere along the way Tilly had given up providing her offspring with more in terms of values. All four lacked discipline, whilst beyond his City job Nathan was apathetic, doing his little best before collapsing on the sofa for sport. Steve sent cheques.

But Harry had bided his time. Patience, the thing he was good at, which she could use more of too. She watches the golden fruit turn rose-coloured, bubbling slowly. Of course at first Harry had submersed his sorrows in nightlife – and oh, how posh ladies loved him! – but soon he realised keeping a country house required work. So he took up law and the role of organiser, stored the Holden antiques and quietly started to pay down debts. All his university days thereafter he mostly eschewed the wild life while Tilly worried if he was alright. But he was only being practical. He knew they could not recover the past or meet their vast obligations. They finally sold Cranfield Manor.

One by one, contents emptied. And on that fateful New Year's Eve when one topic still flowed seamlessly into the next, Harry had confessed his agony at failing. *I couldn't keep it together, I couldn't provide enough, I failed.* And though he seemed to understand it wasn't really his fault, she caught a glimpse of a man haunted by ghosts. Only later did she learn the full scale of his commitments, as Harry, mixing deep belief in personal responsibility with his parents' idealism, had remained determined to continue the family's generosity. Thousands of pounds went to foster homes and children's charities. Such causes must have become more heartfelt after his own loss. And for a while he did manage it all: saving and giving away, building a new nest even without a lovebird to share it. So perhaps it wasn't so strange when they met that they naturally slipped into these roles: husband and wife, provider and dependant, case opened and shut. He was the pillar, and she accepted the traditional lifestyle; they even laughed about it. Then evening excitements gave way to quieter nights, a baby, the move out of the city. It had all happened so quickly. And now how much more time had gone by.

Time enough for all to be sterilised. Abruptly she cuts off the flame. The jars continue to knock against each other, then go quiet. In the silence she stands still for a moment. Almost too much has occurred for half a life. But then there's the other half to come.

The mixture in the other pot begins to bubble again rapidly. She gives it a final stir, shuts the heat underneath. Time to pour the syrup into jars and seal the lot. Now it's just a question of making it all stick.

∞

The usual crowd gathered for the usual event. Suddenly the bell rings, conversations are cut, doors fly open. From a sea of bobbing heads Christophe shoots out like a champagne cork, another four-year-old released from the pressures of school.

'Mama! Mama!' He points to a sticker on his dark red jumper. 'I got star of the week!'

'Wow, great, what for?'

'I don't remember,' he screws up his face. 'Oh, yeah, good writing!'

'Good writing? Well done, I didn't know you could write,' she teases.

'Everyone can. The whole class got a star. But I got an X mark too,' he shows her a red slip, a frown crumpling his face. 'I like curly letters but I can't do joined up writing.'

'Don't worry, it'll come. You have your whole life yet to write.' And a whole life for everything else. She looks around but the woman she was talking to has disappeared.

'No, Mama, they said we have to.'

'They?'

But now he's gone too, fighting for space in the melee of scooters. So much time ahead and here they are filling a little head with worries. Joined up writing – don't they know it will come soon enough? But Christophe's forgotten his woes. Scooter in hand, he's whizzed off with his mates. She tries to catch up, but Jenny's waving.

'Hey there, how are you? I've barely seen you this week.'

'Sorry, I've been busy, gardening, making jam,' she tries to make it come out cheerfully, though hiding behind chores is a way of coping when absence is too much to bear. Absence, always most difficult when the promise of presence has just been ripped away.

She looks away, spots Christophe.

'You okay? You look distracted.'

'No, actually,' she turns back. 'I'm embarrassed, Jen. About Harry, ditching everything, the weekend, the wrecked plans. I know David was looking forward to it, so were the kids.'

'Don't worry, David will go anyway,' Jenny stops herself abruptly, as if that prediction isn't quite the best. 'You poor thing, Harry really is away too much,' Jenny continues, reaching over to press her into a half hug. 'Why not come to mine tonight?

David's working late, we can feed the kids together. If you don't mind, fetch Sophie for me when you get Katya, then come straight over.'

'You sure?' She brightens. 'That would be great, I hate Friday nights alone.'

'Then it's settled, wine therapy!' Jenny dashes after James.

Well, something to look forward to, something to ease another evening. And an afternoon shortened, no time for lengthy projects, though if Christophe stays outside, she can print labels for the jam jars before they fetch the girls. She hurries, but she's far behind him now. Mindful of his every movement, the distance between them is ever increasing. But it will always be that way.

Christophe rounds the bend and suddenly there's no sight of him, panic, but then the sound: a scooter dropped at the hedge, the crunch of gravel under foot as little legs slice the air. She catches him hopping at the door, pushes it open.

'Mama, it smells good, I'm starving!'

As he always is. But before she can hug him, the thump of discarded shoes and he's off to the kitchen. There she finally grabs him, exposes his flat middle, plants a kiss. He squeals and wriggles away, oblivious to the moment, a mother's serenity and bliss.

'What is it?' He points to the pot.

'Soup, *zhurek*.'

Reverting to Polish and the task of lunch, she spoons chopped boiled egg and *kielbasa*, and ladles tart broth over.

'Yum! Shrek! Mama, I love it!'

She laughs. Never mind the language, he's a fan of the food. Especially now that he's well, slurping happily, relating bits of this and that, nothing coherent or intelligible, just snippets that make sense to him. No use interrupting because you've lost the thread of the story, contentment can come anyway, simply listening to the voice. Of course there's Katya too, but her love for each of them is different, as if love could split and flow in different directions, yet soar to the heavens all the same. With Christophe it's a mother-son bond that's embarrassing to admit, because no matter how much she fights it, it grows stronger. A daughter can be a woman's younger self – brave, clever and independent – the feeling for her is proud and fierce, like a caged lioness. She'd never known such anger before Katya came into the world, that violent need to protect the newborn. In an instant, she knew she would sacrifice her life for Katya. But there was no fragility in her daughter, she'd been born ready to go. All a mother could do then was marvel at such self-made determination, a dove taking to its wings. But with Christophe it stayed softness, butterflies. A soul untainted, darting about, unaware of existence beyond the immediate. And though his orbits and constant motion edged him farther away each day, he always needed shielding from being crushed. It seemed impossible that someday he might not need her.

With a clang, he flings down his spoon, a conductor concluding his symphony, big burp for the finale. 'Mama, I'm excused, I need conkers!'

'Krzysztof,' then in English, 'oh go on, but put on your wellies.'

Quickly she washes up, observing him through the window. This is such the easy part of the job. So much harder are the intangibles; creating childhoods for people you've created, replicating the good from your own upbringing, avoiding the bad. For the moment, sheer simplicity: Christophe chasing squirrels and Roobarb and Custard, their cats. The cats so clearly a part of Harry's childhood, some clever cartoons, though she liked the names too because they turned out to be kitchen creatures, perching to watch her cook. With the cats around, Christophe seems to have forgotten all about his conkers. Such a source of hope, this freedom from memory and the things that bind.

She drops the hand towel, heads to the study to print labels. But first, to check email – she's behind as usual. The internet's not such a large part of her life any more, why focus on what's distant? With Harry, there's enough managing that already. Thirty messages, she gasps, but her heart actually skips at the one: Xavier Dumas.

The name ought to give more away, but there's nothing to glean. He's out there – and reaching out.

To: Noisette
From: Xavier
Re: A Reprieve

My dearest Eva,

Out of the blue, I know, but I hope this finds you well after all this time, my dear. Carole and I are ecstatic, as is little naughty Maxime – we're back in Paris!

I can't say we exactly conquered our corner of China, although Maxime's Mandarin is quite passable. Carole never quite adapted to the food, but her sales thrived. Well, you can imagine, her business acumen, the Chinese addiction to high fashion and willingness to spend – let's say a confluence of strong tendencies.

As for me, I'm splitting time between the old, currency trading, and the new, marketing wine in Asia. The vineyard is getting to be too much for Carole's dear old father Armand. There will be a lot of travel back to Hong Kong but still, better to be in Paris most of the time.

How are things with you, my love? It's been too many ages, but you're only a Eurostar away now. Fancy lunch?

X.

Not a single unintelligible line, even in French, but how to comprehend the totality? Maxime *méchant*, Carole's haute couture sales booming, Xavier back in Paris, and now he wants to get together? The mind works furiously, backtracking, five years since the last exchange, about six since he left for Hong Kong, so much longer since she's seen him. The last encounter she was already married but before Katya, in Paris with Harry on a work trip. Walking alone around Vendôme, bumping into Xavier and Carole, a meeting so awkward because of Carole's taunting smile. But something in Xavier's face spoke of another time and she never forgot it. Then he left for Asia. A few emails back and forth, announcing births, then nothing. Radio silence imposed by her or him or by them both. They'd never really bothered with trivial banter, except as a way of masking sexual tensions. They'd always had that silent understanding of how far things could go.

Now reading into this, which surely she must, at least read between the lines, he's called her *mon amour*. It's a shock from which it's almost impossible to exhale. Because after *ma chérie*, my dear or darling, he's said *my love*. Breath recovers but it's shorter, tenser, more intense. A buried determination rising. Two can play this game.

To: X
From: Noisette
Re: The Reprieve?

Xavier, what a surprise! You're right it has been more than ages, a lot happens in five years. I have a boy now too, Christophe, four and a half, and you might remember about Katya, almost seven. But I've disciplined them severely in the Slavic way so they're not naughty at all.

Harry's doing well but working away these few months, so I'm on my own with the children. Paris does seem rather out of the question. Why don't you fly to London instead?

Eva

Meaning the last line as a taunt, or maybe she doesn't mean it at all, it's just the way they always spoke, in tennis-like volleys fast and low whizzing over the net. Word play. She sends it off purposefully in that moment before common sense can reassert itself. So what? What's so good about reining yourself in? It's death, this constant holding back; whereas the act of acting, even recklessly, is more than a burst of confidence. Exuberance is life itself, no?

She stares at the screen. Hitting back does mean the game's restarted, so nothing to do but wait, wonder what shape the response will take, what speed, what direction – game, set, match point. No, they never got that far, more like permanent deuce. He always played to win, she could only keep up, never had the same drive. Well, not in tennis. In the end they weren't that well matched. Love, always zero.

That wasn't true, though, there had been love. And he'd certainly taught her more than an appreciation for tennis. Reviewing the message, her sarcasm isn't that apparent, more like an invitation to cavort. But it's too late. Now there's only the wait. To know. But know what? If she should see him? What for? That last meeting in Paris was disastrous, Carole practically laughing at her. Though that too was a mystery, because Carole hadn't usurped Xavier at all. As the official break-up story went, Xavier and Eva had concluded a truce, rejected each other for the right reasons – not fitting each other's lives – not because as Carole suspected, there was something wrong with their mutual attraction. The sex had always been electrifying. Neither could be in the same room without ending up naked later.

Too dangerous, actually, that's what the situation is. But he'll get the sarcasm. It's what their relationship always degenerated to, each of them hiding behind a protective wall of verbal barbs. Stray from the computer? Check on Christophe? No, the urge is to linger. Like the sex that kept her coming back. A powerful hold.

To: Noisette
From: Xavier
Re: a reprieve, that's all

Oh Eva, you always did make things so easy.

I'm planning to be in London next week anyway. So I take it you'll come to lunch. Let's say Wednesday at the OXO Tower? One o'clock.

X.

She can't breathe. Or think. But she must. She closes her eyes. Yes, conjure him up. Xavier: the dark hair, the persistent gaze, the solid arms underneath pressed shirts. Because there is no doubt about wanting to see him. And it wouldn't be bad for him to see her now either, svelte and toned, and physically, if not emotionally, in the best state she's been in years. No, it wouldn't be bad to observe him regretting a little. To spite Carole and her blonde briskness, her money and insouciance, her tap-tap way of doing things.

To: Xavier
From: Noisette
Re: The lunch

Dearest X,

Okay, why not? But is this a firm plan or are there other lingering commitments?

Eva

She's hit as hard as possible but was always one to forget to complete the stroke. How to get away? The devil's in the details, as they say, never mind duty to children or husband, which didn't even enter the equation, or Harry, whom she might as well push out, since he isn't around anyway. Can Jenny look after Katya and Christophe? This is important, old Eva needs to rise to the challenge, show strength, prove she can still compete. Xavier will be expecting a good game, still be vying for victory, relishing the game itself. As always, when vanquished he'd help an opponent up, just so he could do it again. Forever holding the advantage was his goal. Of course she had loved proving him wrong. Because then came break point, when she made the stronger move – a course in London, a great opportunity – not least because of that irritant in his roving eye, Carole. Separation cloaked in terms of something temporary, so perhaps it hadn't been a true break. Only in tennis is break point the ultimate moment, when the receiver might win the whole game with the next point. But ultimately had it not been a total win for her, leaving him to Carole and other pursuits? But what had he thought? Was it all really down to playing again, like some failure to convert? Was life only that, a game of back and forth, repetition, complex rules you might comprehend but never really master?

To: Noisette
From: Xavier
Re: re: The lunch

Eva, this invitation comes with an olive branch. Please, be gentle.
Remind me, why are you Noisette?
X.

S'il te plait and *sois-douce*. Hearing the voice, her body melts. No need to punish, he's only another lost soul.

To: Xavier
From: Noisette
Re: re: re: The lunch

Dear Xavier,

Lunch would be lovely – nice to get away from laundering and cooking. I'm quite tied to the house these days.

I think I'm a hazelnut because I once made you a fabulous Polish torte. Or maybe I was a tough nut to crack?

Eva

Slow down, too fast, word play's now foreplay, the body taking decisions for the mind. But it comes without trying: the image of him in his spacious flat, the retreating summer, the bustle of Paris outside the window. Both of them tanned, sun hitting warm naked skin.

Then a gust of wind, and nothing. They both knew it would come to nothing, a mirage. But still it hurt, the parting. And months later, meeting Harry, leaving X forever to Carole and his other affairs: end of story. But now this: a reprieve. A handful of words, the smallest of exchanges, and it's as if he's trying to recapture her. Anyone can fume about manipulations but really who hates butterflies?

To: Noisette
From: Xavier
Re: Something else

Noisette, that must have been some good torte!

Tied to the house? You should be tied up in other ways…

Dear, you sound laden down with responsibilities. Get yourself some help, a domestic. Good for the beautiful woman's soul. You should be wearing lingerie, not laundering it.

58

Sadly on this note I must leave for a meeting. But I'll write you closer to the time.

X.

Cut off – and by that appalling presumption, that *dirigiste* manner, what ridiculous comments! But he's always been like that. One can't be shocked by the very behaviour that inflamed their relations to fever pitch; it's the basis on which everything was built. In the end there were no other expectations. It was from Harry that she expected more.

Another gust of wind, from the back of house now, the door slamming.

'Mama! Mama! Mama! Mama! Look how many I've got!' Christophe dashes in but halts in the doorway of the study, a herd of black footprints trailing him from the hall.

'Krzysztof! You're supposed to take off your wellies!' She leaps up, swings him round, marches him back to the kitchen. 'Look at the mud you trudged everywhere!'

Her anger bursts out in Polish, but it's not him. Mud is minor, X is major, in terms of trouble.

'Get them off!'

The command too stern, his little face crumples.

'But Mama, I found all these.'

Conkers fall from the curve of his jacket then, moist from the drizzle that's begun again. She looks. He only found five conkers that he liked; in the whole garden, only five. He must've chosen carefully yet failed in his mission to bring joy because he forgot about his shoes. Now tears form in his eyes and faster than she can think of a reply they unfurl down his pink cheeks.

'Look,' she says softly now, turning him round gently and crouching down, pointing to the tracks across the floor, though she might as well wave them away, wrap her arms around him. 'Never mind, I didn't mean to shout. It was just that, see, now I have to wash everything.'

She adds a hug because it really isn't fair, shouting when you're the one destabilised.

'It's okay, Mama. I can help you,' he says hopefully, dark eyes shining like Christmas baubles. 'I was sad too about my X.'

She freezes, X? Then remembers: his red slip. But like a warning arrow, a stray thought shoots through – X, like a hex, can be a kind of curse.

Still on her knees she brings him closer, to squeeze away his hurt and her own. He gives himself over to her completely, and she gives him everything too, except her doubt. Pure joy, dearest little man, how could you help? There's no one to save her. But then in a flash, another inadvertent thought:

Beloved son, last child, you might be the only one.

Christophe yawns as she shuts the door, although how can anyone wait so patiently and ardently for something so routine? Every night they come out from under the covers, Christophe's toes, tiny morsels for her to kiss. Tonight they stank but it had been too late to give him and Katya proper baths, damp though they were from their exertions. Because they'd dressed up in polyester costumes, raced up and down stairs and jumped vigorously all over the beds in Jenny's house because she allows that sort of thing. Still it came down to a quick wipe with a damp cloth, a fair substitute when children are tired and a mother's in a rush to get them to bed. Because downstairs other pressing affairs wait.

Anyway Christophe will probably be asleep before she finishes with Katya, another ritual of love, this mother-daughter chat that must go on, no matter how late or impatient anyone feels. She enters the room.

'Mama, I want to ask you something,' Katya begins, snuggling into the depths of her duvet. She prepares her case like Harry, launching in quickly then stopping to contemplate, brows lowered, then raised, a row of wrinkles spreading above her nose. 'Because you said we should talk about it later, and this is later.'

'So tell me.'

'The thing is,' she pauses, 'I want a birthday sleepover with Sophie.' She exhales as if emphasis might make it final. 'I'm going to be seven soon, and that's quite old enough.'

'Oh, little dove.' *Holubko,* Baba Kasia's most soothing Ukrainian word, the long ooo in the middle reminiscent of the coo of a pigeon or dove, the word the same for both. Little birds soar from home, even young, they are unafraid. 'Of course we can arrange it.'

'Yes, but when?' Katya continues, happily preoccupied with her plan. 'Since Daddy's not coming home any more…'

'No, Daddy will come,' she swallows the irritation. 'We're just not sure when. He might miss your birthday but hopefully not. We'll talk about this tomorrow.' She turns off the light, her sight adjusting to Katya's profile in shadow. 'Time to sleep. We've got to get up early for Christophe's football. Plus I have a surprise.'

'What?'

'If I tell you, it won't be a surprise.' Why do children always ask?

'Please?'

'No, we want something nice to look forward to.'

'But how can we look forward to something if we don't know what it is?'

Good point. Katya can always find a loophole, like Harry.

'You might be right, but the way I think of it, surprises are good either way. Life's full of them, like the stories we read.'

'But we know how they turn out.'

'Not new stories. They have unexpected twists and turns. You have to be patient.'

'But what if other people's surprises turn out to be something we don't want?' Katya yawns.

'That happens, but I wouldn't do that on purpose. I promise my surprise will be nice.'

'I won't be able to fall asleep for excitement if you don't tell me,' Katya insists, though her eyes are already shut.

'Yes, you will,' she whispers. 'Surprises keep you dreaming happy thoughts. And so will this.'

Leaning in to kiss her then, she begins the angel prayer, the one she recites every night to dispel fears under the cover of darkness. One of the few things Baba Kasia taught her in Ukrainian, this little rhyming prayer, the only thing she remembers fully in that language:

> Angel of mine, protector of mine,
> In the morning, noon and night,
> Be there to assist me.
> With a candle show the light,
> And envelop with your wings,
> Guide me from all evil things,
> Lead me to a life divine.

The rhythm lulls them both to silence. Katya's given up reasoning, she's safe. But a mother is always left lingering in the darkness, to carry on, alone.

Lead me to a life divine, a mighty request, but worth pursuing?

She listens to Katya's breathing until regular breaths tell of

62

undisturbed sleep. She kisses her forehead once more, her inner voice whispering too: *oh, should you be so lucky.*

∞

Hurry, hurry, move along, she can practically hear them saying as she joins the flow of fellow strangers stepping from the train on to the platform. The crush of Waterloo, being alone in a crowd, she braces herself. She'd like to go slow, on purpose, she's on this journey for some resolution, maybe even peace, though that's a common enough justification for war. Because actually only momentum governs most action, especially in war, an inability to stop, and that's what's carrying her forward too, along the platform, in her arguments with Harry, whisking her away like the train ride itself, already a blurred vacuum-packed whoosh past so many squeezed towns. Then immediate deployment into motion: people charging, dodging, almost pushing as they weave in and out of their own trajectories, hand held devices devouring, everyone walking, talking and organising all at once. It always seemed so civilised in her London days, when did all this rushing about begin?

A woman bashes into her side, sharp handbag to the ribs, dirty look cast over her shoulder. Maybe she is the problem: this new, slower Eva, taking measured steps where she too used to hurry. Or maybe the problem of pace infects her whole life-story because she's rambling along like one of Christophe's tales and like Katya she should be annoyed, because who is sure where it's going? Maybe marrying Harry had halted some of the chaos, but now that too seemed a temporary hiatus, another looking back at what was. Because the attempt to wipe away the frenetic, frenzied purposefulness of youth had really only opened up this

63

bigger gap, where one felt more acutely the eternal lack of direction.

On the steps of the station she stands aside, to catch her breath and see if she's already lost something. They really hadn't misnamed it, Waterloo, war annihilating peace. But it was also true vice versa, the understanding of something often only evident in its negation. Xavier. She takes another breath. She needs to get going, though the walk to the restaurant would have to be infinite to provide her with enough confidence and determination. Should she have plotted a course or was it okay taking one step at a time? Which provides the more solid footing? Supposing she can take a lasting view on what to say or do in this situation, can she stick with it? Questions multiplying, never adding up to anything, only the reality: she did decide to meet him, and in a few minutes it will play out.

Crossing carefully along marked paths it's impossible to slow down now, drivers honking, red buses careening, taxis overtaking and pulling over. She scurries to the safety of Sutton Walk and the pedestrian paths of Southbank. Taking in the colder waterfront air needed in vast reserves for this confrontation, putting off the thought of him, Xavier, just moments away, because who knows if she's prepared? She'd studied herself at length in the mirror, as if the reflective act of putting oneself in third person could make you more objective. She'd told herself superficialities like appearance don't matter, but on the other hand, it is important on occasions like this, what to wear. So she'd taken her time. Finally settling on the teal wrap dress, a blue almost the green of her eyes, a natural contrast to the new and more intense auburn of her hair, her whole style not too revealing, not too concealed, not too dressy, not too casual. Not too anything – exactly right for the day. The dress practical and sexy, with slim tan high-heeled boots, also good for walking and warmth, as well as sexy, so she could congratulate herself on good taste and sensibility. Justifications. In reality she'd been trying not to think of Harry, the times he took her to lunch. Luckily or unluckily, those times had been few, having tapered off like so many aspects of their early relations. Still, for a show of solidarity, she put on the engagement ring. That chunky diamond-encrusted sapphire passed from Harry's grandmother to his mother, one of the few things he didn't have to sell. A permanent point of irritation with Tilly, but it had been Harry's to give. The deflector rock, she dubbed it when he proposed, and he said, *what, to keep other men away in awe and intimidation? You mean like a magnetic force field? A clear shield like plexi-glass, so they'll bounce off when they come near?* And she laughed and replied, *okay, if we have to explain it.*

Now in meeting with Xavier the hope is it will work and she won't have to explain it – deflector, point of pride, barrier, reminder to her and Xavier of where they really are. And where is that exactly? Friends meeting for lunch in a restaurant encased in windows. Yes, of course, a transparent place high above the city, OXO, not quite part of the warehouse in which it resides, as if glass walls could offer protection when everything's out in the open, nowhere to hide. Then again, in taking a dare to be exposed, all might become clear.

Stepping into the lift, a moment to go, sweat forms underarm. Will the dress cover it? Is it dark enough? Will he find her as attractive as he did? A flurry of idiotic questions and another flash of guilt, because it's Wednesday, she forgot Miss Miriam! Too late for regrets though, doors opening. She steps out, scans tables. She has to claim that initial triumph: catching him first.

Pausing, knowing. That centring moment: seeing him. His hair speckled with grey like some distinguished actor's, his tall lean body radiating victory, he would be recognisable anywhere. He is the same.

Looking up, he returns the silent greeting, stands up and remains that way the whole time she crosses the room.

'Sorry I'm late,' she sputters first, though she isn't late. After so many years, the concept doesn't even apply.

He looks bemused, as if to retort, why begin with an apology?

'You look wonderful. Come, sit.'

His voice, baritone, deep and fluid, another element she forgot, how it was one of the things that held her. But rules are different now, she mustn't forget.

'You look great too. Not even ageing, despite your whirlwind life.'

He smiles, as if to acknowledge the point.

'You have that right. Whirlwind, I mean, not about the ageing. I have these now, see?' He points to some barely noticeable crow's feet. But he's tan and relaxed, as if it doesn't matter about wrinkles as long as they're done well.

'Ah, yes, it's been crazy,' he continues in quick Parisian French – the words, cadence, stresses, as they were, the pursing of lips. 'A good experience, Asia. But a relief to be back in Paris. I didn't realise how stressed I was.' He smiles again, taking her in. Not so much observing her dispassionately as consuming her completely.

'So it was hard on the family?' She searches for the right words, the right emphasis, shifting legs purposely to embody that cool businesslike person that no longer exists. 'You said Carole didn't really take to Hong Kong.'

'Not so much the business aspect as she missed her old social life. She didn't like the restaurants, the shops, the crowds. My god, the crowds. It sounds trivial but we both missed the parks, the expanse of sky you get in Paris, where you're not hemmed in by skyscrapers.'

Momentarily recalling his flat, not far from the Tuileries, as elegant a park as anyone could hope for, never mind the Louvre at the end of it, how many weekends had she spent meandering there?

Though it was cooler to hang out in the Marais, his circle of friends blowing smoke as they philosophised, decrying all they were. Except Yves Toussaint, whom she adored for having the surname All Saint, who didn't find her strange for enjoying art museums, gardens, old churches, like a newcomer. He'd been the one who took an interest in poems and other things she wrote. In fact, remembering it, quite a few of Xavier's friends had been more substantive than him, in the end.

'So, what now?'

His question shakes her from her reverie. He's still in an absorbing study of her.

She volleys back quickly, 'No, what now, I mean, new with you?'

'New? Well as far as work goes, I'm thinking of getting out of currency trading entirely, perhaps taking over Armand's business. You know Carole, she thinks her father will live forever but he won't, he's eighty-two. We may never move down to the vineyard – I couldn't leave Paris for good – but the wine marketing does need help. Of course, later, management too, though I don't quite see Carole leaving fashion either. But this is where I,' he corrects himself, 'the Asian angle will help.'

He leans in confidentially. 'I don't think there's a Bordeaux the Chinese won't buy, but with wine, like high fashion, it has to be marketed properly. At the moment, they only think Lafitte, but later I hope they will understand the value of smaller producers and burgundy. It's the exclusivity of the thing we need to concentrate on. Chinese upper classes love the best, even if they don't know what to do with it. Some mix wine with cola, can you imagine? But they want to be the only ones affording it, like the Russians. Soviet snobbism, I call it.'

He leans back, lost in his own world, pausing but not registering if she's joined him, and suddenly it's not hard to recall what it was like being with him, *snobisme sovietique* and all the other pronouncements. Why she left. She's about to ask about Yves and the old crowd, but he's staring again.

'And you, what's this business about your husband being away?' He seems unwilling to recall Harry's name though there's no way he could've forgotten it.

'Harry? Oh, he's...'

'Wait a moment, dear,' he motions to the waiter. 'Let's get some drinks first, shall we?'

So back to the endearing *chérie,* as he scans the wine list, smiling, pointing to her favourite, Sancerre. Long ago when she first encountered it with him, she thought it was called sincere, was delighted with the notion of a wine that might adhere to purity and truth. Later she just developed the taste for it, its connotations forever unproven.

Xavier continues his friendly banter with the waiter, ordering salad and fish for them both because he's forever watching his figure, as well as hers, then redirects the trickle of small talk to her. But that too evaporates as the waiter returns with the wine. Watching the pouring, he seems to enjoy this, the silence, the waiting for privacy. Taking his glass, he nods. They each take a long sip.

'Right, where were we? Your husband has run off and left his stunning wife home alone to meet with me.'

'Well, yes and no,' encouraged by wine, she might as well play the game as best she can. 'It has to do with tax, and that a year apart isn't that long. Afterwards we can think about doing something different.'

Purposely vague, but that explanation, casually flung, now seems poor. Hearing it aloud for the hundredth time, having explained it variously to everyone else, it suddenly appears to be a slapdash idea, like adding new shingles to an old roof. Having exposed a hole, messed with something quite sturdy in its original state, the danger now lies in the whole cover falling apart.

Xavier seems amused. 'So it's tax evasion. Quite the project for a man in the legal profession.'

'It's tax conservation and it's legal. Harry's good at what he does and he's needed in Eastern Europe. We thought we might as well stomach the separation and reap some benefit.'

Xavier's eyes are gleaming in a conspiratorial way. 'So how is this, eh, separation? What do you do for sex?'

Finishing the glass, making him wait for an answer – sex? But it's endless cups of tea, I'm English now, or at least a mother in the suburbs. But better to hide such frustration knowing what Xavier's like when he senses weakness.

'Well?'

'It's feast or famine.' Her eyes meet his. He's looking at her intently.

'So are you famished now?'

'I'm hungry alright.' And grateful that the waiter arrives with food at exactly that moment.

They start on their salads, the conversation moving to Yves and others, neutral territory, avoiding the painful beginning and end, the pregnancy that brought her to Paris, the cracks in their relationship that caused her to leave. It's always safe to focus on the solid middle, the lifetime condensed into months, which actually spilled over into a couple of years but seemed longer at the time. Almost possible to forget the rest even, to recall only the good – the art, the tennis, her life as a kept woman.

The main course arrives, but instead of precise little French sips they're drinking heartily now. Xavier too seems happy to have escaped, if only for the day. He'd hinted at the confines of Paris years ago and something must have driven him to his Asian adventure. But then he was too firmly French. He'd never leave France permanently, had admitted it, in the same way he never would have made the sacrifices necessary for her.

'You should come to Paris,' he says wistfully. 'The autumn is beautiful.'

'Carole wouldn't like that.'

'Carole doesn't need to know,' he says flatly, setting down knife and fork. 'Carole is busy with her work, her shopping and her friends, her yoga and parties and spas. She goes to the vineyard at weekends.'

Ignoring the implications, she eyes him. 'You don't go to the chateau?'

'Sometimes, when I need to see Armand.'

'What about Maxime?' Xavier didn't include him in Carole's interests but surely they were both concerned parents. 'Doesn't he visit his grandparents?'

'Yes, Maxime goes with the nanny, or Carole, or me. But now about *you*,' and again, his dark eyes are on her, his voice gentler. 'About you.'

Better to avoid his gaze now that the butterflies have been released. Go for an earnest, cheerful beginning, because the truth can't be dangerous, no need to deceive.

'What about me?' she smiles. 'I'm home with the children. I take them to school, look after an old house, and garden and cook and bake. I help with homework, take children swimming, my son plays football, they start quite early in England, you know. So it's busy being the only one home,' she pauses. 'Sometimes, I travel, back to Poland for holidays. But these days,' she stops. Because it's all babble, trying not to mention Harry, and it sounds terrible anyway and she's not answering the question.

'Yes, but what about you?' he repeats.

Tensile strength at breaking point, suddenly it snaps.

'Me?' her voice and shoulders dropping, gaze falling to her plate. 'I suppose I've been in hiding, Xav. Everyone's come first. I've been last these past years.'

The holding back of everything, even the mention of his name, releases like a balloon in a powerful whooshing breath.

'But,' she begins again, trying to contain the hapless flapping, looking up at him with great effort, 'just as things were starting to get better, now there's this absence to bear.' She pauses. 'Actually,' her voice almost croaks, 'at times it's quite hard.'

The strain too great, she looks away again, though the last bit had come out in low, measured tones. So as not to alarm him. So as not to alarm herself. So as not to crack up completely. Because there's no point in telling Xavier all this, though maybe there is rationale in telling someone who cares, someone who might be able to help. Maybe he is one of those people. Even after all that happened, all these years apart, it's impossible not to believe that. He'd never hurt her. Not after all that. She glances up.

'*Dur ou difficile?*' he asks. Hard or difficult?

He's caught her out. She reddens but he smiles.

'You need to look after yourself,' he continues gently, seriously. 'You are the pillar of the family.'

She stares at him because that's not how she's ever viewed it. In the family surely Harry is the pillar, the steady and strong one. But for Xav?

'What about Carole?' It slips out before she can stop herself.

'What about Carole?' Xavier's visibly annoyed. 'She's not like you. She never committed herself to the family. You, you have given everything.'

So he's disappointed in Carole. Maybe he wanted more children. Or for Carole to spend more time with the one she has rather than her career. Yet what contradictory goals, irreconcilable feats – even if the desire for balance and self-fulfilment is admirable, having it all is simply impossible. Putting a family first – but really first, not just talking about it or scheduling it – demands total sacrifice. Sacrificing other goals and sacrificing yourself, not just juggling. Because by definition, putting something or someone else first means you come second. Or last. More than one priority is an oxymoron. But Carole was never one to sacrifice herself, while Xavier was always good at making great demands and wanting it all. It would have been a tough position to be in.

'Well, you're right. I have given myself over completely,' she suddenly stops, wondering how that sounds. 'What I mean is, I wouldn't mind doing something else, someday – but not now, or there'd be no one around for the children. Like you said, holding it up, keeping it together.'

'Together? But you're on your own.' Xavier presses the button again. *Tu est seule.*

Her body bristles in retaliation, agitation, excitement. He doesn't have the right to criticise Harry.

'True, but we did agree to it – together – and it'll all be over next spring some time.'

'What will be over?'

'The separation, not the relationship.'

Emphatically stated, she picks up her fork, swivels it around and drives it into the mash. She's managed half the course, but it's enough. She removes the fork, lays it parallel to the knife. The signal, like he taught her, they're done.

'Anyway,' she looks up again. 'I'm hardly alone. I mean, many couples stomach separation, it's a feature of modern life. And Slavs are particularly good at bearing suffering.'

'Are they now?'

'Yes, and solitude has its benefits. I have more time to read in the evenings. Now that I'm becoming old, it's okay to be old-fashioned. I'm even tackling Pascal, you remember, *the heart has its reasons of which reason knows nothing.*'

She's smiling now, remembering him in student days guiding her in French literature and philosophy. Her language had become quite good then, though she'd read some of it in translation before which helped.

'I don't think old. I prefer timeless,' he counters. 'And if you're taking up Pascal, why not Dumas?'

Mischief in his voice, it takes only a second to understand. Not Dumas, the writer. Dumas, Xavier.

'Well, I think he was always too difficult.' But she's chosen the right word – not *hard*.

'He was a self-made man.'

'And a good one at that,' she pauses, 'though a certain amount of swagger comes to mind.'

He laughs out loud, fingers his wine forcefully.

Back to playing the game, exchanging glances, wine glasses refilled several times. Chatter and laughter, it's like floating. Beyond the windows an endlessly cloudy sky says nothing but momentarily a ray of sun bursts through in a preposterous show of determination. The Thames glitters below. She gazes at the city as if it might offer an answer to her problems, liberation from dissatisfactions, an escape, *the* escape. That's when he puts his hand on hers.

'Am I being too forward?' He searches her face intently.

The butterflies are flying tight circles, her reply is inadvertent, almost a whisper.

'No.'

∞

Lying in bed, remembering, not thinking, remembering, all those days from the distant to most recent. It had slipped out before she could catch it, that flutter of a reply, a tiny meaningless *non*, too late to recover, too late to understand if letting it go would

73

bring some ultimate harm to the universe. As a child she'd read a science fiction story like that, a crushed butterfly changing the sequence of evolution, the entire world for generations to come. A man on a walkway mindlessly stepping on a tiny winged creature, and she'd been frozen by that thought: that something so small and simple, done so inadvertently, could have such grave consequences. Unintended consequences, a universe altered.

But of course everything has consequences. Allowing him to caress her hand as he did, for as long as he did, a final flimsy excuse uttered, she rising unsteadily to say goodbye. He, rising to be one with her, honouring her the way any gentleman would do, of course, stand upright to bid farewell. Then coming nearer, leaning in, kissing her on each cheek, parting, the way all French do. Of course. *I understand, but it doesn't make me pleased,* he breathed. Not a trace of regret or detectable disappointment, the charge between them obliterated even that. Then moving away, he let her slip easily, so she felt the awful weight of separation.

Je comprends mais cela ne me plait pas. Butterfly released or butterfly crushed? Able to escape, move wings, flutter, as they parted she'd released a smile meant to reassure rather than encourage. But who knows how he took it? In the tightly enclosed space of the lift, descending into a private maelstrom, she'd been baffled, why hadn't the deflector rock worked? But even as the mind tried to push the puzzle away, the answer was clear. He'd caressed the left hand, the one Slavs don't adorn with rings. She'd kept the right one hidden under the table.

Flinging it away now in the mind, this ring along with every weighty barrier, no more deflectors, taking on the passion of his weight, imagining his body on top, hers for the taking. His soul, desire, his hands moving even as her fingers do the work, to forget she's in bed alone, because there are so many memories, of him kissing her, first her face, then back of the neck, then lower, lower, lower, until time stands still. His arms are pressing her wrists,

Xavier's holding her down until she's full body pinned under. No escape, now anything goes, imagination rules reality, he controls everything – force, passion, desperation – it all returns. He's hungry for her in a way she'd never known previously, nothing steady or steadfast about this. This weight of separation, the weight of his body, everything the way it used to be, back when she'd wear a red slip, dance on the bed and he'd fling her down and take her from behind. She'd cry out, hair pulled, protesting, heaving, shuddering, then suddenly it'd be over – over, she left gasping, a drowning woman coming up for air. Yes, over, it's over now, like it always was. Because it never lasted forever, it was never meant to last. He would only ever be her X.

Rolling to one side, she catches her breath, keeps her eyes shut tightly to retain the darkness. Oh, so easy to justify this, the Xavier of the mind, playing yourself to him alone. Because she's alone, abandoned already, so forget more austerity and deprivation, the preaching of religions. This is total desire, another kind of absolute. He's never stopped loving her. Love, this supposed great thing, yet always hemmed in, circumscribed – why? Why should love only flow to one man or woman? For conventions of religion, a man-made world? Who made such rules – share your love equally with children but love only one man? Who's here to judge? Conscience, such a quaint concept from previous centuries, but she's faced chaos, annihilation, death. And life is tiring, so, so tiring, why not allow love in all its fullness?

All those days in Paris, Eva, don't you remember?

∞

She must have dozed off. Lying in the darkness, in the warm afterglow of imagined passion, she must have fallen asleep. Now she's half awake, feels the cold. Where is Harry? She pulls the covers up around her neck, tries to remember. Budapest, Vienna... the thought tripping back to Harry himself, who should be here next to her, his body warmth regenerating hers.

Bringing her feet round to a curled position, yes, where is he? Harry. Mr Heater. Mr Fix-It. Mr Practical Constructive Advice. He never bought into things like red slips, equally happy for her to borrow his pyjamas. Better yet, the luxury of skin on skin, *why bother with lingerie if it's only going to come off?* To which she giggled, *but don't you find it sexy?* Then she'd flaunt something purchased in the sales. *Sure, but I find you sexy anyway, especially in tight dresses, which you should wear more of – you know I like to watch you from across the room.* She probably smiled, *well, I'd wear them if you'd take me out.* Then she'd have waited patiently. *Okay, find a babysitter,* he said, mostly likely not looking up. *You know how little they are, Harry, who can I really leave them with?* And so on and so on. So they'd rarely gone out then.

Of course there had been that party in Soho, when she'd worn that short, tight glittery skirt. Fretting she looked like sausage squeezed in casing, as they say in Poland, or worse, as the English put it, mutton dressed as lamb. Was she already too old for these attempts at youth? Did she look like the kind of East European woman that trawled hotels? *No, you were a hit, Eva, trust me, love, flaunt it while you can. My fantasy is knowing I'll have you later.* So he could be passionate, this Harry. A quirky wild side, and laughter, so often lacking with X. With X, almost too much intensity, no room to breathe. But Harry was easygoing, introspective and diligent, hardworking and faithful. So what's missing, besides his presence? What's missing, when there seem to be no clues?

In the darkness lying alone, drifting toward a blank, maybe to sleep on it, yes, as they say, to sleep, perchance to dream, perhaps it'll be better in the morning, the pull of slumber a powerful maelstrom sucking her down, further, further, like a rip tide, spitting her out sideways, but not to that peaceful place but to the jumbled dreams of the confused. Because Xavier's beckoning outside the kitchen window urgently but she can't come just yet, Harry's rung to say he's coming soon. X is out there, waiting patiently, but Harry is out there too on the platform at Clapham Junction, busiest station in England, the sign says all the connections can be made here. But that's too many permutations and it's to no avail, Harry should know that, because he's waiting for a train that won't come. Today's a holiday, a holiday from the everyday, he should be home already, and she's there, isn't she, so where is he? Yes, she's home, cooking quinces for a party and that's where Harry should be too, but then the sudden panic – she'll never get it right, not this chef's recipe. She's never tried it before, and worse, she's making it up as she goes along and what's the success rate of that? *Have you put in all the ingredients?* The chef prods her from television like a cartoon, pointing a castigating finger, *everyone knows how it's supposed to taste, Eva. You can't take liberties, do as you like, you have to follow the recipe, follow the rules.* The doorbell rings, the phone rings, so much ringing, altogether it's practically church bells, then suddenly everyone arrives, everyone but Harry. Even Xavier's outside smoking, blowing lots of smoke actually, refusing to step into her party, being demanding as usual but not satiable either while Harry continues to ring, ring, ring, to say he's running late. *It's okay, I'll catch the next train, love,* he says, but she's lost patience, reminding him trains don't run on Boxing Day. *No, it'll be all right, I'll just catch the next one,* he insists, and she slams down the phone. She's going out to Xavier, but now he's disappeared too, probably talking business with Armand, so now she has to entertain the whole house of people all by herself. There's no one she knows, not even in her own house, and Katya keeps coming downstairs crying and Christophe's running a fever and to her horror, the great horror of any hostess, she has to ask everyone to leave. Xavier returns then, right at that moment, how perfect, fighting his way against the departing tide, *what's wrong, Eva?* His easy laugh forgiving and deep, anyway he knows this is no big deal, the whole thing's funny actually, her alone, trying to manage while her husband is forever a day late. And Xavier takes her hand and gives her the right amount of pity, all of it in a look that says, *I want you*, and he begins to seduce her, *you poor overworked thing*. His eyes say it as his hands move down her back, so she ignores Harry ringing, again and again, only ringing, never coming, while Xavier presses her against a wall, a wall that isn't her house any more but somewhere in Paris which is also London, Xav saying over and over, *just you wait and see.*

∞

'So how was it?' Jenny busies herself transferring apple turnovers from a baking sheet to cooling rack, the scent of fruit and pastry filling the air.

'Swimming?'

She'd already blanked it out. An afternoon trying to swim *with* the tide, poolside watching children gulp for air, intolerable noise, heat, pulsating humidity. Droning drills, high-pitched screeches, clumps of hair clogging drains. Wet tabloids abandoned on soiled nappies, bins overflowing. The health club. Having signed the kids up over Harry's protestations – *maybe toddlers don't need to swim, Harry, but this is the society we live in, too many long afternoons, exercise does them good.* And the thought she didn't share – *a sure night of solid sleep is a mother's prerogative.* Still it seemed a hefty price to pay.

'No, silly,' Jenny laughs, turning around, licking a sticky finger, pushing her bob back into place with the back of her hand. 'Your lunch with Xavier.' She rinses her hands, sets two mugs on the table and sits. 'Well?'

Xavier, Xavier, another kind of futility.

'Well?' Jenny repeats, looking intently. 'Come on, spill.'

'Nice, it was… interesting.'

'And? What was he like?'

'Predictable.'

'Come on, Eva!'

'Okay, hot as ever.'

'See, I knew it would be dangerous,' Jenny smiles. 'But that's the beauty of the internet, I guess, nothing's ever finished. Anyway, it's not like you met him at night, after all, just a lunch,' then she smirks, adds, '*date*.'

'I'd call it a meeting.' But the tension is too great, the smile bursts through.

'Romantic rendezvous?' Jenny teases.

'Tête-à-tête.' She pauses, now serious, because she needs to ask the favour. 'Jenny, please, would you not mention it to David? I had thought I'd tell Harry, you know, he's not the jealous type, level-headed. He wouldn't have forbidden me, though he'd mock me mercilessly. But lately, the separation, it's a strain. Probably best he not find out.'

'What, you want me to act as accomplice? Sure, no problem. As long as you let me live vicariously through this illicit affair.'

'It's *not* an affair, it was one lunch,' but she can't help laughing.

'Ooh, the lady doth protest. Look, Eva, I'm kidding. I wish I could have had lunch in London too, but noooooooo, slaving away at the Aga, four children tugging at my knees.'

'Stop,' she flashes Jenny another smile. 'I do thank you for taking them. I owe you.'

'No, it wasn't a problem. Have you heard from him yet?'

'No,' her smile disappears.

'But you will…'

'I don't know.' But that's a lie – one of them will write, then it'll be restarted.

'What about Harry?'

'What do you mean?'

'I'm not trying to judge,' Jenny's voice lowers as she falls serious, 'but it does seem if you're having issues, Harry away and all that, you probably shouldn't see Xavier again. It could open a can of worms.'

Or she might feel sexy again. Alive, butterflies, but that's another truth best buried. Because the story of Pandora's box has two versions: you open the box and lose all, nothing left but hope, which is optimism for the future. But that's the positive, Western interpretation. If you're Eastern, Slavic, hope is negative, a last resort. It's what you're left with when all else has failed.

From the top of the stairs, a thump and the sound of Christophe's mournful whine. 'Katya, I'm telling Mama!' Then the front door creaking open, and David's boots stomping. 'Hello?'

'In here,' Jenny jumps up, suddenly registering the time. She throws herself into final assembly, pulling a tray of roast potatoes and sausages from the second oven, draining beans. She dries her hands quickly and bends around the doorway, 'Hi hon!' then calling in the opposite direction upstairs, 'Tea everyone, come wash hands!'

David saunters in, surveys the scene. He's in his soiled work wear, a garden centre owner who never shies away from heavy lifting.

'Fantastic, and what are we having?' he grins, stretching his beefy arms across the doorway, poised to make way below for a horde of incoming children.

'Same, only better,' Jenny says. 'Gourmet bangers and sautéed kale and whatever roasties are left over. Eva, you'll join us?'

'Oh, thanks but no, you two carry on.'

'You sure? Plenty of food, and I'm about to open some nice merlot. C'mon, you can't tell me you have dinner waiting if the kids are eating here.'

'No, but,' she doesn't finish.

'Then stay.'

'Join us,' David says. 'I'll go shower, get out of the way and leave you girls to it for a bit.' He grins again, disappears.

From the hall bathroom excited voices behind shut doors: the children have turned hand-washing into another game. Jenny calls again but returns to her puffed pastries, moving them one by one from the rack to a decorative plate.

'I think this is how I'll serve them at the Christmas party,' she muses. 'Before the kids attack them tonight, I'll get a photo for the website. I've had good feedback on these, might make them a staple on the menu. Then again, catering's such a business of fads, you have to stay on top of new demands, keep reinventing.'

'You're incredible, balancing this with the kids, house. I feel so useless by comparison.'

'You're not,' Jenny concentrates on arranging. 'I couldn't do this if David didn't work regular hours. You're practically a single mum, Eva, juggling everything, how can you be expected to do more?'

'But I feel the opposite, like I'm doing nothing,' she sighs, recognising the guilt that weighs heavily on dissatisfaction. 'Sometimes I feel I could disappear and no one would notice. Like I've dropped off the world's radar.'

'No one would notice? We would – I would! Your kids certainly would,' Jenny retorts. 'Even Xavier would notice,' she smirks. 'Come on, that's just middle age talking. Harry's relying on you absolutely this year – don't be hard on yourself.'

What was it Xav said? The pillar?

Jenny rifles through the wine cabinet. 'Here,' she hands over a bottle and corkscrew. 'Only one way to get back on track: red wine and Abba. *Voulez vous?*' she almost sings. 'Go ahead, open it. I'll get the kids and serve up dinner. We can sit next door, I want to hear all about this ex!' she bustles out.

All about this ex, but it sounds more like: about the sex. Another thing she can't admit, but with X, isn't it the same? And if not, what more is there?

∞

'Mama! Mama! Mama! Mama!'

She hears it from a distance, the never ending mama. Like 'Mamma Mia', here we go again, old tracks on repeat, sure sign you've hit middle age. The back door slams twice, she leaves the study quickly. Christophe and Katya, already in the kitchen, boots in a pile, for that much she's grateful. It's a mistake to be distracted by X before the day is done.

'Look at these!' Katya carefully stacks conkers on the kitchen table. 'These are food for our restaurant!' She hovers by Christophe at their plastic kiddie kitchen, its little oven doors wide open, stove top littered with tiny pots of conkers. 'Here, Christophe,' she continues sagely. 'You can be the waiter, to take the orders, and I'll be the chef.'

'But I can't write joined up!' Christophe wails. 'And I don't want to wait!'

'Not wait, *wait*!' Katya says, but he's perplexed. 'Okay, then *I'll* be the waiter, but *head* waiter,' she continues without missing a beat, 'and you be the cooker. Look here, cooker, these conkers are overdone. You must mix them or they'll burn.'

She pats him on the back kindly and Christophe, easily appeased and not at all bothered by her occasional bossiness, takes to the new arrangement: taking orders from his staff. Katya writes fancy chalk squiggles on the blackboard, then astonishingly, RESTORENT and MENYOO, and in no particular order, letters just as higgledy-piggeldy: ZOOREK SOOP, BRED, KONKER KASROL.

'Wow, that's some menu. What's the first thing?'

'Mama! That's *zhurek* soup, don't you know?' Katya protests.

'And conker casserole and bread,' adds Christophe, not reading but briefed on the plan, Katya whispering in his ear.

'I'll put on dessert, but not yet, because we don't want to spoil their appetite,' Katya affirms.

'You get no pudding if you haven't eaten your dinner,' nods Christophe.

'Oh I get it,' she smiles. Pink Floyd was right about English school discipline. 'Carrots and sticks.'

'No, Mama, no carrot sticks,' says Katya. 'That's not on the menu.'

She chuckles. 'Go ahead and play, I'll go on the computer a bit more.'

'No! You have to stay here! We need eaters!'

She has to concede because it is their time, though five hours of childcare can be an eternity, especially since Xavier's written. But dish after dish of leaves and conkers is served until everyone's absolutely bursting and it's time for real dinner: pork cutlets, boiled potatoes, solid Polish fare. Plus those ever popular English peas that beg the question: why are they considered child-friendly? Always rolling on to the floor, she picks them up one by one as they scatter, mentally willing time forward.

So on to baths, more adventure, as small boats get in terrible trouble from the tidal waves in the tub. Katya and Christophe play naked, safe in their confined space, while she flips through magazines, occasionally glancing up to tell them to stop splashing water everywhere. But really her mind is on his message:

To: Noisette
From: Xavier
Re: Une bouffee d'OXO-gene

My dearest:

Sorry it took a while to get back to you – business, life – really no excuse. It was lovely to see you again, a breath of fresh air, or oxygen, if you forgive the pun – you always were better with words.

Don't worry about the past or anything and if you're ever in Paris, let me know. I may be back in London soon, but I don't know when, sorry.

Until then, I remain yours, truly,

X.

So few words she could commit them to memory. A breath of fresh air for him, but for what? *You always were better with words.* Ha, Harry doesn't think so. And *désolé*, sorry, in all its French ambiguity, but *I remain yours, truly*? A way of signing off or did he mean – *does* he mean – to remain hers, truly? How would that be possible? *Don't worry about the past*? Since their meeting there's been nothing but the past. Dreams interfering with reality, no way of knowing anything for sure, though how can one know, apart from investigating further? But isn't that too but a thin cover for completely letting yourself go? No, go on searching for hidden meanings, the emotions behind phrases, check those tenses, but still you'll return to the beginning, uncertain. She's reviewed these words many more times than intended, but maybe that *is* the intention, unveil what's there.

Anyway, what could she say to his message? Nothing clever came to mind as in their first barrage of notes. She couldn't say, *still missing our days together but overall glad to be here!* Nor could she wish him and Carole all the best, because even if you don't want to see others unhappy, it might sound flippant or worse, a weak lie. Nobody really gains in another's misery. Or so she'd always believed. But maybe you do gain if taking from them is the road to your happiness. She couldn't come to any conclusion on this score, so she left her reply open-ended:

Yes, it was lovely, and I suppose a good thing the Channel separates us now. You were very well behaved. I applaud you.

Enjoy being back in Paris, we'll see what the future brings.

'Mama?' Katya's voice. 'I'm cold.'

Looking up from a page of adverts that hasn't registered, she sees the bath water's leaked out slowly. Katya and Christophe are sitting in an inch of foam.

It's a small thing, only a small thing. It could even be funny. But for the sharp memory, the past piercing through: Katya's bewildered look, an infant in the bath. She'd only looked away for an instant, really. But Katya had slid under, as if the water was her natural home. Her big baby eyes gazing, no breath, just a wide eyed stare through clear liquid, an infant mermaid. And she, the mother – the *mother* – had stared back. Shock maybe, only a split second, but even that was too long, that moment of observation. It might've gone either way. Then instinct, panic – the grabbing, the lifting, the gasping. The permanent guilt.

'Mama?'

'I'm sorry, I'm so, so sorry,' her voice breaks, an apology too profuse for the situation. 'I'll rinse you off.'

Blitzing her own hand with hot water, punishment, to get it right for them, she sprays their sudsy bottoms with warm water, pulls them out and wraps them tightly in fluffy towels. Giving each a hug in turn, she leaves them again guiltily, to run for their pyjamas, another thing she forgot.

She returns and there they still sit, on the mat, squeaky clean and bright-eyed, chattering like the baby monkeys they once saw bathed on TV.

'There, all warm,' she hugs Katya again to make it better. 'Now story time,' she adds, as if they were the ones who needed reminding.

But story time always settles her too. It's a time for nesting, a cure for her distractions and a form of distraction itself, reading stories, the three of them on Katya's bed, she stroking Katya's arm, then Christophe's curls, once so reminiscent of Harry's wavy hair. But then Harry had his cut to suit his image, or the times, so now she only has her son to go by.

Time to get on with the story, Christophe's pulling on the pages, so she releases them both and they're off to fantasy land, that world where children spend their days. A world where a boy dreams: how might he and a star get together and be friends? It would be exciting, wouldn't it, having a star of your own? Think of all the fun you'd have! Then one day instead of waiting and dreaming, the boy decides to go do something about his desires. He sets off on an expedition to catch his very own star. Unfortunately he has to wait a very long time for one to appear and this tries everyone's patience. Finally it does appear but of course it's too high to reach. The boy can't climb up to it or lasso it, and wouldn't you know, his trusty rocket's just out of fuel. Even the birds on the docks don't seem to want to help out. So things are looking pretty hopeless. But as the boy's about to give up on his challenge, he spies a star in the water. He can't catch that one either, but he walks along the shore, patiently waiting again. And sure enough, the star comes to him.

Closing the book, she wonders if they got it, that it's not really a star, only a reflection of the real thing. That actually a starfish washed up, something altogether different. But what's the point of destroying effect?

'See it came after all.'

'Maybe it was because he tried so hard,' Katya says. 'Maybe God sent him the star because he could see the boy really wanted it.'

'Or maybe he got lucky,' she throws in a discussion point, good for them to think. 'Maybe that's why in English you thank your lucky stars?'

'Or maaaybe,' Christophe interjects with dramatic pause, 'the star could see him from the sky and that's why he jumped in the water and swam over!'

He yawns then and she can tell he isn't greatly bothered with his theory, he's happy with the story as it is, open-ended. But he also wants to be like his sister.

'Yes,' Katya adds, 'but maybe it was angels!'

They chatter on, Katya issuing out ever more sophisticated postulations until it's time to tuck them in. They've both missed the point, but it's time to leave them to sleep.

She shuts the door, makes her way to bed yawning. Then it dawns: no, she missed the point. When you try, things do come to you. And patience helps. Or maybe you just get lucky. But it doesn't greatly matter that you can't tell how or why most of the time. It doesn't even matter if dreams come true exactly as you wish. Because it's the fact of a wish being fulfilled, and for that, there is no difference.

∞

Miss Miriam forks a single morsel, chews one bite at a time. It can be painfully slow watching her eat, quite a few cups of tea go down. But she seems to enjoy potato pancakes with sour cream, a discovery late in life.

'Mmm, that was delicious, Eva.' Miss Miriam sets down her cutlery, folds her napkin. 'I've eaten more than I should.'

'No chance of that, you didn't have breakfast, and here it's almost lunch. You mustn't forget to eat,' she chides. 'I don't know what you do on days I'm not here.'

'Oh, I manage,' Miss Miriam smiles, her blue eyes flashing mischief. 'I don't forget to eat, Eva. I wait for the good things to come.' She takes up her tea cup for a long satisfying sip.

'Here, I have something else for you.' Reaching into her bag, she pulls out a jar. 'Quince jam, I made it from the fruits of our tree. Good on toast but also with cheese, especially that Spanish one, manchego. I've pressed some quince cheese especially for that if you prefer, but I think the jam works both ways.'

'Why thank you, you're ever so kind, this is more than enough.' Miss Miriam is delighted. 'Such an international experience I'm having. I'll be sure to have some with breakfast tomorrow. I don't have Spanish cheese, will cheddar do? Oh, I can show Emma what lovely neighbours I have.'

'Emma's coming?' She's never met Miss Miriam's eldest, the one who lives closest. It was a great surprise to find out recently she only lives a few miles away.

'Tomorrow. She says we have business to take care of.' Miss Miriam sighs. 'It has to do with the house. Apparently developers have their eye on it,' she leans in conspiratorially. 'Emma says we should sell soon, something to do with a mansion tax that's coming, or inheritance taxes. I don't know, what a muddle, trying to leave things to your children. But I'm not apt to do anything different from what Charlie said in his will. Property should stay in the family. I can't imagine why she or Philip haven't thought of taking it over, they each have a brood. Though I suppose some are boarding now. But it can't be that much trouble, dividing by two, basic maths. One or the other should take it over,' she pauses, smiling. 'Not that I'm planning on dying soon, but the neighbourhood can't go to the dogs after I'm gone. I see what's going on, the council letting developers do whatever they like, knocking down proper homes, putting up concrete blocks, more and more traffic, just terrible. You can hardly cross a street without cars whizzing at you, almost running you down,' she continues, shaking her head, 'and all these children trying to get to school.'

Wilful civic-mindedness, one of Miss Miriam's endearing qualities. A consummate letter-writer and council-baiter throughout retirement, she was now watching a lifetime of experience and opinions reduced to irrelevance by dint of her age, preservation not being in the slightest interest to young bureaucrats.

'It *is* quite crowded already, I agree, and not enough schools for all the houses they're building. But I'm not sure they'll do anything to reverse it. The government's plan is for thousands more homes to be built in the south-east. That'll tend to fall on areas close to London, like ours,' she sighs. 'Harry's even said we might have to move farther out.'

'Dear god no,' Miss Miriam says. 'Exactly what mustn't happen, respectable residents leaving. How dare they push us out – this is Surrey, not London. If people want to live on top of each other, they can stay in the city. We're not rodents to be squeezed in.'

'You're right but it's a question of staying to fight,' she doesn't add – or giving up, doing what's best for yourself.

'When you live long enough, you hear everything,' Miss Miriam says, a propos of nothing, a phrase she often uses to wrap up. 'Now you mustn't be late for that darling boy of yours,' she taps the table. 'Time's getting on.'

They rise and make their way to the door. She's half way out when Miss Miriam starts mumbling.

'Charlie, I don't know about that will. They might not be deserving, our lot, we ought to rewrite it.'

∞

Waiting for Harry, it's like waiting for Godot – will he ring, won't he, when will he come? – everyone waiting impatiently saying they won't wait any more (though they will), saying there's got to be a resolution (but why, is there ever one really?) because would anyone bother carrying on if they knew there is no resolution? Why not give up? On plays, internet, television, and complicated affairs. Why not stop creating new dramas, filling one's head with fiction, other people's troubles, real or imagined?

She tosses the book aside though she's not finished it. Not so much boredom rising, as fatigue. She thumbs through another book but sets that one down too. So much for literary fiction. No prospects there for resolution, nothing to make you feel good. Of course contentment can't be found in current affairs either – or history or philosophy or religion – quite the opposite. There's only suffering and guilt, inherent and surrounding one's doing and non-doing. Because no matter how many times you set the valiant goal of alleviating poverty/war/hunger/suffering/reading *War and Peace*, who actually does? Like most honourable goals, great tomes gather dust. English masterpieces, Polish classics, French standard-bearers, all waiting bedside – and the Russians, as ever, beyond waiting a turn – perhaps somewhere in this pile there is a path to wisdom. But for instant feel-good, only escapism will do. Besides, it's too late for anything else. Exhaustion's taken over.

She grabs a catalogue from the floor, starts flicking absentmindedly through pages of flowered bags: this one, that one, another one. Though what's the point if it's not clear what you want? Is passage of time only a quest for perpetual distraction? And even if it can be argued to be a basic human desire, surely escapism is predicated on non-thinking. So how can you escape if you *do* think? If instantly you wonder how these companies can afford to exist? Maybe it's because they're asking more than a hundred pounds for something that costs a fiver to make in China. Bags and scented candles, napkin rings and fur throws, distressed hooks, all the same in these catalogues appearing on the step intrusively, making you want to peruse them though there's nothing missing in the house. *Oh, but this key holder will make your life so much more organised. Look, see this woman, how much she's enjoying it? Look how much better her life is now that her keys hang evenly in one place. Look how she smiles, how happy, how much more satisfied she is with her life than you with yours.* This escapism is a fallacy but it's too easy, as easy reaching for a catalogue as a cup of tea. Becoming addicted without knowing to some soothing aspect of life when all else is in chaos. *Here, look,* the catalogue beckons, *see how well dressed and coiffed and orderly life is elsewhere, simply by virtue of owning products with dots, stripes and patterns? Though we know if you buy them, there will be guilt, not peace or pleasure, because life isn't really meant to be stripy or dotty. Or maybe even set in patterns. And certainly not always happy.*

Yet to be able to escape! To be carefree, like these women and their childish wardrobes and sunny houses, with their appliquéd flower corduroy skirts and pale blue polka dot mugs, so far from the worn and faded surroundings to which she defaults. They're real people too, these women, she knows, because she's been in their kitchens – and conservatories and sitting rooms – all chirpy with new catalogue products. But they're never satisfied like their paper counterparts because they always need more: newer candles, fresher scents, a whiter mixing bowl with a better pouring lip, *see how you can match your tablecloth to your napkins?* Until after a while she felt her table might be too Polish-looking though Baba's embroidery had always made her feel safe and grounded. What's all the fuss about if you only take out tablecloths once or twice a year? Where are you supposed to store all this stuff you collect? Because it's not like Christophe's conkers, easily tossed and replaced. She'd been taught to keep things for a lifetime. Because that's how things become important, that's how they become heirlooms.

She sighs, casting a despondent look at the phone. Time's getting on. Harry should've rung by now to give her whatever important news he said he had to transmit. Whatever accusations he might yet throw vis-à-vis household economies at least she can remind him she'd broken the cycle of buying and throwing away. Because after initial mistakes, she reformed, broke with capitalism's new totalitarianism: constant consumption. She remembered Baba and Mamcia cooking the greatest meals from simple spoons and chipped bowls, happy, memorable meals eaten from no matching sets whatsoever. So even as acquaintances and friends who came from modest means claimed to understand all this was surplus to need, they continued buying and spending and collecting all the same. Maybe they felt deprived, that acquiring unnecessary things might make their lives fuller, as if clutter could fill gaps left by troubled pasts. But she'd thought about it and figured out that the new batter bowl wasn't any better than the old one. In fact her pancakes had improved over time no thanks to any bowl, so she gave the fancy one away to a charity shop. It never had such a good pouring lip anyway. Nowadays, she felt practically immune, catalogues not so much an escape as a reminder of what could be lost if you gained too much.

The phone starts, she reaches over. 'Hello?'

'It's me,' Harry's tired voice. 'How are you?'

'Fine.'

'What you up to?'

'Nothing, bed, waiting for you,' she pauses. 'Looking at all the stuff we don't need.'

'What?'

'Catalogues, never mind. You okay? You sound exhausted.'

'I am,' he yawns.

'Maybe you'll have a chance to rest more next week. It's almost half term.'

He coughs. 'That's my news, there's a change on that.'

'Please don't tell me you have to cancel,' her voice wavers. Who could bear the thought?

'No, it's a positive change.' He pauses. 'How about instead of Warsaw – Paris?'

Paris.

'Eva?'

Xavier.

'Eva?'

'Why would I say no to that?' It comes out lightly.

'It does mean you'll have to stay home with the children for the first half of the week, no school or activities, doubly hard on you, I know,' Harry launches in. 'But we've got negotiations in Paris, and while I'll be busy the first half of the week, I thought you and the kids could come out for the second, a long weekend. We'll be staying at the old Intercon, so we can swank it up a bit in the evenings, get a babysitter, go out.'

More promises: Paris, a fancy hotel, free time. More importantly, another chance with Harry. It's been months since they had an evening together. Xavier mustn't intrude, not on this, not family time. Though would she have been so quick to trade eight days for four, no matter what the backdrop, if X weren't there?

'I admit I've taken the liberty of booking tickets assuming you'd want to go,' Harry presses on. 'And sorry I didn't book the train, I know you hate flying, but I have all these spare air miles. It's a short flight, you don't mind, do you?'

'No, I'll manage, it's a stupid fear anyway. We have to fly to Poland for Christmas, I might as well get used to it,' she pauses. 'Speaking of which, I meant to ask about booking BA or Lufthansa, not much more expensive than flying on low cost, what with surcharges, horrible schedules and taxi fares. Instead of Rzeszów I could fly to Krakow with the kids, then drive to Przemyśl with Magda. I sent you itineraries by email. If they work, I'll confirm with Magda.'

'Sounds good, do it,' Harry says, content. 'See? I told you we'd manage. All coming together.'

'Maybe.' It comes out inadvertently.

'Why, what's wrong?'

'Nothing,' she exhales, searching for something to fill the space. 'The kids miss you.'

Harry sighs. 'Eva, I miss them too. What did you do tonight?'

'We read *How to Catch a Star* – again.'

'Christophe's favourite,' Harry interrupts.

'Seems you need to work and wait to get lucky.'

'Is that the moral of the tale?'

'I'm not sure,' she says truthfully. 'Seek what you love, maybe. Be passionate.'

'Never mind working or waiting, I'm passionate about you,' he says, firmly, softly. 'I wish you were here, or I was there.'

'You are missed, Harry.' But she stops from letting go, from saying *I miss you too*. What good would that do? He wants her to hold on. 'Anyway, David's been asking when you'll be back, he wants to organise another cycling trip.'

'I'll drop him an email. By the way, I got one from Tilly, she's going stir-crazy with the renovations, kids. They're off school already, apparently two weeks holiday at half term. You wouldn't mind terribly having her round, would you? You'd be doing me a turn.'

'Sure.'

'Eva, promise me one thing.'

'What?'

'Promise me you'll always be mine.'

She laughs, surprised. 'But I have already!'

'But again.'

'I promise I'll be yours forever and ever. Now you do the same.'

'I promise to be yours forever. But now, I need to go to sleep. I have a meeting at seven am.'

'Go, I'm not keeping you.'

He laughs, blows a kiss, the phone clicks. She turns off the light.

The kids miss you. A half truth put in because it's true in general, not because they've asked about him lately. Sometimes they go days without mentioning Daddy but she doesn't want to remind them, or tell him. Nothing to be done to bring him back immediately, nothing to feel sorry for either, they're in this deal together. Daddy's only away because of work, whereas some daddies go off to war and get in real danger and never come home. Or if they do, they don't have a leg to stand on and still no money for holidays. So we're lucky, very lucky.

It's also right that Xavier shouldn't intrude on family time. But he's there, in Paris, and in dreams, in this bed too. He already does intrude. So the consuming problem now is how to make it all work. Without transgression or guilt: what to do about Xavier, and very soon, Paris.

∞

She pulls back the curtains, takes in the view from the upstairs bedroom, down the street and past Miss Miriam's towards the park. Autumn days are now a rich patchwork quilt of contrasting colours and weather. One day bright canopies reign, the next day the same spot is empty woodland. The sun ignites red maples, turns birches to gold, then wind comes along and lashes them into stark black silhouettes. That's how they will remain for the whole winter, mere outlines of the life once present against an afternoon sky.

Already the deep blue is giving way to clouds; soon it'll be a timeless grey expanse once more, cauliflower soup. She turns from the window, lights the lamp with its money-saving low watt bulbs, hunts for the sewing basket under the bed. Better not to frame this as some dreaded routine, the days she still has to wait, the people she'd rather avoid. Tomorrow Tilly is due up from Arundel with Jack and Oliver, her youngest two. For some reason they have no activities outside school, a private institution providing generously enough during term time but also well equipped with a range of reasons to limit those terms. Even Tilly complained they paid more for less school. Maybe something to pass on to Harry the next time he considered prep over state. She sighs. Yes, a favour to Harry, having Tilly round, though it might have happened anyway, because as long as it fits into her schedule Tilly always feels a duty to act familial. Only the effort tends not to fall on her shoulders. Dinner will need to be prepared, but Jack only eats bread, Oliver only meat. Roast chicken and warm rolls ought to do the trick, with broccoli for Katya and Christophe as well. A simple dinner, but she can shop tomorrow. Today seems better for the mending of things.

Turning to the longstanding pile, she picks up Harry's trousers. Slouched on a chair, waiting weeks to be taken up, of course it's not urgent with him. Jobs that need doing, like the conversations they need to have, weeks can pass. But eventually you do have to get it over with. She lays down the trousers to thread a needle. This is the hardest part, driving this uncooperative, wily strand through an invisible slit. Sometimes it's the only bit that brings satisfaction, her handiwork afterwards never that impressive. But propped against the bed, cross-legged on the rug, a calm feeling descends; she starts on the first stitch.

Harry will be grateful, though it's not as if she owes him, does she? Silent penance for her secrets? Can you gain points being overtly tolerant and generous if you're not being totally honest? Does one negate the other? Surely it ought not to be a question of manipulations or calculations; love should be open and free. Yes, open and free. She completes the next stitch but it runs through. She hadn't secured the first. Open and free. She tries again but it slips through her fingers, she pulls it tight on the third try. The sewing begins in earnest then, the motion repetitive, solid. Like the predictable personalities of Tilly and Harry, easy to know where they stand. Yet their relations are forever unpredictable, because without the umbrella of an older generation there is no buffer for old competitions or new dissatisfactions. Like most siblings, they simply made different choices. Death could have brought them closer, but it did not, and there's no one to blame for that. Unfortunately, Tilly isn't nearly so forgiving, not about perceived inequalities. Adoring Harry with the powerful admiration of a baby sister, she also falsely attributes to him similar tastes, and far more problematically, strange powers, as if the sum of his life were endowed with magic and it's specifically unfair to her that he's more or less satisfied with his lot. Well, less these days. But Tilly's always been selfish in that regard, given to bouts of haughtiness and hypochondria that seem to be ameliorated by making over the house. If her knee's playing up, plusher area rugs are purchased, and if she suffers headaches, elaborate fresh bouquets. She is most definitely a catalogue woman. Her argument that she needs a nice place to recover has never been challenged, though Tilly has never been house-ridden or incapacitated from driving. Her tendency to fill a void with sumptuous objects and treatments, combined with Nathan's obsession with the latest gadgets, often leaves their family financially strained, so they are either scrimping on holidays or parcelling kids out to grandparents, whilst Tilly insinuates that everyone else is luckier for not having to make such sacrifices. The only hope for this visit is that Tilly might be in a good mood. Or that whatever provoked the visit has already receded.

Pulling that stitch tight, she lays down the trousers to take up a dress that's lain around for ages. Lack of occasion plus minor damage, though on closer inspection the tear is only a burst seam. And the material is black, so even done poorly it ought to be an invisible repair. Perhaps the dress can be restored to its former chic state. This garment of many memories, bought in Paris by Xavier. She begins stitch after stitch in rhythmic pattern.

Anyway what's to hide of their past or present? Surely Xavier qualifies as a friend after so many years. An integral part of life at one time, she can't be expected to have forgotten him. And should it be surprising that after making contact they enjoy dropping notes to one another? Maybe not. But the truth is she can't stop herself writing him. It's like a hit from a drug, even the wait is addictive. But what's behind that which makes her feel that way? What's behind that facial expression of his that makes her feel so weak? Mere attraction? Residual love? Both of them coveting what they can't have?

No, delusions must be done away with. Fine, neither of them has forgotten their first wild love affair: she, the fresh faced twenty-one-year-old visiting from Jagiellonian, taking up with a handsome economics student rising at Sciences-Po. He took her under his wing to show her the university, the French way of life, and ended up improving her French until the East European lilt was hardly noticeable. So easy to remember it all, the cafes off Vaugirard, the debates about socialism and capitalism, the role of the state, philosophy, running late into the night. Because what did it matter then, when they were students, free to be intellectuals, happy to take what the state had to offer? The heated arguments, giving way to dissolution in drink, everyone crawling back to cramped quarters and pairing off, usually those in least agreement politically. She and Xavier, in that perpetual game of cat and mouse until they reached his fifth floor *chambre de bonne*, making love under its little round window until the liquor evaporated, the sun came up, and it was time again for lectures.

Was that it – all of it? The vibrancy of youth regenerated? The days when everything still lay ahead? Life before all these responsibilities fell on their shoulders? Before they could all look back and see how free they were then?

Or was there a kind of debt, perhaps still unpaid, because she can never really repay it? For what he did later. Because when he took her in again he was a successful young professional, but she was second-time-round, second-rate Eva: desperate, broken, alone – and pregnant with Adam's baby. Where else could she have gone, fleeing Poland to have that secret abortion? Securing a visa for herself, with his help, because France and more importantly Xavier, provided that moral-free framework for killing an unborn child. It's impossible to deny it now: he'd given her life-changing help. Not just for her, because she too did away with a life, however small and undeveloped and unwanted. Yes, even as she shed Catholicism and sinning, she ended the start of a life, a biological fact. Someone who'd be much older than Christophe and Katya now.

But hey, life's full of difficult choices, how much should anyone let themselves be troubled by an irrevocable past? A clump of cells, what's done is done, no regrets for what could not have been changed, the gnawing question now is why X and why now? Because he sponsored her then, took her in without pity?

Because he nursed that fragile Eva back to health and against all odds they became lovers again? Is that it? Because of that unquestioning acceptance? Is that why she still seeks him? Because now it's always unfinished business?

Maybe. Or perhaps he only feeds a shrivelled ego, a lost sense of self. And that would mean reliance on him is a kind of meanness. A selfishness, against Harry and even against Xavier, because she really ought to search out her own sense of self. Has she really fallen so low that only a man – god though he may be – can give it? Harry's clearly the smarter one. He knows he can't give it, what she seeks, he's waiting for her to come around. And X has no place except to give what she can take, and he'll take all she gives and more. Can she be that desperate for salvation?

Sitting, not mending, lost in thought. Salvation, salvation, what did it mean? Not watching the rain that's begun, looking past it, clutching the dress, and suddenly, the rain, the time! Christophe will be done in minutes – she'll have to race to make it.

Laying the sewing quickly where the children won't happen upon it, she grabs a thick jumper, hurries downstairs. Coat, wellies, phone, keys. But from the family room, shiny plastic sheets catch her eye. The curtains, returned earlier, still in their wrapping. The pleats must've set by now. She must remember to remove the cover.

The curtains, another thing. She slams the door, fumbling to lock up and stay out of the wet. Matters are worse than expected. They've been stitched up to the extent they could be, but the fabric's not weathering well at all. No real covering it up now, the mistake was all hers. She chose. Whatever she does now, conceal weak points, hide errors, sometimes things will fall apart anyway. Not all things are easily mended.

∞

'Ugh, I've been on ibuprofen all day,' Tilly picks herself up from her dramatic slump over the worktop, wiggling on the stool to get comfortable.

'Cup of tea?'

'No, caffeine makes it worse.'

A second drink offer rebuffed, but might as well try again. 'I do have herbal.'

Tilly waves her hand, gives a weak smile.

'I find red wine does the trick. You wouldn't think so but it does, a real muscle relaxant,' she sighs vigorously. 'If only I didn't have to drive back. Traffic around here, *such* a nightmare.'

What can she do but smile sympathetically? It's a struggle to take the conversation further, especially if Tilly's brain is now a muscle. She turns to separate broccoli into bite sized flowerets, though maybe it wasn't the headache Tilly meant but her other catalogue of ailments: back and knees, general fatigue.

'Harry mentioned Jane and Rupert are very busy these days,' she begins again. 'Thinking about university already.'

Tilly brightens. 'Yes, Jane is. Really applying herself, so serious. Well, almost sixteen, I suppose it's time. Rupert's only interested in rugby, though he does have another year. Taking a gap year, you know. Travelling to Bali, what not. At least his friends are acceptable. Quite a few of them intend on St Andrews.'

'Bali?'

'No, Scotland, all the rage. What with Wills and Kate,' Tilly drops the names as if royals belonged to her inner circle.

'Oh, right,' she pauses. 'Seems a long way off. For me, I mean. I can't yet imagine Christophe and Katya... I vividly recall being at uni myself.'

'Yes dear, but time passes quickly,' says Tilly.

'At least it's not showing on you.' She almost stuns herself with the quick comeback, shoring up Tilly's sensitivities.

'Oh you are sweet.' Tilly suddenly lowers her voice. 'But I must admit, I've had a bit of help lately, my first session of you-know-what, to smooth out a bit of forehead. I think it's alright if you keep it natural.' Then in her normal jumpy volume, 'I've also discovered the most *wonderful* masseur, Andre, he really sorts out the aches and pains. I don't know what's going on with my back, I probably need to see him again. But if you want to know real secrets, I never miss my monthly session with Angelica, I told you about her. Her facials are *divine*. I know you don't subscribe to this kind of thing but really, Eva, it's the preparation that counts. Don't wait until it looks like you need it.'

She means it as a compliment probably, but it's hard to know what to say to that, especially the notion that injecting poison in your face might be natural. Best say nothing, Tilly will continue anyway, hopping as she often does from one subject to another without warning.

'But the most exciting thing is that we've *finally* got around to the master bathroom. I know you've had yours for ages, you've probably forgotten what it's like, sharing a loo with the kids, but I can't wait.'

She bristles. Who's forgotten? Who grew up sharing a bathroom with six people, one of them elderly? The whole house in Przemyśl had only four rooms including the kitchen, and for years Mamcia and Tato slept in the living room while three siblings and grandmother shared two small rooms. Oh, she knows what sharing's like.

'So we're going with that chocolate and teal theme, nice dark wood, wenge, and I found this amazing wallpaper at Little Cloud, really subtle fleur-de-lys, so it'll be traditional and restrained whilst modern at the same time. Thank god all the construction and plumbing are done – so much dust, so cold, you know. But after that, we'll do the next bit of the extension…'

Tilly chatters on. Because of previous renovations at Corner

House, it's easy to nod and relate without getting involved. But the narrative lacks sense. If they're short of money, why is Tilly spending so much on beauty treatments? Is Botox even a beauty treatment? And since the older children split their time with Steve and will quickly move on to university, why are they doing a second extension? The house is plenty big for their needs already.

Big enough for their needs, yes, but for their desires? No, one mustn't be judgemental. Everyone deserves an extension, in upper middle class Britain anyway. It isn't Tilly's fault she has no perspective. That she's never seen the poverty of Eastern Europe, or anywhere really, she grew up in that fabulous country house, Cranfield Manor. Maybe she was too young or too inattentive, but her parents' perspective about using money for the benefit of others seems to have eluded her. Later when the elder Holdens died, the building stood but the edifice of wealth came crumbling down. Suddenly they were like other people, people without antiques and a long driveway, and Tilly had a hard time adjusting. Hence the rush to marry Steve the banker, then Nathan the banker, hence extensions – a scramble to recover part of what was lost. Harry got his head down and worked, never spoke about living that way again. By comparison his goals seemed modest. But then the Plan. Consciously or not, it could be his way of trying to recover the past.

'And after that's finished, I suppose it'll be the garden. Ow!' Tilly shifts on the stool again.

'You okay?'

'Yes, no, I don't know why my back's playing up. I must see Andre. I'd hate to think it was *aging*.' She says the word as if it were a disease.

'But you're in great shape,' she holds back the words that would come naturally – for forty-five. 'I agree it is hard to believe we're middle aged.'

'Maybe *you* are, darling,' Tilly smiles as if joking. 'But it's no excuse. Forty's the new twenty.'

She turns to the sink to brace herself. How to counter such mathematical impossibility? Such retarded euphemism? Forty is double twenty. And at forty-one or forty-five, even if you don't subscribe to connotations of middle age – grey, paunchy, doomed and disaffected – surely you have to accept the numerical accuracy of things. She washes her hands vigorously, as if one could wash them of Tilly, then ventures a different thought.

'Well, some aches are preventable with overall fitness. Although mine could be the gardening.'

'I don't know *how* you do it, honestly,' Tilly replies, but not as if she's impressed. 'I could never manage without a gardener or cleaner. Though I suppose ours *is* twice the size of yours. But I just haven't got a green thumb.'

'Green thumb?' She lets out a light laugh. More like hard work. 'Oh, I enjoy it, fresh air, the satisfaction of winning a battle against weeds, even the aches, I suppose, they make me feel like a job well done.'

'I suppose there's that,' Tilly sighs. 'But, of course, you *are* so lucky to have the time. My job takes up *so* much more than part-time. Events organising used to be fun, now it's just time consuming. Though of course we can use my income.' She puts a quavering emphasis on income as if that's what they're missing but everyone else is not.

'I suppose after Harry returns you'll be quite secure, though. What will you do then?'

'Do?' She shuts the oven on the chicken, a few minutes more, better get the broccoli on.

'Well, aren't you planning on a bigger pile?'

Pile? It might be another discomfort, like haemorrhoids, or an Americanism from Tilly's richer friends, something about property, their favourite topic.

'I don't know, if you mean where we live, the issue's access to schools. Sunnier garden maybe, that would be my dream. But Harry and I haven't really discussed it. We're pretty happy here.'

Happy, yes, she turns back to the sink, except he's *not* here.

'Really, darling, boarding is the way to go. Frees up time immensely, you can dabble in work, interests. I can't wait for Oliver and James to follow in Rupert and Jane's footsteps. I have to say, I'm really surprised Harry hasn't considered it.'

'I don't know,' she coughs, hesitating to count children as a job, even if they are. 'I suppose I'm partial to having the children around, even if it's manic at times. The schools around here were billed as very good. But it's not quite what it seemed, so it's true, we're in a quandary now about the future.'

'Well, you have options: going private or moving further out, where there are other state schools *and* you can get the place you want. You don't really have to give up anything these days. Harry was so fond of Cranfield, I always expected he'd get back to where we were.'

Where they were? And where was that? In the direction of the Cotswolds? More upper than middle class? Less work, more play? She starts washing up forcefully. So easy to get lost in these conversations, not being English or growing up rich, because the sense of failure or success about where one fits in society had never entered her mind. In Poland, growing up had been about having enough to feed the household, odd guests and celebrations at holidays, but mostly about working hard and not minding. Because that was life. But the way things were going in England, not just the rich minded work, the lower classes too, never mind middle class resentments.

'When's Harry coming back?' Tilly jars from deeper thought.

'Harry? According to the Plan, next April, end of tax year, Easter,' she pauses, dries hands. Best stick to facts and timetables, things that can be explained without engendering emotion. 'But we'll see him in Paris next week for half term holidays, then Poland at Christmas. Next year at February half term we hope to go skiing, but the rest of the time, unless he visits, I'm here on my own.'

But that's glossing over it, really. The countdown of days, and the many nights she's already passed alone, never mind what lies ahead: all of November, half of December, most of January, February and March. The coldest, bleakest months.

'Paris,' says Tilly wistfully. 'How lovely. I do wish we could go skiing this year too, alas, the extension.'

'I would have thought a break from skiing wouldn't be a bad thing – for recovery, I mean. Your back and knees.'

'Oh,' says Tilly, as if it never occurred to her. 'I was hoping the physio would have me sorted out by then.'

The children rush in at that point, the point at which the conversation might roll back on to itself. Chatter is submerged to the crash of cutlery and plates, the mad dash to wash hands and sit next to favourite cousins. It's like holding a defensive line in an all out assault, keeping drinks from spilling, arguments to a minimum as places are secured at table. Stepping around waving hands, she portions out food, making sure Jack gets extra bread and only a sliver of inoffensive white meat while Oliver gets crispy skin and both wings. Katya and Christophe are served a mixture of what's left over plus a generous helping of broccoli.

'Ew, I hate broccoli!' Oliver wails.

'But look, darling, you haven't got any,' Tilly points out. 'Look, Auntie didn't even give you any, she remembered.'

Oliver looks down at his plate for the first time, then settles down. Katya looks bemused.

'Hey, Auntie Evie, this meat is good, can I have some more?'

'Absolutely.'

Jack must be growing up, last time he only ate bread and butter. She returns to the stove, cuts off more white meat, spoons fatty drippings from the pan. Jack gobbles most of it in an instant.

'I'm *impressed*, Jack,' Tilly smiles. 'I thought you didn't like meat.'

'I don't,' Jack says with his mouth full. 'This is chicken.'

At the stove she suppresses a smile.

'And Auntie makes a good sauce so it's not icky dry.'

'Anybody more broccoli?' she says loudly, but really only to Katya and Christophe, not much chance with the other two. She once tried to counsel Tilly against putting a whole chicken in the steamer, that it wouldn't produce flavour no matter what the health benefits, and that cooking times on labels were generally too long. But Tilly had been on one of her periodic nutritional kicks that dictated puritanical methods. Yet when it came to vegetables, she'd long since given up.

'So, more broccoli anyone?'

'Me, Mama!' Christophe shouts.

'I can't believe you like broccoli,' says Oliver. 'Revolting.'

'It makes your willy grow,' Christophe mumbles between bites.

'It does?' says Oliver.

'Sure,' Katya chimes in. 'Full of vitamins.'

'So?'

'Vitamins make you grow, stupid,' Jack says.

'Language!' shouts Tilly.

Christophe pipes up, 'My willy's way bigger than last time you were here.'

'Krzysztof!'

'Okay, let me try some then,' says Oliver finally.

Looking over at Tilly, who's arching her eyebrows and shrugging, she forks out a stalk carefully. Oliver is Katya's age, nearly seven, but never touched a green that wasn't small, round and frozen in its previous state.

'They're crunchy, like mini trees,' Katya starts to explain, but Oliver's already got one in his mouth.

'Hey, pretty good,' he says, dipping it into chicken grease.

'Of course,' says Katya, rolling her eyes. 'And good for you.'

But the boys dominate and conversation turns to penis size. They're told to finish up fast. Scampering off, they leave a warzone of debris.

'I can't believe Oliver ate broccoli *and* liked it,' Tilly says.

'I got that trick off my other sister-in-law, Piotr's wife, Danka.'

It's true but around Tilly self-deprecation is also instinctive. Modesty is something you must possess in the land of gentry. But she'd also learned long ago it was a necessity around people who spend their life complaining.

'Really?'

'Yes, Danka told her boys they'd shrivel up down there if they didn't eat their vegetables. You've never seen such an improvement in eating habits.'

Her laugh escapes at the thought, leaving out the other one – copious amounts of juice from the roasting pan help. Anyway, it's a compliment to her cooking, and to Oliver and Jack, who seem to be coming round despite the mayhem at home.

'Let me know if there's anything I can do to help while you've got the works on.'

'You are sweet,' Tilly says, rummaging through her bag for her phone, 'but I've got it all under control. Another few weeks and we'll be back to normal.'

It's hard to imagine what normal is in Tilly's household, but she nods in agreement. Tilly fiddles with the phone checking texts for a few moments, sticks it to her ear, nodding knowingly over some message.

'Eva, darling, this has been *fabulous*, hate to eat and run, but you know, the traffic.' She leans over slightly, makes a kissy sound around two imaginary cheeks. 'You're an absolute dear to have had us.' There's a crash upstairs.

Time for the Holden-Hewitts to go. Meaning Jack and Oliver, because Tilly decided to remain Holden while contemplating seemingly endlessly, if she could ever take on Nathan's Hewitt. Apparently it didn't sound right, Holden-Hewitt, though the children had been locked in. Like Jane and Rupert, the elder two Holden-Billinghursts, still clinging to Steve's surname, presumably for financial reasons.

Busying herself in the hallway, Tilly focuses on her phone to the end, her calls for Oliver and Jack repeatedly ignored while she taps in a few more crucial texts. The cousins try a variety of stalling tactics, but promised sweets, they finally get in the car. Christophe and Katya stand at the bay window, waving at the departing company.

'Hey Mama,' Katya says, 'your curtains are fixed. See? No more shreddy bits.'

'Yes, *holubko*, but please don't touch them. The damaged section's got a panel sewn in. But they're going in other places. They're very fragile now.'

'Why don't you buy new ones?' asks Christophe.

'They cost a lot of money,' replies Katya, echoing previous explanations.

'Isn't that why Daddy's away? Getting more money?' says Christophe. 'We can get new ones when he comes back with bags of money!' He smiles, puts his hands on his hips, pleased with his solution.

'No, we can't,' says Katya, 'the shop is closed. Mama said.'

'Oh, you two,' she interrupts. 'We can't get new ones, they're expensive. Anyway, Daddy's not working so we can buy new stuff. We have to make do as well.'

Make do and mend, as the wartime adage says, and clean up the mess in the kitchen.

'But if Daddy's not working for new stuff, why is he working?' asks Christophe.

Katya looks up, intrigued.

'Daddy *is* working to provide for us, but we still need to look

LESIA DARIA

after what we have. Because we don't want Daddy to work day and night just so we can buy new stuff, do we?'

'No, we don't!' Katya shakes her head.

'So when we have enough stuff, then Daddy will come back?' asks Christophe.

'No,' she says, trying to reform her argument, but Katya interjects.

'We have enough stuff, except for I really want gel stickers like Oliver. Do we have enough money for that?'

'What about Daddy!' Christophe jabs her with his finger.

'Ow!' says Katya, 'Stop hurting me! Mama!'

'Stop it, both of you! Daddy will be back in spring. But we'll see him many times before then. And what we have doesn't have anything to do with it. He'll come back when he's finished his job.'

She's annoyed but it isn't the kids, though they should be in the bath by now. Who wouldn't expect them to be muddled by it all? Harry and she, sacrificing their togetherness, their children's childhoods right now for some secure future life. But life as what? Elderly people with nice retirements whose adult offspring are well accomplished and not around any more? Miss Miriam and her sad situation come to mind. But even if their family stays close in the future, Christophe's exactly right. Why is Daddy away now when we have all the stuff we need?

∞

For predictability factor alone, it could be irritating, but it's not. Paris exactly as it should be: clear skies, crisp air and impossibly chic people treading scrubbed pavements, and the first thought is where has all the dog poo gone? If anything, the city seems to have improved in this regard, maybe the Parisians too, looking like they've just stepped out of the theatrical shop windows they pass, only threw on their clothes, ensembles ready, didn't think much of it because they were too busy making love moments ago. She observes them from the windows of the taxi, and in cafes, on corners, these fashionable women laughing at their good fortune, pursing lips to decry someone else's faux pas with a flick of the chin upwards and that *tsk-tsk* that indicates they disagree with what their company is saying. *Mais non, ce n'est pas possible, elle n'avait pas fait ça!* She can't hear them but knows what they're saying – it's not possible what the other one said someone else did – though whatever the person being talked about did to deserve such calumny gets lost in the bee-ba-bee-ba of ambulances and car horns.

Everyone's excited, but the secret is hers: they're in the first *arrondissement*, not far from his flat, and their old hangouts in the second, third, fourth. She knows exactly where she is. They were always Right Bank people. Well, Xavier, at any rate. But then the staggering disappointment of his email returns:

You were always unpredictable, Noisette, and naughty. Sadly, I'm committed to Armand this weekend, heading with the family to the chateau. But I'll see what I can do.

Her fault now – she'd left it too late, trying not to feel culpable. Sending a devil-may-care message the day before departure, as if you could trick the mind into abandoning guilt by pretending it was down to fate. Slippery slope of justifications. But her proposition had been preposterous anyway: *meet at the Rocher for a drink?* Really? The cafes of Montorgueil with children in tow? Now he probably thinks she was begging.

But her spirits lift as the taxi pulls up at the Intercontinental, now signed the Westin, and they retreat past golden lampposts and vast gold doors into a mirrored hall interior with dazzling flower displays. Then another set of glass doors, opening to a fountain courtyard. All her time in Paris, she'd never once stepped foot inside this hotel. This courtyard now, a moment of discovery, as she and the children take in a rectangle of blue sky, white clouds moving in and out. It's a real live picture frame, a perfect screensaver, the sky shifting but perpetually unperturbed in this small enclosure. Xavier's comment about the awfulness of being hemmed in by skyscrapers returns, the preferable expanse here in Paris. Or maybe it's better, safer, to have a limited horizon, an encapsulated vision like this? But Christophe pokes Katya and the moment's lost. Lost to reality, collecting keys and heading to the room.

She opens the door, goes straight to the closet, opens it. Harry's shirts. He's here. A grounding sight, especially after the usual nerve-wracking flight and all the time apart. Soon, he'll be here in person. She fingers a button-down, the material stiff from hotel pressing. One of his suits remains in a plastic cover but she doesn't know if she should release it. It might be for his next destination. She turns away.

At least the children seem at home – or more accurately, like they're at Jenny's.

'Right, now stop jumping, this is a posh hotel, we're expected to behave.'

'Okay, Mama,' says Christophe sullenly, flopping down on the bed.

She sees the note, takes it up.

Eva,

Hope your flight was okay, no turbulence. I'll be free by seven, latest. Meet you here, we'll get kids to bed, then dinner downstairs, Boudoir restaurant booked for 20:30.

Harry

P.S. Don't text, phones off in conference, bad reception anyway.

Checking the time, it's six already.

'Come on, off the bed. Let's go to dinner.'

'Good, I'm bursting for escargots!' Christophe declares.

She laughs remembering another mythical story of the Holden household, as Christophe, just two at the time of a previous trip to France, was introduced to escargots. He'd fallen in love with the notion of eating buttered snails, had consumed half a dozen every chance he got. Afterward he maintained it was his favourite French food, as if that were normal for children, having top foods in various cuisines.

But really who wouldn't be pleased with such *petits gourmands?* Entering the restaurant and knowing what to do with napkins and cutlery, clambering for crème brûlée, munching and crunching and making a right mess of the table, they eat it all. She smiles, watching them, leaning back in the chair, savouring her last sips of fancy tea. The waiter gives her a smile too; she internalises the proud parent moment. All those years of training – *eat what you're given, no such thing as children's food, someone made that up* – finally paying off. With full tummies they ride the lifts and with more energy than before, Katya and Christophe burst into the room.

'Daddy!'

Harry's on the bed, looking down at one of his devices. He looks up and breaks out of exhaustion into seemingly real satisfaction. Christophe and Katya jump on him, crumpling his suit.

'Come here, you too,' Harry barely overcomes the attack, signalling to her.

They fall into an embrace on the bed, edging out the

children. Her turn now: to be submerged by a powerful wave, to be adrift, not wanting to be tethered, for work, or sleep, or anything.

'You look nice,' Harry says.

'This?' she pulls away. 'Wait till I change for dinner,' she smiles. The black dress.

'About that,' then registering her reaction, 'no, it's not bad, only another half hour to go, some niggling details. Let's get these monsters to bed, then you head down, have a cocktail. Half an hour more, I'll break out, I promise.'

'We're not monsters!' Katya protests.

'But I am!' says Christophe. 'We ate whole snails.'

'Did you?' says Harry, running his fingers through his hair. 'Well, they make you very sleepy.' He pauses. 'Good thing it's time for bed.'

'But I don't want to go to bed, we've only just met Daddy. Mama!' Katya wails. 'It's not fair!'

No, not fair. But life's not fair, as they will tell you later. Though that's not a fair statement either. Because sometimes life is fair, or fair to someone else when it's not fair to you.

'Katya, we have the whole weekend with Daddy. We'll even have breakfast together.'

'But that's tomorrow,' says Christophe. 'I'm not even hungry yet.'

'No, of course not,' she gives him a squeeze, pokes his tummy to make him giggle. 'Not with all that food in there. But we've had an exciting day, and it is bedtime, so off you go, brush your teeth.'

The children weigh up the situation, decide they've lost. Two determined parents and anyway lots of mini bottles to investigate in the bathroom.

Standing in the doorway, observing them, she feels Harry come up from behind. He grabs her waist, kisses the back of her neck, a tickly feeling that goes all the way down the spine and front, to the place she really wants him to touch.

'Not yet,' she whispers.

'I can't wait,' he says.

'Mama, Daddy, are my teeth clean?' Katya grins. 'Look, I have two wobbly teeth!'

'Where?' asks Harry. 'Show me.'

'Right here,' says Katya, sticking her fingers in her mouth. 'Rau ere an oer ere.'

'I see,' says Harry, 'very slightly wobbly.'

'But they'll wobble more!'

'Especially now that you're seven,' Harry says. 'All your teeth will fall out and we'll have to get you fake ones.'

'No, Daddy!' Katya protests. 'You get grown-up teeth then!'

'Is that the way it works? I forgot,' Harry smiles.

'Silly Daddy,' says Christophe. 'You need to see the dentist. He'll explain it all to you.'

'Oh he will, will he?' Harry picks him up, Christophe squeals. 'But now the monster needs to go to bed!'

They get into pyjamas and bed, and Harry kisses them goodnight. Then almost as soon as he's appeared, phone in hand, he slips out.

She settles them with the angel prayer.

'Mama,' Christophe says, 'Do angels hear you in hotails?'

'Ho-tails?' she mimics him. 'Of course, angels hear you in hotels. They're everywhere.'

'That's good,' says Katya, 'I'd hate to pray and have no one listening.'

'Someone's always listening. God or angels or saints and people who've died and gone to heaven.'

So they say, but she doesn't add that, because it's the line she's always maintained though Harry says, *no way of knowing it's true, why feed the kids drivel?* Of course there's no certainty,

115

but it's not about science, or even religion and its bureaucratic hierarchies, it's about faith and hope, and where are you without those?

'So angels do the listening if God's too busy?' Katya asks.

'I suppose so,' she smiles. 'No one knows exactly how it works, but I'm sure he delegates. The world's a busy place.'

'But why do people have to die?' asks Christophe. 'Because they're like snails?'

She thinks hard, trying to focus, because she's answered this one before and it's important to be consistent, whilst accounting for the new angle on snails.

'Well, the world would get too crowded if everyone stayed on it. No more room for new babies, who take up even more space than snails.'

'I think everyone should stay put, and tell God to stop sending new babies, if there's no room,' says Katya.

'Still we get so old eventually, our bodies hardly work any more. We all die someday, so babies aren't such a bad thing. They're new people to replace the old ones.'

'But I don't want you and Daddy to die,' Katya starts sniffling, having understood the implications, or maybe just identifying them as old.

'We're not dying yet,' she says it cheerily, though thinking about it, *we all die someday* is a form of stative present, and happening all the time. But to get their minds off it, she adds, 'We're only going down to dinner. Daddy and I want a chance to eat escargots too.'

'No! We don't want you to go!'

There is the listening service if they cry, people at reception to fetch her and Daddy from the restaurant, but that's too much for them to take in, and what if it doesn't work? Tonight will be a first.

'Nothing to worry about.'

A reassuring statement for everyone's benefit, but the children remain worried, so she soothes them further and finally tells them to be quiet, lie still.

Sitting in the darkness she breathes in and out loudly until they're breathing regularly too, then painstakingly she shuts the adjoining door. Time for glamour on the run: make-up retouch, hair clip, tights, dress, heels. Tip-toeing back, she sets the phone in place, then grabs her purse and heads out the door exhaling deeply. Freedom.

∞

The same restaurant looks different after eight, lights dimmed, candles glimmering, jazz playing softly. The maître d' manoeuvres her towards a table in the far corner, offering a view of Rivoli traffic. The profiles of drivers facing right are illuminated momentarily as they pass before being plunged into darkness. It's dark in the room too, heavily curtained like upstairs but a deep burgundy or purple, with modern twists applied to what might have been old fashioned decor. Dark wood furniture but minimalist, showing someone has bowed to a younger generation of guests – *look, we're keeping up, we have foresight, we get irony.* The carpeting is also plum or deep purple, the whole place so dark it'll be a wonder anyone can make out their food. Boudoir indeed.

She signals to the waiter, orders a *kir royale*, but it's impossible to sit and survey surroundings for long when you're alone, you end up looking lost or nosy. Anyway, nothing to see. She focuses on the nibbles and the drink, picking through olives and rice crackers tossed in artful bowls, savouring their flavours because she mustn't devour everything before Harry arrives. Scanning the menu, the next logical activity, reveals a typical selection of French classics like boeuf bourgignon. Though on closer inspection they've been altered, with mousses and jus of this and that and not very French spices like cardamom and ginger. There's even something vaguely English and experimental about it: skate wing and John Dory and lamb roasted with pink garlic. Plates arrive at other tables carrying the signature flourish of haute cuisine: stacked potato slices, elaborately carved vegetables, oversized sprigs of dill and chives that stick out like feathers. Old hat for people like Harry maybe, but if you don't get out much, a treat.

Soon her glass is half empty. Then dry. She stops the waiter, but that can't be right, well after nine, more than half an hour, what to do? Ordering alone isn't polite but if you're starving how long should you wait? Wine, yes, a bottle, she indicates the empty place a husband will fill. He brings it, uncorks and pours. Her favourite Sancerre. To celebrate. But that's not the kind of thing one does alone, so eventually she stands, heads to reception. No messages. Good and bad, at least the children are asleep. She returns, sits down to fiddle with the menu again, sips her wine less delicately.

The waiter approaches. 'Madame 'Olden?'

'*Oui?*' she looks up.

'*Pour vous*,' the waiter lowers his head, hands her a note.

Suddenly it's as if everyone knows: Harry isn't coming. The waiter must know too, he's passing judgement, head down. Not right for a woman to be left alone like this. No self-respecting Frenchman would do such a thing.

'*Merci*,' she reads quickly.

Will be there as soon as I can, please order.

But her hunger's gone. Or rather it's taken over completely, her stomach a gnawing hole. The drinks have gone straight to her head. The waiter's about to leave, she stops him.

'*Monsieur, attendez s'il vous plait, je voudrais commander.*'

But the salad comes before Harry, a lot of wine too. By the time the main course arrives, her hunger's been replaced by alcohol-laced anger. Pushing white flakes of fish around, taking salutary bites of buttered rice, more than a few mouthfuls feel forced. And at least one man keeps turning repeatedly to look at her.

The waiter returns looking aggrieved, throws his glance elsewhere.

Another note?

So sorry, will try to finish up as soon as possible.

But she's already finished too. Putting the bill on the room, she heads upstairs forcefully, mind swirling in arguments and counterarguments, plans of attack, ambushes. The alcohol really isn't helping.

You never get to go out like this. Doesn't he realise it's a big deal?

Of course, but he's working. You wouldn't be here Eva, if he wasn't working. You're lucky, be grateful.

Grateful? For being stood up? One chance at a romantic meal in how many months?

You think he wants to work now? That he'd choose to stay working when he could be with you? Try not to feel sorry for yourself, Eva, feel sorry for Harry. Give him a break already.

Sure, feel sorry for Harry. Give him a break. Always him. What about you? Last to matter. Really, who cares about you? Not Harry, his priority is work. Imagine him telling clients to sod off, that he wants to wine and dine and fuck his wife in a hotel room. Ha, no chance! He's not that man any more, he's lost his balls, just putty in corporate hands.

So what are you going to do about it?

Not wait around, that's for sure.

119

A knock at the door. How long has it been, lying in the darkness? At least she didn't undress. Stumbling over her shoes to the door, she blinks in the sudden light. Another note? Utter disbelief quickly replaced by the desire to rip it to shreds, she grabs the note.

'*Merci.*' She remembers her manners, though her anger means the poor bellhop will get nothing but a half-hearted smile.

But he doesn't go.

'*Il m'a dit d'attendre.*' He said to wait? For what? To humiliate her? Why should anyone witness this episode in marital discord? She tears open the note.

Madame:

Please forgive the intrusion, but I couldn't help noticing you were alone at dinner. Perhaps you were waiting for someone who didn't come. If so, there was never a greater fool.

If you'd be so kind, I'd like to buy you a drink at the bar.

Richard

The man in front of her is shuffling and now she sees he's quite young, really just a boy. Sucking in her breath like Frenchwomen do, exhaling a tiny *oui*, she shuts the door, leans against it. Nothing to it. Harry didn't turn up, she might as well go out. Have another drink, bought by someone who evidently cares. Nothing to it whatsoever.

Sliding back into her heels, she steps out purposefully into the lift where gilded mirrors tell everyone – *hey, you're as good as ever* – though if you're worse for wear, just wait. Only a moment till doors open and you're out. She leaves her blurred image behind, tosses her hair, proceeds on to the marble. Immediately she slows down. It's slippery. She focuses on her feet. Better safe than sorry.

Rounding the bend, looking up she sees him. In the middle of the illuminated lobby – Harry. He's animated, clapping a man on the back, both of them pleased. Noting her but clearly not her expression, his face lights up.

'Eva! Sorry things ran over, but we've accomplished our mission, I'm a free man! This is Ian.'

He doesn't ask where she's been but surely her smile is stretched. Free man?

'Pleased to meet you,' says Ian. 'Well, I'd best be off. Early start on part two, catch you at eleven?'

'Right,' says Harry, turns to her. 'Come on, let's get a drink.'

'What about dinner?' She almost forgets fury for incredulity.

'I'm not hungry. They brought us those ubiquitous trays of sandwiches meant to prop up the working stiff. But we can get snacks at the bar if you're peckish, or was dinner alright?'

He registers his mistake a second too late. 'Look, I'm sorry.' But instead of stopping there and making it alright, he adds, 'but it is a work trip, you know.'

Moving into the bar, annoyed to the extreme, she lets him follow her.

'Don't be angry with me,' he says, but it's too late and he knows it.

Still, no one wants a row in a hotel bar, and suddenly she remembers the curious stranger, the invitation that actually brought her down. She looks around though she wouldn't recognise him, even though she agreed to meet him. Meet him? Whatever was she thinking? But Harry didn't come, did he? No, he wasn't just late, he never even turned up. Never once had Xavier done that.

'Yes, I know, work comes first.' She can't help making it as sarcastic as she can.

'Look, I didn't want it this way,' he replies gently. 'I don't control my own schedule, you know that.'

The ultimate excuse: not my responsibility. So much for choice and free will, free man. No point retorting though because *he* is there now, the man who was watching her. At the bar on the far side, still looking at her. No, more than looking, practically undressing her with his eyes. The way Xavier does. Is it even possible at this age to be attractive to the opposite sex? No, probably he's just desperate. But maybe everyone's more desperate at this age. Or maybe he's had a fight with his spouse. Or maybe he's divorced, or on a business trip, or does this kind of thing when he's away in hotels.

Harry takes her silence for acquiescence. 'Would you like some champagne? I think you deserve it.'

'Actually, that would be lovely.'

Suddenly who's mad? Completely deflated but determined to have a good time because if Harry doesn't know how lucky he is, then screw it. She'll have a nice time regardless.

Sipping the champagne, she feels herself rising above the earth, above all its pettiness and disappointments, not only beautiful but desirable, laughing at everything Harry says while this stranger, this Richard, Stranger Richard, looks on. It's almost pornographic, this voyeurism, except everyone's fully dressed, behaving properly in public, so it's possible to feel all the more sexy. Amusing to this husband, siren to this stranger, and somewhere else, who knows what to an old lover who still seems to want you.

Stranger Richard watches while she and Harry get up to go, but instead of being put off by her obvious rejection, he follows her with smiling eyes. Maybe he likes a challenge. Or maybe he thinks she's a prostitute. Yes, that could be it. Stranger Richard knows about her past, as a dancer, though she never slept with a paying man, only danced in the skimpiest outfits, he must be thinking she's cheap. Maybe she is, and that last thought sends her spiralling down the flute of fizzy highs. Now she's quite sad inside, this other Eva, and Harry practically has to crank her up by the arm to get her back into the room. It's easy to pretend to be stable, but you also know when you're not.

Harry slips the key into the door and pushes it open. An immense rush of relief ushers her in like a wave, the relief of being able to flop back on the bed, Harry wastes no time slipping off shoes and saying I love you and she, I love you, though it's like other people speaking, all these yous, the sadness not gone, only a part of it, the rest a gaping hole that desperately needs filling, and she says hold me, and he does, and just when it's about to get better, Christophe coughs from the other room.

'Mama, I don't feel...' he starts.

And then they hear the sound of vomiting.

Coming and going in waves, as if she'd drunk an ocean, her nausea is like a temporary physical insanity. But Christophe is fine now, running along the gravel under the Eiffel Tower, in and out of its shadows. Child sicknesses only seem to last long enough to annoy parents, although the hotel staff were not particularly pleased with the midnight clean-up, and no one was impressed by the smell. As disgusted as she felt, she'd fought it down, couldn't be sick herself, while Harry kept coaxing Christophe to get it over with. *Once it's out, it's out,* he said. As if that made up for lost time.

No use spoiling the present though, another good saying. She takes in a deeper breath of cool air, briefly feeling at one with the world. The Eiffel Tower, so easy to forget how impressive it is, this hackneyed symbol of Paris. The structure's rather ugly, steel with bulging rivets, hordes of key chain hawkers huddling under its arches. But the enormousness of it, especially when you're right under it, is nothing less than inspiring.

'It's a giant rectal set!' Christophe shouts, running up.

'You mean erector set? The kit Daddy bought with metal plates and screws?'

'Yes, Mama,' he says earnestly. 'It doesn't look like Lego, does it?'

'It would be if they painted it red,' says Katya, 'instead of grey.'

'They don't have to paint it bright colours, it's impressive as is, and at night, the whole tower lights up like a Christmas tree. Come on, let's start climbing.'

'Can't we take the lift?' Katya asks. 'It's ginormous!'

She follows Katya's gaze to the people in diagonal elevators, small animals trapped in cages.

'No, they're expensive, and look, about a hundred people waiting. You have plenty of energy, and we can all do with some exercise.'

A blood rush might even help cure the rest of the hangover. Not half as bad as it could be, only a thumping headache and the sourness of sex that almost was.

They start up the steps quickly, but soon their pace slows. It isn't difficult but takes time, climbing this or any tower: arriving at the first level, scaling the second, where you might try to make sense of what you're seeing. In the distance and on panels before them all the sights of Paris are clearly marked. But the various points of interest don't hold the children's attention. Disappointing after the climb, but not that surprising. They have no past memories, and you need memories to make experiences fuller than the immediate. She too could use someone to share it with, like Harry. Or better yet, Xavier.

But both sets of memories are closed off to be present for the children, so no point hanging about getting beaten by the wind. They descend and move quickly along the paths leading to the Ecole Militaire. Slow down, she wants to shout, such a long way to go, but in the distance Christophe's busy charging at lazy pigeons. The birds waddle at his initial approach, then he attacks, jumping with both feet into their mini flocks. The pigeons launch themselves upwards in panic, only to set down a few feet away. Christophe chortles with glee, marches off to do it again, finally going off in search of new victims. Katya returns.

'Mama, I'm so happy. Paris is very nice.'

'Yes, it is. Did you know your mama used to live here once?'

'In the hotel?'

'No, not the hotel,' she smiles, 'but not far from it, so I know the city quite well.'

'Why did you move away?' asks Katya. 'To be with Daddy in England?'

'I didn't know Daddy then, I only met him later in London.'

Paris back then: never could she have imagined ending up like this, a daughter and son by another foreigner, a man she hadn't yet met. Katya doesn't ask more questions, they walk together in silence, listening to the crunch of gravel, passers-by, muffled traffic. Katya's no longer thinking about the rest of the story, but there are many things she'll need to understand before she grows up: about men, about staying and leaving, about making a life with the right person. Too early to tell her this, of course, hard to know when you've learned the lessons yourself, because is there a set of rules that makes it easy? Even if you create for yourself painstakingly the path you will follow, can you live by a grand plan? Hadn't she followed her heart most of the time?

The heart, yes, but the head too, because in the end, one must think things through. She'd always wanted to consider herself morally bound and good and kind, but she'd always been willing to experiment. Maybe that's been her main problem, the one always leaving her in a muddle. Because if you don't acknowledge boundaries or stick with a system of guidance, charting a course is quite difficult. Even the best explorers find it tough to make their way without a compass.

'Mama, where are we going?'

'To the Rodin museum. To see some famous sculptures.'

'Oh good, I like sculptures.'

'Bless you.' She kisses her head.

'What's that for, Mama?'

She's about to say, for loving art, or being this little person of vast understanding, but that's only part of it, and not even the most significant.

'That's for you being you,' she says, hugging her tight, 'and because I love you so much.'

'Okay.'

Then, like her brother, she's off, running after birds, joining Christophe, who's found an interesting piece of waste amid the sandy stones. She moves to them quickly.

'Please don't. Don't pick up rubbish, Christophe, you don't know where it's been.'

'Yes I do,' he says proudly, holding up a wrapper. 'It's been on an ice cream.'

'Precisely,' she sighs. 'Someone else's food. Throw it away please.'

Christophe runs and tosses it into the bin.

The piece of paper, the bin! She should have thrown it away immediately, last night, but what did she do with it? Maybe she crumpled the note. Maybe she left it on the desk? When she gets back to the hotel she must check, though it's not an incrimination of anything really, only an embarrassing footnote to a sorry state.

They walk, seemingly forever now, stopping to eat at some cafe at a grand intersection of avenues, but even fortified with *croque-monsieur* it seems a vast distance to the Musée Rodin. She'd forgotten how expansive Parisian boulevards are, especially for tiny legs, a lot of prodding goes a short way. Arriving before closing time is a victory in itself, but it's late, they'll have to skip the gardens. Once inside Christophe loses interest almost immediately, but Katya is entranced by the high ceilinged rooms, the wrapped naked bodies, grimacing faces and ethereal mythical figures.

'Mama, look,' she points to an art student on the floor, 'she's drawing statues.'

'Yes, love,' and without thinking switching into Polish, 'lots of students come here to draw because the statues are very famous and beautiful. They're studying curves and light and shading.'

Then like a bolt of lightning: these same floors, and she, a student, not drawing but writing luckless love poems. In this very same room, so many years ago. Maybe under the influence of Szymborska – precise, insightful, fluid lines of reminiscing – more poignant now still, looking back at one's younger self. Yes, she, in the presence of these same statues, which haven't changed at all and never will, only the people viewing them changing. The visitation of art galleries so much like visiting churches, people gathering together but alone, each searching for something lasting, immutable. Hoping it will reflect something larger in oneself.

She walks in silence without Christophe and Katya, who have decamped to a corner to play. But she's got to find the one, the figure that inspired. What were the lines she composed? There was the one poem she wrote in honour of Camille Claudel, Rodin's long suffering lover, but she can no longer recall it. And another she'd composed soon after arriving in Paris, having left Adam in all his complexity, his hard life and new found devotion. She'd sent him that poem, the last thing she ever wrote for or to him. Now the words tumble out, halting and confused, as if released from a long-sealed tomb.

I have already seen you in an old man
His cheekbones protruding – your profile profound,

A far outward gaze, the high arch of a brow
Exposing a thought that only I'd know,
A stiff roughened beard I might still one day touch
Your dishevelled hair, caressed curve of a neck
The round so familiar I could trace it in air...

I watch from a distance
I see it is you
Gone forward in time –
And I long for the dusk, gently aged
To be mine

The rhythm of her native language, soft and sad, and now the image of birds circling the sky, freed from a long-buried place. She'd memorised it in the writing, emotions dormant for years, cadence and meaning forgotten. Such a confusing time, coming to Paris, the abortion, maybe regrets had set in. The experiment of living and hanging on with Xavier would have been dubious then, at the start. He was a new protector, not lover, and the recent history with Adam would have been a vibrant painful reality. That Adam who had saved her first, from certain verbal and physical abuse one night in the club. Then moving from protector to first serious love, as she and Adam grew closer like many young people, wrapped in a cocoon to protect themselves from a bigger world that simply doesn't understand. They'd spent years like that, trying to save each other from demons. And when the bonds of familiarity finally began to chafe, there were already other external problems – and that one grave internal one – both of which made her want to flee. So what kind of future had she imagined then? Which statue had it been?

And I long for the dusk, gently aged to be mine.

Yes, somehow she'd pictured herself in advanced years with him, blotting out failures, though she must've known reconciliation would never occur. Youth's wistful and twisted reflections, the faint hope two lovers might reconvene and live as old couples do, with the furrowed faces and hunched backs showing the efforts of a lifetime. But the baby had gone. It was not to be. Nothing between them was to be. And now here with two children, by Harry, who is to see her through the end of days, and yet with that great hope comes dread, not youthful longing at the prospect of aging. Because with such certainty ahead – death – you want to stop the clock.

Silently, she walks around the room, Katya approaching, slipping in her hand, asking questions that go unanswered because Mama's in this fog of thought. She can't find the statue anywhere, she's telling them or herself maybe, this special statue she's looking for. But it's not because the statue isn't there. It's because it no longer reminds her of that person he once might have been. It's no longer a remembrance of Adam as an old man she might one day see. Adam is now erased from her as completely as anyone could be. And because she can't recognise him, she can't even feel sad.

The note that could have been damning – she needs to find it. Though why it might be damning is another matter. Nothing was done to precipitate it, nothing even happened. But not being at fault doesn't always matter. Jealousy works in strange ways. Even Harry, who isn't normally possessive, what would he say if he saw it? Lately he's showing quite a few signs of strain too, the way he's indifferent or harsh with the children though he's spent hardly any time with them, the way he runs his hands through his hair in desperation, the way his smile disappears faster than it used to even on hearing good news. He even eats in a different manner, though how is difficult to put a finger on, slower and faster at the same time, a different rhythm maybe.

Searching around the desk, under the bed, behind the curtains, rifling through the bin: there it is. Barely disguised, but a relief, Harry wouldn't have gone through the rubbish. Unfolding the note, she rereads it and throws it away again. A non-starter, a story that won't happen. Just a brief melodramatic opening and shuttering of some alternate reality. Yes, the flutter of possibility, the flattery of sex. Though the note didn't even properly identify this Stranger Richard, only that there was never a greater fool than her husband.

She tries not to think about it, turns to the next room, peeking in on the children already asleep, worn out fast by their sky-high climb, the hike across Paris and endless metro steps up and down. She practically had to carry Christophe into the hotel.

A click of the door, Harry steps in.

'Hi,' he whispers. 'Kids in bed? What's this?' He motions to the dirty dishes.

'They were too exhausted to sit in the restaurant, so we had room service. They fell asleep straight after.'

'Sounds great,' Harry smiles and yawns. 'Why don't we do the same?'

'Sure,' she says uncertain, pausing. 'Harry, you know, before tonight, I'd never ordered room service. What luxury lives these kids lead. And us, us too.'

'I don't know what everyone gets excited about, the food's nowhere near as good as a proper restaurant, always cold.' He loosens his tie, stretches out on the bed. 'But I could do with getting out of this suit and not going anywhere.'

A luxury that isn't a luxury then. But he might be right. A bit like staying in, relaxing at home, the closest he gets these days.

'Will we have a chance to go out tomorrow?'

'Tomorrow?' Harry says, unlacing his shoes, kicking them off. 'Yes, sorry, forgot to mention, cocktail party at Hotel Costes. Nothing to do with the deal I'm working on, Paris office putting it on for its clients. But we're invited, want to go?'

'You mean, *the* Hotel Costes?'

'They had to name it after something,' Harry smiles. 'If you mean the music, yes.'

'Wow, you are jaded. Do you think I get a chance to dress up and go to fancy clubs any day of the week?' She picks up a pillow and throws it at him playfully. 'I guess that makes staying in tonight alright.'

'So what do you want?' Harry picks up the menu, scans it.

'How about soup *pistou* and bread, I need something stodgy after today.'

'I'll have steak tartare then – at least it's supposed to be cold,' he picks up the phone and orders, adding a bottle of Pinot.

They lay on the bed in silent half cuddle, almost falling asleep until the knock at the door. Harry grunts.

'Oh, I'll get it,' she gets up.

Same bellhop as the night before, he wheels in the trolley, clears away used plates, sets out the new service. She hands him a tip, double, but he continues to shuffle uncomfortably.

'*Madame?*' he holds out a piece of folded paper.

She takes it quickly. It's in French. She starts to read.

Plans can change, I'd like to see you.

'Richard again?' Harry says, eyebrows raised in amusement.

'How do you know about that?' She looks up before she can finish reading.

'I found the note by your shoe,' says Harry, without a trace of anger. 'You should be more careful.'

Moving her finger, looking down at the note to its ending, she crushes it reflexively, glad for the physical distance between them now.

'Harry I didn't do anything, you were late, this man, this Stranger,' she pauses, 'Richard was watching me in the restaurant, sent up a note asking me down for a drink, which is rather intrusive, I agree, but then I thought I'd look for you…' she stops the lie.

'You don't have to tell me,' Harry breaks into a smirk. 'I know all about Richard – you're not the first.'

'What?'

'Richard's a very wealthy man, he hangs about this hotel. He's, shall we say, not such a stranger but a known predator. Last year he hit on Ian's wife.'

'Oh.' Because it's all she can say, feeling embarrassed and defeated. And it's funny too.

'Never mind then.' Taunting but tense she opens the note, rereads it and rips it purposefully into tiny shreds. Binned for good.

'Wait, what did he say this time, *ma chérie*?' Harry's up and hugging her now, kissing her on the neck.

'You mean,' she's about to correct him, *mon amour*, but continues, 'oh nothing, a fool hanging about, waiting for another chance.'

'I thought so,' he murmurs, continuing his kissing.

She lets go, the tension a great flood, dinner can wait while they make love. It's a good solid love that's playful and full of missed chances, but for her part, tension too, then wine and food, and Harry's right, the soup's definitely tepid even if it wasn't on arrival. Tartare no longer chilled, only room temperature, but that's fine, and after it all Harry quickly falls into a deep sleep.

But she can't relax because of the note. The near miss. Because she caught the troubling bit: not *ma chérie*, but *mon amour*. It wasn't from Richard, it was marked X.

∞

It's like a rising tsunami you can't stop: faulting someone for not getting it quite right, the dread of returning to repetition, inconsequential events. At the window, she hopes for positive distractions, but actually she's already waiting. Waiting for an end to this scene, renewed separation with Harry, while outside there's mayhem, people rushing about in the rain, trying not to get wet, looking not-so-chic under giant umbrellas and folded newspapers. The downpour shows no signs of abating.

So much for plans, a last twirl around the Tuileries, or for matters to have turned out differently with X. She was never able to respond to Xavier's note and she can't even take the children to the park because of the weather. Now there's only packing. She sighs. Boots to wear on the plane, flats and heels into the bag, along with trainers brought especially for the parks. Hard to believe she took so much stuff for one weekend. In younger years one pair sufficed for months, but now four pairs for four days. Because try as she did she couldn't dispose of anything; the weekend held out so much promise. Assembling dirty clothes but mostly unused ones, it seems silly to have prepared for every contingency. The trap of the catalogue woman.

The door opens.

'Daddy!' Christophe and Katya shout in unison, as if their games hadn't held their attention.

Abandoning their animals, they run to him. She fetches discarded Pookie, stuffs him into the bag forcefully. Nothing more hateful than the ritual of goodbye.

'Hey, come here,' Harry says.

133

Pretending not to hear him over the din, she tries to hide disappointment, this repeatedly being resurrected then tossed away again easily like Pookie, one minute the favourite, the next minute forgotten. She wills the distance to harden like a protective bubble that might make the break-away less raw. The distance between them will soon grow greater anyway.

He comes to her, forces her into a hug.

'I know what you're thinking, but we still have time for lunch. Let's go.'

Her acknowledgement is a glazed look, because there's nothing to say. It's been said before. And lunch, as ever, is a pointless exercise in last-minute togetherness: Harry already on the phone, perusing documents, checking emails, disappearing into his text, disappearing, disappearing, before he's even gone. Riding together in the taxi, checking in for separate destinations, children begging him not to go, Harry saying he must. Her stomach twisting in a knot, the familiar final goodbye, one last shooting pain, it's done. He's gone. Gone through security, back to security, back to the world of work.

Sucking in her breath, she puts on a brave face for the little ones, though they aren't looking anyway. They're happy in their imaginary world, anticipating flight. She scans the terminal for a place to sit and wait. They might have gone through with Harry, but who wants to watch someone board when you've got hours to go? Perhaps they should've stayed at the hotel, but that didn't seem a fun option either, staying behind. Any standing still kills pace. And she could doubly kick herself for the brevity of the weekend, the missed chances, Harry's inability to break free. Even the final night, the famous Costes, not the euphoric craziness she'd imagined or hoped for, but a ping-pong match of colleagues slapping each other on the back. The leaden effect of vodka and fizz, that awful mix, the dress in its second outing still no talisman, the clumsy groping afterwards, the damned burst seam.

She looks down at Christophe and Katya, goofing about with their wheelies. They should all go and get a drink, then go through and watch planes. She reaches for her bag but someone comes up close behind.

'You were leaving without saying goodbye?'

She knows before she turns. The depth of the voice sends the shock wave. She locks eyes with him, tightens her grip on the children.

'How did you find me?' she blurts out. 'I had no time, didn't think it'd be possible.'

'No, it was me, I didn't make enough time,' Xavier says quietly. 'I should have.'

'This is Christophe and Katya,' squeezing their hands, she releases tension by passing it on.

'Pleased to meet you,' he replies, and he does seem genuinely pleased. He crouches down to speak or possibly get a closer look at them.

'Hi, I'm Xavier, an old friend of your mother's.' It comes out in heavily accented English, no special emphasis on friend, as if it were the easiest relationship in the world. 'Now where are you two going?'

For a moment his manner of speech is amusing, the English stiff, like him. But only on the outside, of course, the opposite of what she knows him to be like when intimate. The whole scenario *is* funny in a way: him bending down for an earnest appraisal of, or from, her children. But he's a father too, why shouldn't he know how to act?

'We're going home to England,' Katya replies shyly.

'But the plane's not for ages!' Christophe chimes in.

'It's true,' she breathes out. 'We skipped out on the Tuileries because of the rain, so we have almost three hours.'

'Ah, good news finally,' Xavier says, stretching up and smiling. 'We'll have to do something about that.' Extremely pleased now, he brushes past her. 'Come, I know the place!'

135

Viens, always the command, he strides off expecting to be followed. A spring in his step and his trademark loafers, that dressy casual style he adopted as a student because it announced he was either rich or lucky in the world, either way he would command it.

There is nothing to do but follow, so off they go, down the long terminal and moving walkways, the children zipping their miniature wheelies loudly over the metal bumps, having great fun making them tip and crash.

'Where are we going?' she says, catching up and tapping him on the shoulder.

He doesn't stop, doesn't seem to want to give her an opportunity to protest. She laughs nervously. This situation is absurd.

'Trust me,' he says, slowing down to look at her playfully, 'a hotel.'

'No,' she stops, but the walkway's still moving, the children far ahead, so the absurdity continues as they glide on together.

'Not that, come on,' he says grinning, taking her hand as the walkway ends.

He leads them around a corner. A Sheraton sign. They must look like a family, marching together, and suddenly, embarrassingly, it seems less ridiculous, even a relief that Harry's gone.

'See? No good cafes at that end, you have to come here,' Xavier pronounces as they move through revolving doors. The din of the airport vanishes instantly.

They head left to an open bar area, a corner sofa, the whole space beyond silent. People seem to be whispering rather than talking; even the tennis match playing out on flat screens is on mute. The decor resembles an evening cocktail lounge: sensuous curved couches, a bar with art deco touches. With natural daylight removed, it could truly be anytime, day or night. An encounter, a date – except for the children. But Christophe and

Katya seem to have adapted too, taking their animals from their bags, setting up a zoo a few sofas away. It's just the two of them here and now.

Xavier signals to a waiter, orders juices and coffees, looking up to say, '*Ça va?*'

'*Oui, assez bien.*'

'Oh no,' Xavier retorts smiling. 'Only well enough? Should I be ordering champagne? We *should* celebrate. I've managed to catch you.'

'No, it's…'

'Done.'

He signals the waiter back, counters the coffee order while she tries to think what to reply. *Ça va?* Yes, some bits are pretty good but by implication, other parts are wanting. How to explain a mood? That a moment ago, the weekend was over, Harry had gone and life was disappointing. Not only the shape of it, but Harry, for leaving. Maybe it's not his fault there's this gaping hole, but butterflies have filled it, so now she feels gratitude, for the person who *is* here, even if he too can only fill the gap for a couple of hours. But soon he will be gone as well, and this same Eva, seemingly so beloved, will be on her way home to carry out duties alone. How to say that this is the sum total of life? Bearing great responsibilities but feeling discarded? That it's not at all what she bargained for?

'You don't have to tell me anything,' he says, his melodic voice a lull of calm.

She looks over at Christophe and Katya, happy, oblivious. Oh, why not be like them? Life lived simply, choices made by someone else, thoughts connected to the everyday, not beyond. Maybe there's no point in making Xavier understand this. Or maybe he does. Maybe that's why he's here, making the effort, sacrificing whatever else he should be doing.

'To tell you the truth, Xav, I'm shocked,' she finally exhales pent up tension. 'I can't believe you came out here to see me.'

'Not really,' he says, taking her hand.

'Don't, the children.'

It comes out a whisper. But she knows they aren't watching. They aren't registering a thing.

He ignores her protest, caresses her finger. 'Sadly there's not much I can do here,' he jokes, then releases her hand.

Now they can speak of other things: pleasant times, old friends, his business and his travels. Taking in his adventures, she only hints at her life, though there's not much to report – her life is playing itself out here on the sofas where they sit, under the silent match above their heads, and there, where her children are playing. It's plain to see what her life involves. It's all this endless present, the future obscured. For now, he too is here, with her, making it better. Not just more bearable, but shining a light on it. He hasn't even glanced at the screens though it's probably an important match. No, his attention is all on her, and that's so gratifying it's hard to resist.

Soon minutes move beyond the hour, that trickery of time, lost when most needed. Now it *is* time to go. Embarrassingly the children have started bickering, Christophe's desperate to see planes, while Katya's glances seem to ask, who is this strange friend of Mama's anyway? If they were any older this scenario would be taking a huge risk – wait, did that thought actually surface? Such a prelude to deception. No, this thing with Xavier must stay above board.

Friendly and casual, he escorts them to security and they embrace openly like old friends – the old friends they are. But he's also looking at her with a gaze so strong she has to look away. He grabs her arm then, firmly, draws near.

'Next time,' he breathes into her ear. 'I mean it.'

Then he lets go.

She dashes away with Christophe and Katya, running in big S motions around the chains to security. Up to passport control, where finally they all turn to wave. Xavier waves too, like a father seeing off his family. Naturally, seeing them off. And the only thing that can possibly come to mind is: that should have been Harry.

∞

'So good you're back, Eva.' Miss Miriam bustles to make tea but doesn't seem to recollect where her favourite canister is.

'Oh dear, I can't seem to find it, what a foolish old lady I'm becoming. Oh here,' she reaches into the place it's always kept, in the cupboard to the left of the stove. 'Did you have a lovely time?'

Paris, already distant. Though they'd only been gone a short while, a deep fog set in. It's unlike any she's ever seen, only heard of, the proverbial pea souper.

'Eva?'

'Yes, sorry, it was lovely. I was thinking of the weather. You must keep warm, especially with that chest cold. It's not good that it's come back.'

'Ah, a little thing,' but she coughs heavily.

'Here let me help.'

'You'll do no such thing, I am perfectly capable,' Miss Miriam leans for support on the worktop, turns the tap to fill the kettle. 'Thank goodness those kind gentlemen came and repaired the plumbing. Since Charlie died, I'm not good at keeping to such things.'

'The plumbing?'

'Yes, I didn't even know I had a problem. But they knocked on the door and offered a free check. Took the whole sink apart practically and found a terrible leak somewhere. Thank goodness they fixed it.'

'A leak?'

'Well, I didn't notice it, under the sink somewhere in the wall, but they brought in all these pipes and fiddled for more than an hour. Charged me £450, but I guess that's going rates.'

'Miss Miriam!' but she stops herself. 'Did those gentlemen leave a card?'

'Oh yes, I must've put it somewhere,' Miss Miriam starts rummaging by the phone but abandons the effort as quickly. 'I'll probably never find it. But they said they're a local company. Since then, I've had several offers, gardeners, driveway resurfacers, they must all be friends.'

'Miss Miriam, you must be careful,' she pauses, 'not all tradesmen are reputable. Please, ring me next time someone proposes work, I'll come and check their references.'

'That would be good,' Miss Miriam sighs, pouring the tea. 'I told Emma about it and all she did was get very cross and shout. But she didn't come over.' Looking despondent, she suddenly brightens. 'Never mind, you're like a daughter, so attentive. My son,' she blushes, 'my son,' pausing as if trying to recall his name, 'never mind. He doesn't ring.'

'Oh Miss Miriam,' she takes her bony hand, rubs the veins and spots gently. These signs of real aging, softness and fragility not like a child's but stretched out, worn, thin – the hands of Baba Kasia, before she went away forever.

Miss Miriam smiles, bright eyes flashing steely reserve. 'Don't you worry about me, Eva. I've got some fight left.'

∞

She stares out at the fog, its own persistent presence, breaking up but returning the next day, people disappearing like ghosts. It's even altered the psyche of the school run, no one wants to stop and chat. The impetus is to rush home to safety, certainty, warmth.

Shuddering from the cold, she turns to the fireplace, kneels and lights a fire. Only mid-morning, early November, a whole winter ahead without Harry, how much drearier will it get? She stands up and returns to the window to draw back the curtains, though at this point letting light into the family room also means letting in cold. She surveys the room, what next? No, she can't – she can't go back, not to this. A pile of toys in easy reach of the basket, but who wants to tidy? Where's the satisfaction? Please, no more repetition, let's move on. She needs to talk to someone, Harry maybe, but he's placeless, stateless, a man with no abode. She doesn't even know where he is these days, hopping from city to city, seemingly not knowing himself where he'll be. So it's as if he's formless too, having slipped into the mist saying *I'll be back in a little while*, never to return. Ringing him all she gets is *if you'd like to leave a message, please do so after the tone.* But who wants to leave messages? Damn it – an exchange, live people, words, ideas, feelings, excitement, action! That's what she needs. More than a month until the kids' Christmas concerts or any hope of seeing Harry, she cannot go back to the beginning.

From the study, the computer beckons. At least *he's* out there. Xavier, in Paris. Some distance too, but easier to picture him now. In his flat or at a cafe or better yet, that scene at the airport, which inflates spontaneously every time she closes her eyes. Hearing his voice, feeling his solid hold on her wrist, his breath on her ear. The words: *next time, I mean it.*

She goes to the desk and sits before the blank screen. If there must be repetition, might as well fall back to that time, or the best of times, or even the next time, that imagined next place, a darker corner where Xavier will greet her again, from behind, his baritone undulating as he insinuates what he wants. Touching her ever so lightly on the shoulder, he'll guide her, she'll move with him, to a back room, a table as hard as the back of the chair she's sitting on. She's unzipping her jeans like this as he kisses her neck exactly where it electrifies. Moving with him, letting herself be taken away, his hands are where hers are, he doesn't have to undress her fully, jeans down just enough, he'll move quickly, pinning her to the table, the surrender absolute. He knows exactly where to find what she has to offer, the current moving between her legs, that flash of light from which time and distance escape and there is no reckoning. Being. Only being.

Only being, she exhales, fighting her own emptiness. Again. Being, not nothingness.

Eyes shut, the stillness of an empty house, the cold study. She has to imagine his embrace afterward, the warmth that would be there. She'll need another day, like the one that came years before this, not an end, but a beginning. And him, Xavier, holding her, as if he never meant to let go.

∞

'So how was it?' Harry asks.

'Jenny's? Fine. She's planning a party next Thursday.'

'Oh?'

'She's trying to expand her catering, get new people interested in placing orders for when the Christmas season gets busy. Lots of mums are going. Jenny's neighbour Louise will babysit for me.'

'Sounds reasonable, social.' But he doesn't sound interested.

'And Miss Miriam is getting better, still weak but better.'

'Oh, I meant to ask, how is she?'

But she's just told him so clearly he's not listening. She sighs. Even when she related the story about the spate of scam artists, her worries about protecting Miss Miriam, all he could say was *Eva, you can't do everything, she's got family, it's their problem.*

'So how are things at your end, Harry?'

'Not great actually,' he perks up. 'Negotiations aren't going to plan, though hopefully the deal will be done by Christmas. That's the deadline.'

Christmas as a deadline, not a celebration of birth – only someone with their head buried in business could see it that way.

'That means it's unlikely I'll be back this month,' he continues. 'Maybe not at all in December either, I might have to meet you in Poland for the holidays.'

'But Harry, that's more than a month away,' she feels the panic rising. 'The kids' concerts, you said…'

'I know what I said,' he interrupts, 'but the whole team has to be in Vienna the next few weeks. I can't be sure I can break away, so best not to count on me.'

'But I already count on so little,' she starts, though it isn't true but the opposite – she depends on him completely. But he's also missing the point. Marriage is about time spent together, not the assets you bring to the table. She must try again: be lucid, be final, nail it on the head.

'Harry, the Plan's keeping us apart so much it's driving a wedge between us.'

'Eva, we were just *together*, that incredible weekend in Paris, what, a couple of weeks ago? A few more and you'll be in Poland. More to the point, you agreed to this. It'll secure our future. I can't believe we have to go through this again.'

She can hear the stress in his voice but Xavier is a clear and present danger and she and Harry need to have a conversation about what they're doing and why. How this is affecting her and the children, their concept of home life. This *is* about family, *their* family. He should care.

'Okay, forget about the future for a minute, what about the present? Life's not just about the future. It's about living as we are. Maybe we should live differently. So we can be together,' she pauses for breath. 'Long distance marriage is crazy, Harry, it's not like we're destitute, that you have to do this. Another four weeks? Not good for the kids. Frankly, it's all wrong.'

Wrong might be the wrong word, another spark, but he doesn't know about X, doesn't know the peril besetting her and she can't warn him. But she has to make him understand.

'Don't you see? It's just not good for our relationship, or the children, it's not normal.'

'But it's temporary, Eva,' he says in that steady voice he adopts when someone veers from hard fact into spongy emotion. 'Say I come home now, or any weekend, simply because we're both feeling lonely or you're feeling low – we'll lose all we've worked for. All that time away since last spring, all that hardship will have been for nothing, they'll tax me to death. I've got days saved up for home visits, sure, but that's in case of an emergency, you or the kids falling really ill. Remember you have just as much vested in this, you wanted the kids stable. A few more weeks and you'll be in Przemyśl, and I'll be there for some of that. I can't do anything about my schedule between now and then. What more do you want? Why can't you be satisfied?'

She winces at the jab, reluctant to respond with an upper cut. Adam had taught her a few boxing techniques, in case she needed self defence when he wasn't around. But she'd never been much of a fighter on the outside, taking comfort in internal rectitude.

'Eva?'

'It's not about satisfaction or stability, Harry,' she resumes. 'It's about our relationship, our home life. You're always wrongly attributing my discomfort to dissatisfaction emanating from selfishness. But I'm not being selfish. I'm looking after everyone's interests. You'll miss the concerts, the entire run-up to Christmas, that's part of the season too.'

'Right, Eva, we agreed to this *together*,' he drops to low measured tones, changing tack the way he does when he sees he might lose but wants to win. 'But okay, if you want, we can throw it all in, if it's that important.'

'No!' How dare he deflect and dump on her the responsibility for the failure of the Plan! 'No, Harry, we'll see it through if you insist. But I'm just saying, it's not working. This Plan doesn't work!'

He doesn't say anything to that and it's obvious he's seething with anger. Because he's been thrown a problem he can't solve. Because it requires two contradictory responses – come home now and stay there and make it work.

'I've had enough of this,' he says. 'You're cornering me, but I won't go there. So do what you like, Eva. I thought we had this thing worked out. But you're not making any sense. So do whatever the fuck you want. To make this better for you.'

∞

Swaying, heading for the computer – freedom of action is what we need yet so desperately lack. Yes, freedom – to be happy, to veer on recklessness. She's in a dangerous state but who cares? Too many glasses of wine at Jenny's, so much gossip about other people's supposed infidelities, who knew it was so common? He said, do what you want, and even if he didn't mean it, when you're emboldened to tempt fate, why not the internet? Nothing in the inbox? Feel sad, or dare yourself to fill it.

To: X
From: Noisette
Re: à la prochaine

So, my dear. What next time?
Eva

Short and provocative, like her best skirts. Back to the kitchen
for the bottle started yesterday, one more glass, this could take
time. Might as well get comfortable. Virtual life, life on screen,
the lure of instant gratification. Even if you have to wait for that
too, why didn't she grasp it before? Instant gratification,
especially if, with any stroke of luck, a reply does come instantly.
It would be a sign... yes, he's out there. For her. Right now,
engaged with her only.
    Yours, Eva, all yours.
    She types quickly:

To: Noisette
From: X
Re: re: à la prochaine

The next time I see you.
Would next week be too soon?
X.

See? He's there. But take care, squint, letters can be jumpy. Read
it again. Make sure it says what you think. Read it twice, just for
the thrill. Ha, pure escalation, but further than what she had in
mind? How to counter?
    She takes a large gulp, sets down the glass.

To: X
From: Noisette
Re: the next real time

Xavier,

Wow, you do come quickly.

Would this trip be for business or for love?

Eva

She practically spits out the wine, smiling like a deranged idiot. So what, no one sees. Why contain angst, why repress? This is living, dammit. Insanity, stupidity, liquid desire – who cares? It feels good. Game restarting: the lure, the hunt, the wait. The entrapment.

To: Noisette
From: X

Eva, I only come when I'm ready.

And I would do much for business, but more for love.

I don't need a cover, though I have one. Meetings with wine merchants in the City, next Thursday. What's your excuse?

X.

Her heart's beating so hard it actually hurts. On the brink. It's wrong. Being there on the brink is already wrong. But who can't want this? This wanting to be wanted. To be put before business, not after. How dare Harry not see that? Harry. Gone. Might as well down the wine in one go, exactly like he'd tell her not to.

But seriously, think – words are important, not throwaway jibes. No way to meet him in London, impractical. She can't ask Jenny again, Louise is in school, who can a person trust?

Another sip. Dammit, glass empty. Stop. Order thoughts, how to make this work? How not to lose X, or Harry or oneself in this complex equation? Be honest?

To: X
From: Noisette

Dear X,

No excuses but I'm struggling to think of a way to meet. Only three hours free in the mornings. But not far from Heathrow or Gatwick, if you're flying. We could meet somewhere for coffee.

Eva

Coffee? Really? Last time it had already moved to champagne. Erecting ridiculous barriers: trying to be safe in a public place. Will he play along? Maybe not. He's always seen right through her.

To: Noisette
From: X

I am flying but morning won't do, meetings. How about Thursday night, say eight? I could come around to you with some great wine. Corner House always did sound inviting.

X.

Done, almost.

You don't have to ask him, only stop him. Say no.

Just do it already, fuck it, you can always make excuses later. He intruded.

Ridiculous, who are you making excuses for? To whom are you justifying your acts? He can't come if you don't let him. Don't let him.

What do you care for propriety? He doesn't. You both know Harry's gone, one time available. Come on Eva, play the game.

Okay.

∞

Dumping the remains of ready meals, she shoves the containers guiltily in the bin. How can people subsist on this stuff, never mind feed it to children? Just this once, she told herself. Just this once, as she was getting her nails done, just skip the cooking and preserve the manicure, look half as polished as Carole. She used to tell Harry, *my charm is Polish not varnish*, and he'd laugh, but now it's not funny, because maybe these other women have it right. After forty you need to pay attention to these things, even if it's for the first time. It's not easy to compete, and god, we are all getting older. What can be done to halt the process? Nothing. But let's try anyway.

She heads upstairs for what's required: apply war paint to even out the complexion, accentuate cheekbones and highlight almond-shaped eyes. Forget Tilly's invasive injections and incisions, one must draw the line somewhere. And better the line be drawn than cut. Long ago she'd vowed to age gracefully, normally, fully and intact; a face to match hands and feet, body and hair, all remaining beautiful in totality. Because you can't fix things in parts, a person is whole, like Miss Miriam or Baba Kasia, wizened old women with the glimmer of rebelliousness in their eyes. Baba Kasia, who didn't even wear make-up, never had it in those days of war and suffering and perseverance, now falsely cast by cinema as times of glamour and glory in black and white. But it had been hard and grey and beauty came from valour not vanity. What silliness now drives women to pretend they are younger than they are? Yet everyone takes out the concealer anyway, goes on the offensive to defend what's left of youth.

She inspects herself in the mirror. This is the face he will see. Maybe beautiful now but just wait – wait until the chin starts to sag, the face starts to slide and fine furrows turn to deep rows. One day you'll wake up unrecognizable to yourself. Inside you'll feel young but to everyone else you'll be decrepit. What will you do then? Is it possible to remain true or is everyone corrupted by falseness eventually, having plumped and rosied their skin so that only the eyes tell the truth? Because the truth is in the pain and joy, the hope and fear – surely the truth is what Xavier wants too. That's what he's coming for, that's what he'll see regardless, because eyes themselves never change.

Mirror, mirror on the wall, cannot stop a woman's fall. But a reflection only abets what one will do anyway. She catches a last glance of herself, this other new Eva, clicking the mascara into its case. Application not at its best, but what does anyone expect? Nerves, children acting up, cats racing about unnecessarily, everyone sensing jitters, even an ambulance with its mournful background whine drawing closer then stopping abruptly so the children's noise is amplified. She calls out for bedtime, her voice lost in the noise, a robot rattling through prayers and no chit-chat with Katya, though it's wrong, adding the silent prayer they'll both stay asleep, no matter what, and especially no vomiting. Yeah, dear god, I'll do my best, please let me see what this is about, and in this way, you hope to make good what more than a sneaking suspicion tells you is bad. A good bad. A bad good. But life's not wholly in one person's control, is it? Xavier *is* the other half now.

Descending to the kitchen, she pours another glass of wine. Just this one, to steady the nerves, because it's not possible *it* will happen. That unspeakable it. So damned unfortunate she gave up smoking. Just this one second glass. The important thing is the kids stay asleep. Let's all be thankful for swim day.

The solid boom of the brass knocker, the boom that makes every entry into the house sound like an invasion. She takes a deep breath, opens the door. But it's Jenny.

'Oh hi, what is it?' all in one breath, trying to take in Jenny, plus the other emergency, the ambulance flashing down by Miss Miriam's house.

'David,' Jenny pants. 'He's having crushing pains in his stomach. Sorry I should have told you earlier, he's been having these, I'm taking him to hospital, could be ulcers again, or appendicitis, but you know how long hospitals can take, Louise is there now, but if I'm not back by eleven, if I need help, just in case…'

What to say? Without someone around there's little she can do, she certainly can't reveal X now, not at this time of night. Why didn't Jenny call or text instead of coming over? But she's so distraught no point in asking.

'Jenny, I'm here if you need me,' she uses her steadiest voice. 'I can always pop over, to check on things, if that's what you mean. Mine will be dead asleep tonight.'

'Thanks, you're so great,' Jenny's face is grim. She hurries down the drive, disappears around the bend. The sound of a car driving off, David must be in it already, while in the distance the ambulance lights continue to flicker.

Taking in the cold air, she tries to come to terms with what's happening. Because it doesn't make sense. If David's having stomach troubles why didn't they go to the doctor during the day? Unless it's something like appendicitis where pains get worse until you're doubled over, but that doesn't fit with Jenny's report that they're recurring. But it must be serious if David's conceding to go to hospital. And down the road the ambulance, hopefully not for Miss Miriam, she only just returned from there. The cold's coming in, she must shut the door. But a taxi slows beyond the hedge, stops.

Frozen to the spot, she listens to the exchange on the street, the voice reverberating before the vision of him appears, striding up the gravel. That sound, identical to the Tuilieries and Eiffel Tower, why hadn't she made the connection before? All these places, so solid but shifting under your feet. But in this moment, which takes ages, him walking, large shoulder bag swinging at his side, suddenly he's right there before her, taller and more handsome than ever.

'Good evening.' The baritone is a melting caress.

'Come in,' she feigns impossible calm, then instantly cracks. 'A friend of mine was having an emergency.' And without planning to at all she launches into the story, a story to silence the silence and explain why she's standing there, door half open, as if waiting.

The chatter does help extinguish her nerves, though Xavier doesn't seem in the least perturbed by what should be an awkward meeting. Here, in her home, her husband gone, the invisible thing between them.

In the family room the fire flickers in the draught, illuminating little of the room but mellowing its contours. Spotlights would show the curtains' residual damage so she left them off, but now it's too dark and romantic, a setting for what shouldn't be. Even the coffee table has the perfect props, two wine glasses, a bottle, although as promised, Xavier produces his own.

He smiles, looks directly at her. 'Come, I want you to taste what I'm doing.'

He leaves the statement hanging, so quickly she has to find another topic besides what he wants her to taste and what he might be doing. Wine coursing through her veins already, she sits, he too, on the sofa some distance apart, not awkwardly but slightly formal, both of them working hard to keep the conversation casual.

Then time, that great magician working sleight of hand, and everything begins slipping, as it does when you're talking of all the years since you've met. Because actually there's a lot to cover: children and jobs, travel and sport, amusement and art, and politics and economics if you get stuck. Sipping the red, it might be the best she's ever tasted.

'So getting back to this,' she swirls the liquid in her glass gaily. 'This is the real benefit of getting into the wine trade.'

'You mean it makes it easier to seduce?' Xavier jokes.

'No,' her laugh comes easily. 'Well, maybe in your case. I meant it's a more enjoyable way of paying bills and consuming profits. You get to drink the good stuff.'

'I suppose with the chateau producing better, it's a golden horizon.' He sets down his glass. 'Carole isn't that interested though, family ties remain more than anything. Carole isn't…'

With the mention of Carole, she can't help tensing, even after downing so much in the attempt to relax. Maybe he's noticed. She's feeling it. He's looking at her intently.

'A golden horizon, but only from the point of view of wine,' he reaches over, stroking her arm tentatively.

'Oh, why's that?' her voice almost breaks.

'Because it's not like it was with you,' he says in low tones, drawing near.

Such a good thing she remembered to turn the key in the door. *What a terrible draught, doors practically swing open themselves.* Another ruse but also a precaution against the slightest disturbance, little feet descending. There isn't a sound in the house, however. No one will intervene to save her.

He knows it, knows her well, and with that playful stroke of the arm, it begins. He leans in again and places a tiny first kiss ever so gently behind the ear. This time he doesn't pull back, he moves down the neck breathing so incredibly slowly it's excruciating. He pauses, then retreats, then moves in again, leaning ever closer with his whole body now, putting each kiss in exactly the right place, the one that connects right down between her legs. She could protest but he's the master of this game, she's succumbing, unconsciously letting out a small moan even while saying please, meaning no, but please can also mean yes, a word so indeterminate. Trying to hold his hand steady he's taken her glass away, set it somewhere, comes in closer again. This time it's as if he was always there, there already, where he is, was always meant to be, here and there, more forcefully and purposefully. She gave in for just a moment, but now she can't be saved. He's captured her for good.

Without the slightest hesitation, he starts to move aside clothing, kissing her naked collarbone, going lower and lower. He knows what he's doing, done it a thousand times, nothing can hamper a man full of conviction, a man who knows his rights. When she returns the kiss for the first time, it's as if she's dealt him a blow with her recognition. He lets out a moan and now she wants control, to make him beg for mercy. They're tearing at each other, half naked, and only then, when she's pinned underneath, do the words come, *please, please, enough.*

He doesn't want to hear it, keeps going, moving faster, his body's becoming heavier so that protest is uttered again and now he takes note in case he's hurting her. *We can't, not here.*

'Please, not here,' finally hearing her own hoarse voice.

'I want you so much,' he says, his head bent into her neck, hands still trying.

'I noticed,' she laughs and this makes it better.

He looks up, notes her expression. 'You really are something.' But he doesn't seem angry, only incredulous, bemused. He sits back, takes a breath, reaches for his wine.

'So are you, a fine mess you've got us into.' Her nerves come out in laughter. She too sits up quickly, reaches for the bra and blouse. Covering nakedness, the worst averted.

Xavier smiles, fingers his wine. 'If not now, Eva, when? If not here, where?'

'I can't answer that,' she says hotly, indignant. 'Come on, Xav, be serious, you have Carole, I have Harry.'

'So we do, what's wrong with that?'

Where to start? The muddied territory of Xavier's morals: a pointless hike across flat landscape leading nowhere, with pockets of quicksand to boot.

'For Catholics…' she begins.

Xavier holds up his hand and smiles. 'Enough,' he says. 'I've heard this before.'

'None of the major religions have changed their minds on adultery.'

'You're not Catholic any more,' Xavier reminds her. 'Or religious, and certainly not practising.' He emphasizes the last word with a pregnant pause, as if refraining from enumerating all the serious rules of Catholicism she's already broken in the past.

'True, but I want to be good to Harry.'

'You can be good to Harry and good to me,' Xavier suggests with a smirk, leaning in to kiss her again.

Even if that's what she originally thought, coming from him it sounds awful. The sinkhole she's been trying to avoid, pulling her down, Xav going too far, becoming self centred, patronizing. Feeling repelled is the only chance at escape, so she feeds it.

'Maybe in your book you can,' she moves away. 'Talking the book was always your strongpoint.'

'Touché,' says Xavier, not in the least offended. 'Though that's English conceding the point. I'd say we're deuce.'

Still trying, still playing, so she rebuffs.

'So you and Carole have this open relationship?'

It might have been a strained question earlier but they're past that now.

'You could say we've agreed to disagree on occasion,' Xavier says wryly.

'Only it works out less ideally than you'd hoped?'

She can't help pushing it but Xavier looks at her with penetrating eyes and thinks for what seems a long time before he replies.

'Or maybe I just never forgot you.'

Then for a brief second, less than a fraction of a second, there's the totality of hurt in his gaze, a flash in the dark in his eyes, and she knows who caused it. Her. No one won this match. And the game's far from over.

∞

Looking in the mirror one sees what one wants to see. Though it's undeniable too, the glory emanating from secret attraction – the smile, the rosy glow in her cheeks, the spring in her step – doesn't a reflection say it all? Passing other people's houses, cars, she wonders if it really is noticeable. The afterglow of desire, white hot passion unrequited, everything still left to savour, no harm done, really. All those weighty constraints that leave a person downtrodden – morality, conscience – released like butterflies. Why not make yourself happy in whatever way you choose? She'll have the patience for the Plan now, isn't that what Harry wants? He'll marvel in her newfound wisdom and power and sexiness. Because if he were here now, she'd take him upstairs and take him apart. Feeling naughty and virtuous all at once, equal participant but also superior, for having stopped Xavier at the moment when things might have careened out of control. If there's any guilt now, it's for failing Xavier, not Harry. Because Harry really should have known better than to concoct this stupid Plan. Anyway, she's not going to hurt him – why should he even know? He'll only reap benefits later because she'll be more seductive and liberated with each passing day.

She casts a sly sideways glance at the last car window as she approaches the crowds. Being happy, being nice, isn't that what everyone wants of her? The children too are enjoying the by-product of a mother's happiness, because she *is* being nice, not tired and grumpy, going to extra lengths like making Baba's *nalysnyky* crepes with cheese and jam, even for breakfast, with double helpings of honey. Today she's not even late, marching to school for this special occasion, happy face announcing she's ready to take on anything. Yes, that smiling visage helps, the one that says nothing's too much trouble, because let's face it, people do respond better. No one wants to engage with those who look like they might actually need it. An unwritten rule: too risky to inquire how someone is if you might have to sacrifice in return. No, better to exchange like for like, empty compliments, false friendliness, complaints about the weather, even if really, to her, English weather has always been about the same.

Of course, now that too is remarkable – icy, cold and clear, the way she likes it – another reminder of Poland, sledding down hills freely as only a young child can. No responsibilities, no thought to dangers ahead, only sliding down, down, down, high speed, until the inevitable but not always fatal, crash at the end.

Sucking in the wintry air, stomping her feet to stay warm, she looks around at the gathering crowds. Everyone's having a change of heart in the run-up to Christmas. The atmosphere's changing palpably. Though every year is also the same: performances, carol concerts, nativities and mince pies. One might be more Mary Magdalene than Mother of God, but Christ was born to forgive all. He always forgives the tainted, does he not?

First in the queue, she enters and takes a seat near the front, turns around to watch the hall fill up. Mums and dads, grannies

and granddads, and nannies the school calls carers as though
they were looking after invalids instead of children. But she can
sit with pride, her children don't have a carer. She, the mother, is
the one to care. The one to show up and watch, drop off and
fetch, each and every day, the first and last to catch that spark of
joy in their innocent eyes. But then she's always been their
audience, an audience of one. The pillar. How did she miss it
before Xav pointed it out?

So it's worth it, making this effort, not only in mothering but
appearance, her curled hair half clipped so it tumbles down in a
messy just-been-done way. Make-up too, a first for a school affair,
some people seem to be stealing second glances. Good, let them.
Just because she doesn't usually look good doesn't mean she
can't. Scanning the crowd, mainly for Jenny, but it's too much of
a melee, David's aches inconclusive, doctors found nothing,
though Jenny still believes it's beyond the scope of chamomile.
She must remember to ask later if he's feeling better, offer to have
James and Sophie round. Lights dimming now, the hum of
conversations dropping, the show begins.

Elves and bunnies. Dancing snowflakes. Gingerbread men
and candy canes. There doesn't appear to be a storyline, although
Katya was adamant when she came home the other day that all
stories had to follow these, her newly discovered, rules.
Beginning, middle and end, Mama, the teachers said. And having
checked the homework diary, sadly she saw what Katya meant:
National Curriculum, Literacy, Key Stage One. It would have
been too confusing to tell Katya that actually stories don't always
follow this pattern, sometimes they go on and on, you might even
be able to pick and choose parts, and quite often to get anywhere
in life you have to break the rules.

On stage the children are hemmed in, too many at once. But
the singing is sweet, the adapted music pleasant despite inane
lyrics and the odd costume failure. All is forgivable of course, as

anyway the Nativity's missing, so it's all filler. For whatever reason the central event of Christmas was downgraded this year, the focus on this, the immaterial, or materialism surrounding the holiday. When she found out about it at first she felt greatly aggrieved, as if something valuable had been stolen from her. But why was it disturbing, having the bit about Christ's birth eliminated? Just another story after all, they have to vary the programme. You can't do the same thing year after year, bore people with repetition at the expense of a message. Life isn't a morality play, and Christophe's putting on a fine performance as the elf he is, Katya in her snow bunny outfit with the older girls in ever-so-slightly-forming figures, wiggling bottoms just this side of respectable. Some are quite the movers. Thankfully Katya doesn't seem to have this, her mother's one exceptional talent.

Clapping, flashing cameras, more clapping, laughter, and poof, show over. The children have been seen performing, the parents seen watching. A collection begins for some charity or other, a strange ritual, because growing up her parents didn't give away precious money in public, only at church. To help friends and family, or even strangers, meant time given. Or what you could pass on physically until you had nothing left to give. Then you prayed, especially for those people in homes and orphanages, so God would do his bit. But now dutifully she stuffs a note into the clinking bucket, thinking how much softer the sound the more you give.

Katya and Christophe race ahead, disappear around the forest of adult legs. She's caught behind aging aunties, men in woolly hats.

'Daddy! Mama! Daddy's here!'

Lost in the noise, the crowd, other children diving through legs, she can hear but doesn't believe. Then she catches a glimpse. The apparition is real. It's him. Harry. Sheepish grin, tired face, dishevelled hair. Harry in his uniform of travel: crumpled suit, grey cashmere scarf and worn-out Church shoes.

'I would have made it,' he comes forward earnestly, extending both arms wide in embrace. 'But the plane was late.'

She steps into him, then pulls back to study his face. Sometimes he comes through, and he does so thoroughly, it makes her want to laugh and cry at the same time.

'You poor thing,' she laughs as the tears well up. Because Christmas does make you emotional. And she is sorry. Sorry for having doubted, for having strayed, because he tried, he really did. She's been too hard on him and not hard enough on herself. He does try. And Christmas time, so full of weighted expectations, never working out like it should. And yet he came, all the same, like some other famous story set in Christmas. All the same, he came.

'Wow, you look amazing!' he takes her again in a crushing hug, the crowds pushing them together more.

She gives herself over to him, his smell, his warm body. Not asking or even taking, just giving. Every pretence is shattered, a split second expanding into the fullness of time.

'I've missed you so much,' she mumbles.

The words are stifled by his collar, but it doesn't matter that he hears, only that she said it. Because at that moment she means it – really means it – more than she ever has in her life.

∞

'Right,' he says, rubbing his hands together, as if he'd never left. 'So what's for dinner?'

The banality of it returns so quickly: mugs still in the sink from breakfast, stacks of unread post, taking stock of the cupboards.

She's been caught unawares. Suddenly the future is now, as if a whole houseful of guests descended five hours early while you were still in pyjamas, hoovering. Rushing to tidy up, hide the mess, not enough time to prepare and entertain these unexpected people and their expectations. There's a real difference in wanting something and getting used to it once it's there.

'Eva, any ideas?'

'Um, whatever you like,' she turns from the pantry doors. 'We're a bit low on interesting stuff. If I'd known you were coming...'

'I could do with a curry,' he suggests, grinning. 'You wouldn't believe what passes for Indian in Austria.'

'I'll probably never know,' she returns the smile. 'Okay, curry it is.' She stops. 'Except.'

'Except what?'

'As long as you accept that after a curry, my tummy's too full and churned up for...'

'Oh no, not that again,' Harry says.

'You know how those spices are, I can barely digest them. I like the taste but I didn't grow up with this food like you.'

'So eat something mild, like korma.'

'Harry, coconut milk doesn't particularly agree with me either.'

'Crikey, Eva, so it's sex or curry?'

'Well, I don't want to put it that way, but that's usually how it goes.'

'Okay then, sex first, curry later.'

He grabs her by the hand and says, 'Come on now, my little chapatti.'

At first laughing and resisting, because what a nut he is, especially after he calls her tikka masala and tiny bhuna and whatever else, then poppadum, which he thinks seems to suit her best. He keeps patting her on the bum as he leads upstairs, saying poppadum, poppabum, and they're both laughing, locking the bedroom door for a quickie, she steadying herself and giving in, not preferable but if it pleases him, and anyway getting it over with is a good compromise. Because she really ought to learn to eat Indian if she's going to become fully English.

Kids stuffed in the car, they're off to his favourite, The White Tiger. Katya and Christophe come prepared with their favourite animals to survive critical dinner activity: boring parents talk. Harry's relaxed, talking about taking out the motorbike, cycling with David, who insists he is better despite Jenny's protestations. Normal life. All the things Harry usually does when he's around.

Picking at her food, she watches him finish, fold his napkin. He takes his beer and leans back for a drink.

'Just so you know,' he says smiling. 'We've secured the bonuses.' He makes the announcement with pride.

'Great. That's great.'

And she is pleased too because it means he probably won't baulk at skiing during the February half term school break. He'd argued it was a racket, the pricing then double to other times, insisted they take Christophe and Katya out of school early. She said it wouldn't work, they wouldn't allow it, the headmaster was cracking down on family time. *What, is the national curriculum for infants more important than family? What's wrong with this country?* But she was the one under pressure, it would fall on her, the disapproving looks. State schools had ways of getting back at you.

But with the bonus they could play by the rules and celebrate in style: Courchevel or Klosters, and why not? Hadn't he suffered to earn it? Wasn't it what he always dreamed of? Snowy holidays in the Alps, children picking up speed every year. Every man should have his dreams and the ability to fulfil them. She watches him beaming, slurping foam off his beer.

'So you see, it's all worth it,' he declares.

'What's worth it?' then wishes it hadn't come out that way.

'Being apart for a while,' he says, leaning forward. 'It'll buy us the kind of life we want very soon. And I'm not talking holidays or house but the stress of the long term easing.' He pauses as if he might launch into a tirade about the sheer wall of money needed for living, what a great opportunity it's been to save, the dangers of low interest rates, recession. But he doesn't continue, takes another sip of beer.

'But will you ever stop? I mean, how do we know when we've hit the magic right price? Once we have all we need – supposing we get there – I don't quite see you going to an easier job.'

'No, true, I'll still have to prove myself once I make partner. It's a question of career, and that will mean a hard slog back in London. If they call me back, that is. Seems they like me out there.' He says it in a boasting way, not as if he's worried.

But the words *out there* make her think about the prospect: the many more nights she'll have to bear alone, the children too, without their father. Because even if he does return, he's right: he'll be at the office all hours. That doesn't seem a very different outcome to where they are now.

'At some point though, you'll stop working so much,' she says hopefully but without much conviction. 'You have to think about your health.'

'At death's door,' he jokes. 'Let's enjoy it for now. Make hay while the sun shines. I, for one, can't wait to ski. Must be the cold air.'

She'd like to interject that death's door is probably not a great time to start thinking about health, or even death, but she doesn't want to spoil a mood, so they start on the snow already dusting the ground in Poland, the skiing in previous years, the great runs, the gourmet meals, the plush Swiss hotels. It really is so easy to be whisked away to a world of fantasy fun, where everything's dazzling designer white, lunchtime *vin chaud* and après-ski aperitifs sparkling to witty repartee. Then hot tubs and hearty dinners, and afterwards on soft sheepskins, with cognacs in hand, you repose by the fire, finally relaxing long enough to remember to count your blessings.

Her stomach rumbles as Harry signals for the bill. She gets up, races to the loo, barely in time. What *do* they put in this food? Old doubts creeping in too, not only about coming here but everything they talked about, because she'd had none of it growing up – no curry restaurants or fancy trips. They'd skied the Bieszczady on wooden planks and down Przemyśl's single slope having as much fun for nearly free as the Holdens have on a couple of hundred euros a day. It was the monetary difference, not the qualitative, that was staggering. But then she did leave her hometown, oppressed by the thought of repeating the past, ad infinitum, and that had driven her out to the wider world, which turned out to be an expensive proposition. So maybe Harry was right citing school fees, universities, retirement, though that couldn't be all of it, because her parents had managed a good life without stockpiles of savings. Her childhood hadn't been a tenth as expensive as Katya and Christophe's, and in Poland they'd counted their blessings every day. So maybe it was the sum of all parts: activities and lessons, trips and shopping, holidays and house, all draining them slowly. Never mind the future.

In the bathroom, the walls and appliances, everything, a blaring white, a nod to that ephemeral tiger perhaps. The colour should be expansive but the stalls feel cramped, the whiteness almost piercing. Why fall into the trap? Why stay in a race to provide more? Harry's ambitions always seemed a positive thing, but now he was sacrificing life. Her parents' sacrifice had been one of giving up luxury, holidays – they'd never sacrificed time itself. And there hadn't been a feeling of deprivation either, no one looking over their shoulder, not until later when they found out what others in the West had. Could she and Harry ever adopt that kind of perspective or was it no longer possible to strive without being tainted by the exigencies of money? Was money itself the corruptor?

Flushing, as if one could dispose of filth, she exits the stall. Really there was no coming clean; shit only got moved around. Washing hands, she proceeds to the dryer, which ignites like a rocket, full thrust. One of those English contraptions so loud you can't hear yourself think. But they work, that's the main thing, the end point. Not if it's pleasant, only if it works, saves someone money. Like in any experiment, that was the control group – nowadays the successful money-makers. But it was an assumption too, like Harry's preoccupation with the ends and not the means of getting there. And conclusions were always skewed if you set up the experiment wrong. If you used the wrong assumptions, asked the wrong questions, you got the wrong answers.

But no one questioned the premise any more – what life is about, or that hard work, the satisfaction of it, had once been its own reward, *not* something that needed constant, ever more extravagant, rewarding. Work had become too time-consuming, so time-consuming it had stopped being work. It had become a way of being. An existence you *wanted* to escape, as if you *could* escape existence. So all the Harrys of the world were trying to flee the ubiquitousness of work, a trap they themselves had built, an all-encompassing encroachment even as they sacrificed everything to it. Falsely building barriers like ski holidays, in the hope that cell phones buried in puffy coat pockets might be ignored, only to find the world still caught up with you. Because everyone had bought into the technology that made it impossible to run away.

Staring in the mirror, face drained of colour, it seemed at times that you could only ever fall behind. But was that all of it?

A problem of working too hard, trying to save too much money, spending too much to begin with to provide for endless contingencies? Certainly a cycle had formed that couldn't be broken, too difficult to challenge anyway, so the best advice was, don't think, carry on. Harry himself said it on occasion, but then everyone had to carry the guilt, the grumpiness of being trapped in the cycle, of never feeling satisfied because in the end it never mattered really what you owned or did. But who could change this singlehandedly? Would Harry even agree with such an assessment? Weren't they in it together?

The Plan might be rotten, but she's probably taking too long. Hurrying out of the loo, she dashes from the restaurant to the waiting car.

'Sorry for the delay.'

'It really doesn't sit well with you does it?'

'No.'

Her answer is emphatic, flat. Because the important question remains unanswered: why did she ever try to accommodate him on this and so many other points?

∞

Corner House, always colder after his departure, but another week, and she and the children will be gone too. She gets in the car, starts the engine, looks back despondently at their undecorated home. On this point surely Harry had been right: why bother decorating if they're leaving? Still it feels sad. In the same way she's sad for Miss Miriam, whose house also looks unloved since she returned to hospital for an unspecified stay. Increasingly Emma's at the house and other unfamiliar cars, the family hovering, swooping in but with none of the holiday cheer.

And David, the doctor still unsure, diagnosing stress, sending him home to relax, the lack of progress worrying Jenny to no end.

Checking the rear view mirror, visibility remains poor in all directions. The fog is intransigent, the chill pervasive. The coming holidays are blotting out the past, infiltrating the present. But how to integrate the future, what will be? She drives on autopilot to the stores. Katya and Christophe, young enough to have forgotten last Christmas yet old enough to observe English traditions around them, have set her a new challenge simply by being so young. She's had to concoct an elaborate fiction as to how it might work: *you see St Nicholas and Father Christmas stick to traditions where you are. If we stay here, we do things the English way, put up stockings, leave carrots for reindeer. But in Poland St Nicholas comes earlier in the month and on Christmas Eve presents go under the tree. The main event is family gathering, eating a meal all together, carolling, going to church.*

It went down like a ton of coal.

But I don't want to be Polish, I'm whole English! Christophe cried.

Approaching the roundabout, she looks right, as you're supposed to. Seeing no hazards, she proceeds with confidence.

You can be Polish and English, she replied.

But that didn't appease Christophe, until Katya said, *Pinglish and Ponglish,* then they all laughed. But really, what kind of convoluted theories of nationality does she have to develop?

Maybe it's too difficult, this experiment she's embarked on. Yet what to do except carry on? Without coherence or unity, life might only ever be this – a series of boredoms punctuated by temporary excitements, small escapades, fictions with which one might escape if the void isn't too big. Or if you run fast enough, as if by running, running, running to some distant point on the horizon, always keeping busy, you'll fail to notice you never arrive, never know why, the void always there. Yes, ignore it. Christmas, so particularly suited to this kind of hustle and bustle, the shopping and packing, dashing from store to store imagining what the other party might like even if there's no demonstrable need or desire. Privately, someone must be tittering, *actually this is crazy, what we need to do is slow down*, but no one does because everyone's too busy. So supermarkets fill up with near-homemade, ill-starred mince pies, which won't get eaten because the family's already too stuffed on reheated filo spinach triangles.

You know it, but still you do it, Eva. So don't believe what they say – you should have known. Go as slowly as you want. Stare into the blackness and think. Only the act of resistance counts.

But even her conscience hardly garners a transient hearing these days. She gets out of the car like any other mindless shopping zombie, enters the store to stock up on something. The shops are bursting with Christmas specials, and they truly are enticing. There doesn't seem to be an alternative except to do what everyone else is doing. Because she has to share her English life with her family somehow, though if you can't bring brandy cream you might as well forget flaming pudding, a real pity that, because so many Poles don't know about this, a dessert you deliberately set on fire! She casts her eye further down the aisle of assorted goodies. But that's what you learn when you go to live somewhere else, you come to understand the relevant things, like sipping champagne while listening to the Queen's speech and the importance of the Queen, even if you don't pay her any attention most of the time. Her first Christmas with Harry, she assumed the Queen would be speaking for hours, brought in a tray of nibbles from the kitchen. Tilly laughed, *it'll be over before it starts, darling,* and she felt embarrassed but also confused, because what was the point of the Queen if you only gave her a few minutes a year?

It was exactly as Milosz had written: despair, inseparable from the first stage of exile – though if you analysed it, you'd find it resulted more from your own shortcomings than external circumstances. Milosz, another of Poland's great poets and philosophers; always comforting knowing a genius has similar problems. Yet over time she'd come to understand English, and perhaps, the English, only because she herself had changed. Even if no one recognized it, how could she not be different than when she arrived? It had been such hard work fitting in so late in life, not like a child taking in language and culture by osmosis, greeted with open arms for even the smallest effort. No, she had overcome, through adversity, mistakes and rejections, the rhythm of life not a falling in sync but a heavily furrowed field. Now, preparing to jump back, Mamcia and Tato might be easy to accommodate, but what on earth to bring Piotr or Magda?

Scanning the vast selections of foodstuffs, balancing luxury against extravagance, she starts with the first challenge. Really, what to get Piotr? The baby brother who'd grown whiskers and a belly so big he was now a fine representation of rural Polish manhood. Ever the happy-go-lucky lad, universally loved for telling a good joke, children clamoured on Piotr as if he were a permanent St Nick. No one adored him more than his wife Danka, who gave him every opportunity to make an excuse and slip out to the shed for a smoke. Industrious and portly Danka, who also kept Piotr marching along, stoking his residual ambitions for him, though everyone knew he had no desire to be head teacher. Threatening no one, therefore, Piotr had many mates, and Danka's hopes for him could remain an elusive goal, giving them both something to look forward to. Their lot – Marek and Bogdan and little Mila, who must be growing up fast – were a happy household even without certain basic amenities. So it was always doubly hard to know how to bestow a gift – can you even add to happiness?

Then Magda, a prickly question. Sour and difficult from youth. Who knows how things might have turned out if she hadn't clutched her Catholicism so tightly, rejecting unsuitable suitors whose only crimes were losing their virginity on a hot day in a barn. Becoming studious and matronly, a trend that appeared early and developed like a virus, by her thirties she looked forty, and now probably fifty though still five years away. Her preferences were unchanging. Hiding her body in waves of clothes of a middling brown colour, neither chocolate nor milky coffee, hair tied in a bun so tight it made you want to release it just to stop the pain. But Magda had good points, one of which was her devotion to the cause of orthopaedics. And being truly good in the technical sense, she'd brought pride in equal measure to the despair she'd wrought on their worried parents. Generous in an absent-minded way, she was often taken advantage of but never seemed to mind, which was infuriating to watch and hard to protect against. But she was neither openly bitter nor unhappy, only quiet, to herself. A resetter of bones. She'd obviously accepted her lot in life without preaching to others the merits of her choices. It was possible that God found solace in her.

Staring absentmindedly at the cartons of Christmas crackers, time passing, catching up, phone beeping, demanding, she must get going. The boxes of Christmas biscuits oddly seem to feature mostly German characteristics: *stollen, pfeffernusse.* Maybe because the royals were originally German or maybe because modern Christmas is this mixed up international affair. She grabs mince pies and chocolates for Piotr and Danka, a nice English tea blend for Magda, smoked salmon for Mamcia. For Tato she'll find some whiskey or cognac at duty-free. For the children, she'll have to shop later.

Paying quickly and hauling the shopping to the boot, she winces, it's already full. She'd forgotten to drop off at the charity shop. Another English thing that once made her marvel – the many charities populating the high street – now it seemed normal. Even fashion magazines had declared it glamorous to unearth solitary treasures while rummaging, though like so many things, that only really applied to the rich. Only those who can afford to pass over differences identify what's used as treasure. Necessity wears, breeds other emotions, like shame. Except at this time of year, the disposal of last year's goods seemed so routine even Katya and Christophe thought it part of the bargain – offload the old to make room for the new. Perhaps it was self-defeating after all.

Driving back, hitting the gravel, grinding to a halt, she dumps the bags in the hall for a quick check on the computer. Again nothing from X, a form of agitation in itself, but instead a rare missive from Magda:

To: Eva
From: Magdalena
Re: Your visit

Dear Eva,

How are you? You must be getting ready for your trip already, we are all so eager to see you! I must remember to go to the market and find some toys for Krzysztof and Kasia.

But I am also writing you with news, and I hope you won't be offended by what I did. You may not know but I have seen Adam lately. In fact, his son Jacek had a broken arm, and we met a few weeks ago at the hospital. Of course, we spoke of you and he mentioned he would like to see you.

I am just passing that on, then, because he left me his address here in Krakow and we exchanged phone numbers. It seems he has gone back to being Catholic but attends a different church than he used to. His wife Jana also came to the hospital, she is quite heavy and breathing poorly. They also have another boy Stanislaw.

Well, that is all the news. I told Adam when you would be here, because he asked, and I had to give an honest reply, but he did not say anything after that. I hope I did right.

Please don't reply because after this writing I shall probably not use the computer much as it is a busy time. I look forward to seeing you next week however. I will certainly come to the airport. I have all your flight details.

Your loving sister,

Magda

The language so familiar she could trace it in air. *Trace it in air,* wasn't that the poem she'd written? But now a hole has opened up and she's falling through it to a world of new illusions. Seeing Adam? Not possible. Maybe Magda couldn't have done otherwise, not said otherwise in hospital whilst treating him. She probably didn't set out to make a sister's life more difficult. But if the past offered limited choices, who wants to be reminded? She hadn't forgiven Adam for what happened and he couldn't have forgiven her either. Not in the state she was in, not with what she'd planned to do.

For the worst bit of the argument anyway, she had forgiven him. He hadn't meant to hit her. Of that she was pretty sure. He hadn't even hit her hard. Or in the face. Just a backhanded slap on the arm, something someone else would probably have let pass. But for her it had been the crystallizing moment: not good enough. An iron rod ran through her core: *cut the cord and run.* The blow left but a short tingling, the greater mark was invisible. She decided on the spot to leave him, and Poland. And to make sure it came to pass, she told no one in advance.

She told no one about it afterwards either. Though in some ways the scarier bit was what came immediately before – he'd been pummelling the table, steadily losing control, a burly man capable of real injury, working himself up. She recalled not fear but mostly disbelief, especially when he broke down completely afterwards, crying and begging for forgiveness, his physique no match for his emotions. In the babble of a broken man, Adam explained he was livid at her suggestion of abortion. They were both fatigued at that point, arguing for hours – and that part of his excuse for losing control was true enough. But he'd been with the sect for a few months, his strict habits increasingly wearing on her. By the time this moment came to a head, she was no longer feeling so much indebted for his protection as burdened, trapped. The prospect of starting any family life under religious zealots was impossible.

But all that had been safely lodged in the past: his born-again rites, the silly cohort of believers, the praying and singing, the smiling smugness. All that and more, buried instantly. The faint bruise healed quickly. The real casualty was the unborn baby that no one ever knew of. No one, except Adam and Xavier. And X had been the one to put that right.

So many cars, flowers in the window, good news finally: Miss Miriam celebrating her 83rd birthday. She'd been invited by Miss Miriam herself weeks ago and since then relishing the prospect of bringing her this: a combined birthday present and Christmas hamper. Store-bought hampers still confused her with their simpleton extravagance. It was only a basket of food and drink. Even if individual items were of the best quality, when assembled they seemed too expensive, as if the goal had been to transform the whole into luxury by virtue of price tag. She was sure that wasn't the point of it, and anyway pride and generosity in a gift came not from fast phone orders or trends or meeting expectations, but the time putting it together. Homemade *rogaliki* biscuits and fruit compote, preserves and quince jam, all Miss Miriam's favourites.

She waits as footsteps approach, the basket at her feet weighing a ton. This time Miss Miriam will be right – *looks terribly heavy, Eva.*

'Hello?' The door opens to a portly woman in her fifties in brightly coloured and conspicuously fashionable clothes.

'Oh, hello, I'm Eva, neighbour from down the road.'

The woman peers over her shoulder, so she continues.

'I came by, to see if, how Miss Miriam, the birthday party...'

The woman stares at her, says nothing.

'Sorry, are you Emma, her daughter?'

'Yes, I am,' she replies haughtily. 'But I'm sorry, you're too late. My mother's passed away.'

You should have known.

'Sorry?' she pauses. 'I mean, I'm sorry.'

Suddenly she's so very tired.

You should have known, Eva.

'I'm sorry,' then she stops.

Because even if she could make sense of it, it doesn't come together. Everything's shattered, a million shards of glass.

'I'm sorry,' she tries again, looks at the basket, as confused as Miss Miriam. 'I put this together as a... you see, I wanted to...'

The woman glares as if she's committed a searing mistake. The absence of civility.

'No thank you,' she says icily, retreating into the house, closing the door. 'I'm sure you understand, we don't need this right now,' and then, mumbling almost out of earshot, 'we don't need your kind.'

The door shuts with a final click.

She can barely breathe.

Your kind? How dare they?

But surely they know what's best, Eva, they are her family.

Oh, but Miss Miriam! Maybe they have no idea.

A life extinguished. In a few words. An instant, all it takes, to move from life to death. Afterwards, viscous time: tears welling, they must be hers. Her cheeks are wet. She is all aching bones, bending down slowly, in barely perceptible motion, a crushing pain, this simple action requiring a thousand minutes, a million maybe, to remove that well-wishing card. The basket *is* too heavy to lift, Miss Miriam was right.

You should have known.

Maybe it's not English. Or the right thing to do. Maybe it's a waste of effort and time. But in the absence of civility she clutches the card with her final words, and turns and walks away. She leaves the basket there. For them, whoever they are.

∞

The captain's switched on the seat belt sign, they're ready to go. Christophe and Katya in their seats colouring in new little notebooks with faint pencil marks, she staring into space. The plane begins its reckless dash down the runway, lifting them forward, upward, transporting them, up and out and up and out, stomachs pressed down. She closes her eyes, they're entering the clouds. Dense whiteness shrouds the small round windows. All senses, bearings lost. She opens her eyes, shuts them again. This is the part she hates most: loss of solid ground, no notion of up or down.

Hearing voices, Polish and English, all mixed up, it's like her jumble of a life: Pinglish and Ponglish. Harry didn't even find time to comfort her about Miss Miriam, even as she tried to tell him, crying, about Baba Kasia, having missed that funeral too, though at least she'd been invited, how if you don't go, there's no closure, now she'll never get to say goodbye. As usual, he left her to make her own way with the children. Their meetings only accentuate the separation. Her solitude. The pattern of coming and going.

At the end of the day, Eva, there is no salvation, you are alone.

Look at the solid white, we are, all of us, alone.

Fragile, we, us, all, solitary figures,

Making shadow movements,

And to a solitary grave we all fall.

PART TWO

'So you make a sacrifice!' he threw special emphasis
on the last word. 'Well, so do I. What could be better?
We compete in generosity – what an example of
family happiness!'

Leo Tolstoy, *Family Happiness*

The landscape is blanched, a pale almond in icing sugar, the snow is coming down hard. The contours of the road have disappeared into vast white drifts, billboards indistinguishable from one another, their messages obscured by sticky marshmallow clumps. But the wind has abated, so the trees stand motionless, mere brittle twigs against a dense milky sky.

They turn off the motorway, the children's chatter distant, Magda's comments too, because they're approaching the city centre, so much to take in. Krakow, with its ancient cobblestones and brand new shops, an old worldliness given way to a Western sheen, now made quaint again by the blanketing snow. So many years ago when she last drove down these streets, the last time she saw Adam, ill with his child. Magda might have suspected, but no one knew for sure, and in the passage of time she had ceased to think about it. Now the details swirl like snowflakes, how she made her way out of the city with a bag and a secret burden and that one-way ticket to Paris bought by someone who awaited her. Conveniently Magda had been away at a medical conference at the time, so she'd left a note saying she was off to start a new life in France – she had to, it was over with Adam and her job at the academic journal, friends from the Sorbonne had invited her, a Xavier, whom Magda had heard of, and good things mostly. For months she'd sent reassuring messages of this kind, usually to her parents, even when things weren't going well. Then the letters tailed off. Much later when she and Magda reunited at Mamcia and Tato's, Harry was already on the scene. Harry knew most of it. But what happened that particular winter between her and Adam had been buried, then lost. She looks at Magda, studiously mastering the slippery roads, wondering if she ever surmised or even questioned the real reason her younger sister left.

'Oh look!' Katya cries. 'Horses!'

She and Christophe point excitedly at the brightly decorated draught horses pulling tourist carriages in the medieval centre of town.

'Oh, I'd forgotten, but it's also changed a lot!' Her enthusiasm matches Katya's, the scene a perfect backdrop to Christmas.

Magda smiles. 'Changed for the better, I'd say, though you should see what they charge for those rides.'

'Can we, please?' the children clamour in unison.

'We'll see,' she says, deterred mostly by pricing because of Magda, 'but if it's too expensive, we'll do other fun things.'

'Like what?' moans Christophe.

'Like going up to Wawel castle and parks to throw snowballs, like children do here.'

'That sounds fun,' says Katya.

'I like throwing snow,' Christophe concedes.

So it's settled, for a time. The car twists down narrow streets and Magda parks as close as possible, but still they have to heave their luggage through snow banks and up a set of creaky stairs to her fifth floor flat. Suddenly convenient England doesn't seem so bad. Not only for the sheer effort of life here in Poland but because of the many remembrances flooding back: other people's as well as her own, as if the past had settled into the floorboard cracks only to fly out at you like dust when you tread upon them. Magda chats as they climb, passing the third storey, the flat occupied by Pani Zoya, whose hair was dyed fiery red well into her eighties. Pani Zoya too had passed away, like Miss Miriam, unable to fight off a particularly bad winter chill. A new family with small children had taken her place, but Magda hadn't gotten to know them.

The sad thought of Miss Miriam. But that and other hardships are forgotten as they enter Magda's flat, the opposite of a large cold English house. Toasty warm and cosy, Magda's tiny realm is stuffed with the comforts of a lifetime: medical books, old blankets, threadbare cushions and rugs. All of it the same as last time, same smell too. And something's definitely happening in the kitchen, or at least Magda's gone to the trouble of visiting a bakery, because on the counter is a plate stacked high with the little strawberry pinwheels and apricot crescents of her youth: real *rogaliki*. And the kind of black bread you can't get anywhere else, and in the oven, she can see a whole rolled pork, *rolada*. When did Magda ever learn to cook?

'I had help,' Magda says, following her eyes. 'The lady down a floor, Pani Stasia, Pani Zoya's old friend, is a marvellous cook. She showed me how. Of course, mostly I stood and watched.'

She smiles because no matter who cooks rolled pork, it's evidence they heard Eva was coming. She had mentioned it to her mother once, *my favourite, rolada*, so it became obligatory as a first meal whenever she returned. Still, it's incredible Magda remembered.

'On such an occasion as this!' Magda says, setting a pot of water on the stove for tea, pulling out some old Ukrainian brandy.

'Oh, Magda!'

'But a little!' Magda takes the reply less as a protest than a compliment to generous hospitality. 'It's good for your health!'

Even if she can't stomach poor brandy she can't seem ungrateful, and besides, you can't argue with a doctor. Magda pours two tiny glasses of brown liquid and they clink, *na zdrowie*, to health, and down it goes, burning the whole way.

'Ah, very good this one,' Magda remarks, peering at the empty shot glass with satisfaction. 'Now tell me – tell me all about your English life!'

'Well,' that colloquialism they always start with in her family, *nu*, to emphasise what will be said, even if you don't know where to begin. 'What can I say?'

So she begins with the Plan, and Harry and his work, how difficult it is being on your own most of the time with small children, school and activities, the pact of separation, ever more a burden in dark lonely nights. But then not having explained fully about English politics, the economics of it all, she stops, because Magda's nodding but with a look of incomprehension, because wouldn't it be nice to have such troubles, a husband who makes money, a house with so many rooms and children to fill them. True, long lonely nights aren't a monopoly experience. She ought to wrap up her story, ask how Magda's doing. England's not important anyway, receding like a fantasy already, a life belonging to someone else. Whereas Magda's experiences are solid, firmly connected to past and present and future, a life based on years of familiarity, not wholesale disruptions.

'Well,' Magda begins, 'you know there's always politics, even at the Faculty of Medicine,' and she launches into the ups and downs of teaching at the university. 'But I keep certain hours at the hospital, I have to, nice for camaraderie too, and what a coincidence it was, that time with Adam, because it was my only day that month taking patients alone. All three interning students had come down with the flu, and what were the chances of that?'

'So, how is Adam?'

'Well,' Magda turns around to dish out dinner, her owlish gaze diverted to the stove. 'For one thing, he's bald, and much thinner, though his wife's as tubby as can be. Poor thing has diabetes, though it was all preventable. People have taken to eating far too much, especially all this fast food, terrible.' She continues scooping and scooping as if serving up an army.

'Thinner and bald?'

'I suspect those evangelicals eat differently,' Magda fills the bowl to overflowing. 'It couldn't have done them any good. But you know his grandfather on his father's side was bald, they say it skips generations.'

So even doctors resort to common wisdom, though stranger still is the image of a bald Adam after all that long hair. But it seems less dangerous that way, not being able to picture him.

'He had three children but one of them died from pneumonia, a few years back during that bad winter when Pani Zoya went, which I think is when he stopped with that crazy religion that doesn't believe in vaccines and went back to being Catholic. You knew about him losing the child, didn't you? I must have told you. Anyway, took a while for his wife Jana to come around. She really was the more zealous of the two, so they say. But after a lost child… They go to Holy Transfiguration, not Trinity, though, so mostly I hear the odd story from nurse Beata at the hospital, and I don't often see her.'

'Oh,' she pauses, but Magda keeps going.

'The time I saw Adam, he was with his son Jacek, who had broken his arm climbing trees, and Jana, the wife, was there, and Adam said he had another younger son Stanislaw, but he wasn't there. I didn't ask too many questions, you know, Eva, but it was clear Adam wanted to meet with you even before he spoke. Looking like a horse chomping on a bit. When Jana was in the waiting room and Jacek had gone back to her, Adam looked me in the eye, gave me his address and phone and asked when you'd be back. It was the way he was looking at me, so I didn't lie, Eva, I told him you'd be here before Christmas. But you aren't obliged to see him, well, if you ask me, you aren't. It's usually not for the best to dig up dead things.'

Her tone is final, as if it's time to move on. But what can you move on to after death? For a moment, she sits quietly, struck by Magda's choice of words, *not for the best to dig up dead things.* As if she'd known. But how could Magda have known, unless Adam told her? That was unlikely, they weren't in touch, only Magda hearing the odd story, this one meeting in hospital.

Magda continues chattering, a great contrast between the way she writes and talks, because in writing she's terse to the point of being unemotional, while in person she starts off rambling, concerned and open. Until she's gotten to the point – then she clamps down, puts matters put to rest. Like this thing with Adam. It's where they always differed. An erratic contradictory Eva always revisited a problem, even if it might not need revisiting.

Magda sets the steaming plates on the table as the children tumble in. The space is cramped, like any galley kitchen, a folding rickety table rammed right up against the wall, wooden stools tucked under. But it's preferable to be squeezed in now, seated elbow to elbow eating and drinking and chatting, giving into the stodgy togetherness of Polish life. Despite her diabetic warnings Magda forces more food on them than could possibly be advisable: pork and cabbage, boiled potatoes, fruit compote and baked desserts. A day that rolls from one form of heaviness to another, lightness of being displaced by solid sustenance, the promise of eventual escape in slumber. Christophe and Katya's eyes are already drooping.

She leads them to Magda's bed, tucking them in with their prayer, returns to find Magda has made over the sofa and set up her own tiny divan in her small study where she'll spend the night.

'Do you need anything else?' Magda glances around, clutching a book, reading glasses propped on her head. It's the way she's always gone to bed, ritual solidified into way of being, and she looks around slightly nervously, as if to say why would she change now?

'No, all good, thanks. Good night.'

Dobrze, dziękuje. Good, thanks, words of childhood flowing freely now. But she's not tired, only displaced, distracted. Maybe tea would soothe. Indeed back in the kitchen, herbals are stacked high in the cupboard, and at the very back of the shelf, a familiar box: Harrods. Bought years ago, still unopened. A twinge of regret, but being in Poland she doesn't want it either. Time for Polski Lipton, golden-coloured, with lemon and honey. She makes a weak cup, climbs back on to the sofa with its loose springs, lumps and raw woollen covers. She should have known. Yes, she should have expected it would be the same. Magda's never been an adventurer or homemaker. But that's because she'd never been molested by vast choice, marketing. She doesn't know the products out there to smooth over the bumps in life. She's been too busy saving lives and teaching others to do the same. So if the price is a sister's discovery of an unwanted gift, or sleeping on a harder bed, who is this Eva to complain? She and Adam slept on worse, in worse places, and that seemed romantic. Now she's like a pampered English princess with her matching cushions and fine china, but this is where she came from.

She finishes her tea, shuts the light, sinks into the sofa and tries to get comfortable. The past is but a point of departure, no need for regrets, isn't that right? She too had suffered but overcome, and for her willingness to take great risks, now she was in a place where her children didn't sleep on scratchy sofas or wear cheap socks that itch and slide down. What was the virtue in remaining poor? Was there any point in remaining satisfied with what you had if there was better out there? Weren't you supposed to strive?

Finding a cosy position in a dip between cushions, she closes her eyes. But maybe materialism too can eventually bring misery, a different kind of poverty, a poverty of the soul. Maybe in striving for a fulfilled life, the first step is making peace with oneself, one's own past. Maybe that's the meaning of what her conscience is always prompting her: *you should have known.*

∞

Hanging damp clothes on radiators, she hears *Looney Tunes* in the background. Christophe and Katya don't seem to mind old cartoons or awkward dubbing, as slapstick comedy appears to work regardless of language. But so would any television after such a long day outdoors. She places a plate of *rogaliki* and glasses of warmed milk before them, returns to the kitchen to wait for Magda.

The sliver of a window reveals it's snowing again, although the day began brilliantly: bright blue sky, icy cold, the children nestling under their duvet like two intertwined cherubs. Then dressing for the day, which called for the opposite of an unburdened soul: bodies weighed down heavily by coats, scarves, hats and gloves. But those inconveniences were quickly forgotten too as they wandered up to the castle to be awed by turrets high over the Wisła river, then the *rynek*, the main square, and Kanonicza, the side street where they happened upon a little restaurant, *Smak Ukrainski*. Taste of Ukraine. Their luncheon borscht like Baba Kasia's, not the *barszcz* made everywhere else, Baba's sour beetroot soup a lovely rich burgundy, earthy with mushrooms. As heavenly as the mashed potato dumplings, *varenyky* so soft and malleable in the mouth, slathered in fresh *smetana*, the kind of sour cream you can't get in the West. She tried to explain as they ate, about her own childhood, their ancestors, how Baba Kasia came from Lviv, a city that had been in the same country as Krakow then, but a different one now, how brave Baba had been, because it wasn't like modern times Poles marrying Ukrainians or English or whoever they want. But the children weren't interested in tales of the past, they wanted a carriage ride, which they imagined to be a sleigh. So she conceded guiltily while paying the food bill and setting aside something for the ride, together more than Madga would make in two days. But that was economics for you: tourists spending silly money while locals saved lives for a pittance.

Magda saving lives, resetting bones, so vital to holding up a body. So one must be patient, her last day of work before the long drive to Mamcia and Tato's in Przemyśl. About seven hours because the European Union hasn't yet built the motorway so there's traffic all the way through towns and rural junctions. *The route's same as ever but so many more cars now, an hour's delay around Jarosław,* Magda exclaimed. *Imagine, Eva, rush hour in Jarosław!* But it's hard to imagine anything, even the familiar, because the journey will be back through time, and time itself will have altered the reality one meets. What will be the same or different as they draw closer to that final moment, the crest of the hill beginning the snaky descent down Serpentyna Sobieskiego to their childhood home?

The telephone rings, it must be Magda, hopefully not to say she's running late.

'*Halo, słucham,*' her voice gentle: I'm listening.

'Eva.' A man's voice familiar and distant at the same time. Adam. She sucks in her breath.

'Hello, you there?'

'Yes.'

'I didn't expect to catch you,' he says.

She's silent for a moment. 'Me neither.'

'When are you off again?'

'Tomorrow,' she pauses.

He steps in, adamant. 'I didn't mean to disturb you, Eva, wrong of me to call, I know. But I wanted to know you were okay. To hear your voice.'

'I don't mean to be…' but she stops, not sure what to add. She thinks for a minute. 'I'm fine, most of the time. How about you?'

'It's life,' his sigh transforms into a chuckle, and she can envision his whole body shaking gently, the way it used to, when he laughed.

'Yes, it's life,' she repeats. 'And what a life too!' She smiles and suddenly, it seems okay, in her native tongue, her native land. It's only Adam. Thinner, balder, married with children.

'So yes,' he says, more seriously now. 'But Eva, it's been so long – we couldn't meet, could we? Just for a drink somewhere? Tonight?'

More a dare than a request, and a dare can always lead to regrets. But regret itself might be stronger if one doesn't take a chance.

'I'm on my own with the children,' she stalls, then the click of a key, Magda walking in. 'Wait a moment,' turning to her, mouthing, *it's Adam*. Magda's eyebrows go up, she shrugs.

She sighs, turns back. 'Sorry, Magda came by, you were saying?'

'Look, Eva, if it's not convenient...'

Not convenient, maybe not even pleasant, but a chance at reconciliation?

'Hold on.'

She turns back to Magda. 'He wants to meet, briefly,' she whispers, receiver pressed to her chest. 'Could I, quickly, tonight, after the kids are in bed?'

Magda shrugs again. Coat off and hands weighed down with shopping, she walks past to the kitchen to unload. She's right, it's no one's place to give permission. Some things must be decided alone.

She lifts up the phone. 'It's okay, let's say eight-thirty. Is Slava's open?'

'Let's go somewhere a bit more... how about Wierzynek? Anyway it's closer to you.'

'Okay.'

'Okay then.'

He puts down the receiver first. It's done. *Okay*. But is it? Or is that just hope?

Kitchen empty as Magda's gone to get changed, she sits and stares at the wall. Wierzynek is not far from where they are on Reformacka Street, but why did he pick it? An exclusive restaurant, or was, steep stairs leading down to an underground complex decorated with costumes and old weapons, a fancy place for celebrating weddings, anniversaries, big moments. She would have chosen a more casual spot.

Magda returns, opens the bag, pulls out roast chicken. 'I picked up dinner from the supermarket,' she says apologetically, as if guests would expect a full home-cooked meal every night. 'It's very good actually, what I do when I'm on the run.'

Has their stay already been an intrusion? Is Magda cross with her for agreeing to meet Adam? Or did she want her to stay and share the evening? But Magda isn't social, she only ever retreats to her room.

'Oh Magda, it's fine – great – we all love chicken.'

Instinctively she remembers all the chickens she made Miss Miriam, gets up to give her sister a quick embrace. Magda's eyes too have reddened but hers might be the tears from years before, when they were still together at university, before Magda hardened herself to fate and denied herself pity, the tears that said *you always were so lucky with men but what about me?* Magda quickly wipes away the wetness, as if to reassure her.

'Look, Magda, I know this seems crazy, but I think I need to do this. The way I left was not fair to him.'

'I don't know,' Magda replies slowly. 'I could see pain in his face. Be careful.' Then she adds, 'Well, I suppose you have to see his bald head!'

The way she says it makes the situation silly and they laugh, which makes it better. Magda busies herself putting carrots to boil and the rotisserie in the oven, because even a cooked bird might have refrozen after a journey home in minus fifteen degrees. Mash goes in the microwave, though it might be the first time Magda's ever used it, the way she fusses over the dials. But soon the thing starts to hum, the children are called in, and another meal unfolds like the long day, full of wistful sweetness, heaviness bringing on slumber. Sometimes the best one can do is draw things to a close.

'I'll be quick, an hour or so,' she whispers, turning to Magda, shutting the bedroom door.

'Take your time, you'll have much to discuss. Maybe it's what God wills,' Magda says. 'I still have to pack, make phone calls.' She pauses. 'Nice to have you back, it's been a long time.' And with that, she disappears to her study, leaving a little sister to make her way in the world.

She bundles up, leaves the warmth of the flat for the dark freeze outside. What God wills? Or fate? Or choice? Hers or Adam's? Could it be all of these? So many forces bearing down at any moment, how can anyone distil concepts to black and white? Why not accept the idea of guiding force but also free will? She'd argued with Magda about it long ago and given up, not in her own conviction but in trying to convince Magda that both Catholics and atheists viewed the whole thing too narrowly. Conscience and memory surely existed within the laws of nature – every human being proof of it – but conscience and memory also did not seem to be governed by those laws. Pockets of randomness appeared to undermine them. Maybe the universe itself was a contradiction. And if that was how the universe was constructed, why not philosophy, religion too? Could anyone stand on a pulpit or platform and claim to know the ultimate, to argue persuasively either way? It was what she and Tato always agreed on, although she was by far the more prone to contradiction. But observation, experience, invention, the ability to affect change or smash through like in atomic experiments, even if those experiments sometimes failed – that's how humans learned. Yet probability, chance, the element of chaos, seemed to underlay existence itself too, before one could even apply rules. So everything might well be a combination, or even a result of intention – the belief in one's belief. Surely for that people ought to make way for all beliefs, so long as they didn't harm another. Surely for that, it's okay to see if Adam's okay.

Trudging on, heated thoughts repelling the cold, she suddenly stops to check her bearings. The streets in the direction of the *rynek* are familiar, central Krakow so much a part of her old self. But now it's changed too, so it's easy to be displaced. Paths leading to side routes are often deceiving. Only when something's right in front of you can you really be sure. Then the moment of recognition: *Wierzynek.* She slips inside and seeing no one, but hearing something downstairs, she heads down. But one can always regret being hasty; the place looks as if between events. Disconcertingly empty.

Empty, but for him. Alone in a corner. Adam. Truly, physically he's diminished and unthreatening, though still handsome in a fierce-looking rock-star kind of way. Sporting the same goatee she'd seen in his last photo, only now it looks more like a statement, this protrusion of hair on his chin where it's lacking on his head. This combination almost makes him more menacing than in his days as a bouncer, when he was long-haired but clean-shaven. Underneath any exterior she knows him to be soft – except for that parting argument, which makes the doubt rebound: has she been called to set things right or is she walking blindly into blunder?

He's spotted her now, so it's too late to back out. Staring, he's mentally willing her forward. This glare would make anyone want to flee, or at least think twice about coming into a club, but she feels compelled to move towards him, stand before him, even with this rising dread in this formal place. Because now it seems very much like the start of judgement day.

'You're still so beautiful,' he says.

The statement isn't soothing. She shuffles as he gives a weak grin.

She returns the smile. 'You haven't changed either.'

Which in a way is true: his demeanour hasn't altered, his presence still commanding. Something erratic underlying it, transmitting excitement laced with fear, a burgeoning realisation that you'll never fully grasp the person or personality.

'Oh no, look at this!' He clasps his bare head, then covers it with a knitted cap he's been twisting in his hands. The cap almost makes him look younger, fashionable, like teenagers who wear headgear indoors whatever the temperature. 'Now I have to wear this all winter!'

'You would anyway in this weather.' Her smile is frozen now. They've never engaged in such pleasantries, totally unfamiliar territory.

Drawing the heavy chair back an inch, perching delicately, she studies his face for all that's known – two sons, the lost child, a stout wife – almost no longer believable. A waiter emerges from the shadows. Adam seems to know him, signals for a beer.

'Well, life,' he says, 'turned out differently than we planned.'

It's a harmless statement, a declaration of fact. Along the lines of what one might expect from him, but unnerving all the same.

'Yes, we had planned. Then plans changed.' Her voice goes quiet.

'That was my fault of course,' he says matter-of-factly. 'I got caught up in the emotion of seeking a better life.'

'It was fairly unforgiving,' she continues gently, 'that path you were on.'

'So was your way,' he retorts, not unkindly. 'All I ever wanted to know was that you were safe. You only wrote twice.' He pauses. 'You never sent a photo.'

'I,' she stops. She hadn't sent a photo because she wanted him to forget. With panic now she remembers the poem. What had he taken from that?

'Well, it was hard at first,' she forces herself to continue. 'Changing cities, lives,' not adding *lovers,* 'but then one grows used to anything.' She falls silent for a minute. 'Though sometimes you don't, get used to things, I mean. I left Paris, I guess you know that. After two years. I went to London, studied more, worked at another journal, you know the rest.' She stops short of mentioning husband, children, all that her life is now, because maybe that's not what his life is like. Happy families.

'Your sister told me,' Adam says. 'Quite a story.'

'A story like any other,' she says. 'I suppose just different – from yours.'

'Which is too bad,' Adam says, holding his gaze, not moving. 'We could have made it work.'

For a moment she can't imagine what to say. Because when two people have known each other so well, they might have enjoyed this moment – had life not thrown so much at them. But does he really believe it could have worked?

'Adam,' not daring to look him in the eye, 'we couldn't have made it work. You were in the grips of that moron – sorry – that awful Vlad and that woman, his sidekick, and those people.' No point in holding back, no time. 'What could I have done?' She looks at him. 'Go back to Przemyśl with a child out of wedlock? After my parents worked and suffered and saved so I could finish university and start a life in Krakow? Leave the journal, the job they were so proud of? What choices did I have?'

'You left the journal anyway when you ran off.' He takes a swig of his bottle, ignoring the glass provided. 'Okay, it wasn't an ideal set of choices, but there was *choice*, you could have given me another chance. We could have married. It was my baby too.'

The baby. As if it had been born. As if it had existed beyond a few grouped cells. She ignores it.

'I never would have married into that cult,' she says forcefully. 'Never. And you didn't want to leave it. Ultimately our views on abortion were different. But anyway it wouldn't have worked.'

'It wasn't a cult, it was a sort of quasi-Christian religion. But okay, strict. Too regimented maybe, questionable rules. But I realised that too, see, I went back to being Catholic.'

As if Catholicism were such a liberal move.

'So did Jana.'

She means to give him something comforting to hold on to, but her mention of Jana seems to shock him.

'I never loved Jana like I loved you.' His eyes are on fire. 'We only met and started up after you left, left for good. She needed me, and she was part of my life then. When you left.'

'She's not part of it now?' she says softly, trying to deflect his indictment.

'Of course,' he remains calm. 'But to tell you the truth, I'm not the Catholic I once was either. It's out of fealty and respect more than love or moral obligation that I've continued with Jana.'

Now it's the continuous past tense that's jarring. Unsure what to expect with Adam anyway, but definitely not that. He can't be on the brink of another life-altering change. Surely he's not planning on leaving Jana?

'What do you mean?'

'I mean, I no longer support the Catholic Church's view on divorce, or pretty much anything, but I've stayed for the boys. Otherwise, I'd have left Jana long ago. After Eva died...'

'Wait, wait – you named her Eva? You had a girl and named her Eva?'

'Of course,' Adam says, eyeing her, taking a slow sip of his beer. 'Jana didn't know how things were with us. She only joined the group after you were long gone, and she didn't – doesn't – know anything about us really. I wanted to remember you always.'

How to react when you'd rather scream? How could he? But he seems to know what she's thinking.

'Well, it's not like you asked permission before you did away with our child.' And then, as if to mitigate the statement, 'I really missed you, Eva, like you cannot believe. Even after what you did. In fact, it was the thought of you that pulled me out of that other religion entirely. Because I couldn't reconcile God's love with the loss of you, then the loss of little Eva, and when I felt forsaken, I took to drinking, to the death. But Jana stopped me. So I have that to be grateful for.'

Now she sees it's a non-alcoholic beer, *Karmi*, he's drinking. Instinctively she joins in, grips her glass and takes a large gulp of her lager, sensing an instant too late that it probably sends the wrong signal, a dare to his deprivations. Or worse: derision.

'I'm sorry.'

'No, I'm the one who should be sorry.' He doesn't take his eyes from her. 'Like I said when we started, I made the wrong choices. Apart from that night when I saved you from that idiot at the club – it was the best night of my life. I've replayed it often to keep going.'

He falls silent, and she too, because what can you say to that? Words are always inadequate, but shouldn't she try to salvage something? Save what part of him she can? Oh, how hard Jana has worked all these years!

'But aren't you in the slightest bit happy?'

'Happiness is elusive,' Adam says quietly. 'I have my sons and I have Jana, who is trustworthy, even if we tolerate each other mostly. But she does look after us and it's not by far the worst marriage. I have a good job as a restaurant manager, I go out with the girls as part of work, and I can afford to lure you out and buy you a beer.'

He says it almost defiantly, leaning his head back, taking a last swig. Then he sets the empty bottle down with a clink.

'Alas, it's shit,' he shrugs unhappily, and she doesn't know if he means his beer or his life but he breaks into a weak smile as if to signal it doesn't matter very much.

Pain and regret. It couldn't have been different. Parting was for the best, she'd told herself that many times until she was sure of it. But why had she suspected it would be the same for him? Why so sure of a happy ending? Wasn't it clear when she left he was damaged in some way, might never be saved? He'd never regain some idyllic happiness he pictured with her, and seemingly that was her fault. With her whole sturdy English life she had averted catastrophe but there was no way to help him.

Adam starts again quietly. 'I didn't want to make you feel bad, Eva, really, I only wanted to see you for myself again. To see how things turned out for you. Honestly. Magda made it all sound so wonderful, I wanted to make sure it was true.'

He's either being dishonest or selfless, selfless the way he can be, the way he brought her into his life. She could hope he isn't lying. That this is a glimpse of the man who once loved her, who might still love. But as he sighs what comes to mind is the adage that you can't go home again. And it's true, but not for the reasons you'd think, like circumstances or surroundings or people changing irrevocably. It's because you can't rewrite history to make things better, even if you'd like to.

'Look I'm sorry,' Adam starts to say, but she interrupts.

'No, don't be sorry. It's just life. You know, like they say, we don't always get what we want.'

Without skipping a beat, he replies in English. 'But sometimes we get what we need.'

∞

The journey to Przemyśl is long enough to replay the scenario many times. To wonder what the point of it was and whether in the end, she'd said the right thing. If she'd asked the wrong question, or too much the right one, because although it seemed central inquiring after one's happiness, it was only useful if you could wrestle a reply into a neat compartment, tie up loose ends. Certainly she'd wanted to avert disaster but maybe she had precipitated one – fresh regrets for herself and Adam.

Staring out the window, she takes in the scenery without really registering it. Adam seemed resigned to carry on with his life, barely satisfied. But much deeper sorrows were carrying him along like a strong current. And she did feel sorry, not only for him, but for having given him the opportunity to express his pain. Because sometimes there is no satisfaction in revelation. Clearly she'd made the right choice to leave him, to rid herself of the burden of single motherhood, to embrace all that happened since, build a good life. But for him, there was only a different kind of certainty: that she had abandoned him. That was how he felt then, and now, and no matter how hard Jana had worked or might work in the future she'd never make him happy. Which meant the burden of guilt for Adam's unhappiness lay solely with this Eva for the rest of their lives.

The car rolls on, the outside world moving by placidly, Magda's face fixed to the road ahead. They've left behind the wide boulevards of Rzeszów where old Soviet memorials still dominate roundabouts, shops huddling in long promenades that channel blustery head winds against the very passers-by who might be prospective buyers. Here, the last signs of commerce, before the countryside takes over: windows with white wedding dresses, windows with white goods, kiosks crammed with cigarettes and newspapers and thin plastic toys, the kiosks themselves papered in posters for Deep Purple tribute bands, just like the old days, only stuffed with more stuff. And smaller nameless shops peddling to the average consumer: *Angielska Odzież Używana*. Used English Clothing. She winces, but here they are, the new second hand shops of Poland. She'd got used to Oxfams and Age Concerns and hospices, that dumping ground for the Western consumer. But here the clothes look that much cheaper, cast-offs of the West, things perhaps cleverly procured in a charity shop in Britain to be sold on again – twice disposed. One might try to view it ironically – a return to that Soviet system of recycling, the kind of passing on and making do that underpinned the whole communist ruse. Because despite promises of better times under capitalism, not many Poles can yet afford the bright shiny new things displayed in brand name shops. But used English clothing – an advertisement of quality or an empty beckoning to materialism, further inequality?

The car approaches city limits: cranes everywhere, Europe rebuilding what the Soviets let decay. But signs of the past cannot be erased: more tattered posters for heavy metal bands, a feature of life for generations, even if the radio's moved on and is blaring today's English pop. Again, more Europe, in the form of roadside German super stores – bigger than any monoliths the Soviets could have dreamt up – fighting their French megamarket competitors side by side. Part of the destruction of French tradition, if you believed Xavier, but then the French espoused a peculiar form of capitalism, subsidising industry to the point of sclerosis. French *hypermarchés* reigned free, but within that peculiar bubble of self-protection, they were the kind of place Harry loved to stop on holidays for exotic delicacies. Because unlike Tilly and her pretensions toward specialist shops and boutiques, Harry had no problem with the idea of luxe for less. Tilly, Harry, Xavier: figments of imagination. The reality now, sub-zero temperatures and mile-long car parks busy despite the snow, showing either vast need or hope.

But only a few hundred metres away, signs of trouble, economic failure. A new kind of decay taking hold, with half built houses for sale. Reminders of the early years of promise when Poles rushed to borrow abroad in Swiss francs or euros, trying to avoid their own high interest rates, only to find prices of new homes could go down as well as up. When house prices fell at the same time as the Polish *złoty*, loans abroad became unsustainable. Debts mounted even as banks stopped lending – leaving unfinished construction, hollowed shells by the road. With warnings from Harry, though not strictly necessary because of her inherent conservatism, Magda had avoided trading for bigger, further out. It looked like a wise move, staying put in that centre flat.

Magda, focused on driving, not talking, the children giggling quietly in the back seat, absorbed, amused. Nothing for her to do but take in the surroundings, familiar but a revelation, the past bulldozing into an uncertain future. Clusters of houses, not really towns, giving way to a few tentative new buildings, then flat land, then rolling hills, and barely being able to see over the crest of the road before it opens up again to an expanse of farmland below. Used or disused, hard to tell in the snow, another vista opening like the one left behind, another hill ahead, another slope downwards. This road, renamed the E-40, the old rolling road to the last point in Poland, historic Przemyśl, and finally the border with Ukraine. All part of the hope of a new European generation: planned bypasses, better surfacing, all the faster to connect East and West, first and foremost for big football matches in 2012. This infrastructure, roads especially, would be a change of gargantuan proportions for rural communities, lifting many out of poverty, spreading equality itself across Europe. Watching the road rise and fall, it was yet hard to know if things have changed as much as she had hoped or not, or whether in fact she'd wanted it to remain as some distant memory. But this was the essential problem of moving on – the past shifting so you can no longer build on it.

'Time for sleep now, they're all tired,' Katya advises as Christophe lets out a yawn.

She turns around. They've arranged the animals into a long bed, the theme presumably, zoo-transported-across-Poland. She smiles, though how can anyone be so satisfied with repetition? How can familiarity be relief, these replays of life soothing? The same characters finding adventure over slightly new terrain, when really they're only getting lugged across Europe. No thought to the fact that there's no point really, travelling from here to there, only to see what's on the other side of the hill. Because it's only ever the same misery or tragedy or comedy or boredom unravelling, only in a different setting, acted on yourself and someone else.

She watches Katya's face, radiating simple pleasure. No, one must stay positive for the children. Christophe's eyes are already shut, his head rolling.

'It's not a bad idea,' she tells Katya, 'you could have a sleep too.'

'Okay,' says Katya.

She shivers, turns back to the front. The car is really cold, her childhood misery, unheated vehicles. She had prepared the children in extra layers but forgot to prepare herself. She hadn't thought she'd feel the cold. Like she hadn't really thought through that meeting with Adam – had she really believed she could make a difference?

The question is still gnawing, and the answer's not clear. It's like asking what life might have been like if Adam hadn't gotten involved with religion to save himself – them both – from the night life slowly eating them alive. What if she hadn't moved on when she found out she was pregnant? What if she'd gone along with his plan for salvation, then forced him back to normality, like Jana? What if she had been more patient, more daring really – had had the child despite the views of their world? What if she had carried on with her Polish life right then and there?

But that would have been a too far-fetched a story. Like asking her to have been a different person, erasing all that came after. She never would have joined a cult. She'd never been religious. That kind of attachment had been chipped away at an early age by the violence and intolerance and selfishness of the Catholic Church as she'd come to know it, and later, as she saw from a distance in quite a few other organised religions as well. From the very first episode when that nun smacked her best friend Maya with a stick – and they were only seven like Katya – to the merciless treatment of the girl who fell pregnant in secondary school and *that* rather imprinted one's psyche on that matter – and finally, all the mean-spirited Catholics who judged her in Krakow and back home in Przemyśl, the ones who turned their heads in church and cast the first glance because they'd heard she was living with Adam in sin. Those were the episodes that shaped religious views, the edifice of the church becoming too much to bear, a whole body of fervent believers out of touch with realities, far from the compassion and open-mindedness needed in this troubled complex world. On one hand, priests preached kindness but the Pope railed against condoms even as people in Africa died of Aids and starvation. Even before it became personal with the proposed abortion, she'd argued with Adam: *how many more impoverished bodies need to lay down their souls before the Church acknowledges a basic human need?* She couldn't remember his reply but now she would have added, it's not just a *desire* for touch and satisfaction, but a *need*. Yes, the fulfilment of desire is human necessity too. Desire and touch have a rightful place in nourishing mind, body and soul, and so one's whole life. Sex isn't necessarily about bringing new infants into the world, especially a world that for many is one of great uncertainty or very certain poverty. And more, with hindsight, because all the time they preached self-abnegation, some of the most overtly religious were committing criminal acts against small helpless children, priests against boys, all around the world, and as a mother this was something she could never forgive.

Like Adam could never forgive her. Not if he was honest with himself about his beliefs. She stares out the window, the landscape now unchanging. *After all, we are humans, not gods*, she recalled arguing further, when he took up with his new salvation. *What's the point of all this pretend sainthood, why bother with religion at all?* But Adam couldn't see another way out of his dark existence, out of the drinking. In the same way she'd convinced herself there was only one way out, especially once she'd decided the drinking was not normal, and progressively getting worse. When she became pregnant, it'd begun to spill over into everything. He'd forgotten about that. Or maybe not. How drinking had been a factor, the one they hadn't mentioned. The one that hung in the air like a stale beer the morning after.

So ironically religion had saved him – Jana and the evangelicals or whoever, the distinction between religions and cults long since muddied – their deprivations and moral codes perhaps succeeding where rationality failed. Who was to judge that either? Easy enough with hindsight to say maybe all Adam needed was a few sessions with Alcoholics Anonymous, a professional to talk to, like in the West. A more liberal, understanding, dispassionate environment, which could have encouraged them both in the right direction, and maybe a tragedy could have been averted. Two people who loved one another might have married and kept their baby. But it wasn't so. So religion had killed as well.

In the snow unsightly brown patches lie unearthed where diggers and tractors and heavy trucks have come through. But why did it have to be like this at all? The ruination of pure and good. What earthly rules keep humans so tightly bound that they're forced into bad sets of choices? So that the only outlet seems to be radicalisation or escape? Something must be wrong with a world that doesn't permit the gentler option, an option that speaks of love and kindness and well-wishes and true forgiveness, instead of judgement and harsh punishment and guilt.

Looking over at Magda, an older sister trapped in her ways, the steady one. Always the driver, never a passenger. She's engrossed in the radio programme that's been on for the better part of an hour, the one which took over after their conversation fizzled. A relief, because Magda had wanted to know about Adam, but not too much. Not so much as to contemplate life itself perhaps, the strange opportunities that present themselves, the odd routes one takes. Looking back at the children, Katya's head rolling like Christophe's – amazing he hasn't been sick – their eyes are firmly shut, angelic expressions on their faces.

'Magda?'

'Yes, hmm,' Magda suddenly rejoins. 'I don't know if you've been listening, but this has been so interesting. So many people calling in with their problems. They used to go to the priests, but now the confession lines are short and the phone-in lines are long.'

'The suffering of humanity remains about the same. The only question is who deals with it.'

'Hmm,' Magda replies. 'In church this morning the priest remarked on just that.'

She nods, though she didn't go to church with Magda. Children too young to rise for early Mass – true but also an excuse, and both of them knew it. Except for Christmas and Easter, as a favour to her parents, she'd hardly attended a Mass for twenty years.

'I hear Kasia and Krzystof snoring!' Magda says.

'I suspect they're exhausted by all this travel.'

Exhaustion is bearing down on her too, like a weight. As if the visitation of past lives was not only taxing but ageing, a battle against death itself. Maybe the only thing one could do was rest as much as possible between skirmishes. Maybe turning away was the only answer when you're too tired to confront religion, belief. Too tired to point out how tricky it is sometimes for Katya, going back and forth with Kasia, because a name is more than a label, a surface requirement to be called something. It lends meaning, becomes part of identity itself, the emotions fuelling a life. That's why Adam named his girl Eva, to remind him of her apparently. But now that she was gone, what did it leave him with, besides the loss of two Evas?

Magda must not have known. Not about the name anyway, or she would have mentioned it. Adam's dashed hopes, now forming a new guilt, for that Eva of the past who had moved on and changed but who was still an Eva sharing a body with the present one – a cord not quite severed, a tiny feeding tube of guilt. Yes, he'd lost much, this Adam. All she can do now is hope he doesn't see it that way. But that too seems impossible.

'If you're tired,' Magda pipes up, 'go ahead and rest. I don't mind. I've done this run so many times I could do it in my sleep. I promise to stay awake, though.'

She smiles but grimly, her face returning to determination, as if you never knew what foe might be encountered on the road. 'Only two more hours, maximum, even with the standstill in Jarosław.' And with that, she turns off the radio, as if to enforce silence.

Sleep, another tough proposition. She rests her head on the icy window, the car hurdling along a bumpy stretch. Rolling a jumper, she wedges it between her ear and the glass but the buffer is meagre protection against the blows and jolts. The cold is pervasive, the feeling of calm dispersed. Only the sounds of the howling wind go by.

∞

Heat, warmth, the rush to the door; the gush at the sight of who's come, who's grown, how much was brought, and *oh, you shouldn't have!* Tato takes the bags with great show, directing them to rooms, even if they're the same rooms as last year. Christmas homecoming must be the same in every family.

The temperature inside is stifling; stepping from minus to plus twenty makes you want to undress to the lightest of undergarments. But no one else seems to notice. Piotr in a bulky jumper, like his eldest Bogdan, who in trying to be admitted to manhood has sprouted whiskers, though they're well away from his father's formidable moustache. Everyone's talking at once, Danka's still home, cooking with little Mila, and their middle one Marek *was* here but he disappeared with his mates. A flash of memory, being the middle child, the only escape either books or friends on another street. A hard road to travel once you set on it, you can never rest. But the thought's interrupted by clanging in the kitchen.

'Come in here!' Mamcia shouts.

They enter to brief kisses of her turned head, because actually Mamcia's too busy chopping and mixing and stirring. She only stops to pat Christophe and Katya with a greasy hand. They eye a towering plate of pastries.

'Go ahead,' Mamcia says. 'It'll be hours before we eat, six o'clock at the earliest.'

That's only an hour away, but there's nothing to prevent spoiling children at Christmastime. Christophe and Katya grab three crescents each.

'And milk for the little ones and tea for everyone!' Mamcia commands, seemingly to Tato. 'Or they'll dry up!'

Even Christophe understands that and they all laugh, Mamcia shooing them away again to drink *chai* out in the next room, where Piotr's already goading Katya to brave some Polish words, bribing her with chocolate. This won't end except possibly in vomit, but she's outnumbered. Best give in to Polish life, the rule of relatives, rather than her own absolutes.

Upstairs Tato's decrying the weight of the luggage, so she hurries to relieve him of presents that should be in the kitchen anyway – smoked salmon and lemon curd and mince pies – delivering them to Mamcia while Tato continues to bustle around not knowing what to do with himself because he hasn't got anything to do. All the firewood's been chopped for one room and coal shovelled for the others, the house a series of additions and odd flourishes, as Tato, a self-taught builder in addition to his training in theoretical physics, rummaged and collected and fiddled and hammered and nailed and carved until the structure was big enough to accommodate anyone who should enter. *If Jesus, Mary and Joseph, and even the donkey, were to come, there'd be enough room*, he boomed every Christmas, as if to prove that his generosity and wealth knew no bounds.

She hands him his beloved Hennessey which he inspects briefly, undoing the stopper, saying, 'Here we go!'

Stopping to smell the top of the bottle like a wine cork and carefully pouring himself an inch, he takes a sip. 'Ach! That's good!' He motions. 'Here Piotr, try it, but not too much!'

Piotr grimaces because he's used to this kind of pretend rationing where drink is concerned, not just with Tato but Danka, who also expects her warnings to be ignored. And of course it's facade with Tato too, because as abstemious as he is with himself he's always generous with others. Every evening before dinner he pours himself a local brand *konyak* with great satisfaction, then pours for everyone else. He's a man of aperitifs if there ever was one. She once tried to explain to him that all brandies weren't cognac, that it mattered where they came from and also they were *digestifs*, for after the meal, to digest, not before. But he hadn't approved of her newfound foreign advice, so she stopped giving it. Really did it matter what rules were in

England or France when a man clearly enjoys his first drink, whatever it is? As if what followed might spoil initial enjoyment, true pleasure located only in that very first mouthful, like that famous *madeleine,* a little buttery biscuit bringing a man back to childhood, preparing him for wistful memories as he sits down and puts his feet up by the fire. So Tato now sits and reflects, fingering his glass, having come around to better cognac anyway as times changed in Poland, all without any help or interference from her.

'GranTato, did you take so long to grow it?' Christophe approaches Tato bravely. He's clearly fascinated by his grandfather's face, like Piotr's, jovial and round as the moon but a bit frightening for its bushy beard.

'You can call him *Dziadzio.*'

'Yes! You can call me that!' Tato booms. 'I am quite the granddad! Look how many wonderful grandchildren I've got, I've even lost count! Who are you?'

'Krzysztof,' says Christophe, patiently, earnestly.

'Ach, let me tell you, Krzysztof, this beard took so very long to grow. I've been at it since I was a small boy, like Bogdan here, and I've never cut it, I only set fire to the ends and keep warm that way!'

Bogdan blushes because he's seventeen and not much of a small boy, though still lanky and willowy and pale like a birch.

'But that's not true,' Katya chimes in, 'you'd burn yourself. That's not safe at all!'

'Maybe in England you worry about such things,' says Tato, eyes gleaming, 'but here in Poland, we are very tough, and because it's so cold, we set fire to things all the time!'

'Oh stop it, Jura!' Mamcia shouts from the kitchen. 'Before they set fire to your prized slippers!'

Tato laughs. 'See maybe your Babcia should be English too. So safety conscious. Eva, I read in the papers that you can get arrested over there if children are not wearing safety belts in the car. Imagine, what'll they think of next?'

She's about to reply that even in Poland seat belts are becoming mandatory if not already, but Danka arrives at the door with steaming casseroles and Mila, skinny like her brother, carrying plates of cheese and jam crepes far too heavy for a ten-year-old. Then in comes the lost thirteen-year-old Marek, looking dragged in but quickly forgetting his adopted misery to join in the fun of welcoming the English. The din is fantastic, everyone talking at once, and it is good, so good to be home again. Even if now, she is the foreigner.

∞

Sunday before Christmas and church is obligatory. Though church is already obligatory on Sundays so it's hard to comprehend how it can become more so on holy days. But these are the mysteries of religion, and she never planned to fight them explicitly. Because despite scepticism one can still believe some of it – or more accurately, hope – in basics like God, even if you don't think he resides in a building. Besides, if children are to have any grounding, shouldn't they be exposed to positive bits, morals and tradition? More pragmatic than Harry in this respect or perhaps more laden with responsibility for their upbringing, she doesn't want to be hypocritical or hurt her parents. But maybe that's why God forgives hypocrites. Because sometimes hypocrisy is a form of kindness.

They make their way to church in Tato's car stuffed like herrings in a jar. Piotr and Danka are waiting already in front of the Arch-Cathedral of St John, the one that belongs to the Roman Catholics, where they go first, because Tato's old work colleagues do. Though Tato will then head to the other Cathedral of St John down the street which belongs to the Ukrainians, who are mostly Uniate Greek Catholics and not to be confused with the Roman variety and because Baba Katya's dying wishes must be maintained. Anyway Tato prefers to get all his duties done in one day. In this he's more practical than spiritual and Mamcia's had to put up with it for years, his peculiar version of Catholicism, dodging into the Polish church before closing, then over to the Ukrainians at half time. *It's not a football match*, Mamcia says, *you can't just get the score*, but Tato is adamant that God is everywhere or He wouldn't be much use to pray to, and neither he nor God mind this whole business of church going, which is mostly appearances for other people's benefit and not your own soul.

She stands by the steps, buffeted by the wind, Christophe and Katya running about while Mamcia gives Tato detailed instructions of where best to park the car. Mass is already midway at the Roman Catholics, somewhere roughly between the Our Father and Holy Communion, so they slip into the last row. She stands apart at the back, waiting for Tato to join them. It must have been with him that her scepticism began, Tato's way of thinking, the chink that broke apart the rock of staunch catechism taught underground at secret Sunday school. His pragmatism, and perhaps too the seeming irreconcilability of physics and religion, though as he later explained it, only science was rational and experimental. In religion, you could experiment all you want, but in the end, you just believe.

Tato comes in, choosing to stand alone too, ahead a few paces. She stays behind because solitude allows the mind's eye to wander past the imposing architecture, the stone pillars reaching up into darkness, the cold statues wrapped in evergreens. At the moment no light's coming through the stained glass windows, and the visibility on the Stations of the Cross is nil. She turns to the front of the church but no light there either, only the burdened pillars doing their job, holding up a cumbersome roof. She'd always found Roman Catholic churches oppressive, but maybe her feeling wasn't unique, or her scepticism. Maybe that always began at home, growing with outside experience, because in her environment there had been much to shape a doubting sensibility. When she was growing up, Przemyśl was quite troubled, the animosity between Ukrainians and Poles coming to a head in organised religion. That coloured everything, even before she'd been born, because under the Austro-Hungarians during the First World War and before the second, nationalities already seethed. True to her determination young Baba Kasia had married a Pole, but after the brutality of the Second World War – division and nationalism, fascism and communism – all a form of suspicion, infiltrated society to the core. Like many, whose husbands disappeared in the war, never to be seen again, Baba Kasia didn't remarry, and the uncertain peace enforced behind the Iron Curtain belied other acts like the *Akcja Wisła* of 1947, which tore communities apart once more. Poles and Ukrainians took to butchering one another, then Baba and Ukrainians like her were deported en masse, from their homelands on Poland's south-east borders to the north along the Baltic, to places like Słupsk and Olsztyn. There Ukrainians made homes, or more accurately were given houses of Germans deported before them. Some settled but many like Baba did not, waiting until the 1960s when they were allowed to return. But by then, there was really bad blood between the Poles and Ukrainians of Przemyśl. You could see it now, remnants of suspicion, self-segregated churches. She looks around for Tato but he seems to have slipped into the crowd. These are the things she must remember to ask him about, how Baba Kasia never held grudges or desired revenge, so she let her only son marry a local Polish girl. So even as others continued fighting over relations and liturgies, exiling Ukrainians to lead separate lives though they lived next door, Tato took on Baba's characteristics of tolerance, enabling Mamcia in turn to make their household a mostly Polish one. But Tato insisted on paying respects to Ukrainian traditions, and in that way perhaps, more than in deference to any belief, he carried on Baba's defiance of ethnic intolerance. It was quite a feat in this part of the world.

She spies him leaning against a pillar, deep in thought. Ahead are full-sized Christmas trees with mounds of tiny lights, the only thing keeping the church from total darkness. Christophe and Katya are mesmerised, this kind of spectacle usually far removed from their experiences. But for her too, this ritual of religion is foreign, standing among true believers, a congregation of unrecognisable penitents. She searches for familiar faces but most of the women are too old. Although they might only be classified as old, because being forty-one in Poland could have taken its toll, with harder winters, joblessness and making do with whatever's to be found in outdoor markets. Some of these are certainly the girls Tato warned her about, the ones who wouldn't study and go on to a better life. Tato had always been strict on that point. Only he hadn't been happy with how far away it had taken her.

Two women in the last pew titter, tap their lips, cast glances. They seem to marvel at her very being, the essence of which might be her smile, her teeth not grey or gold capped but gleaming like first snow. She dressed up for the occasion in a posh frock and formal English wool coat, so she does look different from the others, even the well dressed ones. It's embarrassing, this disparity, and stupid: being overly fashionable and utterly cold. Brutal Slavic winters had escaped her memory in the packing, and now the chill, as insistent as the past, has gone from a subtle enveloping to a piercing invasion. In her mind too, that more recent past, the succession of times she and Harry came at Christmas, lugging more nappies than clothing. At first, it was to preserve that one baby, Katya. Like the baby Jesus in the manger, radiant but indifferent under a single yellow bulb, only parents gaze so lovingly. And truly there is joy when a child is born, but also many hard years, especially after Christophe. Why had anyone supposed having a second one would be easy? The presumption being that having one child prepared you for another but suddenly you were juggling two small humans, not one, alone in a suburban house with no extended family, how could it not be challenging to an extreme? Why should she have known? Adding to it all, post-partum, a diagnosis not so much a relief as coming too late, the anxiety already suffocating her like a cuff misplaced on the throat. And she, trying to get it all right, even as she battled anger, sadness, voices urging her to end it, overwhelmed by everything because nothing was right. But how could you know what was right anyway? How could anyone? This seemed to be the essential but fleeting thing, a sensibility that always escaped, no matter how informed and experienced and wise one became. Forever you were prone to doubt and disappointment and unknowing. To feelings of failure and uselessness. Because there would always be something you did not understand or could not fix. Like the loss Adam felt for their unborn baby and the unfair fate of his poor other baby, Eva.

She snaps her head away from the manger to the side of darkened glass windows, searching for another view. But it's time. Tato's given the signal. Tapping Katya and Christophe on the shoulder, she shushes them as they make their way out, *what, another church?* Mamcia and Piotr and the rest stay, refusing to participate in the dodging, as Mamcia calls it. But as a daughter whose daughter is named for Baba Kasia, she's determined to see it through. Joining Tato, they move quickly down Katedralna to Franciszkanska Street to catch the service at the other John.

Huddling against the gusts, she grips the children, even this short walk is too long in this weather. But the brutality also makes the relief of entering church that much more pronounced. A bit like managing the winters themselves, or maintaining Baba Kasia's disciplines, that feat of championing ethnic and religious tolerance in this corner of Poland. Like so many areas of Eastern Europe, this borderland seemed to function normally until one day seemingly without warning, it erupted along ethnic and religious lines. She stamps her feet of residual snow but there's nowhere to move for the crowd, even in the foyer. This Ukrainian St John itself had been a mini-battleground, now a grander version of its original Latin-style Roman Catholic edifice. Taken over by the Polish army in the Second World War and dubbed the garrison church, miraculously, post-war the building had been shared by Ukrainians and Poles more or less peacefully as they alternated services hour by hour. Largely that was because Ukrainians had nowhere else to go, having been thrown out of their church a few metres away by the Barefoot Carmelite nuns. It was a story she'd never quite understood – because if the nuns were barefoot, how could they have successfully mounted an offensive strike? Crammed in the foyer of St John, nearly half a dozen other churches in walking distance, one thing was clear: there were no shortages of churches in Przemyśl. No need to argue, you could always find a place to pray. Still at the original Ukrainian church the nuns toppled the dome symbolic of Eastern rites, so Ukrainians took to protesting while sit-ins were held by Poles objecting to its return to Ukrainians. That bit she remembered well, having lived through it in the late 1980s. The conflict finally came to a head and the Pope himself weighed in. Pope John Paul II, now saint, Karol Wojtyła from Wadowice. Half Ukrainian, half Pole, he must have understood the depth of feelings on both sides. Visiting in 1991, in one of the town's biggest historic moments, the Pope decreed the Carmelites would keep the Ukrainian church and gave the other St John definitively to the Ukrainians. So these days the ethnicities of Przemyśl lived more or less in harmony. Because if there was one person Catholics on either side of the cultural divide could never dispute it was the Pope. Just as in their family no one ever disputed Baba Kasia, and for her sake, old traditions and memories were kept alive.

The warmth of so many bodies defrosting hands and feet, the music reaches for a towering high note, falls dramatically to a lull. The priest resumes his intoning, the choir replies, over and over this never-ending beautiful sad Slavic chant, drowning out all else, pulling the soul, beckoning, *come closer, feel.* Tato too is drawn, moves closer to the second main door until they find themselves slipping in from the cramped entrance to the main cavernous interior. There too, standing room only, and she and the children are pressed far into the right corner. The walls inside are bare, except for giant solemn icons far above their heads. Icons that continue around the windows and culminate in a massive icon wall, the *iconostas,* obscuring the altar. In true Byzantine style, there are no statues, only these icons, the painted faces and bodies of saints standing at attention on gold panels. Mary and baby Jesus figure high above the central wrought gates where the priest enters and disappears, and beyond that almost ceiling height, full centre, is the great portrait of Christ in judgement: Christ Pantocrator, his almond-shaped eyes rendered to follow every worshipper in the church. Baba Kasia had taught her Pantocrator meant Almighty or All-Powerful, coming from the Greek, meaning 'all' and 'strength' or 'ability to sustain'. Apparently words mattered when it came to religious definitions because key interpretations followed. The whole schism of Catholic and Orthodox only came down to a few lines about the Holy Spirit. One small slip and you got it all wrong. And the important point about Pantocrator was not about what God *could* or *can* do. It is that He *does*.

Of course in the West, people had mostly moved on. She shuffles in place, looks through the crowd. Not here certainly, but modernity seemed determined to move away from allowing itself to be awed. Nowadays everyone wanted a rational explanation, people like Harry obsessed with logic, as if that delivered the answers to life. But often enough you couldn't rationalise. Not people or events around you, and certainly not essential mysteries. That was the whole point of mystery. And the further East one travelled, the less explaining people seemed to need or want to inflict on one other. Life becoming more mystical from Orthodox all the way to Hindu and Buddhist, services not meant to explain but entrance. Though of course, if you couldn't quite manage that, then being agnostic, doubting and unsure, seemed the best place to be. Although that too perhaps might just be another justification for not choosing either way.

Following the icons further afield, the mind begins to wander again: Slavic fatalism intertwined with religion, everything the will of an all-seeing God? To get to that level of acceptance, that feeling of peace, one would have to stop fighting. Let go of puny will, forget stubborn rationale and submit altogether to a different power. The power of being pulled – that too would have to be accepted – you'd have to accept letting go. Letting go of doubt, uncertainty – tough enough to do with people, never mind some god you don't see – so maybe it was understandable why people largely abandoned the effort. Declared there was nothing in it. Yet with incense and song, eyes closed to take in the darkness, to hold it close, to let it seep in until there's no possibility of escape, for one moment, it's almost possible to stop thinking. To lose track of time and space. That overwhelming sense of self. The selfishness of being.

'Mama, my feet hurt,' Christophe pokes her in the leg.

She sighs, eyes opening. 'It's almost over.'

Christophe shuffles, moans something inaudible.

215

'Almost done,' she says reassuringly though really they'll have to suffer through it. With Ukrainians you stand for hours if necessary, and poor Christophe doesn't have the benefit she does – seeing over people's heads, watching strangers, making connections.

The old woman next to them leans down to say something to Christophe, and she realises the woman is strangely reminiscent of Baba. Though she's also like any other Slavic grandmother in her headscarf, a ubiquitous look, as if getting old were merely a matter of copying how the previous generation went about bent from village life. But the burgundy shade, the paisley pattern, exactly like Baba's, and the woman's stance, bending over to children as Baba used to, a ray of light illuminating her profile in contrast to the severe faces of the saints. It's like a sign. The singing intensifies in a final hymn, an ancient form of the East, this chanting, singing, intoning, replying, under the shimmering iconostas ahead. She looks at the children again, but the woman is gone.

The service ends on a crescendo, but not in time to resolve a thing. For hours they've been singing, and she only got there at the end. The finale came too soon, a moment interrupted. Maybe the woman slipped out to avoid the exiting crush. Christophe's tugging at her again, *Mama, Mama, Mama.* Perhaps that's why they do it over and over, the same service, for centuries. Because that unity is always broken. By children, people leaving pews, the push rippling through to packed aisles, where stopping to chat, exchange gossip and laugh, the people in the foyer finally spill out on to the street, and there winter obliterates any residual feeling of warmth.

She pulls up her collar against the wind whipping in various directions. For a moment she watches others heading this way and that. Then finding her own family in the melee of worshippers, she joins in with the people beginning to disperse quickly. Fighting the winds, the throng becomes a stream, which turns into a tiny trickle, as the devout make their way up and down the cobblestone hill of Franciszkanska Street.

∞

It's still too raw and blustery to stay on exposed banks for long, so she turns back up the stairs and crosses the bridge as quickly as possible, rerouting her walk through the twisted streets around the main square to Cafe Fiore where she'll meet Piotr and the children. She had to get out – not just to escape the house but make space for another meal. She'd forgotten how it is, the countdown to Christmas Eve less an exercise in restraint before big celebrations than a continuous gorging and feverish preparation of ever more food. Maybe if she remembered every year she would refuse tradition. *It's enough for a whole village, what's on my plate*, she announced at Piotr's the day before. Everyone laughed because Danka rolled in just then with a plate of stuffed cabbage rolls, saying, *you can't be finished, look what's here!* As if it *gołąbki* were something that happened to pop out of the oven and she was just as surprised as everyone that they appeared.

Oh, just something to tide you over! But how can you digest properly if the next thing is always arriving to tide you over? She didn't argue, couldn't, *gołąbki* take hours of preparation and you can't insult the cook. Anyway, it turned out she was wrong – the children *were* hungry after playing in the snow. And Piotr patted his round stomach with satisfaction, saying, *you should visit us more often, Eva, the woman starves me year round, but look what happens when you come.*

It was so good to see him again. And after this cold promenade, a well deserved break, entering a warm cafe to be greeted by a colourful array of pastries, the smell of rich coffee. Her favourite place, Cafe Fiore, with its wall murals depicting some imagined serene waterways of Venice, a place so far from Przemyśl it might as well be a dream. Someone had worked hard to create this fiction of Italy-in-Poland. Even the booths' handrails had been shaped like the ends of gondolas. But it had escaped her until now that even in her hometown this fiction was being propagated – everyone being tempted to escape reality for something more exotic, even if only for an hour. Tentacles of desire, temptation reaching out, pulling you in, establishments serving a sliver of fantasy, when in reality they were only doling out slices of pie.

'Mama! Mama! Mama! Look!'

Christophe bounds towards her, holding something.

'Look what Uncle Piotr bought us!'

A motorcycle, a dark blue miniature BMW, resembling the real thing.

'It's like Daddy's!' Christophe's thoughts echo hers, but thankfully in English, so no one else understands.

'See what I have!' Katya joins in. She holds up a pink notepad and a sparkly pen with a wire springing a feathered plastic star. 'Look, it bounces!'

They're clearly excited so she pushes away the thought that these items might have been expensive, the kind of things Piotr would never have bought his own children.

'Thank you,' she gives Piotr a hug, 'but you didn't need to do that.'

'A little something for my nephew and niece.' He sits down pleased while the children go off to inspect the ice creams on offer.

'But where are Mila and Marek and Bogdan?'

'Oh, Mila had a friend turn up suddenly and Marek went off with some of his buddies to carol for school donations. Bogdan's helping a friend with his dad's car.' He shrugs as if to say, *well, what do you expect, teenagers.*

It suddenly occurs she might have made a mistake, arranging to meet in the cafe. Maybe he thought he'd have to pay, didn't want to bring them, though it was her intention to treat all along.

'Let me get you a coffee,' she signals the waitress before he can protest. 'I feel bad, you driving us around like tourists.'

'Don't be silly,' Piotr says. 'You're not tourists, and you're not putting me out. It's great having you back. Holidays, no one's that busy. You'd do the same.' He gets up. 'Be right back.' He goes to the pastry counter to check the desserts on offer.

Yes, she'd do the same, but she hasn't had the chance. No one's given it to her; none of them have visited. At first they couldn't afford air tickets, but they wouldn't let Harry pay either, then they had no time to take the bus, then other pressing matters got in the way. So it's been years of not being able to return favours. She'd even married in England without them, a quick civil ceremony that seemed practical and radical at the time but now stood out as another moment of regret. Not for dispensing with tradition or fairy weddings, but because her family hadn't been there. Of course, at the time there had been good reasons for proceeding. Not feeling able to come back, the shame of the row with the family priest who wouldn't consent to marry her unless she confessed her sins. But she didn't think her affair with Adam was anyone else's business, or living with Xavier or Harry before marriage for that matter. Tato didn't particularly care or Mamcia, but rules were rules and the church wouldn't budge. When the priest threatened to cause local scandal, then suggested money would sort it out, the rift became permanent. Money? The church about money too? She'd turned away and never looked back. In the end, civil ceremonies still counted, and Tato liked to think of himself as a progressive sort. Harry had always been welcome. But forever after, it really was the return of the prodigal daughter, her role in the family cemented.

Of course family roles rarely changed for anyone, in any family. So all of them were locked in: Piotr ever the baby, the carefree one, confidante of sisters. With the income discrepancy now she had to be careful treading a line between generosity and causing offence. An added strain because it required concentration and practice, making good intentions actually come out that way, a kind of steadiness that belonged naturally to people like Harry, not her.

Piotr returns from the counter licking his lips, clearly pleased with the concoction that's arriving, a millefeuille with cream and jellied peaches on top. The waitress sets down their coffees and he dives into his dessert, offering a taste.

'Divine.' The cream layered in puff pastry, fresh and sweet, probably from a local farm.

'Mmhmm,' Piotr agrees. He finishes his pastry in three enormous bites, then sips his coffee slowly as if that were the truly glorious treat.

'Eva,' he says suddenly serious, setting down his cup. 'Magda told me about your meeting with Adam. No wait, don't be annoyed. I know you've never been that open with Magda, but she does care about you.'

Piotr, always the peacemaker, bearing the brunt of her and Magda's arguments, he never could stand it. Her face must've inadvertently scrunched up.

'No, listen, Eva, she does, really. It's just that you don't know all about Adam,' he slows down. 'He's unhinged.'

'I suspected that.' Her comment is flat, non-committal. She shrugs. 'Well, he was with that sect all those years, and before that, he was always different. I thought, deeper somehow, more troubled by the world, maybe that's what attracted me to him in the first place. I thought – not that I could save him – but that I understood him, that I could understand him. But later, I saw he was troubled, I mean, that's why it ended.' She pauses, glossing over the drinking, the pregnancy, the other contributing factors.

'There's nothing now,' she says reassuringly. 'Look, we met up… I'm not sure why we did, just to see, I suppose, how things turned out. He wanted to, and for me too there was that natural curiosity.'

'I know,' Piotr says. 'You hear it all the time. People meeting up, finding each other on the internet, digging up the past, whatever. But it's not the same for Adam. He's not well, Eva. You don't want to get mixed up with him.'

'I'm not trying to get mixed up with him,' she rebuffs. 'Anyway, what do you mean? What are you getting at?'

Piotr can't know more than she, he can't know about poor buried Eva and certainly not of that almost-child of hers with Adam, the one that never had a name.

'I don't know everything, it's true,' Piotr says, as if reading her mind, 'but do you know Adam tried to take his own life a few years ago?'

'He said that he almost drank himself to death but his wife pulled him out of it.'

'No, I'm talking about the accident,' Piotr stops, and registering no recognition, continues. 'Three years ago Adam ploughed his car into an embankment. Eva, there was no reason for this accident. He was sober, no other cars around. A bus driver saw the whole thing. It was like he was trying to kill himself, driving off the edge of the road.'

Processing with difficulty, she says nothing. Piotr goes on.

'The police came and investigated all the scrape marks and what not, and there was no justification for the act, Eva, no cause. He hadn't fallen asleep at the wheel or anything, though it was early morning. He just shrugged and walked off. Miraculously, the car wasn't totalled. It got hauled out and repaired. It made the papers. He refused to comment.'

'Then how do you know for sure he was trying to kill himself?'

'Eva,' Piotr steadies himself. 'He called Magda to confess.'

'What?'

'They've spoken more than once these years since you left.'

She says nothing again, because this is even harder to take in. Had Magda simply forgotten about the other episodes before the hospital, or not made the connection, that he's been trying to reach out?

'Eva,' Piotr continues gently. 'You didn't ask me where.'

'What do you mean where?'

'Where the accident was.'

'You said embankment, so along the Wisła, I assume, or somewhere in Krakow by the river.'

'No, Eva. He came here. To Przemyśl.' He pauses. 'He drove seven hours here, then tried to kill himself in the San.'

∞

Over the town the large black cross looms forbiddingly against the sky; grey clouds hint it will soon snow again. The wind's died down, as if waiting. They started the drive up the hill in silence, not so much because of what was said, because Piotr told her not to worry, maybe meeting Adam finally put everything in order, maybe he'd get on with his life now. But they both knew that did not ring true.

The underlying reality already almost tragic, she'd braced back the tears. Because Adam had no business doing that, bringing her family into it. And what else did Magda know and not reveal? Magda was apt to lock things away when they seemed over, not one to rehash the past, but in that way she also failed to make connections. Maybe the times Adam had been in touch with her previously had seemed inconsequential, or mentioning them a moot point, was that why Magda had shrugged? Why had she held back tears then? For herself or this failed wayward middle child? Madga wasn't at fault, of course. In fact it wasn't her problem to bear. But then how was she supposed to bear this, dig deeper or walk away?

Maybe it would have been good to pray for Adam in church when she had the chance. She could have prayed for things to turn out for the best. Because if you can't understand everything and sometimes nothing at all, maybe there's a god who does? That's the only hope, if you can choose it, because if you don't know anything for certain, who can say there is no God or that prayer doesn't work? Surely it couldn't hurt, even if you hate church and the Pope and despise evil clergy and all the hierarchy that ever was, can't you still ask God directly for intervention? Isn't that the point – trying? Doesn't the act of trying make it better, make you better? Or if that's too hypocritical then maybe she can hope someone else might pray for Adam. Because surely only God can save him now. God, if He's merciful and good like they say.

Hypocrisy and prayer: everyone does it anyway. Praying but possibly not believing, hoping others will too. She certainly does it when Piotr's driving, silently willing him to focus on the road like Magda, instead of intermittently scanning it, distracted by messages on his phone. In such icy conditions it's positively nerve wracking. Almost as bad as flying, sitting strapped in an airplane. Thankfully they're taking the long way up the hill, not the short steep cut near the old fort – the car's unlikely to slide backwards. But Adam?

They loop around, passing the old Tatar burial mound, Piotr gunning the engine into the clearing under the giant cross. He parks against the slope and they get out to walk. Katya and Christophe run ahead with Piotr, who likes to saunter around the hilltop park because that's what you do after Cafe Fiore and all the creamy sweetness, take in bracing air before the next big meal.

She hangs back, takes her time to mount the stairs to the top where the vista opens up. On a clear day you can see all the way to Ukraine, another world, beyond Europe and its fine order. At the moment it's overcast, the only thing visible is the town nestling below, little trails of smoke escaping miniature chimneys. The children point excitedly at the rooftops covered in snow. New snowflakes are beginning to swirl. It is magical really, and their enthusiasm is infectious. Her spirits begin to lift.

Anyway no harm done. Maybe Piotr's right, a short meeting of mutual reassurance with Adam, but best to be cautious going forward. Because sometimes you can't fix what's broken and whatever you do, no good comes from past misery, not even the understanding or peace you hope for. Sometimes, you have to bear the bad, forever, salvation being the ability to walk away. It isn't a great solution, not as final resolutions go, and not exactly a path to peace. But what if there is no alternative?

She stares at the cross, erected by the former town mayor, who spent so much time at regional government soliciting funds for this immense commemorative object to go up in time for the millennium celebrations. After all his work, just as the cross was raised up, the mayor died of cancer. He was only in his early forties, but it was as if he'd completed his life's work, borne his cross, erected his own cross, only to be buried under it in the town below.

A testament to his life, what he had left behind. But what was hers? Which cross was she supposed to bear, which legacy leave for the future? Wasn't that at stake, what's been gnawing at her? Certainly Christophe and Katya, two beings made by her and from her, but surely something aside from simple procreation. Their upbringing, yes, being a steward of their lives, a job that would be unfinished for quite some time, but later, or in addition? Wasn't that what had to be found, what was to be done? Even if Marx had botched it completely, asking the question in economic revolutionary terms, it still seemed a central problem of life, especially if you were in the middle of it. What to do with life? Meaning and method had to be ascribed as one marched towards the inevitable grave. Youth was gone, youth defined by aspirations, experimentation, glib hope, barriers broken, a struggle to achieve first goals. Then that sliding into comfortable routines – nappies and washing and cooking and drying, back and forth to school, to work, to shop – day by day progressing in small steps – but eventually you had to stop, didn't you, and ask, but for what? You couldn't simply repeat, ad infinitum, simple tasks until death. There had to be a higher purpose. And not one defined by society or circumstance, but coming from the individual, from within, from the soul, which would always strive for bliss, a soul that couldn't be put down but which did resurrect and turn towards light, even if there were terrible crosses to bear. The triumph of the human spirit, that was the common saying, but surely it was more than that. A protracted battle against the unwinnable. A continued contest against a losing proposition, death. Conquering it with life itself, the act of living. Defiance in the face of our own end.

She pulls up her scarf to block the wind. That might be the bigger picture, but specifics still beguiled. Maybe one could never manage to answer such questions alone. And if that were true, she must look to the way she's already constructed her life. In her case, surely half the equation remains Harry.

∞

He steps from the platform a vision of a ghost, less tired than frozen. These long journeys can't be easy on him either. But his eyes light up when he sees her; he grabs her in silent embrace.

'I've missed you so much.'

'Me too,' and then despite herself, she turns to the practical. 'Come, I know it's late, but if you're hungry Mamcia's kept some food warm.'

Harry laughs, and it's like bells pealing. She'd forgotten his laugh! She'd forgotten him altogether, though it seems impossible now, squeezing into the car with him, his arm around her shoulder, both of them quiet because the town's asleep and it seems right to maintain this decorum. Through dark, windy streets, Tato drives home, where Mamcia's waiting, bursting with exuberance.

'Come, Eva, he must eat,' Mamcia says, holding out what looks like a whole kilo of sausage on a plate, pickles and black bread piled high.

'*Nie, dziękuję,*' Harry doesn't skip a beat.

'Stefa, don't force him.' Tato instantly sides with Harry, his polite *no, thank you.*

Mamcia's face crumples but resurrects. Bravery in rejection. 'Well, tomorrow then,' and she bustles back to the kitchen to put it away.

Exchanging goodnights then, the house falls silent. The midnight hour. Harry follows her upstairs and she sits on the bed as he undresses, this being from another planet suddenly descended on the room. His English-cut suit from some faraway office day, the stack of hand-held devices, briskly laid down in the efficiency they're supposed to produce, his whole manner in complete contrast to this rustic home, its slow routines. She stares in amazement as if an apparition had floated in, nothing to do but watch as it unpacks pockets, throws its jacket on the chair, sends its tie sailing over like a ribbon.

'You're quiet tonight,' he says, sitting down on the bed, 'come here.' He falls backward pulling her down on top. 'I've missed you so much.'

'Only a few weeks but it seems like ages.'

'Oh yes, ages,' he repeats, 'ages and ages.'

Then he's kissing her as if there's nothing to discuss, and what is there really, they can talk another time. He slides her jumper over her head, unhooks her bra, takes off his shirt and trousers, and they're at each other. Harry taking short breaths, she stopping once in a while to catch hers, he not waiting to get her completely naked, so that somehow as quickly as it begins, it's over. This first moment of meeting and the dream of how it would all be, already receding. Harry goes to the bathroom and she waits, her turn next, but by the time she's back, he's fast asleep.

She turns off the tiny light and listens to his snoring. He *is* exhausted. Maybe not so much by love-making as the travel, the worry he's carrying for the four of them. But she's not tired. Passion wakes her up, especially making love in this room, a childhood space, an illicit pleasure that inflames. Like the biblical apple, what's forbidden always stokes desire, and far from feeling satisfied, there's only wanting more.

Lying in the darkness, waiting for sleep to come, she holds him, and that all-encompassing reality suddenly returns, becomes a feeling of gladness, wells up and takes over. She finds the nesting spot where their curves fit together. This is the man she chose, would choose, again and again. Another desperate wanting now, to whisper, *don't leave me, don't leave me ever*, but she can't wake him to beg this. So lying in the darkness, slipping into an uneasy calm, she listens to his soft chortles as they progress to solid breathing, and tries to get used to having him again. The only thing she has to do is fit him back into her life. But because life is always shifting, this isn't such an easy thing to do.

∞

In the morning, Mamcia takes her revenge: she serves up a dozen fried eggs and *kiszka* black pudding and smooth white sausages and coarse pink ones. Cold sliced *kielbasa* from the night before layered with fresh ham and homemade pickles, and black and white bread and a whole plate of cheese and fresh butter, plus cheese crepes with plum jam or cherry preserve or Pan Staciek's honey. Harry blinks at the vastness of it all, but Mamcia shakes her head before he can say anything because she's heard all about the slice of toast he usually takes in the morning instead of good Polish fare or a full English fry-up. You can see it in her triumphant look, *of course all this, because what kind of breakfast is toast?*

Harry does his duty and as he is hungry, Mamcia gets her satisfaction. The meal is a melee of children clamouring for attention, Daddy this, Daddy that, Harry saying yes to everything but his mind evidently elsewhere, work or maybe a lack of sleep drawing a blank. He sips his tea quietly, as if waiting for the storm to pass. Then coffee is served, with chocolates and pastries, signalling the end, and an air of purposefulness descends on the house. The new guest has been welcomed, so now on to the serious business of cooking for Christmas.

The children groan as Mamcia announces the day's plan. They'd like to stay with Daddy but they're to be whisked away to Piotr and Danka's where they won't be in the way. Danka's sworn she can look after all of them even with her own mountain of preparations because she can't be talked out of bringing more *gołąbki* than necessary. The rest of the women – she, Magda and Mamcia – must stay for the laborious process of making *pierogies,* because now that Baba Kasia's gone, the dough never turns out well enough and it takes twice as long to fill and seal the dumplings. The men, including Piotr's eldest, Bogdan, are charged with finding more firewood. Tato's brimming with glee because this is less a necessary expedition than a time-honoured tradition, sausage and pickles and vodka in the woods and rousing songs to accompany the axing. Tato's especially pleased that Stasiek is coming. Stasiek is the best singer of the bunch although he can't hear, as if he'd memorized all the songs long ago in perfect pitch and deafness didn't constitute disability. Mamcia bustles about preparing a lunch bag because Tato can't be trusted to pack anything himself, he'll forget a knife or the sausage itself or take too little bread or leave off the *shmaletz* spread made of lard and fried onions. As usual Tato complains he barely walks into the kitchen before he gets pushed out, but of course he's smiling, because he's looking forward to the picnic and especially, making Harry drink.

'Okay,' Harry says in a whisper though there's no need, no adults speak English, 'I'm just going outside and I may be some time.'

She laughs as this was one of the first things she learned in England – the famous quip from Captain 'Titus' Oates who froze to death in the South Pole.

'Seriously, I've got my phone,' Harry adds, looking desperate. 'If we're not back in two hours, text me with some emergency.'

Fond of most Polish traditions, Harry still hates *shmaletz*, and being the *real* foreigner, he can't argue against drink.

'At least I won't have to sit in the house all day dodging Mamcia's entreaties to try this and eat that,' he grins. 'So all in all, it's a fair trade.'

'Don't worry. I've got your number and in a pinch Stasiek's dog can lead you home.'

She gives him a peck on the cheek and the men depart in a clatter of equipment and bottles. She joins the women in the kitchen. Mamcia's taken the carp from its ice pack to inspect it, one of the twelve courses served during the Christmas Eve meal. Magda's already deep in concentration over the dumplings, because if you get distracted the filling finds its way on to the lip of the dough and they refuse to stick closed.

'Ah,' says Mamcia, 'This is the moment I've waited for all year. My two daughters, all to myself!'

She smiles and Magda too, for a different reason probably, because Magda spends a fair amount of time visiting home – or used to, as Mamcia now complains, but nowadays only Piotr and Danka are regulars. Mamcia might be right, moments like these don't come often enough, one ought to savour them in the living. The whole of Christmas in Przemyśl like that, you never know if it might be repeated. Harry mentioned once or twice he'd like to do something fabulous, break with tradition, get out of the cold to the Seychelles or Bahamas. *African safari!* Christophe shouted when Katya overheard and explained to him, because a friend of his had gone away and bragged about lions and zebras. But she'd wondered what kind of a Christmas could be spent in foreign places because Christmas wasn't about zebras or vacationing or being exotic. It was about family and home and traditions like the twelve course meal on Christmas Eve and the *pasterka* service in church at midnight. Even in challenging tradition and belief surely there were some constants that ought not be altered.

'Ach, I'm crying,' Mamcia breaks the reverie. 'I never could stand onions.' She brings them to the stove for frying, directs Magda to chop her mushrooms smaller.

Standing over the stove, waiting for onions to go translucent, she stirs in slow circles so they don't burn. Magda's mushrooms go in while Mamcia manages the chaos, remembering recipes, keeping the rotation of tasks going, so no time's wasted. Amazingly the onion-mushroom mixture she's been given to stir is the base for at least four of the twelve courses: mushroom dumplings called little ears, or *ushka*, served up in *borscht*; the cooked kasha and mushroom cabbage rolls, *gołąbki*; the mushroom sauce that goes over them, and another soup of mushrooms, as if having *borscht* for soup, plus ten other courses wasn't enough. Is it decadent or pointless having two kinds of soup? Might decadence be equivalent to pointlessness? Does that then work the same the other way around?

Mamcia continues to move at a steady pace, like all accomplished cooks, doing several things at once and in advance of other things. Setting aside the Christmas cooking, she quickly throws together this evening's dinner: another pot of soup, a tray of chicken and a load of mash – all on four burners and in one oven. Then back to Christmas preparations, so that only minor cooking remains for that day: carp to fry, cold herrings and salmon to set out, boiling *ushka*, and frying up the day-old Ukrainian *varenyky* so they become Polish *pierogies*. Of course, none of that includes what Mamcia did before they arrived: another carp sealed in aspic in aspic and *borscht* itself, because cooked two days in advance it gets richer with time, plus all the baked desserts and compote. Yet when it's over, Mamcia will still be hovering, getting ready to cook again, showing no sign that sitting down is part of the enjoyment.

They continue in silence, filling the rounds of dough with a spoon of mash potato or cabbage filling, sealing the circles into puffy moons: the transformation of dough to dumpling. The outcome of the *varenyky* is paramount, so rather than talk too much radio fills the background. The public discourse is about the role of the Christ child as a personage in history, the slaughter of innocents as Herod pursued paranoid policies of power, how it might be linked to modern political affairs. Her mind wanders, trying to envision this Christ child, put him in historical or religious context. It's difficult even if you know the story. Anyway, weren't they were all communist atheists growing up? Though everyone knew that too was a ruse – atheism, dialectic materialism, all the other isms, then Catholicism too, officially outlawed but tolerated. A bit like early Christian times, one might say, never knowing when you might suffer repercussions. Because the Polish communists were never quite sure what to do about Catholicism as an alternate hierarchy. Never far from the surface, venerated by most, Catholicism returned with a vengeance when the Wall came down. Nowadays you could hardly escape it, the whole country Catholic-mad. Even Piotr complained religious instruction was squeezing out science, much to Tato's chagrin as well. The pendulum of history swinging the other way, though it was hard to imagine it getting worse, it was bad enough then, underground. At covert Sunday school she'd been so traumatised by nuns praying to God to give them a calling that at one point she wailed to Mamcia, *but I don't want to be called!* Later she supposed she'd been aware even at a young age that a life of celibacy was not for her. *Oh, don't you worry,* Mamcia had reassured her, laughing, *I'm pretty sure God's not calling you.* And many years later they had laughed about it repeatedly, trying to imagine Eva in a religious order. But the call to be contemplative had stuck.

In rows of tens and hundreds, and after so much kneading and shaping, the dumplings lie like soldiers awaiting their fate. Their end: the boiling pot. It's almost comical the way they're stacked up, on the kitchen counter, the small table, spilling over next door to the dining table – attack of the dumplings! But like all foot soldiers they're not in control. Mamcia begins dropping them into the bubbling water in batches. They surface in rebellion, only to get scooped into bowls of melted butter and set aside in the larder to cool for frying the next day. The little ears of mushroom dumplings escape cooking for now, left on a floury board to be boiled fresh on the day of eating. The kitchen's cleaned of flour and the next task begins: cooking kasha and whole cabbages for the stuffed cabbage rolls, *gołąbki*.

Gołąbki, in Polish; and in Ukrainian, *holubtsi*. Harry never could quite pronounce the word in Polish, *gołąbki* sounding like 'gowumpki', and she often found English translations too long. So little pigeons or doves, they'll nest in an oven roasting tin. Magda and Mamcia make kasha filling as she pries off softened cabbage leaves in hot water, passing them over to stuff. Now they gossip about politics and health remedies and people in the community, but suddenly there's stomping outside. The day's over: the men are back. They must have come via Piotr's because the children are here too. The whole house is overtaken with noise and the freshness of outside air.

'You go,' Mamcia says. 'We'll finish.'

Wiping her hands on the apron, she lifts it over her head in a final farewell to the kitchen. The men are hanging a new handmade wreath on the door lopsidedly. Harry looks the worse for wear.

'Hallo, love,' he smiles crookedly. 'I didn't quite get to say no as many times as I'd have liked.' He makes a drinking motion.

'Poor thing.' She embraces him. 'Don't worry, tomorrow I'll protect you.'

'You're an angel, guardian angel.' His words not quite slurred but slow.

'I think you'll find you're deceived in that.'

'If so, you're very good at deception,' he smiles.

'Let's not go there,' she smiles.

'Then where? Upstairs? I don't think we'd be missed for half an hour.'

'I can't,' she turns serious. 'I've got to shower quickly and come back to set the table. My job in the family. Anyway it's almost dinner.'

'Good, I'm starving.'

'That'll please Mamcia.'

Harry grimaces, whispers. 'After so much vodka, *kielbasa* and lard sarnies only go so far. Tell you what, they're some champion axers, your dad's lot, especially the deaf one, Stasiek. Split something like ten logs in under a minute.'

'It's the hearty life,' she says, 'not like us pampered English.'

Harry grabs her and pinches her lightly. 'I'll show you who's English.'

She smiles again. 'Okay but later, not now.'

He grins and heads back out to round up the children who've escaped outside again. She hurries upstairs to the bathroom.

Turning on the shower, dropping her clothes on the floor, she steps into the steamy compartment. Hot water, warm house, good food, family – these are the necessary ingredients. So why is so much of life spent pursuing other things? Even Harry, so happy outdoors but mostly trapped inside at work, surely there must be a way back to basics, to remembering that actually hot showers are a luxury for most of the world. She picks up a Dove bar, soap so common now but an unattainable luxury in the past, its creamy texture pure heaven compared with the rough yellowed Soviet slabs. Simple enjoyment, *holubko*, little dove, now so often overrun by what else there is to be had: fancier tiles, fluffier towels, fragranced candles. Money to burn.

Rivulets run down her body, cascading over her breasts like cliffs to her feet below. The water trickles down the drain, the way satisfaction always seems to go, but how to hold on to it? This so-called simple life – is it a matter of finding higher purpose rooted in necessity, rather than self fulfilment in pursuit of luxury? If so, how to explain that to Harry? Because maybe he's part of the problem, even a cause of it, a perceived fall in living standards a reminder to him that if you work hard enough you might have it all back. The Plan, she shudders, turns the water hotter. But being in it together means that if he is compromised, so is she. And if that's the problem to resolve, she'll have to identify exactly what and how. She has so much to be grateful for, that gratitude must underpin any resolve for change. And she must save water for the others. She turns off the taps, takes the towel, dries off briskly.

A knock on the door, she opens it a crack. Harry.

'How about now, sexy?' He tries to step in, gives a light tug at her towel.

'I can't, I've got to get dressed,' she smiles, brushing past him.

'Eva,' Harry says.

'Yes?' she turns around.

'I love you.'

'I love you too,' she pauses. 'And thank you.'

'For what?'

'For my whole life,' she grins.

He smiles, takes a step towards her, but she waves no. She has these other urgent responsibilities.

But shutting the bedroom door, she wonders if these things really are more urgent. Too late to change the moment, the floorboards creaking outside the door mean he's heading to shower. She puts her ear to the door. But it's only enough time to hear him sigh and turn the lock, the release of a not so small groan of regret.

∞

Christmas Eve, Holy Night. *Wigilia* in Polish, *Svyat Vechir* in Baba's Ukrainian. What everyone's waited for: Piotr and Danka and their three children, Bogdan, Marek and Mila, plus Magda and Mamcia and Tato, she counts out the settings, and her family of four make twelve. Like the meal itself, twelve courses to symbolise Christ's apostles, the meal meatless to pay homage to the poverty of the Holy Family. No need for sharp knives, she sets out the cutlery, remembering the correct order from England, where she also first met people who actually chose to be vegetarian. It had been shocking to learn that not everywhere was a lack of meat considered making do. Even if it wasn't your tradition, like Hindus, you could abstain from meat permanently as a supposedly healthier or higher way of being, a kind of forever fast. But she'd wondered straightaway what the gain was in giving things up forever. Because wasn't the benefit of giving up in feeling that sacrifice more poignantly? How poignant could something be if you made it a normal way of life? Actually, far too many people held themselves in high regard for such permanent sacrifices, but that wasn't at all the point of giving something up. It was supposed to make you a more thankful and humble person.

Humility and gratitude, two more abstracts that were fleeting but still worth pursuing – not least because so much else was suspect in today's cynical world. Tonight, whatever humbleness comes to be shown, there will certainly be no making do. Four days of preparation for this feast, permutations of potatoes and cabbage, mushrooms and dough, enough for a whole village. She sets the obligatory extra place for any luckless traveller who might come knocking on the door, because this symbolism is important too, that no one in need be forsaken on Christmas Eve. A day's fast followed by a feast, a dinner party reliving the story of Christ's humble birth. She puts the finishing touches on the table, goes upstairs.

Harry's lounging on the bed, rifling through his blackberry.

'Working? But it's Christmas Eve.' She checks her irritation with a half-hearted smile.

'I'm catching up on old emails,' he says, not looking up. 'Nothing important.'

Her smile disappears. If it's not important why bother?

He continues, still looking down. 'A couple of people chasing me up, stuff like that.' He taps away another minute, looks up. 'Something wrong?'

'What?'

'Eva, is there something bothering you? Sometimes you seem happy, other times you're preoccupied by something. You give me a look, reticent, holding back. Don't.'

'It,' she pauses, wondering if this is really the time. Maybe her problem isn't choosing words but timing. Then again you never know what the best time is.

'Harry, I don't know how to put it. How to order it,' she pauses. 'It's a bit of everything, I suppose – you being away, me questioning life at home,' she stops again, searches for the right words. 'I do feel trapped there sometimes – not because it's a prison, too sparse; but the opposite, too much. Here there's this simplicity, and I want to have that in my life, with you and the children. Only I can't seem to recreate it.'

'Eva, love, life here *is* simpler. Look around – you don't see Piotr working twelve hour days or Danka racing to activities, kids off to organised football, swimming as soon as they can walk. They go to school and that's it. We're lucky to have such opportunities, but it's harder, no question, on all of us.'

'Yes, but that's only part of it.'

'What do you mean?'

'I mean, what are we pursuing these opportunities for? You work more hours, we have these goals, but for what? Just to buy more stuff? A bigger house? Better holidays? Isn't that pointless, when we're not even together most of the time?'

'So that's what this is about,' he says, his arms visibly tightening.

'No, Harry, I'm not picking on you or the Plan, so don't start. You asked the question and I'm answering. Or rather, I'm asking some questions back.'

'But it boils down to you being dissatisfied, doesn't it. You want to live well, but you don't want to make any sacrifices to it.'

'That's not it.' But it's hard to counter that statement, even if it's not true. 'It's just – maybe we don't need all the things we think we need.'

Harry leans back on the pillow and puts his arms behind his head, adopting his most assured posture, the one that signals he can now repel any attack, wait out any long siege.

'Okay,' he says, calmly but through gritted teeth. 'What shall we give up then? The house, the car? The kids' futures at private schools? The ski holiday in February? How about champagne at New Year's?'

He's moved from defence to open attack, tactics she's seen before. Opponents tend not to last and it's a warning sign: she better wrap up.

'Never mind.'

'No, you said it. You said we don't need all these things, so fine, how do you want to live?'

'Harry, please don't. I don't know.'

'No, you don't. You haven't thought it through. Talking in generalities is easy, try providing the particulars. You have no idea of the hours I'm putting in to secure our future. You think this separation is easy on me? I'm the one who's alone most of the time, at least you have the kids for company. So don't lecture me on giving up stuff. I'm giving up plenty already.'

'Harry, but that's just it, we don't *have* to do this.' She's aware she's pleading, but also losing the argument, the threads she meant to weave into the conversation.

'Yes, Eva, we do,' he rebuts. 'You don't pay attention to the finances, so you don't know. Maybe we can make it simpler, but we don't live in a hut in rural Africa, and even there, the issue of money won't go away,' his voice goes hoarse. 'Because the issue of money never goes away – not if you want the freedom to choose your life.'

She remains silent.

'You know after Mummy and Daddy died we tried to keep Cranfield going for a lot longer than was feasible. That was *my* money going to keep mostly Tilly's dreams alive. You know that when we sold it there were major debts. I started late at the firm. Even on my salary I haven't managed to save what others have. This is our big chance. To pocket something that will make a difference to us, our future. I want us to have a good life, Eva, a good life.' At this, he stops and takes a deep breath, sits up.

'Believe me, Eva, Poland is changing too. People here are working harder to have the same as their parents. They see what the world has to offer and they want a piece of it. They have aspirations too – maybe not everyone in *this* house – but plenty of Poles up in Warsaw hustling to get exactly the same kind of things we want, holidays by the sea, things even their parents once had, the simple life as you put it, but which now, costs more for the average person. Want a vacation at a Black Sea resort now? It costs money. And as the market economy here asserts itself completely, even in Przemyśl people will find themselves with less time. Don't forget, this is a holiday you're on, Eva, it doesn't represent life here normally. Or what it will be like in the future.'

Now it's her turn to take a deep breath. Because he's overstepped the mark, commenting on her family, this house. He has no idea what it was like, teenage years under the Soviets, nothing available, only ridiculous queues. Tato leaving at critical moments, driving three days to find shingles for their roof, he and Mamcia alternating nights in the car in minus ten, freezing so they wouldn't lose their place in line for a refrigerator. Then driving to Ukraine for linens – hours, days, all the way back via Hungary to sell them, to make a tiny profit and buy white goods to sell back in Poland, all this trading illegal, and if you were caught you were in big trouble. On top of that, being silenced for your views, her whole extended family, a history of big and small persecutions, toiling in bitter cold and hot sun, in war and peace, people sent away. Meanwhile in post war Britain Harry's memories were of grandparents complaining about butter rations, but post war in this part of the world meant enduring rape, mutilation, killing. Ukrainian partisans, Polish patriots, German sympathisers, the damned Russians and their Red Army. Then the poisonous peace, that Soviet 'order' ushered in by Potsdam:

more deportations, brutality, enslavement, and after that – gulags, camps, and more massacres – *peace* time that was, until the norm was reached and careers and lives could still be shattered by the slightest wrong word. Tato's chances dashed when he wouldn't calibrate his physics to communism, so his destiny – chosen by the state, all the way from Moscow via Warsaw, of course – rural schoolteacher. And just when they'd finally saved a few roubles, the thundering crash of communism itself. Everything breaking apart. She too finishing university to find all she'd been taught had been for nothing – go ahead, start again. *Linguist, economist? Ha, sell yourself to some foreigner at a hotel. Philosopher? Go dance.* The chaos, the struggle, even now, Piotr and Magda helping Mamcia and Tato because their pensions evaporated when the system collapsed. That was it: a whole lifetime of hard work and savings, gone. And she'd never asked him for help – not once – not that they'd have taken Harry's money anyway. He'd only ever seen the tip of the fucking iceberg, and retrospectively. Meanwhile those old Holdens of generations past, everything always in excess of what they needed, even now – new Holdens with money, house, car, holidays – didn't he see? Yes, they needed money, like anyone and everyone, a universal need. But she also wanted to live free after all her family had endured. To be free of the stranglehold of money. To be okay. But he'd never see it that way, maybe he didn't think it possible. So there it was: nothing to say.

'Eva,' Harry says softly. 'Don't be cross with me. Maybe I haven't got it all right. Maybe I don't understand exactly how you feel. But I'm not the enemy. We're in this together. Remember I said, it'll be tough, but *you* said we'd see the Plan through. Now here we are – this is the tough bit. The middle of the journey. The bit where we're all wondering why we're bothering. But we're half-way through, and if you stick with it, I promise there's a happy ending.'

He stands up now, puts his hands on her hips, drawing her closer.

'I'm getting old too. Old for making partner, old for everything it seems. If I'd started earlier…' he breaks off, his face saddened, weary. 'This is my last chance, Eva. Please, stay with me.'

And it's the way he says *please, stay with me*, not stay the course, or be tough, or agree with me about money or anything else, but *stay with me*, quietly, softly, that makes the anger in her dissipate. She falls into his body, putting her head on his shoulder, wanting to comfort him but be comforted too.

'But it's all so difficult.' Her eyes are closed, even to herself she sounds like a petulant child. But how else to sum it up? 'I don't understand what this struggle's for.'

'Eva,' he says, pulling her back, looking into her eyes searchingly. 'When you stop and come out of your hurricanes of activity, you ask yourself the big questions. I'm keeping it simple: matters pertaining to this earth. You're talking about something else entirely. And I'm afraid the answers there, well, philosophers have been agonising over those for thousands of years.'

'Small comfort,' but a smile escapes.

The doorbell rings below: Piotr and Danka and Bogdan and Marek and Mila, arriving for the feast.

'Saved by the bell,' Harry says, and his eyes gleam with such childish enthusiasm and conspiracy that now she too can't help letting out a laugh.

'Come on, Eva, Christmas Eve, we'll talk later. They're waiting. Let's *eat!*'

∞

Tato is *gospodarz*, host of this Holy Night; solemnly he says the prayer of thanksgiving. Then he takes the o*platyk*, the blessed bread cut in small bits and dipped in honey, and moves around the table offering a piece to each guest, making a special wish and exchanging a personal greeting and kiss.

As he approaches her, he says, 'And to you, Eva, who are always welcome.'

'*Christos razdayetsa.*' Christ is born. He says it to her in Baba's language.

A standard greeting, but if you think about it, yes, a child is born. And what is Christmas really but another family day? A day when a baby came to save the world. Coming despite the world's misery or because of it, to save every person from sin. So the story goes. A good concept even if it didn't happen the way they say, because he lived, died and rose from death, for the idea that mattered – not the action, but the principle of the thing – to save people from the very selfish hubris and greed that so encumbers them. For whom more than her and Harry? Isn't salvation most needed when you're so lost you don't know what to believe?

But the thought is lost in greetings and well wishes volleyed around the table, the fray of sitting down and serving up, engraved glasses clinking against dishes, people talking while charging into the first of many fish dishes before them: herrings in vinegar or sour cream, cold mackerel pates, smoked mackerels whole, their desiccated eyes no longer gleaming, and of course, the Scottish salmon she brought, which now looks unnaturally orange on the table. There's a whole carp poached and carp in aspic too, studied by Christophe and Katya and Harry, with looks that say, *avoid*.

'What you no *like* jelly?' Piotr tries his English with Harry. He pokes the aspic on his plate with a fork, makes it wobble. 'You no like?'

'Well,' Harry begins diplomatically. 'Tell him, Eva, I've nothing against aspic, though I can't say I prefer it either, but really I'm afraid of the sheer number of courses following. So I'm saving myself for this delicious little herring right here, and all the rest that comes after.'

She translates, and Piotr smiles and nods, 'But is good with vodka!'

As if on cue, Tato rises solemnly, holds his shot glass in the air. 'Now I make the first toast – to all the family gathered. Even family from afar,' he looks at her and Harry, 'because if the Holy Family can travel on such a night, so can this one, to be here for such a night. And so may it please God, this togetherness.'

She translates quickly for Harry.

'Comprehensive,' he remarks.

'Get ready with yours, no man escapes a turn.'

He groans. Toast-making for him seems a competitive Polish sport, one he can't win unless he resorts to a good joke.

'Okay, how about this: do you know what they call carp in Romania?'

She shakes her head no, mouth full.

'Crap.'

She laughs, almost spits out her fish. He might be right but he can't use it, no one will understand the play on words, and carp is serious business in Poland. Everyone's merry anyway, eating and drinking in earnest, Piotr telling his own jokes over the clanking of cutlery and plates, and soon the first course is finished, or maybe the second or third, depending on how many fishes you attempt. But the counting's lost in the eating, in the living, because what's the point of counting down anyway, it only brings you closer to the end. A meal is something to be savoured.

Danka and Bogdan rise to collect plates and replace them with bowls, while out of the kitchen comes Mamcia, smiling broadly as she carries the pot of mushroom soup, hurrying out and back again with the pot of *borscht,* followed by Mila with a steaming bowl of *ushka.* Christophe looks terrified, grabs his ears.

'What's wrong?' Harry asks.

'I don't want people eating little ears!' Christophe says, eyes wide.

'Krzysztof! Not real ears. *Ushka* for the soup, look!' She points to the mushroom dumplings, Christophe looking sheepish, grinning. 'See, the dough's only been pinched to look like little ears!' She pinches his.

'Tortellini!' Katya says.

'What did she say, torte-who?' Danka says.

'Tortellini, those Italian parcels that come dry in packets, insides taste like sawdust,' Piotr replies.

'You're not supposed to eat them dry,' Danka retorts. 'Anyway, they must make them fresh, over there in Italy. Every culture makes dumplings, even the Chinese.'

'Did you know there's Chinese food in the shops these days?' Tato chimes in. 'Though what you do with it, god only knows.'

'They say they eat cats,' Mamcia says.

'Oh yes, and dogs too and sometimes small children, they breed them specially,' Piotr smiles, giving away his joke, mainly so Christophe won't be frightened.

But the Chinese are forgotten as slurping takes over, though she'd like to point out another thing she learned in England – slurping is good manners when you eat Chinese food. Thanks to it, the red *borscht* has already made a blotty imprint on Katya's dress. She dabs it with a napkin, too late, the children are escaping the table for a break to ogle presents under the tree. Mamcia calls everyone back for the double hit of *pierogies* and *gołąbki*, with the kind of glee that only comes from being in one's element. She serves out the dumplings and rolled cabbages, pointing to the hot mushroom sauce to ladle over, then hurries back to the kitchen to fetch another batch.

Harry's turn to make a toast, he waits for Mamcia, then stands.

'I'm indebted to my beautiful translator,' he looks at her, then Mamcia, 'and Polish hospitality, of course, which knows no equal, not so far as I am concerned. Though I am getting a bit concerned for my waistline. Maybe a few more walks in the wood with Tato might help. But maybe not, if there's so much *shmaletz*,' he smiles, raises his glass. 'But I would like to thank this house, this family, for welcoming me, my family. We are one.' He looks around sheepishly, as if momentarily not quite believing himself: posh-boy-turns-Polish. But Tato's pleased and Harry looks grateful, so she is too. He might not get everything right, Harry, but he does do his best.

She takes a sip of sweet white wine, while Harry's well into his vodka, as is Piotr, the conversations crossing, getting louder. The Polish are trying English and the English giving Polish a go: Pinglish and Ponglish. She can't help smiling.

'Well, I never saw such slow eating,' Mamcia declares, replacing the potato-filled *pierogies* with the cabbage-filled variety.

Harry's plate is still encumbered with a vast quantity from the previous course. He appears to have abandoned the challenge to finish it. Piotr stands. Time for the third toast, always for the ladies. All the men join him standing.

'So this then is for the women in our lives,' he looks around with a grin at Danka, 'without whom we cannot live, though certainly we can't live with them either. So fussy, always making us do things we don't want,' he cringes as she slaps him on the thigh. 'But then they make the world a better place, and where would our socks be without them? Probably still in the laundry, or wandering around the house lonely, looking for their pairs. And they cook and they clean and work hard all day, at home or in office,' he says, nodding to Magda, 'then what do we do? We leave our socks on the floor for them to trip over. But we do respect them, the women of our lives, for they are the beauty and the light. May life bring them happiness and may we show them deference going forward, never forgetting that without them, we are nothing.'

'Hey, hey!' Tato and Harry reply, sitting down, as a small voice says in fragmented Polish, 'But I won't leave my socks around! I promise.'

She gives Christophe a squeeze.

'I don't know what life will bring,' Mamcia retorts, 'but if Jura stops throwing his socks about, I'll have to go out and get a job.' She bustles back into the kitchen gleefully, returning with more *gołąbki*.

Harry lets out an audible groan but Piotr rubs his stomach and looks over challengingly, 'My favourite!' Then taking a large spoon, with a devilish grin, he first serves Harry.

'One's enough, it mustn't go to waste,' Harry protests.

'You mean to waist,' she says, pinching him at the side.

'Exactly,' he says, 'Honestly, I don't know how you people manage it.'

'Genetic.'

But she too is taking what must be her last bite of dinner, stomach full to bursting like it only can be on Christmas Eve. The children really can't eat any more either, and after salutary mouthfuls they head to mill about the presents again. Mamcia calls them back however because it's time for the all-important *kutya*, the dessert of cooked wheat berries, honey and ground poppy seed. It's stodgy and more a porridge than a dessert, but of all the dishes, it is the most symbolic – prosperity and health for the New Year – and therefore, the most critical. Even if you don't taste any baked desserts or drink compote, the *kutya* you must eat.

'All this eating, Mama, when are people going to stop?' Katya whispers across Christophe.

'I don't know,' Harry says, 'four hours and still going, it can hardly go on forever. Look, it's past ten o'clock already, aren't you tired?'

'No! I'm waiting for presents!'

She shushes Katya. 'Let's wait for everyone.'

But no one really wants to eat anything, so Mamcia goes off to fetch chocolates and coffee. Tato hums carols as he pulls out his Hennessey again. This is a special night and usual rules don't apply.

Unable to contain themselves, the children dig in by the *yalinka,* as even Katya and Christophe have finally taken to calling the Christmas tree. Suddenly it erupts: order to chaos. The attentive opening of presents one-by-one unravels into an all-out paper tear. She stands in the doorway, observing the scene with Tato. He sets down his glass, takes something out of his pocket, holds it out to her.

'I know as adults we don't give presents, but this is something I found for you.'

She takes the little inlaid wooden box, hesitating.

'I didn't say I bought it,' he says. 'I found it.'

She opens it readily, a rosy golden cross. Her eyes widen.

'Yes, Baba Kasia's.'

'But where did you find it?'

'Well, you know Baba was supposed to have been buried with her cross, and when she died we put it in this case for safekeeping. I thought I'd left it in the top drawer of my armoire but on the day of the burial we couldn't find it, it had disappeared. So I put in my cross for hers. For years we wondered what happened, then just after you rang in November and said you were coming for Christmas, I found it. In the basement, behind the curtains, of all things,' he grins. 'It was a sign, coming out from hiding, after your call. I think it was meant for you.'

Baba Kasia's cross. The one Baba always wore, a little Eva fingering it when she sat on her lap, leaning in to hear stories.

'But won't Magda mind?' It comes out suddenly. Any potential jealousy would ruin this gift. She never did want to compete with Magda.

'Magda? No, she was here at the time of the funeral, chose a favourite brooch when we got rid of some of Baba's things. There wasn't much, you know, and Mamcia kept what was of value for granddaughters: a wedding band, a set of earrings. That was what Baba Kasia wanted – to leave something to Magda and Mila and you. Of course, she never met her granddaughter, little Kasia, but when she gets bigger, you can pass her this cross. That is the way it should go. I thought you might like to have it now. I noticed you don't have a cross of your own, any more.'

She winces. Of course she hasn't worn a cross in years. But who would've thought anyone would notice? A cross of her own. The image of the imposing cross on the hill, the crosses people must bear. Is wearing one literally supposed to be a burden or a relief?

Tato eyes her. 'You do want it, don't you?'

'Want it? Tato, I couldn't think of anything I could want or need more.'

And once she says it, it's another release, a burden offloaded. She throws her hands around Tato's neck, the first time in years, embracing him like a small child. Her father holds her gingerly, as if he's afraid he might break her, as if the moment might be severed if he moves too quickly.

'You do miss Baba Kasia, don't you,' he says gently.

'How could I not? I lived with her in that room a very long time. I didn't mean to miss her funeral, honestly. That Christmas, I know how hard it was for all of you, but I was,' she pauses, 'very ill too.' She pulls away, wipes a stray tear, finds herself backing into the kitchen. Tato follows.

'We know, it was years ago, Magda told us.'

'Magda? But I didn't tell Magda anything.'

'No, but she understands more than you think. You've never given her much credit for that.'

She stands very still. Surely Magda didn't know about the pregnancy, the abortion, the depression?

'Eva, we didn't know what your illness was,' Tato continues calmly, 'we still don't. We could only assume it was very serious if you couldn't come back. No one's asking for explanations, for you to relive those times. It's in the past. Baba's buried. But maybe sometime you could go to her grave and visit her,' and almost as an afterthought, 'you know, talk to God there.'

She squeezes the box. So this is what he wants. What he hopes. Though it may not be so much about God as that he simply hopes she'll find her way. Maybe they are linked. She looks at the cross again. Handing the box to Tato to hold, she pulls the necklace around her neck. Wearing this cross is something she can do, for him. For herself. Actually, it's the least she can do.

∞

Silence. Being the only one awake, a vast freedom. Although without Mamcia around shooing people away, the kitchen also feels doubly deserted. Two sides of a coin: solitude and loneliness. She puts the kettle on as a comfort. Tato's present to Mamcia, this electric kettle, because he too decided it was time to update from old-fashioned boiling on the stove. Time to make life easier.

Maybe Harry was right: no virtue in doing things the hard way, suffering if you didn't have to. Mamcia and Tato, getting on in years, someday they'd both be too tired for Midnight Mass. Then who will do the shooing into cars? The complex allocation of places, supervising the mad dash and grab for scarves for a few minutes contact with the cold? Even Harry barely made it through *pasterka*, the vodka got to him. He said he'd wait up, but for sure he's now asleep.

She makes tea and sips it – nettle, to soothe. The *pasterka* service, and Christmas, almost over for another year – well, if you were Polish – Ukrainians would still celebrate on January 6th. Their St John's was shuttered tonight as they drove past, the family as always heading to the other John. Until Baba died, they always celebrated twice though, this evening being the first, and now more like a second childhood, the awe of glitz and finery and furs, as extended families pushed into church where it was stuffy and hot and you couldn't hear a thing from the priest for all the chatter and giggling. Then back on the streets, carolling all across Przemyśl and Poland probably, everyone wishing for the merriment to go on forever. Euphoria, celebration, superstition, religion, all acting to the same effect: humanity feeling at one.

Now being alone, and everything wearing off. Everything over save one thing: stockings. She takes the socks snuck from the children's room and roots around in the cupboard for the bag of sweets left by Piotr. She overheard the children arguing – Christophe disappointed because Father Christmas only came in England and they'd already missed Polish St Nicholas Day. She confided in Piotr, helpless to find a solution, but as always Piotr found a middle ground. He concocted this story: *well, this Father Christmas of yours, you know, he often telephones St Nicholas, to see how things are going around the holidays, catch up on world events and the like, but especially in complicated cases like yours, children travelling all over the place and it being hard to catch them. But if you pray* – and then he winked at them – *Father Christmas might meet with St Nicholas and pass on his loot, and St Nick might make a very extra special visit to your socks in the morning.*

She'd stifled a laugh, watching Christophe, wide-eyed, serious, but Katya said, *no, it's not possible. Mama said they're the same spirit. How can Father Christmas and St Nicholas meet up if they're one person?* Logically impossible, even for a child. Already seeped in the rationality of the world.

So she'd stepped in quickly: *well, the spirit of Christmas breaks into different spirits, Katya, that's how it can meet up, like the snowmen who meet at the North Pole with that English boy who flies through the air. All the snow comes apart, then together in the form of snowmen, then melts again to water, which can freeze again, different forms of the same thing.* Infinity divided, reconstituted, whole again, and they had talked about where the spirit might come from, and Piotr assured them it was all a great mystery, like God or Trinity, or love itself, you just had to believe.

Yes, you just have to believe. Just believe, if you want to. That's all there is to believing. Tato was right to begin with. You do, or you don't.

Slowly she fills up one sock, then the other. Lovely and simple, this tradition of fooling children, truth bent to a greater cause. Then children grow up and fool their own children but no one's offended by the lie, these games of pretend, because the beauty of believing in something good can be its own reward. Participating in something more mysterious and powerful than oneself makes you one with the mystery of life. That's what she must take back with her somehow, guard as her new armour: compassion, gratitude, humility, faith. And not faith in religious stories, but faith she can do more. She mustn't give up trying to make a better life for herself, for them, for Harry too. There's time yet to make him see it – that there is time yet for a simple life. But you have to believe in it first. You have to become what you seek.

And she must lead the way – slow down, let it come, be ready to give up to this life force all it asks. Renege on one's own desires, stop being wilful, stop running away.

She takes a final sip, savouring the silence. Tossing in a few last sweets, she lifts the stockings. Yes, how great even the smallest gifts.

And there is no greater peace than this: the quiet after a long meal, the memory of hushed voices in another room, the breaths of loved ones sleeping nearby. No need to make complicated what is essentially simple: that we have but this one life to live.

∞

'He came, he came! Mama, Mama, Daddy! He came!'

Christophe and Katya run in, jump on the bed.

'What?' She's only half-conscious.

'Mama, he came!'

'Who?'

'Father Nicholas!'

'Father Nicholas?' Groggy, she struggles to remember a priest by that name.

'No, *Saint* Nicholas, silly,' Katya corrects Christophe. '*Father* Christmas.'

'Oh,' says Christophe shrugging, gleeful. 'Mama, Daddy, I got soooooooooo many sweeties!'

Harry barely looks up. 'Really? Let me see.'

Christophe proudly displays his wares, tipping his sock on the bed.

'Wow, look at that. You must have been very good,' Harry opens one eye, shuts it again.

'Yes,' says Katya. 'We've been treble good. See, we got three of these and three of these!' She and Christophe begin counting their loot.

'Can I trade you for those?' Katya grabs one of Christophe's sweets and hands him one of hers. 'You can have this one instead.'

'Hey, that's mine!' Christophe complains.

So much for peace and goodwill towards men. And so much for complicated explanations. Father Nicholas indeed.

'Hey, Katya, not fair!' Christophe squeals.

'Katya, give it back,' she intercedes. 'If you want to trade, you have to ask. If he says yes, he gets to pick one of yours. You don't force it on him.'

Christmas Day, and the first thing you get is a squabble.

'Aw, but he got all the good ones.'

'You don't know what's inside the wrappers. You have to investigate, Katya, there are undoubtedly good things in your pile too. But not all at once and not before breakfast, you'll give yourselves sick tummies.'

'For chrissakes, Eva, it's Christmas morning,' Harry mumbles, 'let them have a sweet.'

She looks at him, ready to be cross but relents. 'Okay, if Daddy says it's okay.'

'Hurray!' They start analysing their stockpiles, deciding which to eat first.

Harry turns, puts his arm around her. 'More church and food today?'

His arm is warm, comforting. She smiles.

'Well, don't make it sound so horrible, that's the whole point of Christmas. But it won't be as sedentary; we've got to go visiting. Friends will come by here, and,' she pokes him in the ribs, 'there will be meat!'

'Oh good,' says Harry, smiling, 'I was missing that yesterday. Absolutely starving!'

For a moment, the contrast comes to mind. Christmas Day in England, people at home padding around in pyjamas, presents under trees, breakfast, maybe church, a big roast with family who will come if they're invited. Then after feasting, games and television, hours of old films, children on computers, and somewhere the Queen. Whereas here, it's the second day, sleeping only as late as church allows, and afterwards guests and carollers and revellers will stream from house to house, neighbours to neighbours, family to family, even strangers tagging along sometimes, as hams are cooked and sausages and pates and roasts set out, no such thing as stress. Plans made, plans altered, invitations might be issued even at church. The next day too: more services, celebrations, the spiritual intertwined with the familial. A joy and simplicity in a lot of hard work and tradition, not getting off as easy as you can.

'Come on,' she says, nudging Harry, who's dozing off again. 'We have to get up.'

He groans, turns over, finally opens both eyes.

'Happy Christmas,' she kisses him.

'Happy Christmas, love.'

'Mama, do we get more presents today?' Christophe stuffs his sweets back into his sock.

'More?' she interjects. 'We got so many last night.' She fingers the cross around her neck. 'And you have all this.' Piotr added trinkets to the candy.

'Oh,' says Christophe, slightly disappointed.

'Well, maybe not all,' Harry interjects.

'What do you mean?' she turns to him.

'I might have a small surprise,' he says playfully, pausing.

'Hurray, Daddy!' Katya wraps her arms around him.

'What?' She's as impatient as the children.

'With all my working away I've had hardly any time off, as you know,' he casts her a glance. 'But I calculated and figured I'm owed some days, so,' he pauses dramatically, 'I've extended my holiday and we're going to have another week together. We'll all drive to Krakow together with Magda. I'm not going back to work tomorrow, I'm coming with you.'

'Hurray!' Katya shouts again.

'And I've planned something special for New Year's Eve,' he adds, looking pleased.

'What's New Years?' asks Christophe.

'New Years?'

Momentarily Harry's taken aback. He's not used to children's questions, so basic they're difficult to answer.

'New Year's is the evening,' he says, thinking as he goes along, 'when the old year goes out and the new one comes in.'

'But how? How does it come in?' Christophe perseveres.

'It just does,' he says.

'One day,' she intervenes, 'it's the old year, the last day of December. But the very next day, because it's the first of January, a whole new year begins. It's how we measure time.'

'Oh,' says Christophe disappointed.

'Why, what's wrong with that?'

'But what if we like the old year? What if we want things to stay the way they are?'

She laughs. 'You can keep as much good from the old year as you like, but you can also try new things in the new year. You can make changes for the better.'

'Like not throwing my socks on the floor,' Christophe says. 'You'd be happy for that.'

'Yes, I certainly would, it was a good promise.'

'Or me letting Christophe play with my toys,' Katya adds.

'Yes, things like that,' she says. Or Daddy coming home once and for all, but she doesn't say it.

'Enough resolutions,' Harry says. 'Doesn't anyone want to know what we're going to do?'

'Yes!' they all chime in unison.

'Okay, listen,' he holds his breath for effect. 'I've planned for us to stay in a super nice hotel in Krakow where Mama can have some proper champagne and a bubble bath and dinner and maybe even a dance on New Year's Eve. Because she's such a good dancer.' He casts a knowing look.

She smiles back sarcastically, the children clamouring on top them again now.

LESIA DARIA

'Hurray, I love to dance,' says Christophe, hovering over them, wiggling his bottom.

'Oh no, *you* won't be going dancing, it's late at night, for adults,' Harry says, toppling him.

'What about us?' Katya moans.

'We'll have a special New Year's dinner together in a very special place,' Harry says it carefully, in a way that means he hasn't quite worked out the plan, 'then you'll get to stay up late and watch a film.'

'Ooooh! What film?'

'I don't know, we'll see what the hotel has,' Harry says.

'Cartoons!' says Katya. 'Hey, Christophe, let's see *Ice Age* again. We should get Pookie and Snowy.'

'Yeah,' Christophe says, and they scamper off to fetch their animals from the other room.

Harry turns towards her, registers puzzlement. 'What is it?'

'I was just wondering if you checked this out with Magda.'

'Of course, it's fine. One space in the car if you let me squeeze in.' Under the covers he gives her a pinch. 'And I checked with your father too. Because we'll all need to leave a day earlier than planned. But that's fine with Magda, she's keen to get back anyway.'

Taking it all in, the change of plan, Harry and her in Krakow. He's been there for work many times, was to have come for New Year's Eve anyway. But now they'll have more days together. The gift of time. In a city of many memories already. But hopefully Harry's presence will be palliative, a way of putting a new stamp on it.

'Look,' Harry continues, 'I do have business to attend to, I confess to that. But not until after you're scheduled to fly out on the third of January. That's what spurred me to think, why not extend my hotel reservations a couple days earlier and make a really grand New Year's? Seemed better than my returning to

256

Warsaw for a couple days work, then turning up last minute at your sister's.'

'Yes, no, I mean, you're right, it is a better plan. I had visions of sitting in Magda's kitchen drinking bad brandy. Though I'm slightly worried about her, what will she do?'

'She's a big girl. I think she can figure it out. Anyway, I think she's got other plans.'

'Plans?'

'I don't know what they are, but she seemed relieved when I mentioned the hotel. I was being careful, didn't want to insult her, about not staying at her place, though we all know there's no room for five of us in her flat. But it seems she has a meeting with someone who might be special. Well, that's how it sounded to me. She said she had an invitation she could now take up.'

She sits on the bed, perplexed. Harry's Polish must have gotten far better than he's let on if he's managed to negotiate all this with Magda. But why didn't Magda mention it? It's what she always feared, being in the way, people bending over backwards to accommodate. Why didn't Magda say so?

Probably because you didn't ask.

And the thought once it comes, seems so obvious, it's embarrassing. She hasn't been thinking of Magda at all, only herself. If there's a chance, she should put that right.

∞

Emotional goodbyes and the journey begins: the serpentine road swallowing them up and spitting them out westward, out on to the E-40 and the seven hour drive across this one small section of the great landmass of Europe. Christophe and Katya are full of unspent energy, but Harry dozes most of the way. She, cramped and stiff and feeling like something's coming over her, watches the road rolling up and down again. Poor Magda, less a chauffeur than a voyeur into the lives of the Holdens, forced to catch snatches of unintelligible family chatter. But finally with a smile signalling relief, she drops them at the hotel and drives off into the night.

Cumulative exhaustion now comes in waves.

'I'll just have some tea,' she tells the waiter. '*Mieta.*'

'I'll take peppermint too,' Harry adds in Polish, not thinking twice.

For a while they sit in silence, then Harry speaks.

'Whew, holidays are exhausting. I don't know how your family managed in that house, all those years on top of one another.'

'Just the way it was, I guess,' her sigh turns into a yawn. 'The house was smaller to begin with. Baba and I were in one room, Magda and Piotr in another, Mama and Tato in theirs. They put me in with Baba when I was born and by the time Piotr was born, I didn't want to switch.'

For a moment she considers Baba, her cross, then resumes.

'Anyway the kitchen obviously has never fit anyone but Mamcia, maybe me and Magda if we're virtually standing still. The dining/sitting room, plus basement for storage – normal – actually, better than most.'

Harry thinks about it for a minute, shakes his head. 'And to think, all that time, Tilly and I were at Cranfield Manor, ten bedrooms, most of them hardly used.'

'That makes Corner House a happy middle ground,' she says brightly. 'I'm looking forward to going home, but I wish you were coming too.'

'Me too,' he says, reaching over to squeeze her hand. 'But you'll see, from now on, the time will go fast. I'll try to come in January, and for February, I've got some ideas for skiing. March we'll worry about later.' He drifts into thought as the waiter brings their teas.

'I promised Tato I'd be back this spring, the kids have two weeks off at Easter. Though it's so early this year, beginning of April, the ground will hardly be soft enough for planting.'

'Planting what?' Harry says distractedly.

'Flowers, I'm going to fix up Baba's grave. You do that, before Easter, the Sunday before. It's tradition. But snow usually hasn't melted by the end of March, so I'm not sure how much we might get done. Maybe I should go in May.'

'Yes, yes,' he says, sipping his tea but already thinking of something else.

'But in April, you'll be coming home too. I mean finally.'

'What? Too early to say. So many factors.'

'You said April, though.'

'I know what I said,' he replies firmly, 'but I don't control my schedule. We'll see closer to the time. It depends what they have for me back in London, and other things.' But he doesn't say what those things are.

She takes another sip of her tea. 'Harry, I'm so tired I might fall asleep here. Can we go up?'

'Go on. I'll finish mine and settle the bill. I'll be up in a few minutes.'

She heads to the room, slow in her usual fast routine of brushing teeth and washing face, feeling quite chilled as the water touches her skin. She checks on the kids, but Harry's taking too long. He doesn't come up in few minutes, or even fifteen, so she turns off the lights, climbs into bed. Nice to be able stretch out, one of the really good things about hotels, luxuriating in soft clean sheets, the freshly laundered smell and fluffy pillows, things you never seem to manage at home to the same effect. Moving arms and legs in the shape of a snow angel, rubbing the mattress to warm it slightly, she curls into a ball. Normally it's impossible to fall asleep knowing Harry might climb in at any moment, but the weariness from the journey takes over. Anyway in darkness you get tired of waiting. Fatigue, new aches, last conscious thoughts drift away, she lets them go, falls into dreams.

At first it's all quite clear: one of the St John's. But the church keeps changing congregations and priests, one minute singing in Ukrainian, the next saying Mass in Polish. It's unsettling but seemingly only for her, because everyone else is adapting to the flow of events. But nothing's being said or sung in order; they're making pretence of the whole show. She tries to tell the babushka next to her, something's not right, but a woman says, *oh look, look how small the baby is.* Craning her head to look, panic overtakes: it's her baby! A cold sweat breaks out, she can feel it, but she can't get to the baby, the aisles are blocked, the priest is intoning, and though the child's alive, it's a funeral service. *Vichnaya Pamyat,* they're singing, *Eternal Memory.* She tries to shout *no, stop! It's still alive, you can't bury it, I'll look after it,* but the coffin's making its way to the front, over the heads of the people, like some lead singer of a rock band who's dropped back into the crowd in the shape of a cross, trusting to be lifted up by the hands of a mindless audience. Those people will hand him back to the stage, but no one wants to hand back her baby. She's kicking furiously, trying to get to the front, but the *iconostas* is melting, the wall of icons like molten metal, the faces of saints sliding off in horror. They're going to take it through to the hidden altar! The baby's high in the air now, being readied for ritual sacrifice, priests mumbling about the gift of Abraham's only son, she's screaming *stop! stop!* But the pleading is lost to groans, darkness invading the church from open corners, someone pressing her shoulder, as church figures take on shapes of furniture and she hears Harry, *Eva! Eva!* pressing her shoulder until it hurts.

'Eva! You're dreaming!'

'Harry, they're killing the baby.'

'Eva, darling, love,' he's holding her so close she almost can't breathe, 'You're okay, you're here with me. The kids are safe, next door. You were having a nightmare.'

But it doesn't matter if what he's saying is true. It doesn't make any difference – what is reality, this room, the safety of the hotel – you can always be afraid of what's in your mind. Of returning to church, but still failing to save the baby.

'Sorry I was late,' Harry continues, 'I had to check out something for work but then there was a scene at the bar. They threw out some drunk.'

'Oh.' Half perfunctorily, half hoping it might make her forget, 'What?'

'Some guy shouting Eva, Eva,' Harry says. 'It was unnerving because it's your name, though of course, I know it's common.'

He doesn't say it insultingly – it is common in Poland – but a split second later she sits up wide-eyed.

'What did he look like?'

'Who, the guy?' says Harry dismissively. 'I don't know, sort of a big bloke, well, tall, but thin, threatening, goatee, but maybe bald under his skull cap. I don't know how he got into the hotel, he obviously wasn't a guest.'

She sits still, very still, because now there's every reason to be afraid: she's exposed. This place offers no protection. Harry's out of his depth. But the only thing that comes to mind is trying to link it together. How did Adam know where to look?

It could only have been.

Yes, only her.

Magda.

∞

Only one door to the outside corridor. She keeps a vigil for as long as possible. For as long as one can, but the brain gets tired and heavy from such work, sleep eventually takes over. This time she's wrapped in a foetal position, trying to feel the solidity of her body. At first vision is quite hazy, a mixture of clouds and rain and snow, as though she's flying through a thick cover of cumulus, no way to tell up from down. But even in the confusion, there's a greater dread of things lurking beyond the clouds. But then they open, and hey, it's not bad at all! In the distance there's Adam's girl Eva, whom she's never seen, but of course it's her – hey, baby Eva! – she's holding hands with their unnamed baby, they're sisters, obviously, so they're looking after one another, all wispy white. But where's Adam? Something's wrong with that, he must be with his boys below, she must rest, curl up, go back to sleep, because her children are on earth too. That's where she must return.

Waking up, to the dark, to being alone, but why is she alone? It's urgent she see the children though it's not clear why, then she remembers: Harry said if she was still unwell, he'd take them out for the day. It's daytime. She was too ill at breakfast, had to lie down. Harry said, *probably nothing, you were fine yesterday,* and she said, *yes, probably nothing.* But she's been lying for hours, and still not better.

Pulling on socks, she pads to the bathroom, splashes water on her face. The water is ice cold, her face in the mirror bedraggled, full of fear. Dreams are hard to shake even if your reflection assures you it's only a figment of imagination. Yes, the product of an overactive mind. But it's her stomach that responds with a dull ache. She crawls back into bed.

This is it – the last day of the year. A day meant for touring Krakow with Harry and the children, then meeting Magda for coffee, and later an evening of celebration. After which, Harry hinted, a whole weekend of fun, including promised rides on the outskirts of town, with real sleighs pulled by horses. Harry's Plan. But it won't happen, not according to plan, not if she's ill and Adam's on the loose. Adam! Because it must have been him, even with no proof – who needs proof when human intuition is so good? – did Magda lead him to the hotel? How else could he know? Will he return? No, unlikely. They won't let him. Anyway he'll have had plans for New Year's Eve.

The door flings open. Harry, Christophe, Katya – red noses, happy faces.

'Hi,' she projects her voice cheerfully but it comes out weak.

'Oh no! I hoped you would have recovered by now, but you're not looking well at all,' Harry comes to her quickly. 'Have a bath, love, rest a bit more. I can cancel dinner reservations and the babysitter. We don't have to go out.'

He's being caring but she can see he's disappointed too. He wanted this special night, was pleased to have arranged something that would have pleased her.

'Harry, I'm sorry. I still feel cold, achy, I definitely don't want to go out. I don't even want to go downstairs. And I don't want to leave the children.'

'Eva, you don't need worry about that. This is a four star hotel,' Harry says calmly.

Hysteria rising. 'No.'

She can't say, it's not safe, the baby, they were trying to kill it. Or Adam, he's after me, he's crazy. She can't sound unhinged. Harry's rational, must be met on his terms.

'Don't worry,' he says. 'You shouldn't go out anyway if you're not well. It's just a shame,' he pauses, 'our tenth anniversary.'

That can't be. But of course, he's right. He's always right when it comes to numbers. Calculations never off – ten years since the eve of the millennium – the night they met.

'Oh, Harry.'

He sits by her. 'Look, if you can't go through with it, you

can't,' he says reasonably. 'It's only one night. Anywhere I can spend it with you will make me happy.'

He says it as if he means it. She searches his eyes to make sure. But maybe staying in is the worst option? Maybe keeping on the run is the best way to go? Because if you're on the move, you're harder to catch. But then if Harry is here anyway, what can Adam do? The hotel's flagged him as a problem, if in fact it was even Adam, he won't be let back in. But the damage has been done – Adam has altered her life. She's in hiding now, not free to trust anyone, not even Magda. Maybe it is better to run away, quickly, back to England.

Champagne arrives at the door. She's perplexed. Maybe Harry forgot to cancel it. But he tips the bellboy, looking determined to proceed alone. Such a contrast to the night she met him. Veering off Trafalgar Square mistakenly, away from friends into the millennium hordes, suddenly she was lost. Trying to figure out where they might have gone, heading down a side street to look, and implausibly, happening on a bar that wasn't taking reservations. A place that was still open to the night and all its prospects, glorious or seedy. And a man named Harry bought her a drink and calmed her down, said *don't worry, stay.* And the implausibility of meeting anyone on the eve of the millennium itself became part of a fantasy land where establishments greeted swaying revellers with open doors and even if you were lost you could meet a nice man, he'd buy you a drink and look after you and you'd have a sensible conversation. That fact alone had drawn them together. And closer still, when they each revealed some of their ghosts of the past. So impossibility itself created its own momentum, whereby the thing had to be pursued, just to see where an incredible story might lead.

But some dreams were better off ignored. Fanciful hysteria, self-delusion, like what happened with Adam and Xavier – that should have taught her not to cast her line so far into the realm of impossibility. What had any of that given her except the revelation that she would never be a religious Polish wife or an atheistic French one? All she was when she met Harry was a mixed-up person living in London as one century ended and another began. Her prospects not so much limited by this, as this *was* the whole expansive reality ahead. Yes, ten years ago, she had accepted Harry, a life with him, and this blatant, unquestioning acceptance had pushed everything else aside. But of course, pushing things aside doesn't mean they don't come back to haunt you.

These thoughts now seem too weighty for her head, pounding as she draws the bed sheet into a crumpled band around her waist. Nothing makes sense. She feels sick to her stomach. Christophe and Katya are glued to the television, Harry's engrossed in his work. It's her fault their tenth anniversary has come to this. She's been dishonest with him. Though there didn't seem to be an alternative, because what could she tell him? That the drunk was her ex? That she met with Adam two weeks ago and now he's possibly stalking her? Would Harry believe it? Would he laugh, say, preposterous, you don't know it's the same man. Or what are you worried about? Not your problem. Or maybe he'd be angry about their secret meeting. But the meeting wasn't secret, Magda knew, so by association she wasn't hiding anything either. Was she responsible for Adam's subsequent actions? Of course not. But not taking responsibility is also a form of running away.

That thought from nowhere sends her spiralling further into confusion, because Harry's looking at her intently from time to time, as if he's either worried out of his mind or doesn't quite believe the severity of her condition.

'Harry, can you draw the curtains, please? I don't want people looking in off the street.'

He looks up, startled she's spoken.

'We're high up, Eva,' he says quietly. 'A festive scene out there, people milling about, reminds me of our first night, you remember, don't you, streams of people, the cold?' But he draws them shut as she's asked. 'Bed time, kids,' he takes another sip of champagne alone.

Protests from the adjoining room, the film's finished, but they want a story too. Voices jumbling, then Harry's emerging clearly, like he's on a microphone – why is everything so loud? A story she's read many times, about a little Chinese duck named Ping, who lives with his large family on a boat on the Yangtze River. Each day Ping's family disembarks to swim, and on their return, waddling up the plank, the last duck gets a light smack on the bum with a reed. One day Ping is late. He sees the boy on the plank, and he knows he'll be the one spanked, so he hides on the bank in the reeds. The boat departs and Ping is left behind. At first Ping thinks, what fun! But of course life on the outside is no easier. Soon he's captured by another family who wants to eat him for dinner. He spends a day cowering in a cage, making a narrow escape only when that family's boy sets him free. Speeding off, Ping again hides in the reeds, and the next day he hunts for his boat. But of course, by the time he finds it, he's late again. However, this time, as any reader can imagine, Ping takes his punishment, smack, right on the tail feathers! But that's infinitely preferable, is it not, to a far worse fate?

She uncurls and curls back again, shivers taking over. Hearing a story, knowing its ending, something familiar, a form of pleasure, she's read it to them too, the moral similar to other children's stories. But old narratives also give a new feeling sometimes, beyond what's expected, as she explained to the children, who were initially very sympathetic to Ping's fear of bottom-smacking. *Getting eaten is worse than getting beaten,* she said, *it's important to keep things in perspective, not run and hide. You must be brave.* But how often had she taken that advice herself?

Harry returns to their room, shutting the joining door. The kids must be in bed.

'Harry, I'm sorry,' she speaks quickly, before courage fails. 'This is my fault.'

'What is?'

'That our evening's ruined, we didn't go out. The truth is I do have a terrible stomach and headache, I don't feel well at all. But something else is bothering me. I think I know the drunk who was in the bar,' she pauses but not long enough to falter or for him to interject. 'He was my ex, Adam. We met up a few weeks ago, he called Magda and asked about me, and I thought there would be no harm in it. Obviously, he's not in his right mind, he used to be a drunk, I told you about him. He supposedly quit drinking.'

'Wait, wait,' Harry holds up his hand. 'What are you saying to me?'

'Just that,' she says, not looking at him but at the windows, though the curtains are drawn and there's nothing to see. 'I'm afraid our meeting a few weeks ago may have prompted something in him to come last night.' She stops herself from accusing Magda, after all there is no proof, and the right thing to do is admit one's own fault. 'I didn't mean to start anything, but I feel responsible.'

'You mean to tell me we're sitting in tonight because you're afraid of an ex-boyfriend?' From the tone of his voice he's either angry or incredulous but she can't tell which.

'No, not exactly, I mean, I don't feel well right now, not at all. I'm so tired, I don't know why, maybe these two weeks, or something I had on the journey. But you said it didn't matter where we were, as long as we're together.'

'But you weren't honest with me either,' he says flatly.

'I thought it would sound ridiculous.'

'So you were more afraid of sounding ridiculous than being honest with me?'

'No.' He's twisting her words now in that lawyerly way of his. 'No, I mean, yes, I was concerned how it would sound, but no, I

267

didn't know how you would take it, which is obviously not well, so I shouldn't have brought it up.'

'Not brought it up?' he's practically spitting. 'We're sitting here and I cancelled this wonderful evening because you got worked up about a drunken ex?'

Her mind is throbbing and the way he says it she still doesn't understand – has she overemphasised the problem or underemphasised it? Everything's dislocated, her head feels like it's about to split open.

'This really takes the cake,' Harry says, as if making it clear, though she's still in the dark. 'I'm really surprised by you, Eva.'

'I don't understand.'

'I don't either,' Harry says. 'This,' he continues, fingering something in his pocket, then bringing out a small black box, 'was for you.' But instead of giving it, he tosses it on the bed.

The effect of the backhanded throw is greater than a slap.

'Aren't you going to open it?'

Tears obscure everything, their anniversary, the whole New Year's Eve.

'Under the circumstances, I don't deserve it do I?'

She slides down, under the duvet.

Blot it out, everything, this night, Harry, Adam, the dreams, squeeze your eyes shut, stomach spiralling, head thumping, movement on the sheets, him taking back whatever it is, sound of a zipper unzipped, then zipped up, and footsteps, the door shutting.

Alone in the darkness, anger and sorrow – all directed at him. Harry. The sum total of nothing.

∞

Harry, conciliatory and gentle in the morning, but unapologetic for the evening before, and he hasn't mentioned the black box. Life is one big dizzy spell – what's real, what's imagined? He wouldn't have done something so petty and childish, but he hasn't said anything either, as if it never happened.

She's shivering, back in bed. Breakfast impossible, the ache in her body all consuming, she had returned to the room and was sick, barely making it to the toilet. Climbing back into bed, trying to order her thoughts, is it the flu going around? If that's it, she won't be up for days. But then they'll miss their flights. And they aren't the cheapest, those flights on Sunday morning, two days away. Now even that looks like a challenge. What's to be done?

Wait, didn't someone ask that already? Why of course, Lenin. Why Lenin? The brain seems a muddle of irrelevant things. What was his answer? It seems important to get answers to at least one question. She sifts through buried history, discredited philosophies, something about workers not rising to fight their employers. Yes, that was it. They had drummed it in: no one would become Marxist without a vanguard political movement leading them. *Politics is all of society, workers need to understand more than just their own corner, they must be pulled out of it. That's why times have to be revolutionary!* Were those his words, or whose? The opposite of Slavic resignation to fate, this idea of revolution, no wonder they had to pound it in. Pound, pound. Like her head, but everyone hated what Marxism produced, the only important point out of it was sometimes you had to rebel. Change what wasn't working. Rebel, yes. But only if you were fit. But she can't even get up now. How the hell will she catch a flight?

Harry opens the door, tense. Maybe he feels pity. Or he's bracing himself for what needs doing. But what does need doing? Didn't she already solve that?

'Eva, you're really not well. We have to delay your trip home.'

'No, I'll be alright.' It comes out automatically but she doesn't believe her own words.

'You're ill, Eva,' he says, gently now. 'Really unwell. You can't travel alone with the kids.'

Why not? That's how it always goes. She readies herself for another argument.

But he puts his hand on her forehand, like he's diagnosing a small child. 'No, you can't.'

He gets up, goes out. And in the blur of time, sometime later, he returns with the air of someone who's done what he's most good at, being decisive in an emergency.

'It's sorted,' he says. 'You're staying.'

∞

The rest of the day she's so ill she can't remember ever being so. Sickness consuming the body, she can't even feel it any more, there really is no being, only nothingness, punctuated by retching spasms, being racked with cold, thoughts that can't be ordered. She gives in.

Give in to it.

She hears herself calling, moaning, but surely someone else has made that sound. But no one comes. No one is there.

Maybe you haven't made any noise, Eva.

The day seems to move from one grey moment to another. The winter sky, never a good indicator of time, darkens. It must be late afternoon. When the door was last shut, Harry said he was taking the kids out, so they've been gone for hours.

The door opens. They're back, with Magda.

Only it's not Magda, but a Magda look-alike. A Magda with a short haircut that almost makes her chic. Except for the tell-tale

fortyca

brown tunic. But the bun is gone. But it can't be, it's her trademark, this must be an impersonator, an imposter. But Magda looks at her dispassionately, that much is familiar, though it could be professionalism or dismissiveness or even Magda thinking this is what her stupid sister deserves. But she's so sick she doesn't care, this Eva lying in bed, separate from herself, watching Magda, approaching with her black suitcase, like in old films, a proper doctor's case, ready to give a body a thorough inspection.

'Eva, you should probably go for tests,' Magda says firmly but not unkindly. 'You'll need to give blood, but I'll see what I can get through urine. If you give me a sample now, we can get the process started.' She holds out a little lidded jar, the label for mustard still attached.

'Okay.' Head swirling, legs hot and wobbly, she might not make it to the toilet unsupported.

'Harry?' But he's in the next room, engrossed in one of his devices, so she sits back down on the bed. If she rests for a minute, she might be able to get back up.

Magda takes it as a bad sign but encourages her up again. She must get that sample because a scientific evaluation must be made or things will never be set right.

'Magda,' she smiles almost giddily. 'You cut your hair.'

Clarify, Eva, it looks nice, better at any rate.

Harry pipes up. 'Magda had a makeover for New Year's.'

'It was a resolution,' Magda replies, as if that were an adequate explanation. Then quietly, 'I did it for a friend.'

But that's more confusing than getting it cut for no reason at all.

'Must have been some night too,' Harry adds, trying to be entertaining. 'I tried finding her after breakfast but she didn't get home till after lunch.'

At this Magda reddens, stiffens. 'Even doctors have the night off on occasion.'

'No, of course,' Harry continues good-naturedly, but he's back looking at his device. 'Even doctors need to party.'

Magda says nothing, the episode spinning into the surreal. What are they talking about? Magda doesn't party. Then a moment later, remembering it *was* New Year's Eve, anybody might have a resolution and dare to change, even Magdalena. Today is the first day of the New Year, a new decade, in fact. Start as you mean to go on, they say. But then, for her, this would be a bad omen.

She concentrates her strength and gets up, continues to the bathroom alone. Sitting in the loo in the dark because the lights are too bright, she's fumbling but she must try to catch it, whatever germs she's supposed to catch. Then screw the lid on carefully, rinse off the sides, and there, now it will all be solved. But that's confusing because a pot of urine doesn't solve anything, her reasoning's faulty, but she can't figure out why. Then the last thing, setting down the jar, gripping the door handle, soft carpeting so hard under tender feet, the grey outside the window, the room going black.

Outside the light is sparse and weak, an egg smeared across the sky. A yellowish sunrise signals another short winter day.

But maybe it's afternoon? Not that it matters what time of day you wake up, it's like being on the E-40 again, rolling up and down, in and out of sleep, another series of dreams going by, then gone. E-40, the motorway, though in England, E45 is a brand of emollients and creams, soothing to a baby's skin. That's related, but not, because her hometown is always too far over the next hill, and no matter how long they drive from Krakow they never seem to get there. It's imperative they arrive however, because important things await. That knowledge is a certainty, even if it's unclear what those important matters are.

Comfortingly, children have been filling the sky, soft skin, so maybe they use the cream, floating about like angels in a painting that leads to a next room where the story continues: myths and legends no one need believe, but you can learn some lessons anyway, about gods and humans in perpetual entanglement, usually to the detriment of the latter. But the sense of it breaks up, the images disappear, morph into hallucinations, that much she knows: colours flashing, voices speaking, a brief recognition from time immemorial. Something going into the arm, her arm, then numbness, a needle into her back too, like a hot spear, but painful only when you try to move and she can't. Her joints ache, so really it's better to be still, or the pounding in the head will start again as well. Lots of doctors seem to rush about, Magda and Harry's faces blurred, but if you don't look, you can't panic, anyway she's alive and Magda and Harry must be here somewhere on the other side of her eyelids, though it's not Magda she wants to see but Christophe, the closest thing to floating babies in the sky. Familiar voices say shhhh, Mama's sleeping, but that isn't true, when she opens her eyes there's no one around, only floating babies when she closes her eyes, and she says, no I'm not I'm not sleeping I'm flying. But they don't hear and she falls back into shadows.

Giving in again: another dreamless sleep, everything soft and and cosy and white. If she's lucky – or maybe not – this one might last a very long time. Cherubs are whispering behind the clouds, she can hear them, can feel the flutter of their wings on her paper skin as they lift her up to the bright light. And there they all are! Little Eva and the unborn baby holding hands, half-sisters beckoning to come. But she's afraid. *Resist.* The light's too bright, she complains silently to the angels, she isn't ready for this yet.

Why don't they let her rest? Leave her to be in the dimness a while longer? All this mucking about, so tiring for everyone. The angels acquiesce, let her down gently on to a soft cloud, a commercial for toilet paper, but the padding turns to a rigid mattress and something hard on the face. No, back up to the clouds, floating about, time's on your side, infinity, so it isn't so tiring, really, you can't be tired of infinity, nothing to compare it to. *It's everything, Eva.* But look, it's subdivided too. A wisp of smoke comes up from a gap in the clouds below, and in the gap, she sees the earth, green and lush and inviting. So hard to choose which way to go, but then through the hole comes another wisp of smoke that transforms itself into Adam, who sees but ignores her, though she did get up to greet him. Why should he be rude? Oh, but he's not, he's preoccupied with the children, takes their little hands and walks way. Still it hurts, why didn't he acknowledge her? He looked tired, stooped like an old man, the children were helping him, so he must be okay. Miss Miriam is waving in the distance, she looks happy, chatting with Pani Zoya, all these international adventures they're having, and nearer, Baba Kasia's kneading dough for *varenyky,* admonishing everyone not to call them *pierogies.* Baba greets her with a hug she can't feel, saying *so many adventures you're having too, Eva,* or maybe that's Miss Miriam, but Baba smiles and winks, *let me tell you a story.* Baba begins with the one she used to tell when they shared a room so long ago, a story meant to warn little children about being bad. But she isn't using words, she's mouthing symbols, there are no descriptions, no plot or theme even, just the ubiquitous nature of goodness if you follow that path. *Rubbish, you can't believe that Eva,* but Baba stops her from being so sure before the end and says, *well, it's up to you.* Thanks Baba, she feels herself saying, thanking her, though it's thoroughly unsatisfactory being left in the lurch like that. She tries to embrace her again to feel something solid but Baba is gone. She's alone.

The mattress, a dim room, the room empty, cold. But she is alive.

Rebel. Fight on.

∞

She peers through the darkness but there's nothing to see, only a bare hospital room. Maybe it's night time and this is reality: no one's around because it's night. In the morning, the situation might be better. She tries to sit up, make sense of hazy surroundings.

A voice penetrates. 'Eva?'

Harry? she says, but it doesn't come out in sound.

'Oh god, Eva, lie still, rest,' he instructs in a panicky voice, 'you're on strong antibiotics, they're going to make you better.'

With that he's told her all she needs to know: some kind of infection, but with powerful drugs she'll be okay.

'Harry,' her voice is a squeak, tears welling, throat dry.

'Eva, be still, I'm here,' his voice says, a figure rustling next to her. 'I'm here, please, be still. You're body's fighting off something serious,' he pauses, as if searching for the right phrase to capture his emotions, as if careful wording might act as a cure.

'You've been here a few days, Eva. You'll be here a few more, for observation. But the drugs are working. Your fever's come down.' He sounds more hopeful than confident.

'Harry,' mumbling but wanting to say, please don't leave me, don't leave me ever, but that is too many words.

'I'm here, I'm not going anywhere,' he reads her mind, trying to allay her fears, or maybe his. 'The kids are fine too, they're with a close friend of Magda's while she's been in and out supervising your care. I promise you they're having a whale of a time.'

Tears roll down but in the darkness Harry doesn't see them, doesn't wipe them away. Tears of sorrow but also heartache, missing the children and Harry, life being good and normal, the way it was long ago. The way it was supposed to be.

'Eva, don't cry,' he says, finally touching her cheekbones and stroking the wetness away. 'It'll be okay. Are you in pain?'

Yes, wanting to say yes, in heart, head, body, soul everything hurts, but it comes out a whisper. 'Christophe, Katya.'

'Eva,' he says, taking one hand gingerly. 'They've been keeping them away. They thought you might be contagious. You were in a special ward. But now you're getting better.' Again the voice falsely upbeat. 'They'll come as soon as they can, during official visiting hours. Christophe is so excited. He said you liked apricot crescents. He's going to bring you some.'

The thought of Christophe, a smile, but Harry's speaking in staccato, so he must be worried. This is all so tiring, she closes her eyes. These new eyes that feel like lead curtains.

'Yes, get some sleep now,' he says melodically. 'I'll be right here if you need anything.'

But there's something she feels guilty about, can't remember what exactly, maybe Harry having to spend a night in an uncomfortable chair or messing up everyone's plans, including her own. That seems too trivial but it's important too and the only thing she can think of, strapped here to the bed, the drip, the room, to the darkness that comes and comes. Even with Harry there.

∞

Morning breaks, the sun shining so hard the brightness hurts. She blinks repeatedly. Harry isn't here, but that's not worrying, he'll be back. She just has to wait. Maybe a nurse will come first, she can ask her to draw the curtains. She's certain she'll never be sure which is better now, light or dark.

Closing her eyes, what's with the bustling down the hall? Far worse cases must be coming and going. Yet she must do better herself. But what to do better escapes definition. If you're confined to bed, intravenous drip and too tired to move, how can you do anything? But *she* has been moved, her whole body, floated, it's not the same room as before, and didn't Harry say she's been here a few days? They must have passed in sleep and dreams. Seems a long time ago he said this. In the distance, voices, little children's. Then the steady voice of Harry, monotone and sure, in control. Maybe it's a dream. Or reality about to happen. She tries to prop herself up.

Christophe peers into the room with uncertain big eyes. He's clutching a bag, the promised pastries. Katya is gripping Harry's hand, reserved. But then Katya smiles. She smiles!

She smiles back to signal they shouldn't be afraid. But then they look afraid. Harry too, grim. All that effort for nothing?

'Daddy, what's on Mama's face?' Katya points her finger, her hand freezing midway up.

'That,' says Harry steadily, 'is a rash, which will go away when Mama gets better.'

What rash? Her face feels normal but the children are too scared to come near.

'Please,' she tries to lift her head. But her neck is stiff, hands too.

'Come,' Harry says, 'it's alright.'

Christophe visibly shakes off his fear, puts on false bravado and takes a few steps closer. 'Mama, we brought you these. Because you like them.'

Emboldened by his words, Katya adds, 'You might not be able to eat them now, Daddy said, but they're for cheering you up. Like flowers.' She's holding some blooms, coming forward unsteadily to the edge of the bed. 'Does it hurt, Mama?'

She stays silent, hard to think of how to explain. But also because it hurts to think, to talk. She whispers, 'I love you so much.'

That's when Katya leans over, puts her small hand on her arm, bravely ignoring the plastic tubes and needles.

'Don't worry, Mama. It'll be okay.' Katya stops, then adds, 'I'm being nice to Christophe and Pookie.' She turns around, looks at Harry. 'Daddy's being good too,' she smiles. 'We're okay.'

Tears must be rolling down her cheeks, her eyes too watery to see. Katya brings her hand up immediately and wipes the wetness away.

'Please don't cry, Mama. You'll be better too, you'll see.'

She wants to keep crying, but a nurse comes in.

'Are you feeling worse?' The nurse quickly checks fluid, tops up medicine.

She shakes her head 'no' while the nurse takes her temperature. This must be a regular check-up. The nurse smiles too, better than a grimace of despair, so maybe she is expected to get better. The nurse goes to the window as if knowing a patient's needs, draws the curtains part-way shut.

Now another lady enters, birdlike but not owlish. Like Magda but leaner with defined cheekbones and very short cropped hair. Harry speaks to her like a friend, and the woman takes the children away.

She tries to sit up. 'Harry? What's happening?'

Face serious, Harry pulls up a chair and lowers himself into it slowly, supporting himself on the way down like an old man. He runs his hands through his hair, sighs.

'Eva, you have meningitis,' he says it quickly. Then, as if thinking better of it, chooses his next explanation carefully. 'But you are coming through. You were lucky, very lucky. Magda caught on to this from the first. She gave you antibiotics on the spot, in the hotel. You've been on a drip for nearly a week.'

A week? But that's far too long, far too serious. Then again, Christophe and Katya's reactions were enough to emphasise the severity of the situation.

'Why are they afraid?'

'Who?'

'Children.'

'Because you scared us to death, Eva,' Harry exhales slowly. 'Literally, what you have, it could have been fatal. You've been in and out of consciousness. For a while the doctors thought you might slip into a coma. But you've been fighting hard, love. You've come through the worst.'

He says this, maybe to inspire her, but he hasn't answered the question, why the children are afraid.

'So why are they afraid?'

Harry looks at her bewildered, then asks, 'Christophe and Katya?'

As if there were others. She tries to nod her head, but it's too painful, she stops.

'Eva, you have something like a burn mark on your face. A red patch down to the chin, across your cheek here.' He makes a sweeping motion that seems to cover most of her face. 'It started as blotches, a symptom of your infection.'

Red mark? And the thing that first comes to mind is that marked woman, that harlot with the scarlet letter on her forehead, the one the nuns told her they'd read about. Presumably because it showed even Protestants in America held high morals, and a range of punishments awaited women who ended up like whores. Except it seemed unfair that it only ever applied to women.

'Eva?'

'Hmm?'

'I was talking about the infection, do you understand?' He says it as if she were a child. 'I am talking of your symptoms.' He takes a long breath. 'Meningitis, together with septicaemia, or blood poisoning, are called meningococcal disease.'

He says this in a detached way, the way doctors do. But this and his previous babbling about apricot crescents must be a symptom of his own disease: fear. He continues speaking in simple staccato sentences as if it might aid understanding. But of course, everyone knows what meningitis is – it's the thing you fear for in your children. Reading about these symptoms in the health service offices, when the children were babies, all those dark nights, the children so small and vulnerable, every time they fell ill, an ungodly fear, of them suddenly dying, how does this apply to her? The situation doesn't make sense. *Meningitis is a fast progressing disease that kills if untreated.* It said that, somewhere. She'd memorised the fact.

'As you know it's very serious,' Harry continues in measured tones – he's repeating himself, isn't he? – he sighs again. 'But we've caught it in time.'

She studies his face. Does he mean it? He looks relieved but worried too, as if everything isn't definite just yet.

Meningitis. A memory returns: she collapsed in the hotel. Maybe that's what he means, someone caught her. Caught in time. But the light is still too bright. Harry is holding her hand. It's the most attention he's paid to her ever. But that's such a sad thought, tears come.

Harry looks at her, smiles weakly.

'Please don't cry,' he caresses her hand gently. 'Please, you are getting better, but you gave us an awful scare.'

He is – he is repeating himself. Trying to make her and himself feel better. But this time he wipes away her tears.

'Thank god for Magda,' he breathes out. And as an afterthought, but now looking away, 'and Lucia.'

But the mention of Lucia is confusing, who's Lucia? Her brow must have crumpled even if it hurts to move. Why doesn't he explain further? But he's already thinking of something else, going back to the details of the day, the scheduling of things, matters he can deal with.

'She's taken Christophe and Katya to the park now,' he says, reporting to her and the rest of the room, 'then we'll go to lunch. But I'll be back for the afternoon because I'm getting special permission to sit here, thanks to Magda.'

So much to thank Magda for, she must make a mental note to do it, and this other person too, whoever she is, who's looking after the children. Then the flight they've missed comes to mind, but Harry must have changed it again. She wants to ask what day it is, has he called the schools? He must have, if it's been a week, but then it's bad if the children are already missing school. She wants to see them again, their angel faces, but not have them see her. She wants to see her face for herself first, make sure it isn't that bad.

But it's all so taxing. She closes her eyes. A stray dried tear feels stuck to her cheek. It's all so taxing. Better if Harry sees to it. Sometimes he's good at making things better.

∞

Darkness again, Harry should be here, but he's not. Did she fall asleep on him?

There are people in the room. Men. A deep Polish voice that sounds almost like Adam. She shuts her eyes tighter, blocks out the fear. But *almost* doesn't mean *is*. No, better open them and verify what's true, the only way to know: to feel and to see.

Someone in surgeon's wear is speaking to a male orderly.

'Don't worry, I'm not here for you,' the man says, catching her look. 'You're practically well enough to go home.' He says it jokingly, probably to lift her spirits.

He motions to her. 'Someone brought you a box of red roses.' He points to the table near the window. 'I'm not the usual delivery man, as you can see, but I was passing by.'

Lucidity, absurdity, where are the lines? She has to strain to see them, these surgeon men in white, these roses in red, but she can't turn her neck.

'We couldn't deliver them to your other room, but now you're here, do you want us to read the note? Signed Adam.'

Body tensing, spasms everywhere, she can't stop shaking. Is it only internal? But surgeon man rushes over, checks pulse, readings on a machine. Bleeping noises, she's running out of air.

'No, Adam,' she's taking in gasps, hears herself groan, deeper than her own voice. 'No Adam,' as if possessed, though it's possible she's not making any noise. They don't seem to hear her.

The orderly keeps hold of her, something on the face, a shot of something, dulling, numbing, dumbing down.

'We'll be restricting your guests.'

Wait, not Harry, don't keep him away.

Whisper 'Harry' Eva, so they'll know.

He's your best bet, your only chance.

Have they heard you?

Where is Harry?

∞

Blackness, isolation. Harry, maybe coming, always going. When she wakes again he's not here. Is he ever here enough?

Hours, days. One blackness rolling into another. She's virtually given in. Given up and given her body over to it, whatever it is. The pain, the boredom, either dying or waiting for recovery.

Solitude. Sometimes the mind is clear, lucid thought. Other times, random, snatches of memory, images. She can barely feel the solidity of self, the coldness of the sheets. The physical and ephemeral come, then slip away. Maybe they've put something extra in the drip.

Thoughts hazy again. If she survives, it'll be one more recovery. Like that time with Xavier, after the abortion, when fever forced her back to the clinic. Except Xavier never left her side, he stayed until the fever broke, infection arrested. He'd been interested in her well-being, directing staff to do this and that. Make it better. Ordering infusion teas, fresher meals. But when she left hospital that time, it was too late – she was still too ill to come home for Christmas. She called to say she wasn't coming. Then Baba Kasia died suddenly in her sleep and she missed the funeral.

Baba Kasia and her cross, where is it? She's not wearing it any more, can't feel it. Did Harry put it away for safekeeping? The body, everything, lightness of being, heaviness of soul, she's just a malnourished vessel subsisting on liquid drips. So it's her soul weighing her down, like the blankets covering her lower half. That cross is somewhere. Harry must have taken it from her, this cross she's supposed to wear. Maybe it is a bad omen, bad luck. Like Adam's roses. They *were* there. Now they're not. Was their existence real? Or is all of this some kind of hallucination?

Thoughts too complex, easier to give over to daydreams. Things you know have happened, so far as one knows anything.

Xavier. That fraction of lucidity. Yes. When she was last laid up, he did try to make her better. And when she'd fully recovered, he made her know he was still interested in her. Mind, body and soul. It wasn't immoral then, the freedom to do what you wanted. They were both open to prospects.

So easy to float back to that moment, the recapturing. It had been springtime. An open window. A fresh breeze, sheer white curtains billowing like a commercial for seaside holidays. An Eva of the past, laughing at something she was reading. The springiness of the day made her sigh. She looked over at him.

Xavier. Who until then had been a portrait of restraint. Lying nearby, reading too. Suddenly he caught her looking at him. Slowly he set down his book, moved so close to her it was frightening. And without a word, he'd leaned over and kissed her. He'd meant to respond to her simple happiness. But in that moment, catching her unawares, he seemed to catch himself unaware. A simple act that became a moment within a moment, a tiny bubble of time, becoming what it was about to become. Like a savage released, he started kissing her again and again. Passionately, eating her up, tearing at her. Ripping away months of restraint. As if friendly relations had merely been a ruse. False pretence to be destroyed. Then still without a word between them, he carried her delicately to his bed. Not like an invalid, the invalid she'd been, but a virgin bride. And then he'd acted very much like she wasn't. She gave herself over, completely. Because there wasn't a single thing about him then she'd forgotten in those years apart. Those years that by then seemed like wasted years with Adam, a long wait for that moment with Xavier.

Adam, she should be thinking of Adam. He's around somewhere. But he turned his back on her in that dream. So maybe he's angry. Or maybe he's okay, he's moved on. A few more moments of pleasure, will that hurt anyone? It's all in the mind. No record of anything. Except the letter. The one she kept, the prelude, the guarantee that if she left Poland, he'd be there to look after her. Yes, that's what it was: a series of words that created a reality, a moment that turned into proper time: months.

A couple of years, in fact. Until Carole. Oh, sweet Carole, who took her place in their circle of friends, then slowly made Xavier know she would not let him go. Carole. But a fog shrouds what happened, her loss to Carole. Had that been it? A straightforward win for Carole? Because at the time, she hadn't realised what game was being played. The high stakes. That Xavier was judging her suitable or not. He probably thought she wasn't trying hard enough. Not sexually, but in the thing the French dismissed as *insupportable* – the things she did and said which he simply couldn't stand. Didn't match his standards. As if Xav himself had been perfect, and it were up to *her* to change for him. She didn't even see it coming. For so long forgiving Xavier his tics and indiscretions. Smug Carole. The triangle might have continued for some time. But no. His lazy, steady acknowledgement of Carole's presence finally drove her away. She hadn't been interested in competing with Carole at all. No more than she ever had with Magda. Competition always made her want to run away. So she let things take their course. She wanted Xavier to be decisive. But he let Carole decide. Oh well, that duel settled. She's pleased. There's nothing wrong with her mind.

But that problem was another Eva's to deal with. A distant past that is clear. But this Eva, this one with Harry, is confused. And now bedridden. Harry's decisiveness on the first night led to all the rest. But where is he now?

She opens her eyes, but he's still not there. When she needs tenderness most, he seems to be missing. She's been left alone with her thoughts and they're wandering, getting stronger, going as and where they like. That's dangerous, certainly, because thoughts as often as actions get one into deep trouble. Surely that's why the awful powers of the Catholic Church were always busy stomping them out. Bad thoughts, evil thoughts, contemptible as immoral deeds. Transgressions for which you must ask forgiveness. Because you've already sinned against God if your mind goes astray. *Five Our Fathers and nine Hail Marys,* the usual assignment from Father Benedictus. But still shady thoughts crept in, the next confession worse. *But I don't ask for them, they just pop up,* she retorted, *why on earth am I in trouble for that?* That question never answered satisfactorily either in the confessional box or at Sunday school, where anyway you were mostly too scared to be honest. Just another cover up – ask for anything but real forgiveness – collect your three Our Fathers, two Hail Marys and one of those other prayers to the Holy Spirit. A numerical equation in penance, even if you were still lying to yourself and others. She'd always hoped for a tightly knit theology. Something to square the circle in the end. That was how the Catholic religion worked, pat answer to everything. Even the impossible. But she found grey areas couldn't be dispensed with black and white prescriptions. So she strayed. And the product of that was constant doubt. This, here and now. Big doubt. Whether you were doing the right thing and how you might know. Why something could feel right even if you suspected it was wrong. That was the product of revelation. And the conclusion.

She tries to turn in bed but it's too difficult. Respite out of reach. If only they'd taught it that way, that doubt was okay. That everything might be a matter of intuition, faith. Believing not only in God and the saints and their works, but that within yourself, you might have the answer. No, that's hubris, they said, a trait to be decried – thinking one could even know. But what if that *was* the recognition of the divine within? Who could answer such questions definitively? Not priests or the Pope. No one but God himself, or angels. Like those angels who'd brought her back to life. Like Katya, first to notice and quickly wipe away her tears.

Because if there is one thing that seems certain now, it's that these angels do exist. They are Christophe and Katya, they are helping. They do exist.

∞

'Sorry I'm late,' Harry says, mopping his brow as though he'd completed a race. 'I had to sit in on the last session, then check on the kids.'

What session? Where *has* he been?

'Crikey, it's been a busy week,' Harry continues, 'the kids don't mind, though Christophe has asked about going home. I told him, a few more weeks.'

But a few more weeks is absurdly long, the children ought to be in school by now. She's conscious of feeling irritated by his matter-of-factness, his back-to-business tone, though really it's a good sign. She must not be dying any more. And clearly he's taking care of everything, and for that she must be – no, is – very grateful. Because she has failed them for not getting up in time. On the other hand, a bit more attention from Harry, even a shred of pity, is it so selfish to want that?

She tries to move but a pain of stiffness shoots through her body. A whole morning trying to walk. Everything hurts. The pain is a flash point, another irritation. Harry wasn't here for that. Or the last scary episode, phoned afterwards, and when he came and she told him about Adam's roses, all he could say was, *but there's nothing there.*

'Eva, you okay? How are you feeling?' He finally addresses her directly.

'When will they let me out?' Her voice still sounds like someone else's.

'A few days, last I heard. But you'll have to stay close to hospital for a while.'

He's not looking at her any more but at his phone, checking a message or something.

'Sorry, just this thing,' he sighs, head bent. 'Might be a day or so but you're definitely past the worst. They should have you walking more tomorrow. You've been very lucky.'

This is getting annoying too – being told you're lucky when you almost died. Or *maybe* almost died, because memory fails, her thoughts still feel spongy, detached from one other. One minute she's dying, the next, she's wondering how she managed to get to the loo. A practical consideration, she can't see bedpans, and practicalities do matter. But maybe they don't matter that much if you've survived. Maybe that's the main point – be grateful, no matter what. They'll come and check on normal functions, tell her she's passed. Poke, poke. Yes, still alive. Though that's redundant, because if you're alive, of course you've passed, but passing time is a minimum, and beyond normal functions everything feels flat. She is a discombobulated version of self, sadness enveloping her like a cloak. This whole scenario disheartening, even speaking to him is an uphill battle.

'Harry, what are you doing?' She doesn't know if she sounds exasperated or not.

'Me?' he looks up again. 'After this, I've got to go to Lucia's to check on the kids, then…'

'Wait a minute,' drawing on every last strength. '*Who* is Lucia?'

At this, Harry's eyes catch a sparkle of light and he smacks his forehead, as if he's just remembered something that will tickle her fancy.

'Oh, of course, I'm sorry, I forgot,' he says, smiling ridiculously. 'She's Magda's *girlfriend*.'

∞

She sits in the chair in the corner of the room, waiting to be fetched, discharged back to the world of the living. The sun is streaming in. Maybe Magda will come too. Magda, the newest surprise. Because if there was anything left to hide from anyone, siblings or parents, Magda had succeeded where frail little Eva had been an amateur. Staunch Catholic lesbian, imagine! Except of course the real difference between sisters was that whatever secrets remained, of the two at least Magda seemed to be moving in the right direction: admitting to oneself the essence of being.

And the immensity of it too. The secret – Magda in a relationship with a woman – a scientific doctor and a devout Catholic but in love with a woman, and a woman in love with her. So not only having a relationship but committed to this course of action despite all the battles ahead. Of course there was no reason why being a scientist or a doctor should prevent lesbianism, except Magda's overall unemotional demeanour, so analytical, dovetailing so nicely with her rigorous asceticism, had always slotted in with the bit of Catholicism that didn't permit breaking rules. But maybe her analytical side had helped drive it through. Not a lapse into raw emotion, not a loss of reason, but a wanting to know. The only way to know anything was to explore it, experiment, trial and error, until you're proven right or wrong. It might be reckless to go against Catholic rules of sexuality and risk eternal damnation – not as she, but as Magda believed them – because rules for salvation and sex were tightly written, no room for experimentation. No seeking happiness the way one sees fit. The Church long ago decreed true happiness comes only through God, seeking Him, a kind of happiness not made for this world, only the other. But obviously Magda wanted to be happy on earth too. And why not? Doesn't everyone want to be happy? Doesn't God, if He exists, want us to find that happiness?

'You all packed now?' A nurse peeks her head around the door.

289

'Yes,' she says, getting up slowly, as if there were any other way. She makes her way to the door.

'Your husband is waiting in reception with the children,' the nurse says. 'I'm afraid they can't come down here at this time of day, but I'll give you a hand, if you need.'

But there is no need because they've spent the last few days practising walking. And bending and reaching, and going to the bathroom without a walker. Ludicrous when you're forty-one, learning these things, but that's what happens when you crash, you begin again. She walks to the bend in the hall where the wing of the main intensive care ward ends. So, she's been under close observation the whole time.

'You are a miracle,' the nurse says by way of goodbye, pointing towards the main hall and disappearing through a door marked Staff Only.

She stops. *A miracle. Very lucky.* What everyone keeps saying. Harry, the doctors, Magda, everyone. Everyone astonished, she did not die. No amputations, she can walk, no hearing loss, no real scarring, even the red mark has faded, something she never saw, will never be able to verify, how bad it was. Headaches gone too, only an underlying and pervasive weakness, exhaustion from the simplest motions. And the dread of life itself.

But you're so lucky.

True, what they keep saying, but still she has to repeat it, because deep down, she doesn't feel lucky. Only empty. Timeless, like something's been lost that might not be retrieved.

A nurse comes up. 'You lost?'

Yes, quite, she'd like to say, but she shakes her head no, regretting that too for the residual ache it produces. Time standing still, she standing still.

Move, Eva.

The inner voice prodding, she begins to round the bend to the main entrance.

Christophe and Katya come running. She's so happy to see them she could cry. But she doesn't open her arms, too fragile to brace for a hug, even from these small angels. Instead her hand goes to her face, to hide whatever faint blotchiness might still be there.

Harry walks up. 'Ready to go?' He smiles but as if it's a real effort.

She nods a very slow yes. He produces a coat for her to slip on. It takes so long to do it.

'So where to?'

She means it as a joke. Buttoning up her coat, she looks up. Harry hasn't answered.

Maybe he didn't hear her. People still seem not to.

The children are already far ahead, Harry striding forward to hold open the doors, pretend optimism driving his demeanour. She tries moving faster, to catch up, steps into the cold. The sudden blast of fresh oxygen is a shock. She stops.

He's gone off again. But then he stops, turns back, as if only now noticing how slowly she's been moving. How far behind she is.

'You'll need to rest before we can contemplate how and when to get you home,' he puts his arms around her as he gives this unnecessary summary, 'so right now we're all going to Lucia's country house where the children have been staying.'

So maybe he did hear her. He leads her forward.

'Yes, Mama! We're going back to Lucia's!' Christophe shouts.

'You'll like it there,' Katya counsels. 'It's toasty warm.'

They get in the waiting car and drive out of Krakow in the direction of Zakopane and the Tatras Mountains. Almost immediately she dozes to the jostling of the vehicle, and when she comes to, they're pulling into a tight muddy lane. Harry apologises for the drive as if the conditions were his doing but it's so good to be free of medical smells, out in the countryside, who cares about twists and turns? A small rural cottage appears

291

and this woman, the same cropped haired one from the hospital who must be Lucia, is standing on the porch, waving as if they were her family. The taxi slows, Harry supports her out, stays to negotiate with the driver. She makes her way up the steps with the children.

'Hello again!' Lucia stretches out her arms expansively, hugging Katya and Christophe.

She's foreign, arms waving as she speaks, reminiscent of some famous Italian actress. All muffled, these goings-on right in front of her, and this Eva who constitutes her body seems only an observer who might someday return to playing. Perhaps in the story of her life, Lucia will be played by that Italian actress and Harry by that loveable English actor with floppy hair who's forever in trouble for getting it wrong with relationships. Preposterous. Who would play her?

The thought is trampled by Harry coming up.

'Eva, this is Lucia, who has been a great help over the last week. She was at the hospital but you didn't properly meet. So now,' he gives Lucia a grateful glance.

Lucia smiles simply in return. It's instantly easy to see why anyone would be attracted to her.

'Welcome, welcome,' Lucia says in Polish. 'Please come in, I am so happy you are better,' she continues in heavily accented English, though it's unclear for whose benefit because the children, even Harry, everyone, is jabbering in Polish.

She enters slowly, a rustic but artful interior of carved wood and oil paintings and hand sewn cushions. Giant reclining gouache nudes adorn the walls, and smaller sketches, studies of the human body.

'Please, come sit,' Lucia motions them to the sofas. On the table are books and fresh pastries and a pot of coffee.

'Oh, coffee,' she says, like a child, then embarrassed. 'Thank you for this.'

'This,' Lucia says, 'is nothing. I will do more! I hope you like Italian cooking!'

So she is Italian. Well, with a name like that, but before she or Lucia can say more, Harry interjects, 'Yes, she'll need to eat to get her strength back up. She's lost so much weight.'

Yes, she has, this Eva third person, she's known it for some time, the feeling of wasting away. But the thought strews further confusion, because the way Harry says it, it's like she's a child, and now she feels alarmed, awoken to the severity of her condition, of which she'd rather not be reminded.

'Oh, I am so happy you are here, that I can finally meet you,' Lucia says in a sing-songy way, again in English. 'I have heard so much from Magda, but what kind of opinion can you make from others? Eh? Not much!'

She says not much like naddamucha, and for some reason, this is really pleasing, an expectation fulfilled. The sing song sits well too, the melody of Lucia's speech relaxing, her garrulous nature soothing.

'You have had good care at hospital. Magda is on duty early tomorrow, so she will come for dinner tonight,' Lucia says, as if elucidating plans might create the necessary order. 'She is so pleased with your progress. Now we will make you better still. Please, Harry, come. Pour this coffee.'

In a brisk take-charge kind of way, Lucia has Harry handing out plates of dessert and cups of coffee while the children, who have stolen a pastry each, disappear. Hopefully it's not because of her, hopefully they aren't afraid, but she doesn't know what Harry told them while she was asleep in the car, probably not to disturb her.

'Where have Christophe and Katya gone?' All her strength for this one question.

'They are in my studio painting,' Lucia says. 'I am artist, you see. I am oil painting. I give them some things to keep busy!'

Now it's obvious why Harry's been satisfied with Lucia's care. But a bigger predicament remains: this illness, how long rehabilitation will last, her sister, how she is, how these two met, the core of their relationship and most importantly, whether the Holdens will be in the way. But the situation is too much of a web to untangle over coffee, so she sips the fortifying liquid instead, happy to hold a cup in her hands. Slowly, slowly. Drinking. It's good. With caffeine coursing through her veins she suddenly feels stronger, more able to think.

'Well,' says Harry, standing up. 'I have to go back for a meeting, but I'll return this evening for dinner. Then we'll decide what to do.'

He says the last words as if he means to reassure her, but his voice falls flat.

'I'll be fine here.' She pushes away her disappointment. 'It's peaceful and beautiful.' At this Lucia blushes, as if she's succeeded in what she set out to do. 'Feels like home already.'

Lucia breaks into an enormous smile, but then a crash from the next room – she stands up. 'I will go to investigate!'

She tries to stand up to follow Lucia, but it's too tiring, so she sits back. Harry comes to her quickly, kneels before her.

'Eva, please, just rest, you scared us so much, I don't know where to begin. Please…'

He doesn't finish the sentence because the children come racing back and Lucia, sensing immediately they've interrupted, says, 'Oh, come here, Katya, Christophe, I have to show you something in the studio I found in the woodpile, a little nest from last summer, all dried up now.'

The attempt at distraction comes too late. The moment lost. Harry keeps telling her how much she scared him, but instead of staying he's getting up to go.

'I'll ring you,' he says, squeezing her hands, giving her a last intent look.

With the sound of wheels turning on the gravel outside, she realises the taxi never left. Harry grabs his computer, leaves. All of her life suddenly seems pre-arranged by other people. But before she can decide whether this is satisfactory or not, Lucia's before her, holding out her arms.

'Come now,' says Lucia. 'I've fixed up a room where you can rest.'

Say no, tell them you'd like to stay here. Right in the middle of everything. Don't let them make you be alone any more. Don't let them cast you aside.

Her voice inside wants to fight but she feels feeble. It isn't for her to decide and it's true, she should rest. So she gets up slowly, follows. They move to a side room, a study or spare room of sorts, with a daybed and bookshelves. On the side table, a bowl of fruit and a jug of water, a still life scene come to life but one seemingly arranged for use rather than observation. So she's been invited into their world, their inner sanctum, their sacred space. It's not only churches and temples of the world that house spiritual matters but even small hideaways like these. She must tread carefully.

Think before you speak, love before you think, and put yourself in another's place, before you even attempt love.

That's a good one, actually, she wants to tell her new voice, she should write that one down. If she remembers. Didn't she used to live by useful sayings? Yes, but so many had to be discarded. They didn't apply. It was finding the universal, the beautiful, that was the critical thing.

She lays back on the daybed, eyes heavy again. Fighting off sleep, her eyes fix on the art books on the shelf. Michelangelo. *The Creation of Adam, The Creation of Eve, The Last Judgement.* A whole set on the great works of the Sistine Chapel. Also books on anatomy. They might be Magda's. But whose treatise on da Vinci? Scientist, artist, Magda, Lucia?

Of course. She closes her eyes. That explains it all.

∞

Waking up, her head's clearer than it's been in a long while. Maybe the coffee before the nap – she's been suffering lack of caffeine as badly as anything else. Sometimes afflictions require a jolt of stimulant. Body energised, mind returns to function.

She gets up, goes to the main room. She had some important thought earlier but can no longer remember it. Lucia? Magda? No one around. And even this short journey is taxing. She lowers herself into the leather sofa, repositions her body centrally. This body now so disconnected from her mind. She is here, but somehow she's fallen out of the middle of her life. Her presence is more of a background fixture to the sounds of people elsewhere, the children behind a closed door in an adjacent studio, probably absorbed in an art project Lucia's devised for them. Chirpy little voices full of pleasure. And from the kitchen, Lucia's lively rising voice, and Magda, laughing. Laughing? Yes, the sound of release. They're in there together. Magda's spirits are obviously lifted by proximity to Lucia. Perhaps loneliness and the great burden of a clandestine affair were what made her dour and silent and retreating all these years. Now all that unhappiness whisked away.

The kitchen doors swing open and shut. She catches a glimpse of Lucia and new-haircut-Magda, busying themselves with dinner. No one seems to have seen her, so she's weirdly alone. A ghost no one's noticed. Touching the sofa to make it more real, tangible, the creases and stains showing many years of use, and over there, a cat – had she not noted the cat before? – sitting on the window sill licking its paws. Momentary panic – who's looking after Roobarb and Custard? Surely not Jenny still? She must make a mental note to ask Harry later. Though he must've arranged that like everything else. Like this cat going about its ablutions methodically and carefully, not randomly like some cats do. Now with its tail cleaned the cat moves to one back leg, then the other, finally sitting back on its haunches, holding its head high, as if proud of its orderly ways.

The door swings open again. Lucia notices her, a panicked look caught between swings. Propping the door half open, she pops her head out again more prepared.

'Oh, there you are! I'll be right back with something for you.' Her head disappears. The laughing in the kitchen subsides, hushed tones take over.

Magda comes out with a herbal concoction. 'Here you go. This is very good for your condition,' she makes it sound like a burden. 'For the lining of your stomach, better than coffee.'

'Thank you,' she smiles, though she'd really prefer one of Lucia's silky long espressos. Nothing wrong with her stomach, apart from being empty for weeks.

Magda bustles back into the kitchen, a storm of activity rising with pots and pans clanging. The door swings repeatedly like a clipped reel, occasionally revealing Lucia in her natural element, playful cook and hostess, sometimes Magda, bent over in useful work.

She sips the bitter fluid. Tastes like nettle, but mixed with something far less tolerable. The mind trying to work out something else about Magda and Lucia. So many mysteries these last weeks: roses at the hospital, if they came from Adam, the puzzle of the hotel drunk, if it was him both times. She will need to settle these mysteries soon. Maybe Magda did say something to Adam, though now that seems less likely given her protective behaviour and Lucia's. But even if Magda had mentioned her whereabouts to Adam, it doesn't follow he would start stalking her. It might have been another drunk, crying Eva in the hotel, as undoubtedly there were many Evas in Krakow to cry over.

Yes, perhaps coincidence, the flowers, the conversations. Or just dreams, like so many flights of fancy she's been having.

A boom on the knocker, Lucia sprints to the main door.

Watching Lucia across the room, she feels detached again, the scene slipping away as if she were a faraway observer, the mind's eye a camera zooming in and out, viewing in 3D projection. Surround sound too, but weirdly muffled – oh, here comes the main entertainment – Harry. He's smiling, waving, holding flowers. Now over to the children to inspect their drawings. Lucia takes the flowers, they must be for her, she doesn't smell them, anyway there's a powerful smell already, although you can't smell in a film, so it means the oven must be open. Yes, the scent of Italian cuisine is wafting into the main room, visible on everyone's faces, and before Harry can say anything, Lucia's back, not with flowers but the biggest tray of lasagne ever, Magda bearing salad in hot pursuit.

'Here we are! Oh children, let's set the table!' Lucia cries, as if she suddenly remembered she's done it back to front, bringing out hot food before the table's cleared and laid.

Harry and Magda start sprinting too, back and forth, fetching bread and trivets and plates and cutlery and wine and salt and pepper and napkins. It's a silly film but no one seems to mind the lack of order, the reverse order, new order of things. Having begun to serve, Lucia suddenly remembers candles, runs back to a kitchen drawer, the sound of it slamming shut, doors swinging and she's back with a lit taper, walking slowly, like in church, and the room now resembles a rustic restaurant. Magda goes back for the flowers.

This must be how you throw life together, the art of rusticity springing from a lack of formality on every level. How did her old life become so organised and civilised? So English that she doesn't recall this sort of thing happening back home?

'Eva?'

She looks up.

'Aren't you going to join us?' Harry's standing over her, hand outstretched.

For a moment, it is like home, only the usual fixtures aren't there. The right background is missing: tall bay windows, leaded features, parquet floors, high ceilings, faded curtains. Her memories of a time and place seem to have receded from there. It's all further away now than a period film in the archives.

'Eva?'

She looks up. The cast of characters is different too.

'Eva?'

Suddenly everyone's looking at her. Then the aroma of food hits, a reminder of hunger, real and present and insistent. She stands, lets Harry seat her next to him.

'Mind yourself,' Magda warns as they begin, looking at her. 'Lucia's cooking is very good, but you mustn't overload your stomach at the first.'

Magda means it as good advice probably, she said it smiling, blinking through her glasses. Though this preoccupation with her stomach is strange, it's her brain that feels sensitive.

'Oh, let her eat or she'll shrivel up!' Lucia retorts.

Something Mamcia would say. Mamcia – does she know about this, her illness? About Lucia? She must ask someone, later, when the children have gone to bed maybe, and that other thing she's already forgotten, from earlier in the day. Maybe it'll come back. Mamcia and Tato, surely they know. Did they come to the hospital or not? No one's mentioned her parents but surely they know. Or is Magda still hiding from them?

Lucia looks at her worried. 'You don't like?'

'Oh yes, I'm being slow, sorry.' She lifts her fork. 'I'm fine really, just a little confused.' She lets the last sentence hang but the silence isn't receptive, so to reassure everyone she adds, 'Strange to have lost so many days.'

Because actually it feels like months, maybe years have been taken away. And she's not only watching this film, she's a character too but a character in a series that has nothing to do with reality. As if it's okay to make stuff up, bring old people back to life and insert them willy-nilly into whatever new scene gets concocted. Yes, she's travelled forward in time and come back, only to find herself astounded by what has passed. Passed and surpassed. Harry nodding, devouring his food as though he too has not eaten in many days, and he must not have, his cheeks are hollowed out. Thankfully the children look the same, chewing happily, their animals sitting with them at the far end of the table. When did that start?

She looks down at the plate and forks the lasagne, brings it slowly to her lips. Savouring the creamy tanginess dissipating on the tongue, when did she last eat solid food? She must have eaten something at the hospital, but she can't remember. Oh yes, bread. Then rice, then apple puree. BRAT, who said that? No toast, only tea. Now this tiny bite, one at a time, swallowed down in baby spurts, like Magda and Lucia's banter, the odd word from Harry, the pattering of Christophe and Katya. Pinglish and Ponglish.

It will take so much effort to contribute, but she must.

'I saw in the other room, books on anatomy,' she starts. 'Da Vinci's studies of the body.' She means it as an invitation to tell of mutual interests, but Lucia and Magda are chewing, so the statement hangs in the air for a moment, out of place.

'Oh, they are mine, the books are mine,' Lucia gives an open and disarming toothy smile. 'But Magda likes them too.'

'Where science and art meet, in the person of da Vinci,' Harry pipes up.

She looks at him astonished. How did he read her mind?

'Yes, we got to know each other over something like that, didn't we?' Lucia casts a smile in Magda's direction.

Magda looks up, senses what's expected.

'Years ago, I was helping a friend of mine with anatomy classes,' she finishes chewing. 'I collated drawings and diagrams for a semester or two, looking for some better pictures of bones too. A publisher of medical books invited me to an art exhibit, and there I met Lucia.'

So it had been years.

'Oh yes,' Lucia adds cheerfully, 'but not an exhibit about the body, if you can imagine, well, not anatomy, it was about the form of the body, during early renaissance. Giotto and Della Francesca, the great masters. Art on a religious theme.'

'Bellini's *Agony in the Garden*,' Magda says quietly.

Lucia looks at her. 'Might have been.'

'But the hair?'

It doesn't come out right, she has to reconnect it. 'Magda, you cut your hair.'

Again, awkward silence.

Lucia smiles. 'Ha! That was me too. I've been urging her to cut it for ages.'

'Not that appearances matter,' Magda retorts gently.

'Not to a doctor maybe, but an artist? Besides meaning there is nothing but appearance. Appearance gives meaning, the transition to beyond,' Lucia says. 'Anyway it suits you, you know that.'

'Yes, it does,' Harry chimes in.

'Yes,' she adds, smiling at Magda.

'Thank you,' Magda says, blushing.

Now is the chance to thank Magda for everything, but Lucia turns to Harry. 'Can I offer you some more lasagne? Bread? Here, please, take.'

Harry accepts, reaches for wine, pours for Magda and Lucia and himself, not even looking at her. With all the medication, it'll be a long time before they can return to sharing that. But still she feels overlooked. Like a child.

301

'Well, I'd like to propose a toast,' Harry says quickly. 'Not only to Eva's speedy recovery and strength and health, but to our two hostesses, whose skills in various things, from medicine to cookery to hospitality to calm and responsive action, brought us to a moment when we can be truly grateful.'

This must be for her as well, this toasting a new way for him to express his feelings. She should feel grateful, but Harry sounds worried. She'll thank Magda later, and maybe ask her about the sadness, because when will that end? The uncertainty, the fleeting sense of lost time, something not quite as it was before, because at the end of every moment, each episode, just as she manages to catch it, her memory fades. Then another niggling question emerges, a thought telling her – this can't last – but then that disappears too and she's bewildered again. It's frightening, this appearance and disappearance of disquiet. Sometimes when she thinks about it logically, she can calm herself saying, no, don't worry, this is all true: this table, this dinner, this togetherness. Yes, it will evaporate, but you just have to hold it while you can.

Like staying at Lucia's: forever is not an option. They'll have to go back, to where they belong. Where they started. England. Except it doesn't seem possible to return to an old life. Or to make a new life either. So how do you re-begin?

Dinner finishes quietly, the three of them talking without her, too many spaces between words. Harry ushers the children to bed. Who has been saying the angel prayer? Have they forgotten it? So many questions difficult to verbalise never mind resolve, especially when every clarity that arises seems to disappear. Like the strangeness and not-so-strangeness of new-haircut-Magda, taking her books upstairs to a place where Lucia will undoubtedly follow, Lucia motioning Harry to another spare room on the ground floor. Finally they fetch her.

She walks in, taking in the new surroundings, familiar and

not. A mattress on a low frame, a side table with the flowers Harry brought, the drinking pitcher transferred from the study.

'I hope you will be comfortable,' Lucia says. 'We don't use this room much, I am so pleased we can fill it with family guests.'

'Thank you, Lucia, it's lovely to be out of the hotel,' Harry says gratefully.

Lucia smiles and disappears up the creaky stairs.

'We should get some sleep,' Harry says, yawning. 'You must be tired.'

'Yes,' but she stops. They should talk, not sleep, after all these nights.

But maybe he's still concerned for her frailty, so they go about their rituals in silence, lie in the darkness for a while.

She reaches out.

'Harry, please. Tell me what happened. What will happen.'

He doesn't answer for a long time, the silence not oppressive, only dominant, vast. The overarching reality.

Finally he clears his throat. 'You know most of it,' he sighs deeply. 'You lost consciousness in the hotel, and Magda gave you an injection, called an ambulance, you went to hospital. Treatment for meningitis. It was – indeterminate – for a time.'

He's editing out emotions, breathing in and out steadily. 'You were in and out of consciousness for days.'

'I had crazy dreams,' she offers the detail, pauses.

'Tell me,' he says.

'One I remember there were angels in the sky, taking me to a light where there were people who had died. But I didn't want to go, I wasn't ready.'

'You stopped breathing for a while,' Harry says very quietly. 'You were put on a respirator.'

'Is that why you were scared?'

'Yes, that, the whole thing, Eva. We didn't know what your condition would be... even if you came out of it.'

He's turned to look at her, but they can't see each other properly, or anything, the room is only contours.

'We thought we might lose you, either way.'

'I'm sorry.' It comes out instinctively.

'Don't be, it's not your fault,' he turns his head toward the ceiling. 'It's no one's fault.'

No one's fault. Not even God's – if He exists. People always trying to blame someone, something, ultimately God when bad things happen, but God couldn't have bad motives. So that's the reason He can't exist, people say, because bad things happen. But logically that argument doesn't work, because if there is free will, then surely God's motives are irrelevant. He could be watching all the silliness from afar, hoping for the best. Or like Tato's latest theory, half joke, God might be there in the black hole, just past the event horizon, proud we've come up with the idea of singularity – for thinking up a new idea that He's known all along. But most likely, life is a contradiction which the human mind can't understand. And after all she's seen and felt, she has no problem with that. But she'll have to explain it to Harry some other time.

'Eva?'

'Sorry, my mind was wandering.' She lies quietly, trying to remember where they were. 'So now what?'

'Now? We'll have to see. You need to stay close to the hospital to return for check-ups. We thought about moving you back to England, but they advised against that, travel, air pressure, stress. We'll have to see, a few weeks here, I mean, in Poland, maybe not at Lucia's. I haven't gotten that far in the plan. It depends how you recover. Then I suppose we'll go back to England.'

The plan, the very words make her shudder.

'We? Does that mean you too?'

'Yes, of course.'

'So the Plan's off?' She forces herself to say it.

'I don't know, I haven't been thinking about *the* Plan, I've been worried about you. Nothing's happened to the Plan anyway since we're here outside England.'

'Oh,' trying to remember more relevant things then. 'But what about school?' and in slight panic, 'What about the cats?'

'The cats?' Harry turns again, laughs. 'They're fine, Eva, they're home. Jenny's popping around to feed them, or Louise. Schools have been notified. Don't worry. I know what you're thinking but the kids are only little, they'll catch up.'

That's not what she's thinking, but he continues more confidently. 'The main thing is that you don't have any after effects.'

'Effects?'

'Loss of hearing, fatigue, depression. We need to make sure you're really better before we return,' now his voice falters. 'We might need a live-in nanny or nurse if you're still weak when we get back. Well, there are options.'

But the way he says it she doesn't think she'll like the options whatever they are.

'Anyway, try to get some sleep now, your body needs all the rest you can give it.'

He nestles up next to her, whispers, 'I love you. I am so happy you're here.'

'Me too,' but the words stick in her throat and tears well up.

She didn't want to die. Of course. So why instead of great happiness is there this great weight? Her chest squeezed to its last breath again, the life she's been given like a choker. After near death experiences people usually report how happy they are to be alive. But what if life seems sad, interminably empty? She puts her hand to her throat. Baba Katya's cross is still missing, where is it? Missing in hospital, she kept remembering then forgetting it, another thing to ask Harry about. Did her parents come to the hospital? So many things he still needs to explain. But he's already breathing heavily, sleep overtaking, he must be exhausted from carrying all these burdens. So she'll have to wait to ask about these things. To trust Harry to chart the course forward. To do the right thing, when the right time comes.

When the right time comes. She tries to empty her mind of questions but they keep popping up. There was a black box Harry tried to give her, wasn't there? Had her hand been too tired to reach it? What was in it? Was it real? She drifts into blackness, thoughts mixing with recollections, she remembers flying, but those were dreams, flying through dense sightless clouds, yes, she's flying now, the whir of engines so deafening you can't converse or be heard. She's asking repeatedly, *where is this flight going?* Faceless people shake their heads in agreement, but in agreement to what? She's insisting – I must know – I must know where we're going, I must know where this is all going! But no one seems interested in giving her information. Then the awful realisation: she's trapped on this aeroplane. That's the only conclusion possible. It will all end in a crash. Death. A blank. The fear grips her body, but no one else around is perturbed, nothingness is fine for them. The clouds outside the tiny round windows are thick, but cherubs are out there too. They're out there for her. But now they can't be heard, and the faceless people chat, unaware of their fatal destination but still somehow reassured. Because after all, when it's over, they say, there is always the black box. The black box that holds all the information.

∞

The house is silent, everyone asleep. She wakes in a sweat, hot and cold. Desperate to shake free of it, wash away the vestiges of nightmares and clammy skin, she gets up.

At the end of the landing, a closed door. The bathroom. But inside, another world: morning. Windows facing the forest, beautiful dappled sunlight illuminating patches of snow. A forest room. Fresh towels piled in the corner, obviously prepared for use.

She strips off her wet bed clothes, steps into the shower. She will wash away the bad dreams. Hot water running over the body, a solid move, doing this. She stays for what seems a long time, but then remembers, water for the others. She steps out refreshed. She is alive. This is the feeling. Yes, she is lucky.

She heads out, back to Harry, but in the darkened room he's still sleeping. Suddenly the joy runs off, just as suddenly as it came, and she's sad. No, lucky – she must feel it again. But no, she really wants to cry. Harry's stirring, soon he'll be awake. But after that, what? Another day in this house? Another day of recovery? No, she will be grateful. Listen to the house waking, the creaks and groans of wood floors and beds, the tapping of little feet and giggling, a house responding to the sounds outside, reflecting nature. Remember the forest room. A warm, sunny day in mid to late January, a gift, the snow melting outside. That must have been the background sound to her awakening, the drip drop of water from the roof pipes to the porch. Less audible now with the banging in the kitchen and in the next room where Lucia must be setting out rolls and jams and coffee with the same cheerful abandon as the night before.

Almost ten o'clock, she checks Harry's watch. Breakfast is out there, the children are eating. They must think she and Harry are still asleep. How did they not see or hear her walking down the hall?

'Good morning, love,' Harry mumbles, turning over.

The forest room. She might have nearly died, but she didn't. And even if they can't really hear or see her, she didn't die. Spring is coming, and she didn't die. That fact alone feels like a chapter drawing to a close.

'Eva?'

She turns to look at him. He's looking at her.

'Harry, can we talk, now please?'

'Sure, what is it?' He must have read the troubled look in her eyes. 'Come here, you should be the one resting.'

'I'm tired of resting.' She doesn't move.

He smiles, as if placating a child.

'I know you are,' he sits up. 'But you have to be prepared to do a whole lot more of it. Doctors orders.'

He pats the bed, but she still doesn't come closer. She needs to hear something else first, not platitudes. She needs to be sure of something.

'Harry,' she pauses, trying to find the right words. 'I'm so confused – by what happened.'

He remains silent, so she continues.

'The thing is,' she pauses, 'if I nearly died, as you say, why weren't Mamcia and Tato at the hospital?' It seems like a good question, so she adds, 'I mean, they know, don't they?'

'Yes, of course,' Harry says, looking relieved it's a factual question. He pats the bed again. 'Please, sit down. You can't stand in the doorway and have a conversation.'

She doesn't know why not but she sits down. On the bed, the place where recovery starts. Though already it has seemed a long time. A long time even since the forest room. Outside the window icicles are dripping into pools of water.

'Eva, they know,' Harry breaks her slide into reverie. 'They were told about your condition. Not about the respirator, not at the time, but afterwards. It all happened so quickly. Magda didn't want to bring them out, have them drive, worry the whole time on the road. For them to worry about us and vice versa. The weather turned very bad that week. Magda insisted they stay home. She rang every few hours.'

'But if I died or stayed ill in hospital for a long time, they would have had to come anyway.'

'True, but it happened so fast. Even if they'd gotten on the road, seven hours, crikey, you could have gone either way by then. They would have known nothing. So we all held tight. They stayed by the phone, they understood...'

He doesn't add *the futility of coming,* but she can hear it.

'Magda didn't want them to come here,' she says flatly.

'Maybe. Maybe there was that too,' Harry says quietly. 'I think she has her life here the way she wants it, doesn't want to give them any trouble. They're getting old, you know.'

'So it's better to be thought a spinster than a lesbian?' But once the words are out, they seem harsh, ungenerous. How much has she spared her parents?

Harry ignores it. 'Eva, we prayed. We all did, even me, and I don't believe. But I didn't let them bring in the priests. The last rites or what you call them. Not that.'

So she'd been that far gone. Almost time for Benedictus and his ilk.

'Anyway, there wasn't time, you were conscious, then you weren't, then back again, so we kept vigils, Magda and I, while Lucia sat here with the kids. All we could do was hope or pray. Your parents trusted our judgement on this, they stayed in Przemyśl, waited by the phone. We all waited.'

So that's how it was. One can hope or pray. Then what?

'Eva?'

'So they won't be meeting Lucia, ever?' For some reason it seems important.

'That's for Magda and Lucia to decide, isn't it? I mean, they know about Lucia in a sense, as a friend who looked after the children. They know what happened over the last week or so. They just don't know the true nature of that relationship. But that's not for us to decide.'

'Of course not.'

She agrees, though it means Magda's still hiding. But aren't they all?

The smell of coffee is suddenly overpowering. She's desperate for a cup. How could she have launched into such a conversation without a cup of coffee first? Harry must be suffering too.

'Eva, these things aren't important,' Harry reassures. 'You've got to remember to take things slow, no resolutions here and now. Now's the time for you to build strength, get better. Later we'll move on. Go to Warsaw or back to England, I don't know, the important thing is you don't slip back.' But he doesn't say what she shouldn't slip back to.

She closes her eyes, and in that dark instant he puts his arm around her shoulders. It feels massive, heavy. She must have become very slight during this ordeal. She opens her eyes though she doesn't yet want to see the truth of it.

'My body,' is all she can manage before the tears come.

'Your body is amazing,' Harry whispers, leaning her back gently on the bed, stroking her temples like a child. 'Your body survived all that – and your mind, your spirit, your will. Now we've got to keep you going, to get stronger. Give yourself time, Eva. Don't be impatient.'

It's like when he said, *don't try to compete*. Good advice, only so hard to put into practice. Especially when you're not competing, you're only running away.

'Oh Harry,' she buries her face in his chest.

He doesn't loosen his grip on her body now.

'It's over, Eva, it's almost over. Eva, it's okay, it's going to be okay,' and over and over, 'Eva, it's going to be okay.'

∞

Her first day alone, she stares out the window. So many days at Lucia's, the initial warmth has dissipated into routine. Like the thaw itself, brief, a false teasing, the world again subsumed by snow. No way to leave the house, nothing to do but wait – for everyone to return, for the hospital to give final dispensation – to allow her to leave, to resume life elsewhere – for Harry to organise it all, make it fit again into some grand plan.

Lucia's on a trip to a gallery, Magda's teaching, Harry's at a meeting in town. The children are at lessons. She counts them off, as if she'd assembled the lot. But it was inertia that did it, inertia taking hold of the Holdens, which finally convinced Magda and Lucia to spring into action, enrol Christophe and Katya in a local school. A school that didn't require forms and dispensations or fees or guilt, a miracle, they were taken in with pure kindness as family, so a family – this extended odd family of Holdens and Magda and Lucia – could carry on.

She pulls the covers of the blanket over herself, looks around the room. This study, so familiar now with its daybed, books, water pitcher, fruit – the whole thing a still life in which she must participate. Get up, get showered, get dressed, eat, decamp to the study. Though nothing will happen there, only more rest. This room is her life now, all movement external to it and to her. It's like being in a cocoon but it is action she wants now more than anything, not rest. Even the smallest distraction – the children home making noise – is something to look forward to, but they're told to be quiet, let her rest in peace. But to rest in peace is death, she wants to shout, so the only way to escape solitude is to ring Mamcia or Tato. But Mamcia's voice is fraught with worry, and Tato's, faking unconcern, *don't worry, Eva, come back when you can*. Neither help. Maybe they're fighting to acknowledge what happened. Maybe not making her promise to return in the near future makes it easier for them to ignore how close she came to death. The way Mamcia babbles about this and that, Piotr's comings and goings, his new business running garden tools across the Ukrainian border, Mila's trials in her dancing troupe, Marek's progress in German, Bogdan's new girlfriend, one might wonder if they care at all. Though of course she ought to be forgiven for no longer caring how many cheese crepes Danka brought for Tato either. Their life events are unrelated to her rhythms, and vice versa. But maybe it's always been like that. Her emergencies, rare appearances, always more disruptive, a source of worry, something to be tolerated rather than enjoyed.

The phone rings next to her, the mobile Harry procured for emergencies, as if they could stomach more of those. The name flashes, it's him.

'Hello?'

'Hi, just checking in,' he's cheerful. 'My meeting's gone well, I should be home in an hour or so, snow and traffic permitting.'

She doesn't reply. There doesn't seem to be anything to add to it.

'Eva?'

'Yes.'

'I've got some good news too – the hospital rang to say your last tests were fine. We can go home. Whenever we want.'

Home, and where's that?

'Well, aren't you pleased?

'Yes.'

'And, to help us all in the transition,' he continues merrily, 'I've arranged for an au pair, a daughter of a lady in our Warsaw office who's been helping me here. She'll be coming to England, until you're really well again.'

An au pair. Not for the kids, but for her.

'Well? Eva?'

'I guess I'll need one.'

'Of course, you won't be able to do any housework or school runs, not initially.' Harry's voice is confident, strong. He's happy in that world where he can fix things with one stroke.

She has to agree after all. He's tolerated her resolutions, like refusing to wear the cross when he presented it back to her. The doctors had to remove it before the respirator, he explained, obviously hoping it would make her happy. But she didn't have the courage to put it back on. As if it might posses a strange spell. So it went back into the box to the bottom of the luggage, where it must wait for a more suitable moment in the future. When she'll stop being afraid of its special powers. She hasn't been able to tell him of the more fearful thing that's appeared: the fear that she might never stop being afraid. That the future will never be what it should.

'Eva? You there?'

'Yes,' she sighs.

'Aren't you happy?'

Happiness is elusive. Someone said that once.

'Eva, can you please stop it? Stop wandering off, mid conversation, it scares me.'

'I'm sorry, I didn't mean to, I was just thinking.'

'Would you mind waiting until you're off the phone? I am trying to sort something out with you so I can finish here and get myself home.'

But he doesn't mean home, he means Lucia's, he's interchanged them.

'Alright, what?'

'It's about the Plan, me coming home, never mind, we'll talk about it later. I'll sort out the tickets. I've got to run now, catch Ian before he leaves for the airport. I'll see you in a bit. Okay? Bye.'

'Bye,' but his phone has already clicked.

The Plan, they'll discuss it later. And so many other things, presumably. The black box for instance, maybe he's waiting for a time more suitable to bring that up too, a time when it's better for them both. She has resisted tempting fate, asking for it, because why did she survive, if not to get better, if not to do better?

But the feeling of stillness, stillbornness, undeservedness permeates. Maybe that is her cross to bear. Because she didn't particularly deserve to survive, not more than anyone else. But if all that remains of life is to do better, won't it remain as sad and empty in the future as it was in the past? If you can't move forward from that, then all you can do is stay in the present.

Stay in this bed, in this country cottage, snowed in, until it's time to re-enter some old life. But that time, the future, the time to return to normality is already upon them. Arrangements have been made – a Polish au pair for Corner House. Harry will still need to go back to Warsaw as much as he can though, so it's not clear if he ever meant to abandon the Plan. Or whether he might have, if only she'd come closer to death.

She looks out the window. The day is fading, it might snow again. If it does, she'll be snowed in, alone. How would the children return? The fatigue of too many questions rolls over her, the cherubs back to whispering behind the clouds, no answers there either. She's trying to grab hold of something solid, something she can announce is real, something worth pursuing. But it escapes like the wisps of white that dominate this new flight into sleep, the black infinity of the sky, always the final backdrop.

Magda sets down her bag with a thump. Her bag sags against the sofa, such a weight for her shoulders she should think of jettisoning it anyway for the sake of her own health. But actually she shouldn't be here at all in the middle of the work day. Magda, surveying the room, why? No one else is around. From her face though, it's obvious something's wrong.

'Eva, I have terrible news.' Magda motions for her to stay seated. 'I can't put it in any good way, so I'll just tell you straight out. It's Adam,' she blurts out, wiping her eyes. 'He's dead. He committed suicide.'

Dead, the word hangs in the air like a devil. But *suicide*? The word is more a question, a disprovable proposition, unbelievable, and therefore unreal.

'What?' Her voice is another Eva's, a voice from the past.

'Eva, you know he tried before, I know Piotr told you,' Magda's speaking in staccato. 'They found his body in the river. A week or so after death, but I only just heard.' She slows down now. 'Apparently, he killed himself sometime around the New Year.'

Think, think, think – though this information can't be processed. Her emotions are raw, like skin frozen to metal. There is a threat here. Her internal life flow is in slow motion, seeping away, she can feel it, like being in hospital again, thoughts congealing so she can't form sentences.

Magda rushes to her, puts her arm around her.

'I'm so sorry, Eva. Really, you've had more than you can take.'

The blackness almost takes over, but pity pricks her like a pin, makes her jump.

'Did you tell him?'

'Tell who, what?' Magda looks startled.

'Did you tell him I was at the hotel?'

'What hotel? Who?'

'At New Year's, Magda, did Adam know where I was staying?'

Magda looks baffled, as if the questions make no sense.

'No, of course not, Eva, we'd only just driven into Krakow. After I dropped you off I came here for New Year's. Why would I call Adam?'

'Then how did he know?'

'Know what?'

'That night, New Year's Eve, a drunk came to our hotel bar. The description fit Adam, he was shouting my name. Harry told me later, I was upstairs. He didn't know about Adam but I suspected it was him. Then he, or someone, brought me flowers to the hospital, I swear, I saw them. Then he committed suicide, just after.'

Her reasoning is already failing, because of course maybe the drunkard hadn't been Adam, maybe all these events in life were a string of coincidences, random chance, like the universe pitted by the scientists, organised and beautiful, but not really. Maybe there was a string of Evas to cry over and she was only one of many. But she doesn't believe in coincidences, that's not how stories flow, not how most of reality goes, there must be causal links, consequences, reasons, how can one take absurdity as a basis? Even endlessly waiting, waiting for God, Godot, anyone, you have to make sense and try to understand it. The world might be baffling but there's something bigger out there, and she must work it out.

Magda continues to study her. She's thinking too.

'You know it's possible he found out,' she says, 'After all it was always the plan for us to come back to Krakow after the holidays. Maybe you mentioned it when you saw him, or I did. Or maybe he heard you were in hospital, many people knew. My church, his, the university. Krakow talks. Anyway, what would it have mattered? A determined man can do anything, a determined man *does*.'

She sits still. Not the ability, but the realisation of action. Not *can* but *does*. And that has always been true of Adam in particular, nothing ever stopped him before. Not in his pursuits of something, not even the Eva he loved. She begged him to stay away from that cult but not even she had been able to keep him safe. Not then, and not later. And certainly not now. Maybe her latest refusal of him, the lack of reconciliation, drove him over the edge? Or had he heard she was in hospital? Believed she was dying, concluded there were no more Evas to live for?

'I didn't tell you this previously,' Magda says quietly. 'Because until now, it didn't seem that important. I mean, a man has the right to search. But after that time I saw Adam in hospital – for his son's broken bones – I started attending a series of lectures on St Augustine's Confessions. Well, you know,' Magda coughs as if embarrassed, 'the Faculties of the Soul: memory, understanding and will. Adam was there too, looking awfully like he needed an answer. But his persistent questioning made the priests uncomfortable. He seemed to want some kind of certainty, beyond even what Augustine could give.'

She pauses. 'Eva? Are you alright?'

'I'm listening.'

'What I am saying is, even then it was as if he was passing judgement on the world. Finding it lacking already. And such severity and dogmatism, even I,' then she stops. 'Well, even I didn't know what to say to him after a while. And as you know,' her voice drops, 'it certainly would have been hypocritical of me to pass judgement.'

She waves Magda's worries away. 'But where is he?'

Magda seems surprised by the turn of questioning. 'Who, Adam?'

She can only nod.

'If you mean where he's buried, he's not. Apparently, he's been cremated already. No service either, not public anyway. You know the Church condemns suicide as sin but I don't know if they couldn't get a proper service or burial for him or didn't want one.'

Magda says *they* and *him* as if these are distant people, Adam and Jana and their children. But after saying this, Magda looks down, adds quietly, 'Not that it matters what the Church thinks. Poor Jana and Stacek and Jacek.'

Then it hits. It's over. For the children, his own children – no more Adam. And no public mourning for anyone else. Nothing she will ever attend. He's been put in a black box, curtains closing behind him as they lit the fires. All that can remain of him is ash. It's over.

Ashes to ashes, dust to dust.

And the wisps of smoke from her dreams return. The dream of Adam appearing as smoke, holding hands with his departed Eva and her unborn baby – *his* unborn child. He had been speaking to her, the adult Eva, but he'd already gone to the other, little baby Eva.

Yes, he'd gone over to the other side. He had decided. No more new Evas. He'd finally found a way to be with Eva and that other child they lost.

PART THREE

'Supposing, then, that I cannot see this Saviour and
Salvation stuff, supposing that I see the soul as
something which must be developed and fulfilled
throughout a life-time, sustained and nourished,
developed and further fulfilled, to the
very end; what then?'

D. H. Lawrence, *A Propos* of *'Lady Chatterley's Lover'*

She stares at the clothes on the laundry room floor. If she can start again, accomplish this one task, maybe she'll get through. *Keep at it*, though this new mantra isn't any more convincing than the last. Too much *carry on, try harder, apply yourself*, which hasn't worked before – why should it now?

But you go on: picking through finer knits, deciding which to wash, as if the process of careful selection might guarantee a better outcome. But *does* choice matter? Because more often life is shaped by the discarded than the chosen. Her past seems to reaffirm it, for having parted with Adam, then Xavier, they both reappeared, like lost socks whose pairs remain mysteriously elsewhere. Reminders of a bygone era, ghosts of the past as powerful as the present, because although Adam is dead, his ghost might be considered alive, how the discarded and departed live on, in the memories and dreams of those who keep living. Ghosts, a dark energy, particles that slip in and out of existence, and even Harry, the chosen one, is like a ghost, sometimes here, sometimes gone. So it's hard not to think of them all as equals. An uncomfortable coexistence.

From the washing machine she plucks wet items, reshapes Christophe's damp jumper and lays it next to Katya's. The dryer's broken, another thing to fix. Another thing requiring energy she doesn't have. Ghosts are taking up most of her time. Sometimes it's Adam haunting at night, asking her questions she can't answer, like *why, why did you do it,* but never answering the same in return. Sometimes he ignores her pleas while other times he reassures her: *everything ends up for the best*. But everyone knows that's not true – things don't always end up for the best. Repeating platitudes does not get at universal truths. Yet Adam insists, *I'm safe with the girls now.* So maybe it's true for him, flanked by cherubs, smirking the way he did so long ago before life's tragedies with babies, when he was happy. But then in waking hours his ghost lingers as a sadness, and it's clear he was never truly happy. Even together, that old Adam and Eva, even with the light there had always been the darkness. The darkness that swallows the body whole between sharp flashes of the strobe, a freeze-frame obliterating human motion, negating the beauty of dance. In his birth the seeds of destruction had been planted and maybe there had never been an exit for him except a fall from grace.

But she'd played a part in that too. So now a chasm of guilt remains. As it does with Xavier, who stalks at night in the passionate embraces she lacks but remembers, so increasingly every awakening is accompanied by physical aching. At night in dreams where Adam is absent, Xavier comes. Surely such reminiscences are just a savouring of sweet memories, a time when there was hope and promise for recovery, when she tried so hard to fit into his world. Xavier is no saviour, of that she's fairly sure. But she can't blame him either – for how could they continue if there was blame to be laid? The scales have tipped in his favour now, she's the eager one, consumed by guilt, desire for restitution, as if Xavier's propensity to take back and the ease with which he brushes over the past, could make up for other losses of forgiveness. For what happened with Adam before and since.

And then there's Harry. Staunchly practical, responsible Harry. Supporting the entire framework on which this rests. Who said she was a pillar? If it weren't for Harry where would she be? Still alone working long hours in a dingy London office to return to a dingy London flat? Where would university degrees have taken her except more hours of translation, editing, deadlines? Repetition and dead ends, only of a different kind, a different kind of emptiness, a childless life she'd never imagined either. Sometimes it's easy to imagine oneself happier elsewhere, but in her case, where would that be, that unknown place of promise? She can't conjure up a life that isn't Corner House and the past offers no solutions, only questions, so she must be grateful to Harry, for the way life has turned out. For his carrying of burdens and heavy loads, that do not include the laundry.

She submerges her hands in the filled basin, wrings out her own wool jumper. These are the things you can't trust Gabriscia with, tasks like hand washing delicates. Gabriscia's only nineteen, good natured and frivolous and rotund, the way many young girls are these days. Forever on the phone chatting, downloading and laughing. Her English nickname Gabby suits her perfectly. She does her best, but there are jobs you must do yourself. The first time Gabby ruined something, it was impossible to show anger for the sake of maintaining peace, keeping to these carefully constructed living arrangements. So she was forced to devise an alternate plan of which Harry knows nothing: give Gabby a string of responsibilities of little consequence so there is no possibility of disappointment. Gabby now, not so much the great help envisioned, as someone to be kept for emergencies: help for housework that's too physical, for when she's too exhausted. Because aside from school runs there's not much to entrust her with. An au pair can't raise children, only take up some of their time, play and giggle, transport them from one part of the afternoon to another. Even speaking the same language Gabby can't set values that guide and teach. No, the big heartbreak, the really hard work, is always left to the mother. So that left Gabby with only one other purpose: to take the edge off *her* solitude. That was an awkward turn of the Plan, that acknowledgement of her loneliness. And a good reason for further resentment. Because Gabby was assigned a job that actually belongs to someone else: Harry.

She leans over the machine for support, suddenly too tired to stand. Why can't he see it? It's not the place of a young girl to keep a grown woman company any more than it is to raise her children. Having someone around isn't the same as sharing a life with a spouse. But all this was put into place in those lost dark hours, hours that only wax and wane like the moon, never so much disappearing as being part of an infinite cycle of sadness, her existence a totality of inconsolable melancholy. She braces herself, tries to straighten, but her shoulders seem to want to hunch. From somewhere the phone rings. She doesn't attempt to get it. She'll never get there in time.

Standing still she hears the faint, insistent bleating, then the faraway answer voice encouraging someone to leave a message. The person doesn't bother. No, why bother? Why should anyone bother with her? Angrily she sets another thing to soak. Of course doctors warned depression might follow meningitis, one of a long list of things that could happen. But it was on the advice of those doctors, Magda included, that she must live slowly and carefully, saving energy for things that matter, that she had begun to sink so low. This default position, engulfed in a cushion from which she can't get up, whole days retreating into thoughts and daydreams and night dreams so vivid there's no trace of the path she'd been on before. It doesn't seem she'd been going anywhere in particular.

But even this, laundering, is but one of endless small tasks. A part of a series, a permutation adding agony of past losses to the nebulousness of what should come. It's all just a never ending chain of being trapped in a perpetual present that offers no hope. Maybe it's this present that is the crippler, a nagging weight, in which menial jobs can only move the day forward incrementally but never alleviate the great suffering of guilt. The greater suffering of not-knowing.

Another thing wrung out, but nowhere to flatten it. A basin of sodden items, and always another one to take up. Like Gabby, another being in the house to look after. Another thing Harry doesn't comprehend. That her own memories of being nineteen are still vivid, the hopes and pitfalls still ahead, hours devoted to writing and phoning and keeping up ties elsewhere in case you return though really you're building a new life already. All these trials and tribulations are the same twenty years later, just with newer and better technology. So Gabby is a reminder of the way she once lived too: happy and free, a girl coming of age.

Maybe that's why they step lightly around one another. This diminished Eva in the vast space of middle life, who must be careful not to be too critical or demanding with Gabby – because of the inherent fragility of youth. Because with all the hopes and promises will come great disappointments, the Adams and Xaviers she'd like to warn her about but can't. The contours of Gabby's life are not yet set, they are for her to determine. Maybe she'll make something of herself one day. She's done well looking after Katya and Christophe and they've taken to her like a house on fire. Another English saying, though not a particularly comforting metaphor, because surely if your house is on fire you should run as far and fast as possible. But maybe there's something else to it. Gabby's popularity, welcome on one hand, but on the other, usurping the one thing that might keep a mother going: preoccupation with her children. But then she can't argue with Harry, she does need help, the disease is lingering in unexpected ways, and she hasn't got the same energy as before. So she must accept this Gabby person in her life and live with her.

She hangs the last bra, its fastenings loose from years of use, and especially more recent wear. No reason to shed practical beige. Just because you can identify resentment building and know you need a change, doesn't mean you'll know what to do. Rising panic, escapist thoughts, doctors prescribing anti-depressants, she was adamant she had no stomach for those. *I'll hold out for other ways of getting through*, she told them.

But how? Survival tactics like changing one's life course or finding adventure or soul searching can adversely impact those closest to you. Because saving yourself is a form of selfishness, not without consequence. And embarking on any path is predicated on the premise that you can hold on long enough in the darkness not to drown in a river like Adam.

Don't drown like Adam.

Conscience, a tinny voice cracking down a line connected somewhere far away. She leans on the worktop, breathes in the smell of fresh detergent. A false spring. This is the dead of winter.

Suicide is meaningless, Eva, pointless, random. And randomness robs you of value, freedom. It gives you no choice.

That had been Xavier's argument too, long ago. Pointing out that even the doctrine of nothingness didn't give you the right to do yourself in. So what had it been for Adam? Why did he think he could find solace that way?

Tell us, Adam, what was it? What robbed you? What did you find?

She shakes her head as if to get rid of the muted inner dialogues. They keep taking over, as if she, an unwilling actor in someone else's life, is merely going through the motions of daily life. But this *isn't* an act – being wrapped in numbness, repetition, waiting – waiting for what? Her own death? Why *not* end it now like Adam instead of waiting?

No – Katya, Christophe. Maybe nothing stopped Adam, but her children stop her. She'd confessed as much to the counsellor: *there's nothing else.* She said it off-handedly, as if child-rearing kept a person very busy, the void beyond the house offering no alternatives. She didn't say what she really meant: *there's nothing else keeping me from the journey to the bottom of a river. The void is already too close, and it's closing in.*

Like Adam.

No – not like Adam. She must fight. The children come first.

Hard-won anyway with that post-partem depression disease, so like this one, overlooked, dismissed, almost robbing her of life twice. She'd contemplated plunging herself to the bottom of a river then, stepped away before it was too late. So she had won once before. The question now was how to battle and win again.

She leaves the laundry, but again, where to? A mystery as great as any other. To the family room perhaps, or the nearest sofa? But that doesn't answer the question, ultimately what to do, how to conquer?

Oh try writing, the counsellor said. Sure, writing, that magic cure-all. As if putting insanity into words could erase it. As if setting emotions in black and white could obliterate greyness. *But it is a method, Eva,* the counsellor insisted, *try putting down your thoughts, then you'll see them for what they really are. You might be able to do something about them.* She did, but no poems came, only flat phrases, and *Dear Adam,* the first important thing that sprang to mind, but that was false too, because how can you begin anything positive with a letter to a dead man? How can that be a statement of anyone's life? How can you put into a diary, *hello there, you're gone, but here I am, in crisis, look at poor selfish me* – as if anyone ought to care. So she left the entry like that, unfinished, guilt-ridden. Like so many other paths, stillborn.

Was it possible to write for oneself alone? Maybe, but it seemed pointless. Somebody had to be there to listen. And it's not herself or Adam she wants to talk to anyway, but someone who might give a reason for going on. But who boasts such powers of wisdom? Certainly not the notebook with its blank accusatory pages. Beckoning, challenging, *see what you can do.*

She takes up a pen, lays it down.

Forget it, they're right, you're not good enough.

Why fight inner accusations, voices in your head, when you know what's coming?

Pain sears her chest, tears bubble up in great swells, roll down her face. They keep coming, rolling over, these tears, for this emaciated body which doesn't want to put on strength. For loneliness, and Harry's suffering, for their flashing anger with each other. For Adam and the lost baby – yes, even that unwanted infant and poor hopeless Adam – for all the senseless dying in the world. Miss Miriam, her empty house a constant reminder of the irrevocable nature of death; Baba Kasia, that even if one could turn back time, nothing would be different. For them, that time had come. And tears roll for this frightening numbness submerging her like a cold current, pulling her further and further from Katya and Christophe. Can't anyone see she's drowning? And tears for the guilt, the escapist thoughts of Xavier, which bring nothing except the further deception of Harry. But mostly the tears roll for what she was. For the lost weeks and months that will never be recovered. For the things one cannot go back and correct.

God never answers the way he's supposed to, so what can you do? Might as well turn to second best: what you know, what feels good. Writing to X is certainly that, though no one would call it real writing. She clicks on her emails. A jaunty back-and-forth frisson of secret notes, more an exercise in futility, churning up past euphoria, cheap thrills. Like any intermittent long-distance correspondence, this exchange can only hold the line. At some point one of them will have to push forward. Because that's what happens in any long siege, one side makes a move, if only out of boredom or belief in advantage or to see the next vista clearly. Because one must see clearly in order to conquer. And if she's going to win herself back, she'll have to dominate this possessive thing.

She scans through the messages; sadly it *does* help. A burst of excitement here and there, something irreverent, something illicit, something even approaching honesty at times. In her last email she admitted what she could to Xavier in thinly veiled frivolity, her *condition* now not a visible disfigurement but a self-loathing, which she carefully termed *feeling down*. Maybe he'll lift her suffering from her all the same. Relief – that's why one goes through the repeated waiting, isn't it? Because Xavier's reply might make time itself worth waiting for: waiting for laundry to dry, for the kettle to boil, for him to return from Hong Kong.

She finishes scrolling through unwanted messages but there is no reply. Despite what she always believed, that he couldn't cause her more pain, there is no pretence here either. Only the reality: her own staggering disappointment. She rereads the note she sent.

To: Xavier
From: Eva
Re: The Reprieve, deuxieme partie

Dear Xavier,

Hello again. I'm writing at the point of half-term – or should I say, no return – Harry's staying away next week. The children break for February one week holidays, we were supposed to go skiing but I've been told to stay put and rest until I'm recovered, whatever that means. I'm no good at rest and recovery.

Never mind, how are you? Do you know when you'll be back in Paris or London? Seems a long time since last time...

Eva

She shifts in her seat. She isn't holding back much. He would read it as an invitation. But he's been on and off again for weeks travelling around Asia. Like Harry really, with his interminable travels, sometimes on or off radar. She glances absentmindedly at the stacks of post addressed to him. Poor Harry. Dropping in now and again to shore up a situation or problem, putting in time they both think is necessary for family life. But the real constancy belongs with Xavier now. Because Xavier's never here, he's never missing. She can't make demands on him, so in that respect she can't be disappointed. In that he's got an unfair advantage over any husband, but then Harry really ought to know better than think it's okay to turn up once in a while. Stupid fucking Plan. It might be unfair, inconsistent, even self-delusional, elevating Xavier to Harry's place. But one has to hold on to something in the void. And consistent underlying resentment of your partner can do just that – keep a soul alive. Maybe it's even better than the gripping but fleeting joy of children.

Children! Christophe! She forgot – Gabby's in the shower. She jumps away from the desk, grabs a coat, rushes out the door. Instantly she realises she won't be able to keep the pace. She slows.

This happens all the time now. Starting off at a gallop, only to feel internal exhaustion reining her in like the sharp pull of a bridle. On the opposite side of the road, Jenny's chatting with someone, James in hand already. They rarely seem to be on the same school run any more. Gabby's mostly taken over this lunchtime dash and for some reason, in Jenny's case, her mother. Maybe the long stay in Poland began the awkwardness, or Jenny found more in common with other mums, but when they see each other it's not like old times. Jenny's concern for her is overt but aloof, as if she can't handle any more turbulence. Did she remember to tell Jenny she couldn't make it to lunch today? She couldn't face the thought of ladies lunching, smiling, complimenting cakes. Still for Jenny's sake, a twinge of regret – which might become a vast ocean if you let it, so best push it away, fasten on the plastic smile that's come to define her public face. She waves, hurries by.

A bell rings and the wave of human traffic reverses. Parents and children begin dispersing quickly. Must be the second bell, the gates behind her already closing, the groundkeeper jangling his keys. She presses on to Christophe's classroom, he's one of two left. A bemused look on his face says, oh Mama, you're late, how silly, but he doesn't embrace her, dashes past before she can even plant a passing kiss. She looks at the other boy who's last now, his face crumpled in disappointment. She'd like to say, don't worry, your mummy's coming too. But she doesn't know this boy or who's coming for him, not when or even if.

Christophe's far ahead, she won't catch him now. Exhausting trying to keep up anyway. Everything's tinged with failure. Like the disastrous February half term she wasn't quite truthful to Xavier about. Another poignant failure on her part, as Harry, ever eager to get back to normal and so excited about his beloved ski trip, insisted a change of scene would do her good. But she had balked: *I don't want any more diversions, Harry. Sitting on a terrace watching life go by, everyone else at high speed, is relaxation a solution to my problem? It's like death, taking holidays, resting. I need life, Harry - action, something to electrify me back into existence.* He didn't answer. Maybe the words didn't come out right. Maybe they hadn't come out at all, another muted dialogue. Harry, at the other end of the line, undoubtedly casting frustrated looks at her intransigence. And it was true, she was being ungrateful, acting like a spoiled child, though really she only wanted him home.

But that argument killed it. Killed the trip, and more importantly, the sex they might have had. But how can anyone give of themselves if they don't feel free? Raging at her own impotence, the binding recriminations, Harry perpetually annoyed at her lack of initiative, as if slow recovery was simply

331

her not trying hard enough. In retrospect it was stupid and both their faults. Harry, furious at her demands and the threatened loss of his favourite vacation, *we're counting days, Eva, I'll be home for David's 50th birthday party at the start of March, I know you can't ski, but you can rest, it's beautiful, you'll take in fresh mountain air, it's only a flight away.* But she retorted spitefully, *you know I hate flying.* Then he said, *fine, I'll go by myself.*

Both of them had forgotten the children.

Christophe, waiting patiently ahead, kicking something in the verge at the intersection where Jenny's house appears in the distance. Humiliating to think of it now, but in that moment of fury, lashing out at each other, they had actually forgotten about the children. She hadn't equated her refusal to travel with the fact that Harry would not get to see them, that they wouldn't see their father for another month. Presumably Harry in his anger had forgotten too, or maybe he was used to not seeing them. The children were never asked. The flights and accommodation had not been booked, so afterwards they could put it down to something that never materialised.

Now it was too late. Embarrassing and too late. The last day of school, half term upon them, all she can do is stomp ahead to quell the anger. But what did anyone expect? What can she do but withdraw if she feels like a failure? Lately every attempt of hers at anything is a reminder of how badly she's failing. Not only as friend or wife or mother, but even as a mentor to Gabby. That she is a failed daughter has never been in question, and her failures as sister are too big to enumerate. Yes, she is a failure, and this is so encompassing it's impossible to take part in anything.

Turning away from Miss Miriam's house to the safety of her own door, the weight of a school run badly performed, another failure to bear, the best option now is to lie low. The bedroom, once shared with Harry, now a place of hiding, another fallacy that's easy to recognise – this hiding as an escape – because you can't shed an old life by hiding, as if resting for ages in a used cocoon will enable a new you to emerge inevitably, a new life with wings. A new life doesn't come by accidentally, or even by grand design. Building a new life is bloody hard work. But who wants to be reminded of that? Difficulties, challenges, more possible failures?

'Mama! Mama! Mama! Look!' Christophe's running upstairs, Gabby's thudding steps in tow.

The tepid winter sun is fading across the bed. Even her thickest blanket doesn't preserve warmth. She sets down the book taken up, pulls the prescription glasses from her face. These glasses, another thing, like so many things ageing her, showing off new debilitations.

'Mama!'

They said her hearing might go, but instead it was her eyesight. As if her body, that sum of all luck, stubbornly refused to cooperate with any prognosis, desired defying medical science. She'd got used to it, glasses for reading, computer work. Probably it had nothing to do with meningitis. In all likelihood her eyesight had been weakening for years. She'd just been too busy to notice.

'Mama!'

He's waving a paper over his head trying to solicit attention.

'What is it?'

'I forgot to show you, Mama, look, I got star of the week!'

'Oh?'

'Yes, Mama, look.'

He comes forward, slightly unsure, having been told often enough not to disturb her when she's resting. She takes the certificate, squints to read the lines: *for good progress in catching up.* Catching up? The implication being quite clear: he'd fallen behind. Where do they get off, judging her children? Of course they'd missed a lot in those weeks, but a mother nearly died – no thought to that though, instead this: a reminder of past failures. She looks at the certificate sullenly, then at Christophe. But he's beaming.

'Well done,' her false happy voice interjects, the one that accompanies the plastic smile. 'You're catching up, and only a few weeks into term.'

Gabby comes forward, head still wet, speaks without really focusing on her. 'Second *half* of term, soon they get grade cards. I forgot Friday when I take him from school, teacher tell me to tell you, about star, and good progress in his writing curlies.'

Curlies? Gabby insists on practising English at the weirdest moments. Cursive writing is how the pressure starts – 'joining up' before you can do a straight line.

'I see. Anything else?'

'He might need new uniform,' Gabby reverts to Polish as Christophe slips out. 'I found a torn one yesterday in the drawer and a few of his trousers are too small. He's really growing!'

Gabby means well, but a mother might as well feel bad again – this resting Eva has failed. Failed to be the first to notice. Sitting there stupidly, being reported to, being told what to do, life in hiatus seemingly forever while this girl takes over. A bang in the kitchen, Christophe or the cats or both. Gabby turns to leave.

'Thanks, I'll take a look at those clothes. You might want to get Krzysztof his lunch before he breaks something in there.'

Gabby looks back for a second, not so much injured as inured to the ways of the house. She's learned not to be chatty unless there's a clear signal otherwise. But on the stairs she resumes her giggly nature, calls to Christophe and their joint peals of laughter reverberate.

Abruptly she gets up from the bed, propelled by anger. Yes, she's been petulant with Harry, but he should be here. Yes, she's been short with Gabby, but who can blame her for being cross when she's in a rut? All this life is going on without her, and how long will this blessed recovery take? If she's become unbearable, self-loathing undoubtedly makes it worse. But life *is* sucking life away. Nothing's happening fast enough, it's all going the wrong way, and pretending life is easy and fun and fulfilling is crap. But where the hell is the way out of that?

∞

She runs the water for the children's evening bath, a bath like so many others, calculated to pass the hours between dinner and bedtime. Passing easier now with a glass of wine, that liberating liquid to soothe nerves, eradicate pain and get through evening routines. For when children get too loud or splashy, for when life's lonely or Gabby's out or hooked into earphones. If recovery isn't going to come, she'll be proactive about it. Of course, a bottle used to last, but now it goes by midweek – one glass with dinner, one after, sometimes a second, or is it a third? Surely a minor indulgence. Another Holden house rule altered. But these days, rules aren't so much relaxed as in free fall.

Free fall, like time itself. The children sliding back and forth forming tidal waves in the tub, how long have they been in there now? Whatever, it's enough, they never want to come out. She doesn't want to wait any more either, time to pull them out. Yanking towels from the heated rails, *Katya, Christophe, enough now*, names, instructions, echoes of the mind, someone else doing the talking, until suddenly they drag her back.

'My turn to pick,' Katya says.

'Aw, you always pick,' Christophe retorts.

'No, I don't.'

'Yes, you do, you *always* do.' His voice goes into a high pitched whine. 'Mama!'

'What are you two arguing about?'

'Stories, Christophe thinks it's his turn to pick. But he *always* picks the boring ones.'

'Do not.'

'Do.'

'Stop it, both of you. No one *always* does anything. And if you argue, I'll pick.'

'Okay,' Christophe consents. 'You pick, Mama. You're a good picker.'

That's doubtful in the extreme, but it's decided, she'll have full power to choose. But which story to tell?

The children settle on to the bed, she hovers at the bookcase, crammed with so many choices. Children's books, each so enticing and easy to judge by its cover. Morals clear cut, the perfect escape, she runs her fingers over worn, familiar spines. Time for something new, but children prefer what's known anyway. Maybe there's wisdom in that too.

'How about *Madeleine*?' she holds up a thin hardback.

'No, that's all *girls*,' says Christophe. 'I want aventure.'

'*Adventure*,' Katya corrects. 'And magic.'

'Here, how about this? No magic, only a bit of adventure. It's about real life, but it's magically written. *The Little House*?'

'Okay,' Katya says, and Christophe assents with a sleepy nod.

So she begins about the little house that lived in the countryside, the house that had a very happy life, a family that lived inside her. But the house also wondered what it might be like to live in the big city in the distance, where grand lights flickered and tall buildings shone. In the country, the seasons passed in glorious colours. Children played under trees, and the changing weather brought spectacular views to her garden. But after many seasons, the children grew up and moved away. City roads stretched nearer and diggers cut closer to the house's garden, and soon more traffic began rolling by. Then other houses and apartments encroached, and bigger, wider roads. The little house watched all this from her hill. More buildings came, taller and taller, closer and closer, even taller, extremely tall, until one day, long after she'd been abandoned, the little house found herself completely surrounded by sky scrapers. It was lonely and dark, and she could no longer see the sky or moon or stars. All the seasons passed by, just about the same.

So this was the big city she always wanted to see, and the little house was sad. But it had been decreed she could not be bought or sold for silver or for gold, so there she had to stay, becoming more worn and decrepit with time. Until one day, along came a descendant of the original owner of the house, a lady who recognised the little house as her own great-great-grandmother's, and she decided to rescue the little house. With great effort, the house was lifted up and transported back to the country, where they found a spot like the old one, a round hill surrounded by apple trees. New foundations were dug and the little house was set down, repainted and repaired, for although she'd been empty a long time, she was just as good a house as ever. The little house smiled, relieved to be able to live in tune with the seasons. Never again would she wonder about life in the big city.

'*It was spring, and all was quiet and peaceful in the country.*' A good last line for any story.

'She wanted a hill with flowers,' Christophe says dreamily.

'Mama?'

She looks up at Katya.

'The little house was happy with what she had at the beginning, wasn't she? She tried the city, but it wasn't at all what she hoped for.' Katya lets out a yawn, nestles against her.

'Yes,' she says, afraid to think about it further. She sighs, loathe to move, but duty calls. 'Yes, she wanted peace and quiet. Come now, time for bed.'

Tucking them in dutifully with the angel prayer, she grasps

337

at some kind of nostalgia, that short-lived calm, the sadness already spreading. She pads downstairs in her slippers. The phone rings as she reaches the refrigerator.

'Hello?'

'Hi, it's me.' Harry's steady voice.

'Hold on.'

'What are you doing?'

'Pouring a glass of wine,' she wrestles with the bottle, the fridge door.

'Eva, you shouldn't drink alone.'

'I'm not, Gabby's around somewhere. I'm relaxing.'

Defiantly, the wine rises to the rim. He's perpetually telling her what to do, how to live, but can't be bothered to join in.

'What were you saying?'

'Eva, the drinking,' he sighs. 'It doesn't mix with depression. You know that.'

'What else is going to get me through? It's not like you're around for brilliant conversation.'

'Dear god, not again.'

'What? What do you expect me to say?'

'Eva, we could have been together for a week in Courchevel, you said no. I'll be back in a couple weekends for David's 50th. What is it you want? For me to come home tomorrow?'

'Don't bother, I'm fine here.'

'No, you're not. This isn't working at all.'

'No, it's working just fine, Harry. I have my routines, I do what I can, then you come home or ring up and treat me like a psychiatric patient. No thanks, I don't need that kind of help.'

'Eva, please.'

Gabby walks into the kitchen, looks uncertain.

'Gabby's here now. What did you want to talk about?'

'Nothing, I was just checking in.'

Checking in. Checking in, what a life. It's like a fucking

airport – just checking in! Make sure everything's in order, no left baggage, no broken rules, all the right forms!

'Everything's fine.' Her false happy voice takes over. 'I've accomplished my maternal duties, the kids are in bed, and now I'm going to watch TV, or go read. Or sleep. I haven't decided. Life's too exciting here.'

'Eva, please stop.'

'Stop what? It's fine for you. You're not stuck in the house all day.' She's seething – it *had* almost been fine after story time, some kind of calm, but now he's ruined it.

'But that's what Gabby's for, to give you a break. Use her, Eva, go into London for a day, do something. I know it can be monotonous but you don't have to live that way. Take a break, go to an art museum, you used to be interested in that.'

'Yes,' she scoffs, 'I used to, like so many things.'

'Eva, I'm only trying to help,' he says exasperated.

'Really, Harry, it's fine. Whenever you come home, it's fine. When you're not, it's fine too.'

Gabby leaves the room, maybe she heard the argument, but maybe not, her earphones were clamped in. But it's a good excuse to get away from him. What does she get from talking to him anyway? Talking is pointless when everything's the same, all these problems insurmountable for being unseen, undefined and amorphous things that lurk after every positive emotion evaporates. Black thoughts, always ready to drag her back into darkness.

'Eva, I love you,' he pleads. 'Really I do. You think I'm at fault, but I signed a contract here, don't forget. I'm in the middle of three big projects. We always knew this would be tough, it would be a commitment. But you said we would see it through.'

'That was before I almost died.' She chokes on the wine. 'As if you cared about that.'

'How can you say that?' But his voice hardens. 'We were at Lucia's for weeks, even *you* said you'd had enough. We had the discussion, move us all to Warsaw? No, you said no. Not for the children. Back to England, you said, back to normal life. We accommodated you, the children. I've done everything I could and can to make you comfortable.'

'Except be here.'

'Alright, fine,' Harry says. 'You know what? You're irrational. We could have been together, but you made me feel like I didn't count. But fine, I'll quit my job and come home tomorrow. Okay? Say okay, and I'll do it. For you. You decide.'

'No! I will *not* decide. You're not going to make me. It's not okay, but I'm not going to be held responsible for this… fucking Plan.'

'I don't understand you,' he says. 'I don't know what you want.'

'I want you to decide, Harry. What's really important to you?'

'That's what I'm trying to do, take your wishes into account, only you keep changing your mind. You keep changing your fucking mind!'

'Fuck you!' Then more bravely, 'Fuck you and fuck your job and fuck our life.'

'God, you're so nice, I can't wait to come home, Ev…'

She slams down the phone, a satisfying clunk, being first. The darkness is almost complete. It is just like the old days, when the little ones were babies. No beginning, no end. Just endless, fucking repetition.

∞

To: Eva
From: Xavier
Re: re: The Reprieve, deuxieme partie

Dearest Eva,
Sorry for taking so long to reply, I hope this finds you better.

I really don't know how you've managed to come through this terrible ordeal, but you're exceptional. I've always thought that.

I'm glad to hear you're recovering, but take it easy, be patient, these things take a while. And look after yourself. February and March are always dull months, especially if you can't ski, but sun is around the corner, must be, even in rainy England.

I'm back in Paris now, business moving at a dull rate. But given the crisis the world's in, moving at snail's pace is better than being stuck or going nowhere at all. We're all lucky to stay afloat.

Write again. You know I'd like to see you, Eva. No expectations just see you. Just say the word.

X.

Just say the word.

Waiting days for this, weeks. No, months, maybe years. Finally it comes. Less taunting than expected, gentler. But is it a new offering or appeasement?

Seulement te voir: only to see you, or solely to see you?

Put a stop to it now, Eva.

Lost voices, a mumbling, so hard to hear clearly, but who wants conscientious advice when it's help you need? A dramatic save is what everyone's after. It's normal wanting it. She wants it like anyone else. She wants.

Be human, Eva. Fail and get over it. Let him in, let him love you, let him.

Buried thoughts unleashing something else again – touch. The possibility, the memory, because it *is* real, has happened before, him touching her, and now there's the flutter, perhaps of crushed butterflies, wretched brittle wings, or maybe the first flicker of something soothing, new baby feathers.

Abandon it all, Eva. Lay yourself bare.
Forget consequence. Body, mind, and soul. Lay yourself bare.
Forget the world and all it was supposed to be.

To: Xavier
From: Eva
Re: on commence

Xavier,

I'd like to see you too. Say how and where and when.

Eva

∞

Was there ever a question of outcome? The simplicity of words belying the power of suppressed emotions, a note holding back everything she might have said: about wanting, needing, the interminable wait. That their failings don't matter any more.

But she mustn't think about the past, or even the future, only concentrate on this, the present: getting dressed. Every act she does, she has to do slowly, on purpose. Even slipping on this lingerie, a lacy black set which hasn't fit for ages, but now on a thinner frame is her only nice thing left. Over it, a fashionable beige chunky jumper – to hedge bets – so no one in the audience that won't be there can say she provoked him. He simply saw through it.

Specious moves. Self-delusion. She pulls on her sheerest black tights. Because if one isn't ready for premeditated acts, there has to be a cover up, or at least the possibility of a way out. The deflector rock won't work, the ring's too big, hangs down helplessly, slips off by itself. But sheer tights, bulky jumper, these are neither protection nor invitation. They don't scream, don't touch me, or here, have me. They say nothing at all. Indeterminate, necessary items, neutralising only somewhat the very sexy pencil skirt. Well, she has to give him something, doesn't she?

In the vanity mirror, eyes glaze over as she shuts her lids half way. Apply low tones to creases and shimmer to highlight the brow bones. Outline the curves of almond eyes with liner, exaggerate lashes with mascara. Finally, a dusting of false rosy colour to give her cheeks some life. It's the first time in ages she's bothered, and looking at her reflection now there's this better version of Eva, stuffing too many things she won't need into her bag. Stopping short of packing a clean thong however – no premeditation, this is life without a plan – *que sera sera.* Though of course, this plan depends entirely on Gabby, left with a heap of instructions. Outsourced responsibilities which spell freedom for someone else.

Yes, freedom that's been purchased, not inherent. She blanks out the march to the station. Through the drizzle, the ride, the stream of houses tacked together on flatlands, obscured by dirty windows. The first carriage is swallowed by the gaping mouth of Waterloo, then another, until the great shadow of the roof engulfs the last container and the disgorging of passengers begins. She changes flats for stilettos, to stand taller, but also because heels throw the hips forward. This way she can rid herself of any trace of that slumped creature that usually inhabits her body. It's important he see her like this, graceful and composed. The one who walked out in confidence, not a weakling seeking refuge. Though really who is she trying to deceive? Xavier can sense weakness in a minute. Why meet him at all if she doesn't want to be saved?

Too late to reflect, take control; in the human crush, a tap on the shoulder, two bodies in instant contact. He takes her hand wordlessly, leads to a taxi stand where babbling customers ring last minute apologies. But Xavier stands unapologetic, as if her coming were his rightful due. As if she'd done it just for him.

And she has, of course. Simply by coming she's made him happy. And this feeling wells up and mixes with the butterflies, submerges. He's as handsome as ever in his slim suit, his shirt the kind of intense Moroccan majorelle blue that never goes out of fashion in France. His hair is cropped shorter than last time, dark interspersed with more grey, his eyes fixed alternately on her and the length of the queue, as if his impatience might only be tempered by the fact that she's already here. Whatever prompted her to break up with him? She doesn't want to be reminded, then hopes very much that she will be – of everything.

Xavier opens the cab door, helps her in, gets in and sits down. He leans forward, hand pressing her knee for balance. For the electricity of his touch, she misses what's said. But it's the thought that he's dared, that he will dare, that's important, not the destination. Who cares where they're going?

The car stops on a side street, they climb out.

'I thought we'd start with something delicious,' he says. 'Come.'

Viens, the command issued in a way once infuriating, but it's the first thing he's said directly. *Come*. It reverberates. She follows up creaky stairs to a low ceilinged space, a private dining room with only six or seven tables of which all but one are taken. Again, failing to catch the name of the place but it's likely the whole day will pass this way, in the form of the thing, without names or addresses or details of any kind. Because this meeting would be possible anywhere, its delineations not mattering at all, only the substance, the force, what happens.

Xavier orders for them both, knowing her tastes anyway, no need to pretend otherwise.

'So,' he says, sipping his Vichy water as the waiter leaves to fetch the wine. 'You are subdued. To be honest, Eva, you look stronger than I imagined, thinner, yes, but not in a bad way.'

Like Carole perhaps? Bony, tsk-tsking Carole? Maybe all along she's been comparing herself to the wrong people. As French women go, this new Eva might be average.

'I've put on a few kilos since I returned. I – it was rather dreadful back in Poland,' she smiles.

'Then we shall have to fatten you up,' Xavier says, returning the smile, 'but only in the good French way.'

He leans in conspiratorially then breaks away to the menu. A bit of distracted banter and she, a willing collaborator. The wine arrives and escargots, a struggle to remember when they last made an appearance, the memory of many things, seemingly important, escaping now. So she might as well return to the moment, pick greedily at the crusty bread, dip into garlicky parsley butter, swallow these chewy little morsels of meat.

'It's so good to see you,' he says, fixing his gaze on her. 'Oh, you don't know how good it is to see you.'

The French, so lovely and melodic, his eyes intimating the deeper meaning: he was worried. Very worried. He cares. Wine going straight to the brain, mixing with euphoria released from some lower part that feeds animalistic drive. Everyone's so relieved she didn't die, isn't she lucky? And so good to see him too. To see him happy, to be carefree. To be taken out, to be taken seriously, to be taken care of. To be taken, full stop. Not end of story. Smile, play the game, it means you're getting better. Because to play you must be alert, mentally and physically fit, show no sign of weakness as you vie for control.

'So?' he says.

'Yes, so exactly what are you doing in town this time?' Her wry smirk turns into a real smile.

'Ah, the wine merchants of England,' Xavier returns the

serve easily, sipping his wine, setting down his glass. 'To be taken seriously you have to maintain old contacts. But it's not important, this business. I mean, I'll have business here, there, everywhere,' he looks at her intently again. 'Really I've come to see you. Are you surprised?'

'Well,' she stops, surprised only by the return to seriousness. 'Yes, and no.'

'For one, I had to see for myself you were well,' he continues. 'Are you better?' He puts the question searchingly, eyes penetrating.

Where to begin? She leans back, remnants of the first course cleared, a pause not nearly long enough to equip her with a clever answer. It's all weakening, this resolve to appear sturdy, giving way to a shakier truth. Where to begin? Like Miłosz: *To Begin Where I Am.* Yes, start there: where you are.

'I am getting better, I think,' she pauses. 'No danger of slipping back. Only the recovery is quite difficult. But Xav...?' And inadvertently saying his name, she mentally has to will back the tears, count one, two, three, swallow, nothing. Why is it coming up so soon? Not his questioning but this weakness.

'Sometimes,' she continues, because *difficile* doesn't quite cover it. 'It's hard...' but that word, a hoarse whisper, *dur,* is the start of a sentence incomplete, hard to do what? What is this hardness?

'Then why do you wonder that I would come?' His voice is quiet but determined.

He seems not to want to let her wallow in pity, extends his hand, takes hers. 'You aren't in danger of slipping back into illness, but,' he fingers her palm, 'maybe you could slip back in other ways.'

He says it not quite flatly, with a hint of inquiry. Is it a statement acknowledging her depression or an invitation to something else? He's staring and the butterflies are looping crazily, but the main course arrives, separates them again. It seems to have come too quickly, though Xavier doesn't seem to mind, as if he'd wished it. And now she has this vision of him having fixed everything: the driver, the chefs, the tempo of service, whatever they happen upon next. He's said, this is how I want things to be. And that control is more than soothing, it's utterly gratifying.

Xavier inspects his plate, says jovially, 'Come, try it. This is their speciality. It'll give you some energy.'

Not just energy, pure delight. Duck breast, a seared exterior mellowing to pink inside, rosy like the tangy berry sauce, a perfect complement to the richness of the meat. When did she last eat real potatoes dauphinoise, those creamy stacks that melt in your mouth? She might as well ignore the medley of green and orange vegetables, one can get nutrients another time. Health isn't about only doing what's good for you but the freedom to choose what makes you feel good, even if might be bad in large quantities. She starts hungrily, but the food seems to stick to the top of her stomach. She'll never finish. At other tables French-looking women are leaving their plates half-eaten. Like the old days. Except then she'd been the odd one out, good Slavic girl to the last crumb, leaving nothing to waste. Maybe now she's finally becoming French after all.

Becoming French – it catches like a dare. Xavier sips his wine carefully, watching her bemusedly, she can tell he approves. The waiter comes to clear plates.

She takes a small sip, smiles. 'So then?'

'So then what?' he taunts back.

'If I've eaten all I can, like a good girl, do I still get a treat?'

It's like a blitz. He laughs out loud.

'I don't know,' he muses, stretching his hand across the table, taking her fingers again and caressing them. He doesn't ask, he does. 'Is it really something sweet you're after?'

'I'll settle for a strong coffee, but with sugar, to kill the bitterness.'

'There is no bitterness, Eva,' he says, softly, and motions to the waiter, already hovering. 'I have another place to show you, you don't mind? You have time today, yes?' he says, more business-like now, but soft too, the question like his stare, hard and critical one minute, inviting the next.

'Sure,' although for a split second she isn't sure. A flash of incredulity – how could it all have led to this? But uncertainty doesn't negate consequence, and it never erases outcomes.

'I wasn't sure if you'd be tired after travelling,' he muses, 'so we can do something restful,' he lingers again, setting up the deception. 'Unless you'd like to take in a museum or something. Fantastic exhibit at the Tate, so they say.' At the last suggestion, his voice drops.

It's nice he's offered but who needs escape when the mind's humming with the beauty of life? Life after white wine, red wine, strong espresso, hand caressed by someone who knows how to caress it. It couldn't matter less where they went.

Xavier suddenly folds his napkin, pushes back his chair, stands up. She catches the moment like a photographic still, shirt open at the collar, his body's hardness revealed in the fabric's crinkles. He's as good as ever. And it's a pleasure and power to watch him, to observe him in this moment of departure, exchanging words with someone else, nothing passing hands. So it's as she thought – all of today is a special arrangement. He's the conductor of the orchestra, she, a string to be played.

They slip out on to the street where the wind's picked up, clouds moving quickly in layers of pale and dark charcoal grey, the whole sky hurtling in one direction forcefully but offering up light and dark in alternations. Only the weather is fighting with itself to decide which way to go. Down a way from the restaurant they walk into unfamiliar territory, a neighbourhood waiting to be gentrified. He stops abruptly, presses her against a wall and deliberately and steadily leans into her body. Kissing her, his lips on hers. A briefness that is slowness, the hard wall behind, body hard in front, her insides dropping away in between. His firmness a gentleness, evident only in retreat.

'I had to know if you agree,' he says, barely above a whisper.

She must be nodding ever so slightly, not so much agreeing as surrendering, her whole body aching for him from this one trigger. With a motion of his arm, a taxi pulls up and he pulls her in. Either unable to restrain himself or wanting to be sure his quarry won't escape, he pins her hand down firmly while his free one searches up her legs. Higher, higher, ever higher to the danger point, she can't even look at him. The moment's liquefying. The taxi stops at a hotel, another unidentifiable place of the day. A hotel like any other, revolving doors, lobby ferns, gold elevators. Props to brush past.

He unlocks the door with a swift slicing motion, gently pushing her in. He's still kissing her, stripping her of clothes, all the unnecessary cotton, cashmere and synthetic barriers between them. It's irrevocable now, this falling away, but then he pauses for a moment, beholding her in her lace. Then slowly, playfully, he leads her to the bed, and starts undoing her straps. Almost roughly he throws the lingerie aside. Yes, everything is to be discarded, all interferences, it's always been this, this desire, until they are bare, intertwined with only a thin sheet half pulled over. He's kissing her everywhere, mouth, face, so she can't breathe. Then he stops, for a minute, an infinite minute, and takes in her presence one last time.

'My god, you are beautiful.'

But it's not only beauty he's speaking of. He means her, all of her, her very being. He smiles and his finger begins again provocatively along her spine, as he leans in to kiss her neck, breasts, then stomach again. The slowness, the restraint, the excruciating wait. His hands begin to move more quickly again, along her back and front, his mouth moving lower, testing every part of her, and he deserves every part, just for that, for saying that one bit of truth, or lie, it doesn't matter which, to make her feel loved again.

He says nothing else, kissing between her legs, lower, higher, she resisting, giving in, breaths swallowed, barely taken, split second measures, getting him back in places she remembers, which he guides her to again. And then without warning, he pushes inside her, filling her up, cuffing her wrists, hovering over and inside her. She gives in to it entirely. This feeling, the agonising emptiness that wants to be filled. Neck craning backwards with pleasure, desperation, guilt – push it all away, the agonies, suck in the pleasure, this moment, because this moment is just for her, him, them, all of us, the whole universe – this feeling of being wanted. The pulling upwards inside begins, the great pulling, a moment stretching to timelessness, a pulling almost too great to bear, and then lightning strikes, the orgasm bigger than any she's ever recalled. With him or anyone. A whole life spilling over, hers, his, a wetness outside but also in, she's moaning softly. It's been so long, but maybe this is what they were all like. Xavier too, groaning as he retracts ever so slightly, pushing in one last time. Then motionless, his tensed muscles in overdrive, he comes. His totality remains static. Above her for this split infinity. Trying not to crush her, but then in the stillness so absolute, a tiny shift, ever so slight but unmistakeable, a crumpling in time. His hold loosens, she's released. He falls to one side, burying his head in her shoulder, body curling into her curves, but he's still holding on, saying, oh my god, oh my god.

Mon Dieu, mon dieu. But what does God have to do with it? Nothing. Only the incredible tensile strength of the wait has snapped. Xavier to the rescue, as she always hoped – no, believed – he would.

∞

She must have dozed off. Maybe he did too. On waking, he's stroking her hair. She lies very still, taking in the strangeness of this situation, this tender, intimate action he's performing. Justifiable but unnerving, because it should be Harry, the soothing motion of his hand, his arm pressing down. No matter what, she can't shake that.

You've cheated on him, Eva.

So? Where is this husband of yours in your great hour of need?

You've broken your vows, Eva, you've deceived. Call it what it is, a tawdry affair.

Not an affair. Xavier. He loves you.

So he's your lover now?

Don't play games, names don't matter, nor words. Only emotions: he loves you, always has. He cares for you, he is caring for you.

You should be taking care of yourself.

Fuck off.

Rolling over, away, not to confront him but search out her own intentions first, she feels him move out of bed after a quick post coital kiss on her shoulder. Some feeling is already withering, but the butterflies have escaped, can't be stuffed back into a neat container. Flying crazy. She lets them go.

Free, free, set them free. But still it's embarrassing, Xavier going about his business, neither of them quite knowing what to say. It's back to the game, though, isn't it, no gross naiveté allowed. She's got to play coy, stay cool, pretend nothing's happened. Fate or whatever. Even though she feels *complètement bouleversée,* no easy words in Polish or English for it, being turned upside down inside out whirled about so you don't know

351

up from down. Maelstrom, maybe? Blown away? Like being pounded by wild surf, that moment when you can't surface, can't breathe, can't identify up or down.

But then you emerge. Then what? To do what, for what? All for nothing? Because nothing has changed. Only a certainty of knowledge, the knowledge of the power of their mutual attraction. But they knew that anyway. So it comes precisely to this – nothing. Nothing to be done. As Xavier used to like quoting: *freedom is exile and I am condemned to be free... I am free for nothing.*

No, that couldn't be, one had to be free for a reason, a purpose, for something, for everything, not nothing. Xavier, standing there naked, checking his phone. Is he actually? So she was right. He too never embraced nothingness, only ran from it, filled it here and there, and now with business as usual.

He returns to give her a peck on the cheek, as if this were the most normal circumstance in the world. As if this kind of thing were bound to happen, because it's just a part of the fabric of their lives. No, stop! The darkness, she wants to shout, tell the world, her conscience, him: it's only neediness, desperation, a failure of ego, *damn it, I'm not like you.* But that's not true either. And that he's not similar isn't relevant. She's met him to match point, again. She closes her eyes to think. He's come closer, he's rubbing her shoulders.

You're even. Love all.

No, Eva, rules don't allow you to love all. The world is not constructed for the love of men but for fidelity.

She opens her eyes feeling his absence again, he's by the door, beckoning her to join him in the shower. Now she must choose.

She shakes her head to buy another moment to think, but he shrugs his shoulders as if to say, suit yourself, no consequence. Was that the choice?

Listening to him, the water beating down, echoes of an old ballad, a singer long forgotten. A simple soulful melody, Xavier humming, but suddenly she realises it's the song Yves used to sing, 'The Two of Us'. Student cafe days stretching out before them, Yves always watching her carefully as he sang, strumming the guitar, Xavier the commanding presence but not attentive to lyrics or music, or sometimes even to her.

Even now he's humming only inadvertently. But the repetition of words in her head is as possessive as his disappeared embrace.

We'll never be one again, the two of us,
The chains that bind we left behind
With memories that hurt,
But we each made that choice alone…

I'd like to tell you nonetheless,
All I am, I confess
You were the one who discovered me.

Maybe you thought I'd go, come back someday,
For awhile I did – I hid and bid
Farewell to things you'd say,
But then you made that choice for you alone…

I'd like to tell you nonetheless,
All I did, I confess
You were the one who uncovered me.

When Time came, my love, you were already gone,
You'd packed your life, to run from strife,
To liberty unknown.
But perhaps I pushed you to that choice alone…

I'd like to tell you nonetheless,
All I could, I confess
You were the one who recovered me.

Now you're gone, I hold on to what's left of you,
Dreams, too late, to meditate
On what's done, regrets.
But I wonder if we'd make that choice again...

I'd like to tell you nonetheless
All I am, I confess
Forever you're the one who covers me.

The fading refrain '*I confess*' precedes him emerging, naked in his glory, proud of his body, his endeavours, the damp on his back like the beads of sweat he washed away.

He stops, looks at her. 'You can stay, you know. Have a bath. I only have one meeting. I'll be quick, back within the hour.'

His voice is that hypnotic baritone but what he's said has broken the reverie – didn't he say earlier he'd come only for her? But of course, how could she have been so stupid? Yes, maybe he did still care for her, was ready to cover for her. But now she'd forever have to cover for him too, even though they'd never to be together as one. Permanent futility – nothing to be done.

So where to go? Because if nothing can be done, you can't sit and wait – it's the waiting that kills – no, she has things to attend to as well, a life to get back to, *tell him Eva, don't leave it open ended*, but the words don't come. Look: already he's leaving, preparing to get dressed, preparing to leave. It's turning into a cheap act, this scenario a stage, even the curtains, shoddier than they should be, the whole facade of fancy hotels belying the fact they're only rest stops for the weary. A necessity away from home, but no one builds a life here. She too is becoming part of the backdrop, and the afternoon's fading fast, darkness encroaching. She can't tell him her life in Surrey is shattered bits, no wholeness to return to. Nor can she decry there's nothing in this hotel room beyond faked homeliness. The play is done. He doesn't see it. But she does. There is no salvation, only distraction. For a moment, to feel so briefly alive. Then invariably you come down from the highs, tension slips, worry and disappointment seep in to fill its place. Every climax is only a temporary fix. A peak that might be reached again elsewhere, with someone else.

She tugs the sheet around her body, curling into a ball to repel the dark clouds already moving in. Didn't it mean anything at all?

'Eva.'

He comes over, covering himself with a towel before sitting down, as if now afraid to be overly exposed.

'Eva, I want you to stay. Please, I only have this one meeting. It justifies the whole trip.'

'Does it?' She turns, eyes on fire. Who hasn't heard this kind of thing before?

'Eva, on a completely practical side, I'm appealing to you,' he laughs, maybe at the idea of her being practical.

'You have the au pair, we have the rest of the night. But I do have two colleagues waiting for me in the lobby. If I'd known before lunch, how things would go, I would have cancelled. I'm not as calculating as you think. Well, maybe – but it would have been rude to change at such late notice, it was part of the set-up, coming here. Anyway, I'm not going anywhere, a quick chat at the bar, I'll be back. Then we can stay here, or go out again. Anything you wish. Anything.'

Anything or endless nothingness? The more he protests, the less it's possible to consider what he's saying. She's shutting down, plotting her next escape, the atmosphere changing palpably, a sudden pressure, it looks like it'll rain hard and fast. What about the children? She can't let an approaching storm come between

355

her and them. They've never been left with a babysitter overnight. What can a nineteen-year-old do in an emergency?

'I know what I want,' Xavier says, in that condescending tone that always irritated, especially when it turned out later that he didn't know at all what he wanted. 'You have a think, have a bath or stay naked. I'll take you either way.'

He plants a kiss and dresses quickly, as if in a rush to escape more emotional scenes. She smiles. This is all so reminiscent of their old dealings. Xavier slipping out to the famous Harry's New York Bar a few streets away from his flat, usually after an argument, or more accurately at the peak of a stalemate like this. Harry's was familiar, American clients always asked for it as if it were something special, sitting in a dark wooded interior untouched by renovations, a time warp to Hemingway's finer era. As if it might rub off on them too. But Xavier was calmed by things that knew their place. Women, decor you could count on, taking whisky the way he liked it, and he'd return superior, the memory of her challenge to him assuaged by the mellow liquid or the experience of laughing at porky Americans in their shapeless cottons. But the funny thing now was what he didn't realise then: that as he ran away to Harry's to forget his troubles, someday so would she, but to a real Harry, who would make things okay. Most of the time. And Xav would be left with Carole, who'd stormed her way in. Yet what had he really wanted? X always seemed willing to sidestep the Eva who became an obstacle to his visions for *la grande vie,* yet now he wanted her to stay.

'See you later,' he says, pulling his tie sharply, stepping out. The door clicks shut.

She unfurls in the bed, kicks off the covers.

Once again they haven't promised each other anything. Later can be such a long time.

∞

His back is to her, he's alone, settling the bill. Preparing to return to her. The weight of nerves shackles her entire body. She stops, but she has to do this quickly. She lays her hand on his shoulder. Almost surprisingly easy to touch him now.

He turns around startled, as if not often caught out.

'I thought I'd find you back in the room,' he starts, searching her face, then registering her coat and bag. 'Oh Eva, don't. What will I do for the rest of the night?'

What will you do, exactly, as if it were only about you – but this irritation, always coming unexpectedly, is a perennial source of strength.

'I need to get back to the children.'

'Phone them, say you're spending the night with a friend,' Xavier says smirking, trying, believing, he still might get his way.

'I would, but Christophe's been sick.'

The lie escapes so easily it even takes her by surprise.

'Sick? I'm sorry, I hope it's not serious,' but he doesn't press further. 'So I guess that's all I get, for now?'

'All you get,' she repeats quietly though already she's wavering, weakening.

Get out now. If you stay too long you'll lose him, or yourself, to this fear, to the wanting.

'No, you're right,' he says kindly. 'You return home. You're such a devoted mother. But I'll miss you tonight.'

'Me too.'

The truth can't hurt now, can it? But it's not just truth she's feeling but fear – fear of guilt and unforeseen consequence, so often greater than desire. That maybe, she still has it wrong. Maybe leaving is wrong.

'This won't be the end,' he adds gently, 'we will find a way.'

She puts out her hand. 'Though we'll never be one again, the two of us.'

'You know nothing's changed, Eva,' he starts, either missing the reference completely or deliberately, strangely embarking on the explanation they both seemed keen to avoid. But maybe this is what happens to lovers. They have to be put in place, afterwards.

'I don't expect you to give up Harry either. Things with,' he skips her name, *Carole*, shrugs. 'It's good. But you,' he pauses, 'you are extraordinary.'

Even as he leans in to say something else or kiss her again maybe, she pulls away. Squeezing his hand, looking him in the eye, knowingly, playfully, half-willingly, she withdraws.

Crossing the marble floor to the spinning doors, the thought echoes like the click of her heels. Maybe he hadn't pushed her into the choices she made. Maybe although she didn't know it at the time, it had been the other way around. Maybe she had been the one who was always too cool, she the one who pushed *him* away.

∞

She shivers as she rises from her vigil, crosses the room. It's because she made light of it. Illness. She used him as an excuse, that's why Christophe is sick. She tempted fate and now she's being punished. It's how all fables go, ending on that false but endearing conclusion, perpetually and readily embraced by the human mind, that one's transgressions must have consequences, perhaps even wider than one can realise. Having strewn bad karma, what do you expect but reverberations? A heavy stone thrown into a pond, concentric circles of water emanating to the farthest reaches, doubling back, no longer orderly, ripples out of phase with one another. To the naked eye, a random jumble, but the universe knows better. The turbulence will subside, peace will be restored.

But will it? Looking at it another way, the universe also drives itself to disorder, and that deterioration is certain, the only question is, will it triumph this time? A question of probabilities then, Christophe asleep for some time, she kneels and touches his feverish head, damp from sweat. The fever might be breaking but she makes an inner plea all the same. *Please let him be well, he's done nothing, spare him.* She doesn't say it out loud because it's for the forces of the universe to hear, this plea. Always the same regardless of plot or actor, age or stage, because no mind can absorb irrationality, fear, unfairness – it *can't* be so, everyone argues, not the child, it can't be him, the one who gets worse, dies. She's no different, taking herself out of the action to become this other, objective, rational, third person, but still praying to powers that be, because who needs or wants a god who punishes severely? Love is what we need, the belief that Christophe will get better, the balance of goodness reinstated. This shivering little being is her whole world and she owes him and Katya everything. They have given her life more meaning than anything else she's done. Creation, any form of it, the ultimate letting go. The will of the spirit to carry on.

Christophe snorts, she rushes to put her hand on him again. He's still sweating, this second night, his little breaths barely audible, so she has to lean in quite close to feel that puff on the cheek. This fragile puff, the only thing guaranteeing human existence. Though of course doctors don't believe in fine lines. But maybe that's because they have to cross them so often.

Kneeling, she sits back on her heels, takes her anger a few inches away, as if he might sense it. The illness came on violently from nowhere, like the news itself, text on the train. She'd been on her way home, one moment fantasising about Xavier and what more might have been, the next finding herself praying fiendishly. Like Christophe, one minute playing, the next complaining of headache, fever. A change in fortunes so sudden, she found herself pleading right away, *oh god, not meningitis, not my boy*. An outpouring that wasn't logical but not crazy either, because these things do happen, unexpectedly, without reason. Gabby had done her bit, then she came home and rang the out-of-hours clinic but they don't listen, do they, just say *keep a watch on him, Mum*, and the next day, the same, the GP: *let him rest*. Rest? Just rest? Rest isn't the *fucking* answer. But all she could do was rage in silence and wonder if that's how it had been for Harry. Told to sit and wait, *let her rest*, wringing hands in gnawing uncertainty. But one can't wait forever, not when a fever spikes, so she left Katya with Gabby and took Christophe to emergency, though by the time they arrived, the fever was coming down and how to explain in the false cold brightness of day that she is *not* being hysterical, if it's meningitis they *must* catch it right away. *No rash, Mum, no adversity to light, no stiffness*, all the symptoms, right down the list, so familiar and condescending, she found herself hating all these clinicians and their diagnoses because don't they understand? They *can't* let him die.

Arching to stretch the stiffness in her back, she gets up and returns to the armchair. She won't abandon it, this place where so many stories were told, of heroes and bravery and boys who overcame fears. Over time the three of them grew too big to squeeze into it – it was always meant for one. But alone, it feels too big again. When you're alone, everything's too big. In the darkness, impossible to know if Christophe will overcome this illness, impossible to draw on life's lessons to some conclusion, because always there might be something more terrifying and unstable lurking behind the scenes. Something that can snatch you away at any moment. How can anyone fight that alone?

Under a flimsy blanket meant only as a temporary cover, consciousness gives way to exhaustion, dreams. Adam again, not so much waving goodbye as turning his back on her, disappointed, but no matter, because Xavier's there to pull her to safety though it's to a dark alley where he means to take her. The pull is too strong, she gives in, feeling at every moment there's nothing else to do but go along. Xavier's leading to a basement packed with strangers drinking dusty chateau wine, acting as if they were familiar with one another. But it's a ritual, this wine drinking and talking, the dust a metaphor for something, maybe quality now, as Xavier brushes it off, hands the vintage away, returns to her. He's running his hands over her legs, looking searchingly into her soul, she's following, willingly, watching from a distance, she sees it is her, gone backward in time, to an earlier Eva playing coy but one with the Eva on the table. She's wishing him on her though everyone's still watching, and Xavier, sensing vulnerability, starts in and they do it right there. Half-naked on the table, devoid of tenderness, like sport. People are clapping, wasn't *that* entertaining, why don't we try it too? But as others line up to take turns with their partners, who aren't partners but strangers, she hurries away trying to dress. Someone claws at her skirt, tries to lift it further, she tries to hit back, but one of her arms won't work. It's numb. But she must get away, it's getting cold, she's waking, aching arm drained of blood, heavy from propping up her head.

Shaking her arm, she crosses the room to Christophe again. Embarrassment of the dream gives way to frustration, helplessness. Passion wants to be stoked, but there have been no words yet from Xavier. He hasn't written since their encounter, so she has this, only this weighty responsibility, Christophe, and her steady relief, Katya, sleeping soundly in the next room.

Kneeling by the bed again as if in penance, she clasps his hand, it seems cooler. She leans in. His breathing is nasal but regular. Maybe she ought to go back to bed herself, truly rest or she'll be no good to anyone the next day. But she can't leave like this. So even though he's asleep, she says the angel prayer, asking for help, a light to guide, from all evil to a life divine. A child's prayer, so simple, but what for her? She's as far as anyone from salvation. Is it too hypocritical to pray?

Then again, why should hypocrisy be some kind of ultimate evil? Why should every hope forever be met with cynicism? Why let eternity mock? Why not participate with choosing?

She strokes Christophe's hand barely perceptibly, she herself now like a butterfly's wing, and suddenly the counsellor's office comes to mind. That worn, faded adage taped to the wall. The paper so thin and tattered, it looked like a discarded thought, to be kept only in case. But in case of what? A case like hers perhaps: a failed person. Yes, a laughable, pitiful case like her. Mistakenly relying on truisms and platitudes, mantras or similarly weak men, though she'd always known none of them could help. She'd always wanted something greater: the infinity of truth.

Undoubtedly it had been there a long time, this notice, going unnoticed. But as it was a first time for her, she'd memorised it. Now there's no one around to listen, no one to ridicule or berate her. So she recites it silently in her own head:

God grant me the serenity to accept the things I cannot change, the courage to change the things I can and the wisdom to know the difference. Please that, especially that – the wisdom to know the difference.

∞

To: Eva
From: Xavier
Re: what can I say

Noisette,

Sorry it's taken so long to write, I seem to have stepped – no fallen headfirst – into mayhem. Work, home life, I won't bother going into details but it's all taking over.

It was so great to see you, and that lingerie. Must I add anything to that? Only my deepest regrets you had to run off so quickly.

How is Christophe?

X.

To: Xavier
From: Eva
Re: re: what can I say

Xav,

Thank you for asking – Christophe's still ill but on antibiotics. Flu combined with ear infection, but recovering. An unlucky year for his health, I guess. Some kids seem to catch all the germs. I can't complain really, recovery is all that matters.

Alas, lingerie – but a brief interlude in life. Yes, it was – so very good to see you too.

Eva

To: Eva
From: Xavier
Re: re: re: what can I say

Noisette,

Recovery is all that matters, I agree. And interludes leading to nakedness are always fine by me. Even if one has to wait.

X.

To: Xavier
From: Eva
Re: wait?

X,

Waiting can kill, but I'll do my best.

Eva

To: Eva
From: Xavier

Noisette,

Waiting mustn't kill, because there will be quite a wait coming up. We're off on a bit of a getaway, Carole wants somewhere warm this Easter. So we're heading to the Maldives in April. Then I'm off to China for at least another month. Good for business, bad for love.

But don't worry, I'll come to you yet. Before the big trip I might squeeze in another London meeting, middle of March. That's only a few more weeks...

X.

∞

'So how are you? Christophe?'

Harry's voice is tentative as he braces himself, the way he does these days, trying to negotiate the minefield of her potential replies.

'He's okay now.' She shifts the phone under her ear, shrugging automatically, as if that might shift the weight of guilt and responsibility from her shoulders. 'I took him back to the doctor's yesterday, insisted they check him over again.'

'Poor little man,' Harry adopts a sympathetic tone. 'You're doing the right thing. But how are you holding up? It doesn't sound like you've had much sleep lately. I'm sorry you've had to deal with this all on your own.'

Sorry? But she's always had to deal with it on her own. She sighs. The phone makes strange clicking sounds. She doesn't even know where he is – Kiev this time, supposedly. Farther than usual, so what could he have done even if he had been in touch? And she's hardly been on her own: Gabby, Xavier, his sympathy, and quite a bit more. She lets out another sigh.

'Eva? I hope Gabby's been a help.'

'Yes. She was there when it all started.'

'You said. You were in London that day. But you never told me about it. Where'd you go? Did you have fun?'

He's only trying to inject something positive in the conversation but she winces.

'Eva?'

'It was fine,' her voice trailing, 'I wandered a bit. It was good.'

'See, I told you, you need to get out, use Gabby,' he continues reassured. 'As soon as Christophe's better, go again. I can hear it in your voice, you're less tense. You are regaining energy bit by bit. How about we do something similar when I'm back?'

She winces again. He is trying. She has to give him that. But maybe he was always trying.

'I'd like that.'

'Eva, I can't wait to see you,' his voice softens. 'I promise, it'll be okay. I know I've not been around much, but…'

'Next week, David's.'

Harry brightens. 'I'm really looking forward to it. Imagine, the first of our group to hit fifty. We'll have to watch and see how David does it.'

'And after that, not much more time until Easter,' she adds. He pauses. 'You know I'm sorry about half term, I...'

'No, it was my fault,' she interrupts. 'I should've gone along with your plan. It was stupid of me to insist you come here when...'

'You've always gone along with the Plan, Eva,' Harry says. 'But we're almost at the end of it. I might have been more flexible. Saving days for emergencies, I thought you were better. I mean, you are getting better, with every day – but still it's too much. Gabby's no substitute.'

Her ears almost sting at the words, tears welling up before she can stop them. But why is she crying? It's just Harry being reasonable. She's always known that about him.

'You okay?'

'Yes, I feel,' she swallows hard. 'I'm glad you understand. Sorry, my emotions are all over the place,' she stops, winces again. 'You know, about Easter, I've been so preoccupied I completely forgot – I promised my parents I would come home.'

'I know you did, but you were right, you're not really fit for travel. I told them months ago it might not be possible. We'll have an English family Easter, at home.'

English Easter. She's never done it. Like Christmases, her Easters have been traditionally Polish, church with every passing holy day, so many, you lose track: Holy Thursday, Good Friday, Holy Saturday until the culmination of Easter Sunday, when tradition demands a basket laden with food be blessed by the priest: ham, sausages, butter and eggs, and all the other symbolic rich foods given up during Lent. A great feast to end a long fast. But what had she sacrificed this year? Nothing. Plenty of self pity, and with Xavier, indulgence, then broken promises all around. So many things to be rectified.

'Eva?'

'Yes.'

'I promise, you won't even miss the sausages.'

Her laugh escapes inadvertently. The old endearing Harry. Her Harry. Even if he doesn't have a clue to all she's upset about.

'Shall we invite Tilly and Steve and the kids? It's been ages since I've seen her,' he adds.

'Yeah, why not.' She owes him – and far more than that.

'Great, I'll email her,' he sighs. 'Eva, I'm so sorry, but I've got to run. Only two minutes till my next call, but I'll ring back later. What time's best?'

She searches through the day's activities, things not relevant to the conversation they should be having. But what can she say? There are only ever routines to return to, and somehow long standing love and merciless guilt must combine to pave way for reconciliation.

'After eight, when the kids are in bed.'

'Fine, talk to you later,' he says, kissing the air, hanging up.

She sets down the phone.

It's no more a satisfactory ending to a conversation than any in the past. Like other times, her resentment is recalcitrant, defeatist, contradictory. A pull of anger versus virtue, victory of passion over indifference, her knowing – so much bigger than his ignorance – yet inner strength also seems to give way so forcefully to resignation. It must be coming.

She rushes to the bathroom, catches the first spot of red. Her insides spilling out. In an instant, deliverance, and a flood of relief. The period explains her moodiness but it's also a sign: she's been given another chance. Despite her transgressions, she won't be punished. She didn't think it could happen anyway, but you can never be sure. But she isn't pregnant from Xavier.

Blood that takes away the sins of the world, the Catholic refrain, how did it end? *Blood that takes away the sins of the world, Lord grant us peace.* Blood that takes away the sins of the world – yes, literally, miraculously, impurities gone, wiped clean!

But it's also true. Because blood can stain. But blood also washes away.

∞

Now that they've started talking, she and Harry, everything is worse. Contradiction, old feelings creeping in, feelings that can't be stopped: guilt, love, remorse, old angers lit and extinguished. Has anything changed?

She pulls the covers to her shoulders, trying to pinpoint that restful spot where she might finally give in. Pinpointing where she is in the scheme of existence seems to be the essence of the game, but she's been trying so hard without success, is it time to give up? Time to let go? No, she can't. Because it's not as if this previous interlude with Xavier was some other Eva, a crazed lunatic who momentarily invaded her body, and now here's this new Eva, or the old Eva back, replacing the sour individual who laboured there before. No, she's upset, raw, confused – but also still drawing on that secret well to make it better: being desirable. The knowledge of the powers of attraction – that's part of what's made it bearable. But that was presented by Xavier, not Harry, so Xavier *has* made it better. Can she be expected to stuff that back in a box and hope it never finds its way out again? Never mind Harry's imminent return, or her guilt. At this moment her heart aches for X, her whole body for all of his, this torment all encompassing and present. And what if it's like this forever?

Yes, the fear of that: the future, of the torment itself. Particularly acute at night in this dream time before sleep, recalling and wanting him, an agony that comes to a head in this expanse of empty marital bed, as Xavier's body comes on to hers. She kicks back the duvet to the farthest corner, turning over, her legs hitting too far. A cold patch not conducive to passion, she has to warm it up, but slicing legs back and forth is reminiscent of children making snow angels. Back and forth, she retracts to foetal position. To that spot slightly right of centre where she always sleeps, even if Harry's not there. As if he'll creep in and resume his place at any moment.

But leaving a space for Harry doesn't trick the mind. Xavier's got new ways of infiltrating. Because now there are so many variations of the past to choose from: the easy days of Paris before Harry, perfectly romantic in the way of a film, blocking out bits that might jar with the cinematic version, billowing curtains, sunny cafes, a rough Brittany coast or imposing Alps as a backdrop, the ruggedness of rocks and sea a precursor to their lovemaking, and maybe a symbol of their demise as well. And Xavier comes in sad memories of illness too, her muddled recollections of the first recovery as well as the last, when he made her know he wanted her still. Always the same – X – he made her know. He never took her for granted, no *you should have known*. No, by his very being – his very *existence* – he made hers impossible to refute. She can't just exorcise him, whatever the intention or belief in rectitude. Because there will always be that moment: on the coast, the sofa, in Paris, Waterloo. The electrifying touch of hands and legs, the waiting.

Her hands go there now, where he caressed her in the taxi, making her ready for what came after: undressing, tearing away, tearing apart. The parting of legs, the forceful invasion of body and soul that was planned, anticipated. And so unbelievably good in its badness. He does it again and again, he will do it again and again, as long as she'll have him, taking and giving exactly what she desires. The build-up, always the build-up, that moment a moment away, an infinite progression or perhaps its negation, a regression, his coming again and again. Her fighting back is only pretence, and as he enters, that pretence is stripped away.

Give in, come on, Eva, give in, give in again. Eva, he's coming again. He will come. Again. He will come.

She exhales with a moan, hard. Conscious of silence.

Only after the flash of light, always this: the darkness. Lying still, breathing hard, insides warm, the cold returning quickly. She restarts the process of warming the bed's nether regions, moving legs, curling back into herself.

Dreams are specious, she must think. Because the entirety of their relationship attests to two people desiring but resisting each other. Two who *didn't* give in, who wouldn't. They weren't destined to be apart, they'd chosen it. Yet desire remained. Sometimes raging like a fire, other times kindling like scattered embers, ready to reignite at the simplest blow of the lips, the lightest touch. It's impossible not to recognise that this will be the end of things. Whether she ends it or not: permanent suspended hiatus. Each of them will now forever be open to suffering, a different kind of infinity from the peace she sought. Yes, destined to be denied and disappointed after each high, because that's what any affair is, a self inflicted state of high and low. Exciting and dramatic only because it's unstable, a euphoria that can't exist in the daily grind of life. It must be the same for him – didn't he say his life was intruding? – like she with Harry, he will always return to Carole.

In the dark she sits up, takes a sip of water. Suddenly the realisation comes: she doesn't even know what Xavier's real life is like. Does he still drink *verveine* at bedtime? Does Carole make him breakfasts at weekends? Do they go out together much? Are they loving or incessantly arguing? What does she do for him in bed exactly? Never mind. Does Carole really exhale chic effortlessly, as she appears? Or do hours of preparation also go into the creation of her, *la femme française*?

She flops back on the pillow, tries both sides, finally turns right. She'd never been jealous or interested in keeping Xavier on a lead. She'd always given him plenty of slack. But maybe it was precisely that, realising too late – only now? – that Xavier probably wanted to be roped in. Maybe he enjoyed playing the kept man in the same way Carole liked being a kept woman, the very vigorousness of their independence pretence to assuage insecurities raging underneath. In that they'd suit each other perfectly. Assigned, recognisable roles, deviations in script unknown to each other. All so French. She'd sworn she'd never be like that, yet she too had been ensnared. The part of French mistress. How could she have been so foolish?

Good for business, bad for love – c'est la vie. Continuing like that the distance between them might ebb and flow forever: Paris, China, whatever. No different to life with Harry. No, big difference: Harry is her husband, father of her children. She chose Harry, not Xavier. Yet foolishly she'd been preparing to give Harry that feeling of beauty and desire and reconciliation, as if he could be a direct beneficiary of Xavier's lavish attentions. What a delusion. She can't keep meeting with Xavier. She'll have to tell him, write him, warn him of the dangers besetting them both. That even in a world of hate and suspicion and death, where in the scheme of crimes against humanity and husbands, making love is no crime, they mustn't carry on. Not like that.

And she mustn't rely on Xav to save her. Their love isn't the issue. No, it's the central issue – because it's not just for love of Harry or her own sake that she must tread carefully. But for Xavier too. For his soul, his love. She made the mistake of carelessness with Adam, and some things you can never put right. But going forward she must make the right choice. Exactly as they say: wisdom to know the difference.

∞

'Please don't make a mess upstairs,' Jenny says, the children dashing by her. 'We can't stay long.'

A feeling of hurt flashes through – why deny them, why her? This is meant to be time to reconnect. Though of course it's wrong to make claims on Jenny when she could have done more herself to reach out long ago.

'I thought we'd have some tea. I've baked *placek*.'

Jenny follows in silence although normally the word *placek* would elicit an excited response. Jenny loves Baba Kasia's messy apple cake.

Pouring tea in silence, she studies Jenny's face. Because it's evident something's wrong. Not only in the reddishness of Jenny's eyes but her nervous tic of looking over her shoulder, as if something terrible may have happened from where she came.

'Jenny, sorry, I can't help noticing but you don't look happy or well. Are you okay?'

Jenny sits, staring elsewhere, remains quiet, as if trying to decide what to say. Then she shakes her head sideways.

'No, I'm sorry, Eva. I should have told you long ago. But I couldn't. You weren't, you know.'

'What? Here, have this.' She sets down the tea and cake with hope. Tea, the English panacea; *placek*, the Polish one.

Jenny touches neither, as if it were another heavy load to lift. She's thinner too, drawn, the opposite of the cheerful fleeting impression on the school run.

'Please, it's me, the old Eva. I know I haven't been a very good friend,' she pauses. 'I am sorry. I guess I've been tired, down. In the last month I've barely left the house.'

Jenny says nothing to this confession, so she continues. 'I don't mean to justify my behaviour, but I really have not meant to ignore you.'

Jenny shakes her head, 'No, I know. That's why I didn't want to burden you further.'

'Burden me? With what?'

'David.'

For a split second, she runs through the possibilities: business trouble, leaving her? Impossible. But something traumatic, Jenny's shrunken figure and manner tell the story.

'He's ill.'

'Oh, Jenny.'

'Cancer.'

Jenny looks away, trying to hold back tears.

'How? I mean, how long have you known?'

'Since around Christmas,' she sniffs. 'So not long, really. Oh, Eva, it's been such a blur. But I heard more from the doctors this morning, that's why I'm so dazed, I'm sorry. So much new information to take in, I'm sorry.'

Pointless apologies but motioning them away doesn't help, Jenny's tears spill over. She's choking on her breath, swallowing hard to continue.

'Remember the night I came to your house? The night I had to take David to hospital? That's when it all started. Tests, late November, his pains started before, of course, but you know men and doctors. He'd been complaining for weeks. Finally I had enough, the shooting pains got so bad he couldn't even sit up properly. I told him that night, that's it, we're getting this checked. He must have had aches for months and not said anything, thought it was work stress. Money's been tight and the garden centre...' she trails off.

It seems out of nowhere but really it's not. She hasn't been paying attention to Jenny.

'So we went to hospital,' Jenny wrings her scarf, knuckles going white, 'that night they didn't find anything, sent us home. But it didn't get better. I was worried, but we didn't really tell anyone, how bad, went to the GP, right up to Christmas, into January, when you were away, repeatedly to the doctor's, irritable bowel syndrome, stress, etc. Finally they ordered more tests,' she pauses, takes a deep breath.

'When they found it, it was not too late maybe, stage one, so they thought. Mum and Dad came up from Cornwall to help look after the kids. You were back by then but I didn't want anyone to know. David didn't either. He thought he could beat it, I suppose. Tell everyone later how he'd beaten the odds. Then with you, your thing,' she seems unwilling to say the words, *meningitis, depression*, as if it they might be another black spot that could rob her of life. 'I didn't want to bother you, trials of chemo, all that. You'd been through such a terrible ordeal yourself.'

But another's burden can be so much greater than one's own. Yet what effect would saying that have now? For Jenny's sake, she ought to have bothered.

'Only it hasn't quite worked,' Jenny lets out another deep breath, hanging her head as if embarrassed. 'It hasn't worked the way it was supposed to.'

She sits very still, Jenny not meeting her eye, as if she's seeking strength elsewhere, in an un-pinpointed distance.

'The first round of therapy didn't go as well as we'd hoped,' Jenny takes a breath, steadies her voice. 'Maybe they misdiagnosed him at the start, who knows. Now they say it's further along, and we have to cancel the party because he needs more chemo, and this new drug,' she breaks down. 'I don't know, Ev, I don't know. I just can't imagine myself without him.'

Suddenly Jenny's crying. Not weeping but heaving like a wounded animal, gulping strident wails that speak of raw anguish that cannot be assuaged.

She freezes. No – not death. Not more victims. Her own tears spring as she moves closer to Jenny, pressing her small shaking frame into her own. But it's not enough. There's not enough of anything to transmit love and hope and belief in the eternal when faced with this.

'I'll help you,' she whispers. 'I know it's not much, but you can count on me and Harry. Don't hide, ask, whatever you need, we're here. You understand?'

'I do, thanks.' Jenny tries to pull herself together.

But the facts are still missing and she wants more details, to make it more real, to alleviate disbelief. How much chemo? Did she get a proper second opinion? How could they misdiagnose? Where is the cancer exactly, what new drugs? Why didn't they really say something earlier? David and Harry, such close friends, surely distance superimposed by the past year didn't count. But then the Holden rollercoaster, *they* must have seemed inward looking too, like Jenny and David, hoping things wouldn't take a turn for the worse, spiral out of control.

'Oh god, pass me a tissue,' Jenny says, hearing the children upstairs, trying to fix a smile. 'I've cried so much, I seem to use up boxes of these. Now this, you know? The news we didn't want to hear. But there it is. I'm not prepared for things getting worse. You're told, so you know it, kind of, but still you can't believe it, because it's crazy. And David's so unwell today. In bed at his dad's, where it's quiet, so many painkillers. But now I'm so afraid, Ev, of that day he goes to hospital and doesn't come back.'

Jenny gets up and they stand there holding each other tight.

Doesn't come back. The words ring. Is it right to acknowledge the inevitable? But if they lose hope, what's there to believe in then? That the spirit survives? That we all continue? Is that supposed to help?

'Jenny, I'm so sorry.' Her squeeze produces more tears in them both.

'Sometimes, I can't stop crying,' Jenny says.

'Nor should you, cry as much as you want.'

'God, that's a lot.'

She smiles, pulls back, blows her nose hard.

'I know this sounds stupid but I've been balancing all this bad news with work,' Jenny waves her arms in frustration, 'because believe it or not, having a few hours to cook and plan something else seems to keep me from going over the edge. It's not only that I have to take it seriously now, because maybe someday I'll have to earn for us both. It's because I can't stand to sit around and watch David in such pain.' She blows her nose again.

You don't have to justify yourself. Say it. Tell her.

'So my mum and dad are helping and David sleeps at home at night but during the day he goes to his father's for a few hours rest, then comes home, like from work.'

Oh god, then the kids don't know.

'I don't know how he does it but that's how things are,' Jenny says, hesitating. 'We haven't figured out how to tell the children.'

And then, although she's been trying hard not to cry, tears start rolling down again. The noise of the children grows louder, they're coming down the stairs. Jenny starts wiping her eyes rapidly in vain, they're too puffy to disguise.

'They know something is wrong, that Daddy's not well, he's lost his hair, he's tired. But that's far from what might happen. So it's not that we haven't figured out how to tell everyone else. We just haven't figured out…'

How to tell the children.

∞

Harry's not answering his phone, she's left him another message, *it's urgent,* why doesn't he return the call? She must stay awake, to tell him, not only unburden herself but figure out a plan of action. To do something – anything – is a way of carrying on, isn't it? Although what can you do when it all might be futile?

She rolls over in the darkness. All the times they went out

together, she and Jenny, David and Harry, so long ago, those parents' nights at the pub, dads in the park on Saturday mornings trying to figure out their toddlers for long enough so mums could enjoy a break and soak in the bath. All those times, seemingly tedious, frivolous, engulfed in an instant: light disappearing into a black hole. And yes, being in the dark about it, David and Jenny trying to keep up appearances as if it should matter what other people think. But then who was to blame for letting silence take over?

She turns the light on, blinks at the bedroom, the furniture, possessions, trivialities, the party cancelled, Harry probably already en route, and bigger issues, like Sophie and James, because surely David and Jenny ought tell them, give them time to prepare. Then again Jana and her boys had no preparation, no idea of what was coming, so maybe it doesn't matter about the preparation. Not when the outcome is the same: permanent. She always felt sorry for Harry losing his parents suddenly, not like Xavier, as if contemplating the idea had counted. But maybe she'd been wrong. All these fathers being whisked away: Adam, David. Maybe the preparation didn't matter that much.

Her stomach tightens into a knot. No, one must fight the fear. The preparation for death surely counts. Asking the questions and acting with meaning before it's all over. She stares at the phone willing it to ring, but she doesn't know where Harry is. Another thing she must correct going forward: keeping track. Because accidents do happen and as much as it seems incredible, it's all statistically possible: so many deaths per year. Airplanes crash. People die all the time. She herself was almost a statistic. Though it seems easier, fighting for your own life rather than watching another's possible passing. She feels frozen. It must have been like that for Harry, watching her, waiting, time standing still. The waiting being infinitely preferable to things going the wrong way. Maybe some deaths were easier to comprehend, Baba Kasia, Miss Miriam, a sad but natural order, but Adam was still incomprehensible. On the other hand, he did choose it. But David – David is having this battle thrust upon him, the worst kind, odds not good, the whole thing spinning into the absurd. Because even if ultimately we all die – the stative present, the state of existence – surely one must do something.

Fight, yes, but how? Following mottos? A philosopher's bidding? The priest's incantations? What can they say now? Be stoic? This is part of heaven's great plan? Yes, you've been given an infinity inside you, mankind, but oh well, you get death. What the fuck good is death?

The phone rings.

'Harry?'

'You asleep? I've ten missed calls, what's up?'

'Harry, bad news,' she pauses but can't really choose words carefully. 'Harry, the party's not happening, David's been diagnosed with cancer. He's in chemo, new medications. It's serious,' she breathes in and out, finally slowing to impose order on the jumble. 'Harry, he might be *dying*.'

The silence, the line a vacuum of time, space, breath.

'Harry?'

You expect him to ask reasonable questions, how, when, why, where, but he says nothing. Please no, not the wrong words again.

'Harry, did you hear what I said? David…'

'I heard you,' the voice without emotion. Complete devastation.

Wait. He'll say something.

'This isn't working.'

'What?'

'This isn't working, Eva,' his voice is shaking. 'Eva, are you okay?'

'Harry, it's not me, it's David and Jenny…'

'I know,' he interrupts. 'But can you hang in there, please? Help Jenny as much as you can, I'll see how fast I can manage this.'

'What?'

'I told you. This isn't working. It's over. I'm coming home.'

∞

The room's dark. He's probably asleep. Although he said he'd wait up if she wanted to talk. And she *has* wanted to talk. Because they need a clear discussion of David's condition, how to help Jenny. And what's happening with Harry's job, their future. Even the status of the Plan. Because surely he hasn't quit his job? But it's all unclear, it's waiting time again – waiting for Harry to tell his story in full, in his own time.

She crawls into bed, listening for indications of his breathing, tries to bring the covers higher for him, so inexplicably exposed. She can't fix the tangle of bedding without waking him, however. It's like nothing ever happens as you wish, or quickly enough, then when you do finally get what you want, it's never as you imagined. Just another bind. Harry home, but in the shadow of illness, possibly death. He'd spent hours badgering her for information, as if facts might shape a different outcome, as if erasing uncertainties would produce a better result. The way he tried to grab on to tangibles, even as he changed planes, airports, trying to get home faster, she could tell he was furious. He kept asking if she were okay, as if his absence, their separation, were now a worse thing to endure because of David's battle. *You sure, are you sure, are you up to it?* As if it was about her and not Jenny. *Of course, it's what anyone would do,* she assured him. *I'm fine, helping Jenny look after the children. I have Gabby.* But maybe that was a reminder to Harry that she too was still unwell.

He stirs, puts his arms around her, they lie like that in silence for a long while.

'The thing is,' he finally begins. 'Until I heard about David,' he pauses again. 'Until I saw him this evening, I thought I had all the time in the world.' He pulls the sheet over his bare chest. 'I really did.'

Then he lapses again into silence, the kind he now seems prone to, and it's hard to know what to follow with. Because on one hand it's totally predictable what he once would have said – *bad luck, all of it, damn it* – and that's true too, not just about David, but Harry's own homecoming. It should have been a thing of joy. An event awaited so many months. It should have taken place with balloons and champagne, maybe even that pie-in-the-sky trip to the Seychelles. Instead, it's come out flat and indifferent, in so many ways a defeat.

'So you see,' he continues, 'you work hard and then it gets snatched from you anyway. So what do you end up with?'

This moment. Just this moment.

But the words don't come out. She breathes in and out. Some things he must find out for himself.

In the meantime, she can do this tiny thing, to bridge the emptiness, the stillness between them: she puts her hand on his chest. Ever so lightly like a butterfly's wing, to feel his skin, the beating of his heart. Her touch seems to warm him, arouse him, and he responds ever so slightly in return, a slight groan escaping. He must know, must understand, it is about this moment. In the midst of all the possible losses and possible letting go, he too must choose to let go. Let go of all that ails him. She moves closer, wanting more than ever for there to be no space between them, to be rid of the bad and the guilt, maybe the good too. Infinity, the sum of all things, but its absence as well.

He moves on to his side, his hand caressing her absentmindedly, she can feel it, knows the difference between mental presence and absence, even in the darkness. But then his despair slips away, or maybe it's despair driving him, because he focuses on her, becoming more adamant and forceful, surer than she can ever remember him. It's as if he's fighting for his life, and surely he is, because what else is there to ward off death except life? Life, in its most vigorous and passionate form. And he dispenses with loveliness, the tentativeness that usually colours their first times together and pushes himself inside her, and that's when it becomes tenderness again. A sudden overwhelming weakness taking all humans beyond the realm of animal. Something bringing knowing and glory beyond the physical. A recognition, temporal and not, of what it's like to be part of something else.

She gasps and drops back, another person, a being falling to a place she so rarely goes, not so much existing as dissipating into liquid loveliness, no form at all, this she, only space, which returns to a body that holds him tightly, even after his breathing has gone shallow. Oh, no, he's sobbing, she puts a hand to his face, but there's nothing wet, he's curling into her, burying his face in her breasts. She holds him until she hears regular breathing.

He needs to rest, he must. The battle is still ahead. But some part of the ordeal is over. He's with her now. He is home.

∞

'Harry, I'm sorry,' she looks out the kitchen window. 'It's really awful, how did it get to this state?'

On both sides apologies seem to tumble out easily now. For her, a sense of duty prodding: do something to stem the chaos. And the garden's always been her focus. Harry's overwhelmed anyway with his daily visits to David, working from home, trying

LESIA DARIA

to catch up on a year's worth of house affairs – all whilst trying not to show the strain.

Soon critical eyes will be on Corner House: Tilly. She'll note that only the approach to the house is neat, the vistas behind it tragically beleaguered. Though maybe that's always the family secret – front for show, back a disaster. Yet even by low standards, what a mess: branches broken, overgrown grass bent from recent snow, muddied pots, decaying leaves, so many untended things. Can she rectify it in time?

'I'm ashamed,' she turns back to Harry, engrossed in old post amidst breakfast debris that covers half the table. 'It's absolutely destroyed out there. I haven't even kept up with basics. Christophe and Katya have been asking why we haven't planted beans like last year, I feel like I've failed everyone.'

Failed – admitting to it openly now.

'Honey, you aren't failing them because you haven't planted vegetables,' he says reasonably, head still buried in papers.

'But they expect it, and I want to give it to them,' she turns back to the garden, 'I mean the children, but now Tilly and Nathan, all of them, coming in a few weeks. The garden looks so untidy, unloved and forsaken, sad to look at and be around.'

'Nothing we can do about it now, but I agree, we should get a gardener.' He tears through another envelope.

It's not the answer she's seeking, throwing money at problems instead of crafting solutions. She tries again.

'That isn't the point, Harry. The point about gardening is doing it yourself. Growing, nurturing, you don't get a feeling of good if someone else does it. It won't be my work, restoring things, making them better. Like with the children, Gabby's helpful, yes, but not the same as putting in time and effort yourself.'

Harry sets aside a letter he's about to open, another envelope she hadn't touched though it looked important and curious, local

382

solicitors contacting them. She'd judged it the kind of thing best left to him.

'Well?' she says. 'Do you think it's normal?'

He looks at her curiously. 'Eva, what's normal? What's normal about our lives?' He sets down his mug, notes it's empty, signals for more. 'Aren't we winging it? Taking chances, hoping decisions are good? No guarantees in life. Look at David, no promises or expectations, we're all just hoping for the best. Some say hope is pointless, a wasted emotion, but I'm taking inspiration from him. Why be negative? Fight on. And you're doing the best you can. You can't do any heavy lifting now, turning over earth, carrying sacks, digging roots, hours of weeding. Let things go a bit.'

She winces. It's the advice she would have given him the other night about his own preoccupations, so much easier to dispense than apply to oneself. She watches him at the kitchen table fighting her own feeling that maybe again she's being swept away, from person in charge to person on the periphery. Sometimes it's as if he never left: the endless cups of coffee, strewn mail, bits of traded philosophy, bewildered looks when she goes on about something in her head he's never even considered.

'Do what you can,' he continues, 'but don't worry so much about everything, what anyone else thinks. Our garden's fine. I'm sure Tilly's is in a right state, it always is. Diggers are practically a feature in her garden, it's not like she'll notice. And in a few weeks the Easter bunny will come just the same, even if the garden is a shocking mess, which it isn't. Just early days.' He extends his hand for her to come over, maybe sit on his knee, like she used to.

'But making life beautiful makes me happy too,' she says softly, not taking up his offer. He might be right about Tilly, and seasons coming and going regardless of the state of the garden, but what if it's not a cycle but a progression? Not early days, but late in the day, far down the spiral, and they are already there, much later on, with everything changed so much you can't recognise it any more?

'I like things the way they used to be.'

Harry sighs, lowers his hand. 'No use longing for the past, Eva, or worrying about the future. Not beyond what we can do. We'll do things differently, get a gardener for a while, you can work together, he'll do jobs you can't. You can still be creative, get the kids involved, do fun stuff like plant seeds. But don't wear yourself out. And don't get down.'

As ever he's being practical and this concern makes her smile.

'Okay, I'll get someone to help.'

'That way you can keep up with the post too,' he half-jokes. 'You're allowed to open things with my name on them you know. Bring me some more coffee, love?' He reminds her gently, looking back at the solicitor's envelope. 'What's this anyway? Post marked January 15.' He tears through it.

She brings the coffee but he's already absorbed by the letter.

'Sorry, I only left it for you because it seemed like your area of expertise, legal stuff.'

'Well I'll be damned.'

'What?'

'Miss Miriam left us her property.'

'What?'

'In her last will.'

'That's not possible – is it?'

'Yes, odd but possible – but also being contested by her next of kin. Look.' He shoves the paper over, but the words are legalese and Latin.

'Can they contest?'

'Sure. They're questioning the legality of the will, which

means, her final state of mind. Which is what I would do too, if I were her offspring.' He takes the paper back. 'You have to ask, why leave that property to neighbours? It's worth seven, maybe eight hundred thousand, at least, with a garden that size. Substantial money even after inheritance tax,' he looks up excitedly. 'What made her do it, your visits? Eva, is there something you know, aren't telling?'

She pauses, sucks in her breath. 'No, I'm as shocked as you. I did visit her every Wednesday, take her lunch, sometimes other things, weeding, watering, between her gardener's visits. Other times I would pop over, see how she was doing, we were friends. Close friends, I thought, but there wasn't any agreement or anything, she never mentioned...'

'Well, it's highly unusual.' He runs his fingers through his hair, his mind working furiously.

'I don't know, Harry, I think they fell out, Miss Miriam and her children. They never visited her much when she was alive, she was critical of them for that. Though I can't believe they'd ruin her reputation, trying to make her out to be demented.'

'To claim that property they'll do more than that, they'll legally declare her insane and overturn the will in court. If it gets that far.'

'I'm sorry,' she breathes out, pauses. 'But Harry, are we really entitled to it?' It slips out before she can stop it. 'I mean, surely, you'd expect... I mean the house and property *ought* to go to her children and grandchildren.' She doesn't add, even if they're selfish, uncaring old coots – the sharp memory of Emma shutting the door in her face.

'You're not seriously saying we should give this opportunity a miss?' Harry's voice rises, his forehead a wrinkled frown. 'This is more than four times what I've been trying to save this past year, which is not in the bank yet, and look at all the hardship we've endured. This could be like winning the lottery.'

She pauses. He seems to be forgetting that the odds of a lottery win are abysmal. But when she brought round the basket what had Emma said? *We don't need your kind.* It sounded like pure bigotry, but what if Emma had been angry because she knew then about the will? What if Emma thought this neighbourly Eva had stolen the house from her?

'Harry, what if Miss Miriam wasn't well? Not fully?'

He looks at her evenly. 'Are you *not* telling me something?'

'It may not be significant but Miss Miriam did sometimes talk to people who weren't there. Her dead husband Charlie, for instance. Towards the end, she mumbled odd things, had little lapses of memory, like old people do, I suppose, sometimes.'

'How little?' His voice hardens, not a pleasing thing.

'I don't know. I'm sure her family knows better, the health visitor.'

'Eva, crikey, I totally forgot – that episode with the scam artists, remember? You told me about some workers who took advantage of her forgetfulness, that might be another indication,' Harry shakes his head. 'Something they could use against her.'

So like Harry, not to forget a thing, even if at the time she thought he hadn't registered it because he'd brushed it away.

'But Harry, we don't need this,' she sighs, meaning another thing coming between them, but he's gathering up the letters, his coffee, heading to the study.

'Maybe not,' he says, turning around. 'But with a solicitor involved, writing to us as beneficiaries, I can't ignore it either.' He continues to the desk, starts setting down his things.

'But what are our rights and obligations, Harry?' she calls after him, refusing to follow. 'Are they only legal or moral too? Are we only ever going to try and take all we can get?'

He looks up and starts back towards her. She's afraid he's angry but he stops, straddles the space between the desk and the doorway.

'Eva,' he says calmly. 'Sometimes you can't straighten out one area without creating problems in another. The way I see it, the devil's in the details. Ultimately, we may not even have that much choice.'

'What do you mean?'

'Miss Miriam must have gone through some process for a valid will. She must've gotten witnesses, an executor, the lot. It was her property to give, I presume, unless her children were still dependents, in which case, they might be owed part of it,' Harry pauses thoughtfully, working aloud. 'At the moment, it seems like a valid will and we haven't been served court papers, so that's good news for us, because either we win outright, or if they do want to question her mental state, we can fight or negotiate a deal. In other words, split the assets and everyone goes home happy.'

'Is that likely?'

'Well, I can't see how they wouldn't try to contest this and try to get something. But the bad news is, if they think they have a very strong case, medical evidence, etc., instances of *lapses*,' he stresses the point with his hands, knuckles hitting palm, 'and they take this to court, then we're talking one to two year litigation and costs. I couldn't handle the case myself, not only because I'm not here enough, but because we'd need a specialist on it. Even using someone else in the firm, a significant portion of the assets would be lost in fees. So it's better to negotiate these things. Not to mention, you can never guarantee a win. And if it looks like we made a claim in bad faith, we'd pay not only our costs but the opposing side. So we could actually lose money. You follow?'

'Sort of. Basically, it depends on whether she was sane or not, how much her family will push back, and who's being honest.'

'In a nutshell.'

'So it'll take a while,' she breathes out. 'But what about David?' She can barely bring herself to add. 'What about the Plan?'

'David? Eva, I can't do anything about David, just wait like everyone else, hope he makes a solid recovery,' he comes closer, leans on the doorframe. 'He's stable and not giving up, so that's good news. As to the Plan, only a few more weeks and we should be through. Thank god I saved up time. But I have to go back to Warsaw for another meeting next week, though not for more than a few days.' He turns his back now, grabs the papers.

'But this – this will take some doing. Whatever our rights, whatever we choose, Eva, we've been dragged in. We'll have to fight.'

∞

It's absurd having to sift through this stuff given what else they have to worry about. But frankly, she shouldn't have deferred it all to him in the first place. She studies the mountain of paper on the desk, a product of those seemingly innocuous slivers of post pushed through the door every day. No one asks for them but still they come: a couple of letters, then some more, a flyer here and there, a weekly, a circular, each one a tiny component of a much larger invasion until you're totally snowed under. Harry now gone a few days, maybe a week, still worried about everything: Miss Miriam's estate proceedings, letters, bank statements, credit card bills, her. All the things she let slide, to which she could add: parent-teacher consultations, family birthdays, marriage. Big and small, they'd all have to be worked through, and she's got to do her bit. But first the pile of messages on the computer. Her eye falls instantly on the most dangerous:

To: Eva
From: Xavier
Re: Repatriation

Noisette,

*Heading back from unexpected jaunt to Shanghai, will be
over your way soon. Be warned.*

X.

Sent from his phone. So he's on the road. No urgency then. She
had meant to write to him, relate her resolution, even if her
resolve is still so often weak. She can't remember what they last
agreed, they'd left it open-ended, hadn't they? So what to say
now? Explaining their situation is as futile as appeasement. But
she'll have to write him something. When the right words come.

For now she can resolve something else she left open-ended.
Something far more straightforward but no less important.
Magda, the sister she's never properly thanked.

To: Magda
From: Eva
Re: Something long overdue

Dearest Magda,

*It's almost full spring here, quite blowy, raining on and off.
The snows of Poland, the icy cold, Christmas, New Year's,
all seem a lifetime ago.*

*There's no excuse for my not writing sooner, though I
suppose we all get busy and distracted, then time moves
faster than expected. But my recovery is slow, my energy
often wanes. I find I want to move ahead with projects but
fizzle out. I probably ought to rest more, as you always
recommended, but I don't much enjoy it.*

Lately we've been hit with another big worry: a friend of ours has cancer. We're all waiting, but we don't know for what. It's rather dreadful, treading water like this, though it does focus the mind on the things one ought to do, one of which is to thank you properly. I should have done it long ago.

So I'm writing to thank you, Magda, for all your help, and Lucia's too. If it weren't for both of you, I doubt I'd be here. Your quick thinking, the care you took of me in hospital, the care you took of our whole family, certainly none of us have forgotten, the children especially. We'd love to see you and Lucia again, maybe in the summer? Perhaps we can come out to Krakow or meet at Mamcia and Tato's or even Warsaw if Harry's still making trips there.

I know we haven't always seen eye to eye but I do enjoy the times we've spent together, and I hope we can have more of them. Stay well and please write when you can. Give my best to Lucia, and again, infinite thanks from my heart.

With love,

Eva

Suddenly she knows exactly what she'd like to say to Xavier – no, shout at both him and Harry. It *isn't* the waiting that kills but the countdown of days. Counting the hours and weeks and months, the omelettes one will eat, the number of cafes you've sat in, calculating the money earned and the nights until we meet and love again: therein lies death.

The doorbell rings, she leaves empty the reply-to-sender note to Xavier, a message still without content. She goes to the door.

Where she can see clearly through the window: it's him.

Xavier.

Not possible.

But really, it's him.

He rings again.

She opens the door just wide enough, heart beating madly. 'Hello.'

The deep, satisfied voice, fluid and serene. But he's looking casual, in a jumper and jeans. He smiles and flicks a bouquet of tulips up from behind his back.

'Surprised?'

Still no words.

'May I come in?' He continues to smiles wryly.

'Sorry,' she opens the door fully, her eyes probably as wide as can be. 'It's just that,' she stops. 'I only just got your text or email, literally a minute ago.'

'Then it was fate,' he says, making his way in, setting his things down. 'All the better as a surprise, don't you think?'

Nerves give no time for the brain to plan, she lets out a false laugh. But it's not funny, this scene. He shouldn't be here. Harry could be back any time. And her appearance! Registered in the hall mirror: not showered, oldest jeans, sleeveless top covered by a ratty cardigan. No make-up, not even a smudge of foundation, nothing to hide behind. The list of offences is long – no, complete. He's caught her in her own element alright.

'You look wonderful,' he says, leaning in for the French exchange of kisses, the prescribed pecking order of one-two-three. '*Au naturel*,' he exhales, handing over the flowers.

'I did think of giving you more notice,' he continues, pausing, luxuriating in his ruse, 'but my meetings got turned around at the last minute. I certainly didn't want you to dissuade me, so I took a risk.' He's staring at her now. 'Did I do wrong?'

'No.' Half truth, half lie, is there any other way?

Xavier smiles broadly. He seems to have taken her response as meaning it's safe, she's agreed, Harry's not around. But of course, she hasn't gotten around to telling him about Harry's return, or David. He steps forward into the hall.

'I'll put these in water,' she steps away.

His presence fills every space, following closely on hers as they move into the kitchen. She fetches a vase, trying to keep as much momentum and distance as possible. She needs a plan. Or at least an inkling of what he's thinking. Even if he didn't know about recent events, what the hell made him think he could come here?

'Lovely in here, Eva, so light, tall ceilings. A beautiful home. It was a bit dark to see properly, last time I was here.'

Last time, like a frequent visitor or proprietor, as if he had the right to be here, to come anytime, take ownership.

'Beautiful garden,' he comes up close behind her.

'It's been a lot of work.' She steadies her hands from the fear, the intoxication of his daring. Half-arranging the flowers in the vase, she moves quickly to the sink.

'So, more meetings in London?'

'Yes, I mean, no.' He doesn't touch her now that she's fled, looks out the window instead, distracted or pretending.

'I did already, have meetings, and unfortunately I have to be back in Paris later today. I flew in yesterday, went straight into the city, worked, crashed at the hotel. I thought of calling you last night, but I had this slice of morning free. When you might be – free – also,' he leaves the words hanging, closing in behind her.

'A flying visit then.' It comes out emphatically, a touch sarcastically.

'Unless you want me to stay longer...' His voice trails, his hands back on her shoulder.

She turns around to look at him. The fear is coming on in waves. What is he expecting? It's gone half eleven in the morning, in the house she shares with Harry and Katya and Christophe. In half an hour, she's got to fetch Christophe and James. In the cold light of day, what the hell made him think he could come here?

You, Eva. You didn't stop him before. That's why he's here.

He's leaning in already, the fear of what might come already melting into the present, into a fear of different kind, paralysis. She has to stop him.

She presses her hand on his arm. 'Xav, we need to talk.' It comes out quickly, then with resolve. 'I'm in a difficult situation.'

'I know.' He caresses her shoulder, moves closer, so she's pressed against the sink at the waist, his body on hers. She can feel the hardness. 'Maybe I can help?'

She holds him on the arm more firmly, edges her body to the right, slips away. 'No, let's sit in the other room.'

The family room, not registering until they're there – the sofa – oh god, the same sofa! Scene of a previous crime, though as it turned out, that meeting wasn't a crime, only a prelude to a much bigger offence. But maybe the hotel wasn't a crime either. David's state, that's a crime.

'My closest friend Jenny,' she begins, Xavier looking at her with some concern. 'Her husband, David, has cancer. We're all very close, David and Harry and Jenny and I, so it's a difficult time. I'm trying to help her and I have to fetch Christophe and one of her children soon, Christophe's best friend. They'll be here the rest of the afternoon, later Katya and Sophie as well. But it's not that, what's difficult,' she pauses, slows down, trying to undo the knots of foreign grammar.

'It's that now again, there is this heaviness, waiting, not wanting to know the worst but wanting the truth as well, even if it is the worst. And so I feel like I must do the right things, to stem the chaos. But I can't seem to fix anything either, the randomness and with us...' her voice trails.

Normally he would have kept trying. Disregarding her in a playful way, he would still be trying to touch her. But he doesn't move a muscle. She breathes in and out, wills herself to look him straight in the eye.

'Xav, you remember when we used to argue about existentialism? And I said I could accept most of it, facticity, despair even, but it wasn't possible – nothingness – it couldn't be an answer?'

He nods, his perplexed looks turned serious, attentive.

'Well, I feel like I am battling it, still. Fighting hard against the nothingness, the jumble to make sense of this, beyond death. I almost fell there myself, and now people I know,' she holds back about Adam, 'like this friend David, it's getting worse. But I don't understand. I no longer feel *free,* and I don't know where to put the suffering. It seems to be taking over. Whenever I get better, it comes back. I'm so sorry, but I don't think you can be the one to help.'

She looks away. Xav isn't a vessel for her to pour her suffering, that's not why he came. But she's sure her thoughts came out in disarray, blurting out something so hard to put right.

'I'm sorry to hear that,' his voice steady but earnest. 'And if I think I know what you're talking about, I have to admit it's been a long time since I opened up to any of our old philosophy,' he speaks slowly, thoughtfully. 'I think my old favourite would have said escaping nothingness is futile, bad faith to run from what you are. But on the positive side, there's no nothingness without being either. So maybe in your anguish you are fulfilling that absolute acceptance of your freedom to act.'

She looks up again at him directly. Neither of them move, his eyes boring into her with infinite sympathy.

'But don't you ever wonder, I mean, how do you reconcile your life now?'

Oh crap, that really came out wrong.

He laughs. 'I guess like most people, I don't think about it very much,' he pauses. 'Except when confronted by the extraordinary,' his voice drops. 'And that is you.'

His eyes show a great sadness now, tinged with regret or

wistfulness. 'I'm sorry, Eva. I shouldn't have come.' He says it without an ounce of self pity.

'No,' her hand instinctively goes to his. Then in English, 'It's okay. I mean, not really. It's not ideal, but I'm not sorry you did, *come.*'

He laughs, maybe because her French was so twisted or he got the English pun.

'Not at all,' she adds, smiling, reverting to French, 'though your timing is awful.'

'Then nothing's changed.' He smiles, turns serious again. 'Eva, you *know* nothing's changed.'

The way he says it, she doesn't know if he means his feelings, or if he's trying to steer her from becoming too attached, or wants her to know he wants her all the same. Maybe all of it.

'I know,' she hazards a guess, choosing honesty. 'Only it is anguish, Xavier. I do miss you, still.'

'And I miss you,' he clutches her arm reassuringly. 'So very much, I always will.'

He leans in quickly, kisses her gently on the cheek, pausing enough to inhale the air close to her neck. 'God, you smell wonderful.'

'*Au naturel,*' it comes out instantly and he laughs.

Oh god, how to push him out? How to get him out the door, never mind out of her mind, or her life?

But he makes it easy. He stands up to go.

'Eva, is there anything I can do?'

'Not these days,' she says. 'Write sometimes, but maybe not too often...'

'I'll do more than that, you know that. You tell me when.'

Just say the word.

But he says nothing more and silently she follows him to the door, he, already dialling for a taxi, back in professional mode, putting away the phone, finally turning to face her, to take in the whole of her, as if perhaps for the last time. And you never know, it could well be. Every time can be the last.

'I'll always be there for you, Eva. Remember. Take care of yourself. You're the pillar of the family.'

Maybe, maybe not, but she must be strong, if only to withstand all these separations.

He smiles, turns, and then he's out the door. Striding down the gravel, purposefully, not defeated but proud, as always. She shuts the door, leans back against it, drawing another mental blank.

He's gone. That's it. She bursts into tears.

No way to stop them now. No way to stop them or to want to stop them, the tears and bottomless pain.

∞

'So,' Harry says. 'It's been tough lately.'

His opener isn't a query, but flat, defeated. She looks at the worn surroundings of the restaurant. No irony here, no dark corners or showy lighting, no pretence to following modern trends. The table's been set properly to traditional standards – simple flowers in a vase, chintzy tablecloth, a stapled booklet menu – hallmarks of a by-gone era. Though it's far more fashionable these days to write menus on chalkboards, she's grateful that element is missing. Too much like school admonishments. Chez Nous is just an old fashioned place. A simple setting that might provide excitement, but only in the way of a remake of a classic film.

'I said, Eva, we've had a tough time lately.'

She looks up from the menu. He's watching her with concern. Already they're playing these familiar parts, words not quite ringing true. Or maybe not yet. But the desire is there, for resolution and reconciliation, the hope to get there together in the end.

'A tough time, yes, maybe,' her voice falters.

'Don't be modest, Eva. I know it's been difficult. But we're coming through this. It's just been harder than we'd imagined. A lot harder.'

His earnestness makes it difficult to breathe. But she mustn't cry. Yes, it has been harder, but what did they imagine? No one thinks through marriage at the start, what it might be like, endless togetherness or endless separations, always not enough of one or the other. One doesn't count on difficulties, illnesses, death, infidelity, the tense sucking sound of money. They'd embarked on the Plan like most people – jumping in, holding hands, hoping for the best. Now in hot water or maybe ice cold, trying to get back to shore, not so much together as in contact now and again. Was that all it was ever meant to be?

'Yes, it's been harder, but we're almost through.' She looks around to find something else. 'Thanks for booking this table, Harry. Nice to be out again.'

He had been generous. Within minutes of arriving home, he'd presented everyone with what they most wanted: the children got hugs and airport souvenirs; Gabby, a bonus the day before she left for holidays, and for her, a reservation at this tiny bistro in walking distance to Corner House. So they can spend this first evening if not romantically, then at least away from home worries, dirty dishes, prying eyes, routines.

'Come on, let's talk about the weekend,' he says, trying to brighten the mood, pouring the wine. 'I realise it's a bit much to put on you. But you know Tilly isn't much of a cook, and there's no way I could stand going to her house. Besides, I want to be home. God, am I glad to be home. So tomorrow I'll get leg of lamb and green beans and mint, and what else should we make with it?'

Easter Sunday lunch, focus on what he's saying, a family meal the English way, even if really she should be in Przemyśl. By now even Baba Kasia's grave must be showing signs of life. Baba Kasia, resting alongside so many others, a residual pang of guilt, because it is sad she's missing it – the tidying of graves, an experience spiritual and cathartic in the way that all good rituals are. It would have been good to put things right, dig out weeds, plant flowers, wash down the family markers. Then they would have walked together, with Piotr and Magda and Mamcia and Tato, among the cobblestones and crooked paths of the beautiful pine forest, the graves at every angle as you mount the hill of the Główny Cmentarz, dappled light falling through old trees on to stones, inscriptions a reminder that time passes, we all die someday.

We all die someday. Yes, that obvious statement, almost a platitude, a sentence that's a perfect example of the stative present but also a deep truth that infects everyone's life story from start to finish. Like a buried inherent sadness, this stative present, similar to the sadness of missing a particular time and place, of family working quietly alongside, and a long lunch afterward, then Easter, which isn't one thing but a whole succession of smaller moments, each lived in a kind of continuous present: dressing up in new clothes and going to church on Saturday, hauling baskets laden with pork and *kielbasa*, boiled eggs and horseradish, salt and butter, all the symbolic foods of plenty, to give up the fast, the basket all the more beautiful for decorated Ukrainian *pysanky* eggs, carefully saved by Baba Kasia, embroidered cloths and fresh flowers tended in the garden for exactly this occasion. And the solemnity of it all: candles lit, priest intoning blessings, making holy that which you eat, a party the next day on Easter Sunday at breakfast at her parents', then Easter Monday, another celebration, a moment complete in itself, going to church prepared to be soaked, because it is called Soaked Monday, a separate holiday in which people leave services expecting to be drenched. Children with water bottles waiting to squirt siblings, gangs of boys loitering to ambush girls passing by, baptism by the masses or a maybe a washing away of all that came before, hard to recall the exact meaning, but wet and happy, they'd retire to another relative's for lunch, and years later that place was Piotr and Danka's. Then after lunch back to the cemetery, to light candles and pay respects, and again forty days later, on the Feast of the Holy Spirit, Baba Kasia would insist on returning to the cemetery for what Ukrainians called Green Holidays, bringing baskets of food to leave with the ancestors, Baba telling stories of Ukrainian villages where they picnicked right there among the graves. People eating and drinking and singing the continuity of life, after death. Yes, missing all that.

'Eva?'

She looks up.

'I lost you there for a bit.'

'Sorry, I was thinking of Easter in Poland.'

And suddenly the thought comes: it's Good Friday, right now. Yet here they are, out to dinner – on the most sorrowful day of the church year. The day after Holy Thursday, when they read out the story of betrayal in church, Judas, the forever sinner. Good Friday, the day to fast and pray and repent. Good Friday, good grief, the day when supposedly all hope had died! Today you were supposed to wallow in it, that infinite grief.

Harry clears his throat.

'Eva, let it go. You're always putting so much on your shoulders. Your parents understand. I told you already, and months ago I told them, you wouldn't be in any shape to travel this spring, probably not till summer. I only hoped in February,' he changes tack. 'But we'll have a nice Easter and I'll do most of the cooking, I promise.' He looks at her pleadingly. 'Please give me a chance to give the kids English traditions. They're not so bad, though I will need your help.'

Harry, banging on about English traditions, though he's spent the year as far away from England as possible.

LESIA DARIA

Eva, let it go – not just his words but her conscience repeating – *Eva, let it go.*

'I promise. The cooking might even be good. Don't look so worried.'

She smiles. 'That's not what I'm worried about.'

'Then what?'

Not yet, she can't let go, she takes a deep breath.

'I feel as though I *should* have gone back, Harry, after all that's happened,' but her voice trails off.

She means Baba Kasia and the promise to help tidy family plots, but also Adam, Miss Miriam, all the people who've gone, maybe even Christ himself, that tragic figure, because isn't the main point of this moment, Good Friday, that ultimately after death one transcends? That Easter is meant to be a time to reflect, mark respect, fulfil the need for penance? Even Xavier, almost less a choice than an abetting of chaos, letting passions rule – had she been too weak to fight or was that too an excuse? Sitting in front of Harry, it's almost hard to believe it happened, and he's looking at her so intently, so gently, not so much disappointed as worried, she's about to cry.

'Look, how about end of May, or summer? You can go back then. The kids will be off school, the weather will be lovely. You can go to Przemyśl or come to Warsaw with me.' He pauses. 'If I still have to go back.' He puts his hand out to her, across the table, a motion so much like Xavier's, it startles.

'Eva, for all your faults, quirks, everything, I love you,' he continues quietly. 'Your kindness, generosity, I always love you. But please don't set your standards of existence so high. Life isn't perfect. You're not perfect, me neither. But it's still okay most of the time,' he grins.

'Like this place,' he adds, and the waiter arrives with the starters then and Harry dives in.

Harry focuses on his food as though he hasn't eaten in ages.

Maybe he hasn't. He seems not to have put on any weight since her ordeal, and now David's. She looks down at her chicken salad. True what he says, this place is *okay*. One of those little town restaurants that pop up and often shut as fast, or conversely, survive as local institutions that no one can ever remember *not* being there. But what engenders that kind of longevity? Sometimes it's mediocrity – no question, or no questioning – settling into a pattern of good enough, no surprises. At which point some people wonder: *who actually wants that?* As if the aim of life were always get the best to be had. And surely there was something in that too – you could only blame yourself if you resigned to adequacy rather than demanding superiority. But then demanding people too fell into a pattern, they too used the unremarkable stand-by now and again. Maybe it happened to everyone, everything, eventually: wanting not so much something exemplary, as something passable, good enough. And perhaps the beauty of the extraordinary only came out then – in the acceptance that there are other, more important things. One could argue it wasn't good to give up on ideals but so many ideals in the world weren't even shared – look how differently she and her siblings turned out. For some, Chez Nous might be a very good place, more than okay for dining, especially if you haven't been spoiled by better. You can only agree on a point if you ally yourself with like-minded people. So how to judge anything? How to know if she herself has gone beyond bounds, simply wants too much? Has she been too demanding of others, not enough of herself?

Harry sets down his fork. He's watching her, noted she's hardly touched her food.

'Eva?'

Inquisitively, he puts his hand across the table, takes hers.

'Let me help you.' He caresses her hand gently. 'We've a lot of catching up to do, yes, we've both suffered, but you're the one for me. No regrets. Please, no regrets.'

How can he say this when he doesn't know the awful truth? Trying to look him in the eye but with her whole being, she's deceived him.

'I'm so sorry, Harry. So sorry.' The tears come tumbling.

'Oh, don't cry,' he says. 'You can be difficult, it's true, and I hate when you get tense and shout. But let's just forget it, let's move on.' He emphasises the last word, smiling as if he'd handed her a dare.

She nods, meets his gaze. She must let go, forget her sorrows, think of him first. Wiping tears, she smiles. 'So about this lamb and the Holden-Hewitt-Billinghursts, how many can we expect?'

'Four of us, six of them, so ten,' he sighs. 'We can manage, can't we?'

'Don't be ridiculous,' she says curtly, as a joke, but Harry looks panicked. 'Of course, we'll manage,' she adds quickly.

He didn't get the attempt at humour. And it might be a long time before they understand each other like they used to. But they must keep trying.

'We'll do an Easter egg hunt too,' he interjects hopefully, then assertively, 'in the back garden.'

And so the digression begins: where to hide chocolates, what brand to buy, what to serve with lamb, how to serve it, all the things a husband and wife might discuss when family time is approaching and arrangements have to be made. Banalities, banter, sometimes so irritating, other times just the thing to ease, bridge first course to main, which predictably is only passable, but instead of recriminations, bad food can be an excuse to laugh and order more wine, because when food isn't great, there's always wine. Even Christ knew that.

Drinking, laughing, she can't even remember about what, Harry having drunk with some speed, a prelude to an unsteady saunter home for them both. Walking hand in hand, she wobbles in her heels, giddy, elated, no longer feeling discomfort. Having purchased these shoes because she'd convinced herself she was worth it, but was she? Rushing out to satisfy, responding to whatever beckoned, but the thing about appearances was that one could concentrate on polishing the outside without working in to any depth. And suddenly that became a new problem. Like Xavier, soothing on the surface – though that wasn't honest either, there had been depth there – but what had he really recharged in her apart from smoothing over for a time the knowledge of futility? *Extraordinary, beautiful,* but if Harry said those words, did say them this very moment, as they walk home, would it last longer, make her feel better? How long until that empty feeling again?

The emptiness, always and forever out there lurking. But it helps, Harry being home. Maybe he's finally realised that's the thing she's been longing for. His presence. But even if he doesn't have a clue, doesn't understand, surely she can give him the benefit of the doubt. Even if she's not sure what that buys her. Because must it buy you anything? Can't you simply live without expecting in return? Surely, that was the way, the only way to rebuild – by your own effort. That must be what makes the lasting difference.

'Harry?' she looks up at the sky, the stars, the infinity beyond.

'Hmm,' he follows her gaze.

'Beautiful night, isn't it.'

'I was thinking the same.'

They continue again in silence to his measured strides, finally reaching the gravel. The loose stones are too difficult to manage but he slows his pace automatically, supports her arm as she negotiates the shifting ground, stumbling.

'We mustn't wake the children,' her voice comes out a slightly slurred hiss. She's surprised, her thoughts felt so coherent.

'You okay or should I carry you?' He's joking, or maybe not.

'You could, don't the English carry the bride over the step? You missed that bit.'

403

'Okay,' he says, lifting her up as if she weighed nothing at all. 'Hey, you're getting heavier.'

'You're not supposed to say that, you're supposed to say I'm as light as a feather.'

'But in your case, it's a compliment, I like this weight better.'

She clasps his neck, bringing her head closer so he doesn't bang it on the stairwell. The smell of his aftershave is overpowering, the musky one that's always made her wish all the air in the world smelled like that. Harry heads upstairs with her unsteadily, her shoes dangling, falling off one by one, before the bedroom, where he deposits her lightly on the bed.

He hesitates.

She shuts her eyes – he mustn't stop, not to talk, observe or negotiate. Please, just take.

'Eva.'

Don't say anything, please, no words. She doesn't say anything either, puts her fingers to her lips in a shhhhhh motion, her other hand on his belt buckle, forcefully pulling it back. He responds as if to a jolt. Pulling off clothes as quickly as possible, fumbling with socks, grinning, she can't help smiling either because he's slightly ridiculous, this Harry. But he's generous and true and he's upon her now, and expertly, in the years that have honed their lovemaking, they begin again.

∞

Guests! She sits up looking around wildly. But all is calm. Only half past eight. She lies back. The sun's pouring through a crack in the curtains on to the bed, a warm space left by Harry. Relax, he said he'd handle it, the preparations, everything. There will be no hoovering in pyjamas.

She gets up to open the curtains fully, then climbs back between the sheets and covers, savouring the peace and quiet. The heat of a small illuminated band of sunlight has opened into a large swathe. Easter Sunday. Yet life's problems quickly return: David, the Plan, Miss Miriam's property, the lawsuit, the onslaught of Tilly and Nathan – and James, Oliver, Rupert and Jane. Windfall or start of another long unpleasant siege?

Let it go. Forget troubles. Easter morning. Let go.

Voices reverberate downstairs: the children, him, Harry. The sum total of her whereabouts. She has him to thank for all this. He's back, taking charge and helping. Spouse, partner, the way things are supposed to be. Surely he's remembered about the eggs, his tradition after all, and now the children's. Children growing up so very differently from their mother.

Curiosity and desire for coffee overwhelm. She goes down in her nightgown and bare feet to the kitchen. The floors are cold, the back door's ajar, his back to her. He's emptying the dishwasher, a broken glass testament to his efforts. He turns.

'Good morning there, sleepy. Coffee?'

'Yes, please. Where are the kids?'

'What, don't I matter?' he says, holding out his arms, ushering her into a hug. He's a fair bit taller and so much more massive there's no chance of escape, not that she'd want to. That warm feeling, being encased, protected.

He whispers in her ear. 'You were fantastic last night.'

'Oh that,' it comes out sheepishly. 'A bit of wine goes a long way, I guess.'

'If I'd known that I'd have started getting you drunk a long time ago,' he jokes. 'Who thought I'd be so lucky, two nights in a row?'

Still holding her tight, the last bit of aftershave mixed with his body smell, she can feel his happiness. She buries her head in his chest.

'So?' he says, gently prying her away.

'Yeah, so,' she smiles. 'Where are the kids?'

'Where do you think? Enthralled by the electronic babysitter,' he points to the sitting room, the door closed. Now she notes the television's singing.

'We could go up for a quickie,' he suggests with a smirk, more hopeful than convinced.

'But aren't they waiting for the Easter egg hunt, or have they been?' She points to the door.

'No, they're so excited I had to placate them with cartoons. Besides I needed to get out into the garden unseen. They've been up since half six.'

'So it's all ready,' she takes her first sip of coffee.

'Of course, critical for the man of the house to impersonate the Easter bunny,' he says lowering his voice, 'English tradition.' He gives her bottom a squeeze.

'Is it really?' she smiles. 'You're so not like a rabbit.'

'I'll show you rabbit later,' he smiles too, lowering his voice. 'Come on, let's get them, they've waited long enough.' He opens the door to the family room, shouts over the telly, 'Christophe, Katya, come tell Mama good morning!'

'Mama, Mama!' Katya comes running out. 'The Easter bunny's come today! Daddy said! And Oliver and James are coming later too. We've been waiting for you!'

Christophe zips past to the back door, starts stuffing on his wellies.

'Out you go then, Daddy's the expert,' she smiles, and he smirks back.

Her nightclothes are too thin to join them so she watches from the back door as they rush to the ends of the garden. These crazy English in pyjamas and robes and wellies, Christophe and Katya squealing with delight.

'I've found one, oh, another! This is easy peasy!' Katya shouts.

'The Easter bunny wants you to find them, I suppose,' Harry says. 'But you have to look really well. We don't want any chocolate left for months under the flowerpots. I mean, if that's where they are.'

The children squeal again, scurrying to the empty pots lining the back of the house.

'Come join us,' Harry shouts.

She motions okay, shuts the door, turns off the telly and heads upstairs. The robe is on a hook on the back of the bedroom door. She grabs it but feels a hard lump in the pocket, pulls it out.

A black box. *The* black box.

Inhaling deeply and letting the breath out slowly, she studies the solid velvety case. It's the same one, old fashioned but with a stick-on gold bow that wasn't there before. Before, when was that? Before the illness, before the hospital, before everything. Is that why he wanted her to come up? Did he want her to discover it, to bring it down? The temptation to open it is immense. Should she join them? It doesn't seem right to interrupt, not with this, it seems right to be alone. She drops the robe, goes to the window where the sun's giving off heat. She opens the box.

Inside is a pair of fine earrings, green teardrops touching like a kiss, a set of rounded diamond studs. Not ostentatious, not large at all, but beautifully crafted. The green's too strange to name, not emerald but a colour that's deep and changing, while the diamonds are bright white, a sharp contrast. They must be near perfect, catching the light, sparkling playfully, casting coloured shards on curtains, ceiling, wall. She sits on the bed, staring. The stairs creak.

'Eva?' Harry walks in.

She turns halfway, eyes watering.

'They're so beautiful,' she pauses. 'But I don't deserve them.'

'Oh yes you do,' he says, coming quickly, putting his arm around her shoulders.

'You deserved them a long time ago. The day I met you,' his voice grows steady, quiet. 'You deserved them the day you made each of our two beautiful children, the day we should have celebrated ten years together. Before you got so sick I nearly lost you.'

He's holding back now, a lump going up and down his throat. 'Eva,' he brings her face up to see his, 'You've always deserved them, and you should have had them. I'm only sorry I waited so long.'

With that there is no way to stop the tears. Tears for regrets and sorrows, faithlessness and mourning, for letting him down, but also Adam and Xavier and Gabby and Magda and Katya and Christophe and Jenny and David and so many others. But these sparkling stones cast off a thousand beams in the morning sun, as if to further glorify the day. As if it, or any other day, needed further glory.

'Come on, don't cry, it's supposed to make you happy,' he says, holding her more tightly then releasing her. 'I know Easter's important to you, so I left them where you'd find them. You'll wear them today, okay? No more waiting.'

She shakes her head but lets her head hang. She ought to hang it lower for all she's done, but there's no way to tell him this.

'You know,' he continues, 'at first I thought about getting something to match the engagement ring, sapphire, blue. Then I thought no, green, emeralds. So I searched hard to find the right colour, something to match your eyes, but it wasn't emeralds. It's this semi-precious stone, tourmaline,' his voice trails off, then again. 'I added the diamonds, for perfection, well, for me you are, and I wanted something for you, Eva, not typical or traditional. Not something you'd save for best, put away. But something made just for you, for every day.'

The silence, the light, the glistening teardrops in her hand and on her face.

'Harry, I'm so sorry, the ring's loose, you know, otherwise I'd wear it too,' she pauses. 'I didn't want to lose it, that's why I put it away.' A half lie, half truth that can't be changed, but might someday be forgotten, altered.

'Oh never mind,' he says, squeezing her hand, getting up to go. 'You can wear these instead. In the meantime,' he smiles, 'we'll just have to fatten you up, in the good English way.'

∞

Maybe there will be no hoovering in pyjamas, but she can hardly leave the mud tracked across the kitchen. She sighs, the kids already arguing over who has the bigger stash of chocolate. Like Christmas, now Easter too, not so much about Christ's blood washing away the sins of the world or death traded for resurrection and hope eternal, as who can increase their personal hoard the fastest. Ever encroaching materialism, always threatening spirituality, and yet, Harry's gift was for the right reasons, even if she really doesn't deserve it.

She mops up the last traces of dirt, maybe a trace of hangover too, then catches herself – what is there to regret? That she hasn't done things differently? That Harry doesn't and won't ever know about Xavier? That the kids will keep arguing, even when they too should be grateful? So what if faithless myths satisfy the masses, Easter bunnies, Christ, she's still not sure what she believes and who's to know what is harmless fiction? Is any of it actually harmful? Is the selfishness of materialism worse than the selfishness she's shown to fellow man? The search for self, another form of selfishness? After all, who is she to judge? How faithful has she been?

Let the one who hasn't sinned cast the first stone. Let the gods of the earth pronounce.

Yes, really, what is there to say or act on beyond what human conscience offers? About this day, about traditions discarded, new ones inserted, about what she can or cannot offer Harry. It is simply time to let go, to make amends. To recognise that beliefs are only that, beliefs, just as the precious stones of life are simply reminders, of what it is to be anointed by love, generosity and tenderness. Reminders of how you can short-change someone, but still they might set you an example of how to do better, even if they're not perfect either.

She puts the mop away, dumps the blackened water down the sink, refills the bucket to rinse it. Outside the window, the garden is awash with light. The sun's momentarily broken out from behind a cloud. She stores the bucket, makes a mug of strong tea, unsure what to do next. Fortify her foggy mental state yes, but how else to help things along? Harry in the next room setting the dining room table, as if it were a task with which he was familiar. It's impossible to recall him ever doing it but today he's organised – lamb in the oven, new potatoes in a pot, packets of ready-trimmed green beans and bags of pre-washed salad at the ready. Asparagus oiled, to be grilled as a starter, parmesan already shaved as a topping, and defrosted shop-made salmon pastry parcels lined up on a baking tray. English family Easter: half prepped, half packaged, simple, *done, sorted, in under an hour,* as some TV chef likes to say. Not so bad, is it? Surely not every celebration has to be hard work, hours and days of preparation to bring family together. Maybe there is something in this stripped down English method, the getting-on-with-it, no-fuss attitude, leaving grandiosity to grand occasions that might merit no expense be spared. After all, their lives have been hectic. If anyone deserves ready-washed bags of salad, surely it's she and Harry. Two people trying to keep a life together.

She gazes at the garden, the sun's tentative moves growing stronger. Maybe he's right about that too. A matter of keeping things simple, working but not agonizing over every detail, taking help where needed, taking pleasure in the unexpected, not worrying about the rest. In the sunlight, the dew is sparkling, reflecting, disappearing, like the tiny snowdrops already been and gone, a reminder that winter's almost over. The garden doesn't even look that bad. And not just because of the odd crop of crocuses but because of the memory, the one she almost consigned with negativity: children shrieking happily in the mud, uncovering small treasures, bringing the outdoors in.

Treasures, and for her something new too, *tourmaline,* even the word is a kind of melody. And perhaps in the same way she forgives the children their transgressions, and that Harry so often forgives her, she might forgive herself? Then she can further forgive Harry his obsessions – money, income, stability, security – because she handed these worries to him long ago. So now they must work together, not at odds. But guilt still has its hand on her throat. How to accept what's been done, what she has done? How to transcend it?

To accept, Eva, you must let go, and for that, you must keep being honest. Not only with others but yourself. Don't hide from thoughts and feelings, no matter how contradictory. Face the cynics, dig deeper, be more reckless. For you are greater and wiser than the sum of your parts.

There is always room for more, Eva. Not material goods but wisdom and forgiveness. There is always room for a new beginning.

'Hey, I'm back,' Harry says, grabbing a clump of mint from the windowsill, moving to find a chopping board, a knife.

'Looks like you've got everything under control. In the kitchen, I mean.'

'Yeah, why?'

'This is going to sound silly,' she pauses. 'But I'd really like to go to church.'

Harry looks up from chopping. 'But the Catholic church is miles away, they'll be here soon.'

'No, I mean, the English one, down the road. Twenty minutes, tops.'

He looks at her strangely. 'You okay?'

'I'm fine, it's just – I haven't been to church since Christmas. Before everything. Now it's Easter but it's not about religion, I promise, I just feel I have a lot to be thankful for. I feel, well, I'd just like to go, please, for a bit. Fresh air, a little walk.'

She puts in the last bit so he'll understand. This isn't what normal people do. Though of course, some English people *do* go to church at Easter – it can't be that strange.

'You sure you're alright?' Harry sets down his knife, looks at her intently. 'Do you want me to come with you, the kids? We could all go. I'm almost done.'

'No, I don't want to throw a spanner in the works. Anyway, I'll be quicker without all of you.'

With that he seems relieved. 'Alright, I'll keep the champagne chilling.'

∞

You walk into a church expecting to find people but of course it's after services, they've all gone home to their families and their

412

Easter Sunday lunches. An empty church could be a cold shell on such a raw spring day, hollow and forbidding. But surprisingly it's neither. Not welcoming but indeterminate: cool and airy rather than damp, not quite warm but perhaps having benefited from winter's thaw or the bodies recently packed in. She's never been inside, never even thought of going into an English church, having been too busy avoiding Catholic ones all these years. Except those obligatory services in Poland, where church is so much a part of being Polish, being family, it's not so much religion as tradition. To be here now is actually disorienting, why did she come?

She picks a place on the back pew: to sit, to wait, unsure for what. The windows are beautiful, yet she's never noticed them before, driving or walking past. These stained glass panels showing the blues, reds, greens and yellows of a hundred years, though the light itself arrives from the sun in a few minutes. Time folding in on itself. But of course one is only privy to the effects of illumination when sitting in the darkness.

'Can I help?'

The voice startles her. She turns around. It might be the vicar. But this man is in a T-shirt, *Lazarus Lives* emblazoned on the front. Weirdly, he resembles Adam, in early days. No goatee but long hair, wild-shaggy Jesus. He moves ahead of where she's sitting, and suddenly it's frightening – the light pouring through the panes of glass, a ridiculous display, kaleidoscope of colour, broken shards and patterns distorting this man's image from beyond his body, his face in shadow. Not Jesus, not Lazarus, not Adam for sure, but so very like him: a contented, hippier, happier Adam. One she never knew.

'Don't get up, though I'm afraid you have missed the services,' he says, kindly. 'No harm in it, though, you know, staying a bit. A little prayer, better late than never, we always say.'

Even the voice, familiar. A kind of flat weightless tone that's neither deep nor high, just patient. Infinitely patient. As if you'd expect that too. She's positive it isn't Adam, it can't be, and it's definitely not an apparition, just a man. Just a man but so like Adam, his gaze on her like fire. But why is he staring?

'Are you the vicar?' she finally stammers.

He laughs. 'No, I'm just helping out today. Crowd control, you know, they get in the extras.'

He tugs on a big metal cross around his neck, not one she'd noticed at first, though how could she have missed it? Immediately it reminds her of Baba Kasia's smaller cross, gone again. Where did it disappear? Either she's becoming forgetful or that cross has the power to come and go at will.

He laughs, motioning to the empty church. 'Well, there *were* more congregants earlier, biggest day of the church year, Easter Sunday. People like life after death. Personally though, I prefer stripping it down to basics. My favourite is when they read,' he pauses. '*In the beginning was the Word. Says it all, really, and the Word was with God and the Word was God.*'

He resumes looking at her. 'You looked dressed up. Have you nowhere to go?

Nowhere to go. In the beginning was the Word says it all. Her thoughts jumble. It's stupid to sit here in silence. But a bouncer for a church?

'No, I do. But is it okay? If I sit here, for a minute?'

'Okay? Stay as long as you like,' he smiles. 'Make yourself at home. Peace, I always say, is a process. I've a long way to go myself before I rest, but first I have to dust off that organ.'

He shrugs as if to say this is all of no consequence but it's mesmerising, this meeting, making her mind work furiously to figure it out. He bears such a striking resemblance to Adam, but he doesn't really look like him, so it's not that, but something else. Strange. Dusting the organ after services? No, something else.

The man disappears up the creaking stairs at the back and then there's music. Music like she's never heard before, not a

FORTY ONE

tune you'd call familiar yet a well known melody. Heard but not easily named, a wave of ups and downs, crescendos and quiet lulls, like existence itself. So although the whole song takes about a minute, it has summed up her life. Then the music stops as suddenly, followed by a rustling at the front of the church, like birds' wings, the coo of a dove. Then silence.

It's impossible, all of it, too dramatically false to be true. She turns around to catch sight of him again, to tell him, hey, something's trapped in the church, or, you look like someone I used to know, anything really, to bring the moment down to earth. But she hears a door closing and another man comes out from behind the screen by the altar.

'Hello, can I help?'

He might be the vicar. Definitely a man of the cloth, but it's really too silly to ask again. She stands up.

'I'm sorry you've missed the service, it was at nine,' he continues. 'But I'll be doing an evensong tonight at six, if you'd like to come back.'

She finds her voice. 'So *you're* the vicar?'

'Yep, not a bad job either,' he says, stretching out his hand with a big smile. 'Tim. Welcome to All Saints.'

She extends hers, *All Saints*, something in that too.

'I'm Eva,' she pauses, trying to find the right words. 'I live up the road. Lapsed Catholic, I'm afraid, but full of good intentions.'

'Oh, we like those,' Tim says jovially.

'Who's your organ player?'

'Pardon?'

'I just wondered who your organ player is,' she says trying to strike a casual note but probably failing.

'Oh dear, I'm afraid we haven't had an organ player in a long time,' Tim shakes his head. 'The thing's been broken for years. No funds to fix it.'

Then suddenly she knows exactly what it is.

415

∞

Of course she didn't tell him, Vicar Tim. Maybe the music was only in her head, maybe a half baked dream, the sound of the dove too, like other muffled things in previous months, the illness, the mind playing tricks. Always that possibility, doctors said so. Nobody but a child believes in ghosts. Well, there are adults who do, but even as she runs through the rational alternatives she knows they're equally improbable. Nothing wrong with her vision or her hearing.

No, you're well enough, Eva, seeing what you do, Lazarus lives. Hearing's fine too. It's your listening that's a problem. What did he say?

In the beginning was the Word.

Long way to go before he rests…

Peace is a process – that was the last thing. Remember that. Peace is a process.

Only cynics and hypocrites argue about attainment. Peace is a process.

Over and over, sitting on the bench outside, *peace is a process*, until it sinks in. There is nothing absolute about life at all. But it's not sad as philosophers have made it out, only a relief. Because far from being pre-disposed, conditioned or trapped, she is free to do as she chooses. But not a freedom to do nothing – freedom to do anything, everything. To believe or not. To stand up or not.

She stands. She *chooses* standing.

Her feet, they need to get her home, to Harry, to Katya and Christophe, it's been more than twenty minutes surely. Tilly and

Nathan and the clan will be there by now, kids starving, stuffing themselves on crisps. She takes a step, stops.

She smiles, she's stopped. She's chosen stopping. For something, or nothing at all, or for everything, the universe.

Here are daffodils, trying their best to come out. So early in April, after such a cold wet winter, such a brave act of defiance. Their petalled heads bowed, their stalks edging the paving stones, a cheery path towards the inevitable church graveyard. These golden heads, tilted towards the sun, concentrating a vibrant orange in their inner circles, as if the conical centre was meant to be a conduit for sunshine, not just stamens of reproduction. And higher up, new shoots on trees. She stares. Tiny green buds on branches, waiting for the right temperature and moisture, the right amount of light to encourage them to open. Here is life, trying to come through. But you'd have to stop, to notice. Choose.

Freedom, hope, choice, belief: all intertwined. If one had freedom to choose, then one could choose hope, a positive. Not something you were left with because there was nothing, but a great welling of belief: faith. Not something granted as a gift but a choosing to be part of something greater: life.

That's why she hadn't been able to conquer the sadness sooner, conquer her failings, and stop the guilt – for Xavier, Adam, the baby, Miss Miriam, Baba Kasia, all these people lost, yet not gone. It was all looking the wrong way. Guilt was the wrong emotion. Because these people might be gone or dead, wronged or forgiven, but these people were alive and a part of her, all these people who'd lived, whom she loved, now in memory, sometimes far, sometimes right before her, like Harry. So it's not a sad, existential cold hearted indifference – nothingness – but its opposite: life eternal. Maybe like they say in church, though perhaps not a literal rising up of Lazarus or Christ, simple Bible stories told to children. But the thing itself. *The Word is God.* Because stories are only metaphors for the real thing – the thing being the essence of existence – mystical, fleeting, not as it seems, not even in its fleetingness, because everything *is* alive and that it remains so, this existence, eternal, despite anyone's lack of comprehension, is a miracle. It's a miracle that the deeper she's dug, the more real it has become, this infinity within her, in the expanse of the universe without her, this infinity revealed where things like guilt and regret do not apply. Because God or no God, the only attribute of infinity is calm. A pervasive peace, a divine within. Unattainable knowledge, the recognition of something without end.

She begins moving, feet going faster, the body moving independently, mind in a fog. But in the place they call soul, there's something akin to clarity. Corner House, she reaches it, the calm already fading, to the noise leaking from inside, to the traffic mounting behind her at the crossroads, she doesn't want to go in, only stay on the step, in this moment forever, holding this feeling. But she's back, on solid ground, it's going, going, gone. There will only ever be the memory of it now – connectedness, belief in self, faith, hope to keep going. She can't stand there anyway, she must carry on.

She rings the doorbell, a hypnotised stranger.

'Oh, it's Mama! Mama! Mama!' Katya shouts, opening the door wide, throwing her arms around her. 'Mama's back!'

She savours the moment of Katya, the existence of Katya, her messy plaits, her powdery smell. She buries her face in the warmth of her hair. Harry appears, exasperated.

'Eva, where have you been? We thought we'd have to send out a search party!'

'Sorry, I lost track of time,' she begins.

He waves her comments away. 'Never mind,' he leans in and whispers, 'Tilly's in the champers already. Sorry we couldn't wait, but there are some hors d'oeuvres left.' He gives her a quick peck on the cheek.

Holding Katya's hand, she finds herself trailing Harry into the kitchen.

'There you are, darling,' Tilly says. 'We thought we'd lost you to God. So when did this start? You're not going religious on us now are you?'

'Oh,' but it comes out in a tiny whoosh of breath that pushes it out. It's all she can manage. Strangely deflated, hopeful, high, giddy – no, not God or Jesus or even Holy Ghost, just All Saints, she wants to say, though that sounds equally absurd. Anyway, the moment's gone, nothing to do but try to feel at one with this next moment. And the one after, and the one after that, absurd though they may all be, this reality and all the other moments that will take her forward until the next time, when she might be lucky enough again to be touched by infinity.

Nathan hands over a flute of rose bubbly, as if instinctively meeting a female need, and disappears to the sitting room for car crash TV. Some middle-aged presenters are wrecking their automotive toys, *not to worry, though*, they laugh, *someone else will pay*. She hears their voices, boys laughing.

Harry looks up from his stirring. 'Eva, you okay? You look like you've seen a ghost.'

Wanting to laugh, scream, cry, she smiles. She chooses smiling. She shakes her head, as if to say never mind, don't pay me any notice, though she's been trying to get his attention for months.

'I'm fine.' A sip that buys time, she'll get giddy on champagne instead. 'Tell you later,' she adds in a whisper.

And pretending *is* fine: the screeches of younger cousins upstairs, in the next room *Top Gear* moving up a notch to *Formula One*, Tilly babbling on about builders. Real life demands pretence, people hanging their attentions on action, dialogue, minor ups and downs, big developments, none of which have any bearing on the great unknowing. Only those who choose absolute solitude get away with endless reflection. For the rest the test is in living.

'So, as I was saying,' Tilly continues, 'I could tell they were doing it all wrong. I mean, I'm no expert but I've been going through the process long enough to see when something's not right. They were trying to cut corners. Bet I should have had Polish builders, hmm, Eva? I hear they work hard.'

Harry throws her a shut-up look, Tilly returns one of bewildered query.

'So how have things been for you?' Tilly shifts gear, up or down hard to tell. 'Recovering? You look well. Tell me the secret to weight loss isn't falling deathly ill, I'm not sure what to try next. Oh, those earrings, fabulous, are they new?' She emphasizes *new* as if she hopes they're old but not antique.

'Yes, I mean, no.'

'What Eva means,' Harry interrupts, 'is they are a present for our 10th anniversary, of the day we met. But she only got them today.'

'How extravagant,' Tilly issues a compliment that's clearly disapproving. 'Nathan, did you hear this?' But Nathan doesn't hear anything, the sound of motorsport is drowning it out.

She probably shouldn't have worn them, at least not in front of Tilly. But Harry had insisted, and she wanted to please him, please herself too. What was wrong in that? Why not be happy? Be generous, please yourself now and again, accept but let go, allow contradiction? The very essence of human existence seems to demand it. Better than cowering in the corner, emerging only with clear arguments, strong and rational enough to confront the day's battles. So what if she wanted to go to church, hear an organ? Why not let life *be* deconstructed so it lets freedom back in?

'I guess I'll have to drop bigger hints then, or louder,' Tilly says futilely, in the direction of crashing cars. 'Anyway, Eva, I glimpsed your curtains, honestly, you can't tell there's been a stitch-up. If it holds, really no one will notice. Speaking of which, you should see our latest improvements, you wouldn't recognise parts of the house! The extension's finished, we're tackling the top floor bathroom,' she lowers her voice, 'wasn't part of the plan, but you know, *finally.*'

Trying to follow Tilly's renovations now is the real impossibility. Not that it matters, Tilly won't notice a response or lack of it. She's still talking.

'Of course, I'm hoping it'll be done by the end of summer term, and if I can't get the tiles on sale, I'll have to buy them full price, nothing else looks right. You know how it is, darling, when you have your heart set on something, you can keep looking but nothing else will really do.'

Maybe, but not the way Tilly means. Because it's not about things, the matter surrounding, that's not at all what matters. Life is the emotions people engender, the goodness we can return, that's when nothing else will do.

'You're awfully quiet today,' Tilly observes, picking at a salmon parcel.

'She must be in shock I'm home,' Harry interjects, trying to lighten up the conversation. 'Doing the cooking and cleaning, what a first.'

He's trying – she ought to help him.

'You even set the table, I bet that was a challenge,' she rejoins in that good-natured teasing way they adopt when things are good. Their own version of the game.

He returns her smile. 'It would have been, had I been left to my own devices, but thankfully Katya seemed to know where everything was.'

Welcome home, your lordship, she used to say, when Harry seemed befuddled by details of the home. But it's no wonder he forgets things, he has a lot on his mind. Anyway what's the big deal about knowing where fancy dinner napkins are kept, demanding he remember the exact time kids finish school? There are plenty of other things he keeps in his head. Plenty of other things he does. He didn't forget their anniversary, the moment of meeting, she botched that up. And plenty else besides. But he came through. He waited and came through.

Let it go.

Let
it
go

And suddenly she knows exactly what she'll do.
'Eva?' Harry is touching her elbow now. 'Are you really okay?'
She looks up. Everyone's gone through to the other room.
'Sorry, my mind's wandering.'
He gives her shoulder a squeeze. 'Hang in there.'
'I will.' She claps her hands together. 'What can I do?'
'I think the meat's almost done, would you mind putting the salad out on the plates? I always dump it but you manage to make it look good. You're so creative.'
And though the thought is there, she can't quite get it out – thank you, Harry, for that. You wouldn't understand if I told you, but those words mean more than anything else you could have said.
He's goes out, carrying the meat through to the dining room. So now she can get on with what she planned to do next. No one will believe it. But she'll do it anyway.
She arranges the salad quickly, slips upstairs to find the box with the engagement ring.
Easter Sunday. Harry gave her these earrings, but before that this ring, which belonged to his grandmother, then his mother. Now it belongs where it lends most meaning. That's how she would feel if it had been in her family, Baba Kasia's cross given to her, which one day she'll give to Katya. The ring belongs to the Holdens, and mistakenly it went to her. But she can fix that. She can give it to the rightful heir. The granddaughter and daughter who should've received it: Tilly.

∞

The kettle whistles, she pours hot water into a mug, moves the tea bag around, takes a sip. A new choice this green tea, they say it's good for you. Grassy tasting, but maybe you get used to it. Yellow in the cup, not green at all, like the lawn outside, even now in late April, how verdant England is. Harry was right: the gardener has helped. Several weeks in, he's turned over the soil in the vegetable patch, added compost nutrients, cleared side beds of dead leaves and branches. He's even lifted up the old ceramic pots and scrubbed them clean. Still no true colour and a dearth of foliage, only the evergreens give off signs of life. But soon the garden will again be at the height of its flowering: the blooming exochorda, the so-called white bride, with its delicate flowers cascading, then weeks later the mock orange, adding its white flowers to the scene just as the bride retires. Later, honeysuckle and asters will come to life, and in this way the garden will continue, moving from white to bursts of colour, spring to summer, as she observes detachedly, like the little house in Christophe and Katya's storybook, their new favourite tale, an old familiar one.

But all that is still ahead. Some things must wait. She sets the mug down to cool. The expanse of grass was all weeds, too late to kill them, new seed already sown. But potatoes are chitting in the pantry, no later than usual, so they'll manage a second late summer crop. And looking on the bright side, she and Katya and Christophe finally did manage to plant beans. They set them out in small pots on windowsills around the house, so even with delays, there will be a start to summer, the beginning of a renewed cycle.

In the stillness of the house her sip is almost too audible: life echoing, resuming its order. After Easter, that climax of the

Church calendar – and several for her and Harry too – afterwards it always does seem less exciting. But you carry on because real life does, and it might be banal, but at least there's good weather. Harry now out cycling with all the children, Sophie, James, Christophe and Katya, soon he'll return to pore over financial papers and litigation, while the children will come in and run about and hover over the cats as if they'd been gone for days instead of hours. Then this, her small slice of solitude, will fold away, recede into the past. But not yet. She wants to hold on to it. Because she used to panic in such situations, too much thinking, as if a small crack in the universe might open up to a bigger void, suck her away to the blackness beyond. But now she's tackling things a bit the way Harry does – when he's being wise – one step at a time, do what you can, everything can't be tended to at once. Actually it's not far from that therapist's saying, the one Harry joked was trite when she mentioned it, *the serenity prayer?* he scoffed, *bandied about alcoholics' meetings.* But her first thought was it was unlikely to have saved someone like Adam. Sometimes words help, sometimes not.

Might as well be a prayer, though, Harry continued, *people don't bother with church any more because they find solace in therapists and sayings like that.* His point was like Magda's about confessionals versus phone-in radio lines, Harry more cynical where Magda was sorry, resigned to loss of faith. But maybe the era of self-help too was passing if a saying like that could be deemed a cliché to be passed over like once-important Bible readings.

Taking another sip, she winces. Strangely bitter, this tonic. Because it had struck her straightaway that the precept was actually quite difficult to enact. People could be as disdainful as they liked, but they were far too cynical anyway. The only easy thing about life was being dismissive about what was difficult. Long ago she'd decided that trying to understand the impossible wasn't a sign of mental weakness. It was strength, to do battle at all. And the bit about the wisdom to know the difference was key to the whole adage: if you didn't know the difference between what could and couldn't be changed, you wouldn't know whether to fight or accept something. If you went further and tried to apply it to every situation – fidelity, infidelity, annoying sister-in-law, disease – how to spot the difference in what can and cannot be changed? No guidance there. As a young girl she'd been taught to pray for understanding, but once you rejected that for nothingness or headstrong logic or vicissitudes of fate, you fell on a rockier path. Why not then pray for guidance, serenity? The road ahead would forever be strewn with obstacles, daily chores of choosing what to keep, what to discard. Surely everyone needed wisdom.

And for her the moment at All Saints had brought it. However briefly, the wisdom of waiting for wisdom. Not a new mantra per se, but a letting go which in it its fullness says: *let it go so you can let it come, in another form.*

She pours the infusion down the sink. Easy to let that go. Though other things fired mixed emotions: Gabby gone, having rung a few days before to say she wasn't coming back, her father had fallen ill. Through Harry's office connections they could have found out whether it was true or not, but they decided that too was better to let go. Maybe Gabby had been driven away by the unpredictable old Eva or guessed Harry's continued presence made her unnecessary. Gabby had left little of value behind, but it was possible, her being so young, that she had little of value on her person. That her life wasn't so much valuable because of the contents of her suitcase as in the places she would still go.

And Tilly, who wouldn't keep the ring, regardless how hard it was pressed it on her. An Eva trying to let go, but Tilly wouldn't take it. Maybe it was shock. Or fear of Harry's reaction. Or because it was a used engagement ring and Tilly had two big ones already. Or maybe there exists that bit of Tilly that remains selfless despite

425

external appearances. So there too, a new bond has formed. A new beginning, which of course, perversely, the English call closure.

She didn't tell Harry, though, not about the ring. Because he seems nervous, more concerned for her welfare, especially after the episode in church. As if bells started ringing in his head, *she's slipping back.* Walking into the family room, she eyes the sofa. Why not? He's always telling her to rest. She sits, tries to get comfortable. But maybe she shouldn't have told him the story about Adam either. Above all Harry is rational and she hasn't been able to reassure him it didn't seem like a ghost. That for her the thing with Adam isn't so much a past event as a background constant present.

She leans back, closes her eyes, the way she did when she studied something difficult, trying to get it to stick in the brain. Like English tenses, when teachers said the past imperfect had largely been superseded by the progressive or continuous present – an action in progress that is never completed. *He was waiting in that church.* That's different from a permanent state of being, the stative present, *we all die some day.* And Adam had not gone – has not gone – away as much as he seems suspended. Never here, never gone. Soul in limbo, the church might say, and they had a point. Not about his chances for damnation or resurrection, but the way he seemed neither here nor there. Alive, he'd taken life to extremes, but if anyone now blamed her for his act of death she'd have to disagree.

She opens her eyes, casts her line of sight to the world outside the window. Adam had been on a bigger quest, played out alone. Yet even knowing this, that we all play it out alone, the unknowing had still gripped her. And it wasn't boring semantics not being able to lay down with certainty the reason for his death, her role in that. Because that unknowing was what had caused guilt to suffuse and ripple through her for so many years, for many other transgressions. She had been prepared to go through her whole life bearing that uncertainty, because if you have to bear something, it was uncertainty and not guilt you'd choose to bear.

Then All Saints: a moment of clarity, forgiveness, and as a result some kind of certainty. Her hand absentmindedly runs over the sofa's soft faux suede surface. Peace from somewhere and nowhere at the same time. From no one, yet from Adam, random words from a stranger and the guilt unexpectedly vanishing. Replaced again simply by unknowing, but also *hope*. Not despair but infinite, immense hope that this is what Adam would have wanted. That maybe she can meet everyone's expectations, even Xavier, if what was exhilarating can become manageable, put down to a series of encounters in the past. Not the continuous present, but firmly in the past. *It happened.*

Running her hands on the cushions, it's almost like flirting, stealing this moment to indulge, almost too decadent, resting, when there's so much to worry about and do. As ever the room is in such a state. But many millions of miles away the morning sun is making its trajectory to the northern hemisphere's midday. A force of warmth and a force to destroy, highlighting its own destruction. The curtains are shining gold. The perfect contradiction. Like a near perfect ending. That damaged, worn, they remain as beautiful as ever. So what if forever they might tear and it'll be a lifelong challenge of monitoring this delicate state of fraying? Or that some day, no amount of effort will hold it all together? Nothing is over yet, and before any moment of finality, she will always be grateful for this: the moment to think.

∞

Pots full of soil, seeds already hidden inside, she shakes the dirt from her hands.

'Harry, can we take a break? I'm feeling tired.'

She looks up but he's at the far side of the house, drill in hand, about to take on the stickier project of a hydrangea whose thick woody branches have solidified toward the windows. They've been working separately but together, he probably hasn't heard her. There's the low buzz of neighbours' lawnmowers, the noise of kids at the bottom of the garden, and silently Roobarb and Custard lolling about in the sun. She smiles, dusts off the last of the garden implements, shuts the shed and goes inside. She returns with drinks, hands him a beer.

'Break?'

'I haven't started yet, but alright, thanks.'

He takes the bottle, mops his brow, lays the drill next to the saw. He's been preparing to hedge his bets. With enough screws in the brick wall, the hydrangea might be coaxed to climb in the right direction, a less drastic option than severing it.

She stands there, sipping, wondering if it'll budge. At least they got lucky with the weather. It really is a beautiful day, especially for an early May bank holiday, a pleasant surprise for most people. For them too, if it weren't for the holding pattern: David back in hospital, echoes of the Plan, a new tax year, Warsaw office calling. She might as well ask now.

'Harry, forgive me but I keep thinking, I don't get where all this is going.'

He takes a long sip, sits on the edge of the lawn, looks perplexed. 'I don't know what you mean exactly.' He grabs an offending weed, yanks it out, flicks it away.

'You know, where will we end up? Not finally, but in the near future, on the practical side of things.' She hesitates to mention the Plan because maybe it's not over yet, just a hiatus.

'Hard to say,' he takes another swig, motions for her to sit down too.

She joins him, and they sit for a while, no one apologising for the silence. She finishes her lemonade first.

'Well,' he says, finally diving into his thoughts, 'if you mean the Plan, then all I can say is, I still don't know. When we embarked on it, the Plan seemed achievable. Okay, tough for a year, but others had done it, why not us? We'd been under pressure anyway, it didn't seem the situation could get worse, and we'd benefit from the sacrifice.'

She says nothing so he continues.

'Then David,' he sighs. 'Obviously, it made me upset and angry – for him, Jenny – but also for us, because it throws everything into stark relief. How hard we work, how futile it can be, ultimately. I mean, David's going to make it, we hope. But I've been working myself to death and what *is* the point? You work hard and what happens? Someone comes and pulls the rug out from under you, death or taxes.'

He takes a long swig, practically draining the whole thing.

'But you're asking about practicalities, and I have been thinking, not just doing numbers but trying to calculate variables, uncertainties. By sheer madness, Eva, it's going to get harder for us, not easier.'

She pauses, breathes out. 'How exactly?'

'Everyone's talking about austerity. Fine, I agree. Time to rein in, for everyone, but especially the bankers who are at fault for a good part of this mess. Their bonus schemes were always a travesty, being able to cash in no matter what happens to the deal later. But beyond that nothing's clear, only that we'll be hit too, where it really hurts: fifty per cent tax and now some bloody mansion tax proposal. A four-bed family house in our area might qualify as a mansion, Eva. That's crazy, we're not talking Cranfield Manor. So I *am* frustrated. Because whatever we do, we're going to get punished.'

He tears at the lawn again, ripping up weeds. 'Of course, they'll say they're going after the rich. But the joke's on us. Celebrities, pop stars, footballers, whatnot, they're heroes, untouchables. They don't pay much compared with what they could and billionaires can always leave. Anyway most of them live in limbo, where tax authorities can't get them, domiciling here, there, multiple residences, a class without nationality, a nation-state of its own. But we are *not* them. Their wealth and status is ensured permanently. We had one chance. Now we're stuck. We'll be the working stiffs left to shoulder the pain – taxes, interest rates, inheritance – all of it going against us. But just you wait, *we'll* be the ones made out to be the bad guys. Not the *really* rich, don't you see? No one's going to care, Eva. The joke's on *us*.'

He looks at his empty bottle, tosses it aside and stands up abruptly, signalling the break's over, though it wasn't much of one. Taking the rope, he flicks out his knife and starts cutting sections roughly. He's always felt better doing something.

'Sorry, I don't have the luxury, in my profession, constant self-edit, here, do you mind? Hold this,' he interrupts himself, scans the wall. 'I don't think I'll need to drill, enough screws.'

He hands her a thick branch, ties a loop around the end.

'So now the Plan's over, new tax year. But the government might still try to take everything we tried to save this past year...'

'Wait, wait,' she feels rising terror. 'Is that the joke? You mean to say it was all for nothing?'

'No, what I'm saying is, they will hit us going forward, maybe retroactively too, they're backtracking fast, recalculating days, and whilst in theory I should have spent enough time out of the country to be eligible for exemption, that's according to *old* rules. But if they're going to change rules midway through the game, keep changing them ad infinitum, on income, property, what can I do? What can anyone do? How can anyone plan their life if they keep changing the rules?'

She stands holding the branch, listening.

'And it's always random who gets audited, another

uncertainty, bloody hell, we won't know for years. We were on the edge, even without my coming back early for David.' He studies the wall, trying to figure out which way the branches should go. 'Actually, that bit I'm okay with.'

She doesn't know if he means the shrub, the Plan, coming back for David or being on the edge, but he continues.

'And here we are, days before elections, more uncertainty and change ahead. All I can say is I wouldn't mind paying tax, really, not so much, if I felt like with our contributions to charity that I knew our money was going to good causes. But what's it all for? Where has it been going, our taxes? To pay vast debts, years of overspending by airy-fairy politicians, drones clocking in and out of the state sector, and they're doing *nothing* to change that.' He's vehement and stops for a breath, stares at the wall.

'And I *don't* mean doctors, nurses and teachers, I'm not talking what's forked out on the odd missile, and I certainly don't mind helping the destitute. But I am damned sick of my earnings being doled out to paper shufflers. Useless jobs at every level – supervisors of supervisors – make-work jobs in new initiatives that successive governments dream up to solve big problems like poverty or unemployment or crime, programs with optimistic names that have no impact whatsoever compared with what they're taking from individual families.'

She interrupts. 'Harry, I know your views.'

He looks at her blankly. 'Yes, you do, modern government: a massive circular make-work program, usually leading to stagnation. With private enterprise breaking its back so we can fund *them*, the bureaucrats.' He snaps at another piece of rope. 'And now, with the banking crisis, the final irony: we taxpayers will have to fund bonuses of bankers who will now try to undo even worse debts created by other bankers.'

He lets out an ironic laugh. 'You know for so long I kept my head down, worked, while politicians made pronouncements and bankers cashed in. But now the arrogance is starting to wear on me. All of them, they seem to have forgotten they created this bloated system we now have to finance.' But his voice drops, he sounds resigned. 'A bit like being mobilised for a war you don't support, don't want to fight, you have to do your duty, but you're narked at how pointless and stupid.'

Having waited so long, she won't interrupt, even if what he says is both true and not. Even if he is focussing too much on the tangible world, as if it held real power. Even if his sacrifice is not comparable to the military's and he too might be accused of adding to the mountains of paper being shuffled around the world. Then again investments in Eastern Europe by private companies had brought improvements to the lives of millions – she'd seen it – and that couldn't be done without a legal basis. And as bad as lawyers might be perceived, they weren't only making money from money, or worse, inflated debt.

He strains higher, pulls harder. The end of the branch slips from his hand.

'Bloody hell, this damn thing. Sorry.'

She's still holding on to the bigger bottom bit, wondering what his next plan of attack will be. Anticipating, she steps forward, pushes the branch towards him with her weight. He grabs the end, reaches higher, finally hooks it on to a nail in the wall.

'Okay, let go.' He steps back to survey the job.

'No, one more, almost done.' He moves aside, secures a few smaller branches with rope, takes another big branch, plots that course.

'So the time bomb, David, you know? What a hand to be dealt, why him? Of course it gets me thinking, it could have been me, of course, it could have, like it was with you, I mean, why you? Who actually *gets* meningitis? It's all so absurd and random.

So yes, Eva,' he emphasizes, as if she'd been arguing with him, 'It became too much. I needed time to think. So I took this leave of absence, weeks, maybe a month if I can stretch it, to help David, and to think. Because we need to think of what to do.'

She can't disagree but instantly the thought worms its way in: now or never to make him understand.

'Harry, I'm not trying to be selfish, but did you never worry, after Adam,' her voice drops lower, 'that depression too can slip into dying?'

He lets go of the branch, turns toward her with a stare, as if he's fighting off thoughts, or worse, emotions. He steps forward, then stops, as if the space between them might protect them.

'No, I didn't,' he looks at her evenly. 'Except when you were,' he pauses, unable to bring himself to say it, 'except then, in hospital, you've always acted fighting fit. That you'll either win or go down trying, and only afterwards might I know.'

A note of incredulity enters his voice. 'I've been confused by your anger recently,' his voice goes more quiet, 'but after Adam, it's true, I was frightened. What did you think?'

She remains silent, swallows hard.

'From the moment you fell ill, Eva, I've never stopped being afraid. Not a fear of you dying, mostly, but other things. Maybe I don't fight my fear the right way. Or the way you do. Or express it in a way that's good for me or you, or both of us. For that I'm sorry too. But you know what I do. Carry on. Fix what I can, hope for the best, dismiss the rest. That's how I learned. Being English.' He practically spits out the word.

'Harry, I,' but she stops. He's turned back to the job at hand.

Anyway she's been out of line for asking. She'd never explained how bad it was, never been fully honest either. She still doesn't want to mention the things he doesn't know, the things she hopes he'll never learn: how post-partem almost turned post-mortem, standing at the edge of the river. Or Xavier, and the near casualty of their marriage. If she's kept these hidden, how could he have known?

'But Harry,' she pauses. 'I did need you.'

'I know,' he sighs, not turning around. 'I know, and I needed you. I need you still. But once the ball got rolling, once we got into it, our choices were limited. Mine maybe more than yours.'

She winces. Freedom of choice, limited. Yet it was she who abused her liberties.

'Harry? Please. Look at me.' She's afraid of his reaction but needs the answer. 'I have to ask now: was there ever any point in the Plan?'

He turns automatically, one eyebrow arched.

'I mean, obviously we need to be, ought to be together. And we can't turn back history like the pages of a book. But if we're going to have to pay taxes, a certainty like death, then there's no point avoiding it. Might we not be better off accepting things we cannot change? Even if we don't agree with the waste and stupidity and absurdity, half of what you earn, if we have to, because *then* we can be free. We can be free with what's left over,' she stops breathless. 'That's where the difference lies.'

He studies her for a moment but doesn't look incredulous.

'You're right. Absolutely. And I'm sorry for the hardships too, but the past is gone and whatever else we could have done, it's the future I'm worried about. Of course we'll pay tax. I'm not going to break any laws. But the devil is still in the details: how we manage, what we choose.'

He turns back to work, starts tying the last knot. She sighs. He's never liked rehashing the past, even if that's where the depths of forgiveness lie. But she doesn't want to go back there either. And he's right that you can't move on if you don't discuss the future and make some kind of plan. She shudders at the thought.

'Okay, so what are the options?'

'No easy answers there either.' He wrestles with the biggest branch, trying to press it this way and that without cracking it. 'There's the obvious: I could try to stay home, ask them to affect a transfer immediately. Or apply for a new job in London, whatever impact that may have on my career and income. Or,' he presses against the branch himself, almost to the wall, pulls the rope tight, 'I could try to bridge the job in Poland, extend this leave of absence until David,' but the top of the branch flies through the loop, flings down.

'Shit,' he groans, grabs the branch further down and tries again. 'Which means going back to Poland but trying to come home permanently as soon as possible. Or the fourth, very last option,' he heaves forward, hooks the branch.

'Got you, finally,' he steps away from the wall, wipes his brow. 'I can't believe how hard this was. But at least I didn't have to sever it.'

'The last option?'

Now he turns, looks at her steadily. 'You and the kids move out to Warsaw with me – we make a new start, quickly, after the summer. We leave the UK for a while.'

She breathes out. So that's it. Together finally, but not at Corner House. All these months apart only to give up on what they were trying to achieve in the first place: a nice, stable life in England, peppered with the odd luxury, backing on to a golden horizon.

He reads her quizzical look. 'No, it's not running away – the way I see it the Plan taught us something. Learning the hard way what we really want, which is not to be apart. But the truth is that unless I press very hard on this transfer, with major unforeseen consequences, they're not keen to move me back to England, not yet. They'd rather I stay in Poland and help build up the practice, it's almost a pre-condition to my making partner.'

He pauses, but not long enough for a response.

'For me, outside career, I'm neutral. But the year abroad has changed me too. I quite like your country, sometimes more than you, I think. It has positive can-do attitude, a social cohesiveness, a work ethic that appeals to me. The situation here in Britain is ridiculous, riddled with class prejudice up and down, only getting worse as politicians exploit emotions when times get tough. Those stuck below are always resentful, they want to keep their entitlements but also fight those above, the system they view as entrenched. And they're bloody right – Britain's never had the kind of wars Europe had to shatter its class system. Meanwhile old money is oblivious and new money feels entitled – to bonuses, houses, cars, whatever – and it's too easy to get caught up in it. Between them both. And now I feel, in the middle, I don't identify with either end of the spectrum. But I also feel like I have no voice here in the middle. That the voices of reason have gone silent.'

He suddenly looks at her. 'What it is it?'

'I'm sorry. I guess I always focused on the opportunities here. Is that last option your real preference?'

'Eva, really I don't mind where I live as long as you and the kids join me. So we can live as a family together. But I have thought that for you personally, it might be better too, in Poland. If you wanted you could start working again. I see it, you need more, this housewife thing isn't for you. Over there you could get interesting work, use old contacts.'

'But you're the one on which everything rests, Harry. What do you want?'

'Eva, I have what? So many choices at my age? What I want doesn't really come into it,' he sounds frustrated. 'I'm *not* going to risk going down a wrong road again and I am *not* the one on which everything rests, you have equal say. We have to work this out together.'

She stays silent for a minute. The two of them: one pillar.

'Okay, but what about Miss Miriam's property? Say we win, wouldn't that make up for loss in income?' She can't believe she's pleading now, but suddenly her fear is rising. The biggest challenges would fall on her. 'Then we could stay here, even if we have to pay half your salary in tax…'

'It's not about money, Eva. And Miriam's property hardly matters in the scheme of things.' He's exasperated now. 'In a minute I'll throw the question back to you – what do you want?'

He pauses but she says nothing.

'If you need details, yes and no is the answer on Miriam's property too. Because there'd be tax on her property as well. Her house will likely be sold whoever gets it, because inheritance tax must be paid and no one's usually got that much cash lying around. So we'd only get what's left over anyway – after paying more tax. Don't forget we're in negotiations, the will appears legal but she might have had mental issues. None of us wants a court fight, so at the moment we're trying to see how to divide it. How much they're willing to let go.'

Or how much *we're* willing to let go, but she doesn't say it. She's not sure about letting go herself any more.

'Well what about David? And Jenny? What about them, our life here?'

'That's a major issue,' says Harry. 'Obviously I don't want to leave if he's still…'

'Lying around?' she interjects. 'Oh, you mean, we should wait until he's dead? That's great, Harry. Very kind. But what about Jenny? She's the one who will need help for a long time, but especially if or when…'

Harry says nothing.

'I mean, Jenny's my friend, Harry. Won't she need more support if David dies?' She can't bring herself to say the word *when* again.

'I'm not expecting him to die,' he says quietly. 'Not anytime soon. But I had thought of that. So you're right, no question. Whatever we choose, we'll be sacrificing something.'

Of course, now he's the one who's right. Harry, as ever, so

good at distilling the truth. It is a question of sacrifice. Ultimately no new life can begin without it.

∞

She sets out mugs for tea, *placek*, the fruited sheet cake Baba Kasia used to make when there was fruit and sour cream to use up, when everyone needed cheering up. Because even though it didn't work with Jenny last time, it's all she can think to do now that a grenade's been thrown into their carefully constructed lives. They'll go to Warsaw and Przemyśl for the summer for sure, but the big issue is what they will ultimately decide. She never did answer Harry's question. What she wants. A Pandora's box of uncertainty if ever there was one. All of a sudden it's like back to the beginning, when they weighed up the merits of the Plan. Do they owe anything to friends like Jenny? Should they let roots deepen here or uproot and start over? If they go, is a permanent move better, selling the house, abandoning hope of return? Or better to hedge bets, let the house, come back in a few years' time? Or best of all to stay here regardless? Return in the autumn, to school and friends, this well-ordered life, whatever the costs? But what *is* the cost of any decision, not just in monetary terms, but in the price to be extracted from her and him?

Maybe Harry's right. Time for bigger change. Like the new coalition government voted in, on which Harry's pinned some hope. Though of course pundits immediately attacked with cynicism, predicting collapse and doom before the politicians even have a chance to start. Harry's waiting but mostly for her. And lately she's been thinking that if he can't radically change the course of his life, maybe she can alter hers, and maybe *that* will add to the sum of their happiness. Whatever the politics or economics of it all, he might be right: life might be easier in Poland. Certainly the children's language would improve and she'd work there more easily, though not until the children are ready. Christophe still can't dress himself properly and in Poland he wouldn't even start school for another year. And Harry, always working late, weekends, often on the road, would they see each other that much more in Poland? Haven't they already learned nothing's easy? Wherever you go, carrying on in life is difficult. Only the alternative is so poor.

Opening the oven, she sticks in a toothpick to see if the dough's done. The plums are bubbly hot, a few more minutes yet. No matter, she's gotten good at waiting too. Seeing life itself as a kaleidoscope, because there is no unified solution, more like a series of questions: what's best for her, for Harry, for marriage, for the children? Sometimes there doesn't even seem to be such a thing as the Holdens, no whole, everyone disparate individuals, every question producing varying, contradictory answers. Surely Harry's leaning towards a move, better for his career, but for her, having to begin again? The children definitely want to stay in England, familiarity of house, garden, friends. Of course they'd adapt and benefit from broadened horizons, but who can say that with certainty either? For her and Harry this would be another episode of middle age, a mid-life adventure. For the little ones it would be a complete re-making of their lives, a refashioning of identity. Is giving up on being English the right thing to do?

She stares outside, at the garden, the living world, as if it might hold out an answer. Surely it comes down to them, the children, whether they go to live in Poland or not. Whether she goes to work or not. Whether they stay or not. Isn't their welfare the overarching priority? And not in an obsequious pampering way, like so many adults giving kids too much say, too many choices, but in taking their needs into account as stewards of their lives. What kind of future *should* they have? Wisdom to know the difference – paramount – and exactly what makes parenting so difficult. Not the little tasks, tedious day-to-day responsibilities, but the weighty lot of decision-making over the course of a lifetime. Isn't that the essence of the role she's playing? And yet, if you can't finalise big decisions, you can at least accomplish the small stuff: bake a tart so the family has something good to eat.

She peeks in the oven. It's not obvious with a flat cake when it's done. It doesn't really rise, so you have to keep checking. Especially if the recipe's haphazard, flung together by memory, instinct, a bit of experience. Yet the small satisfaction of making time to do small things, making time to enjoy them, surely grows into something bigger. That's what makes children happy. Things that might make adults happy too, if they had the presence of mind. These essences of life, not things normally embarked on, like shopping or working overtime for holidays or trying to look or feel better, but things you *don't* usually make time for, like baking and reflecting and really listening. That's reverting to simplicity: creating a little space for peace.

Like Harry fetching Katya *and* Christophe who's finally finishing his first full day at school. She didn't have to tell Harry to hurry up, though he used to say, *nothing will happen if they have to wait.* She didn't have to remind him, *but it's a different kind of waiting than for you and me, it matters.* She no longer has to wield that hard-won mother's perspective, harking back to tears seen in boys left behind. Because he's started to learn it matters. It matters because he's living through it, while in a short time, David may not.

Yes, if they leave, they will lose all this: what they had. And no need to lose it. But maybe it's less complicated than that, less difficult than holding on. Maybe it's like the flat cake, coming out of the oven, the essence of life wherever you are. She sets it to cool on a rack. Because what is there if not the resumption of the order of things? Life, both a letting go and a repetition of life itself, wherever they are or will be, details that bore but also enrich, a dichotomy, of boredom and ecstasy, and however late she's been in discovering, surely it doesn't matter so long as she's seeing, perhaps fully for the first time.

From the cupboard she reaches for the plain white plates, but the blue china set above catches her eye. Cups and saucers and plates, all top shelf, unused in the cupboard for years. A wedding gift deemed too fragile, too formal, for daily use. She reaches for a cup, turns it over. *English fine bone china.* Even the words, so delicate. The golden rims, hand-painted lines. Why not? Why not today, for their family tea party? What's to wait for? Life's for living, stuff's for using. It doesn't get better than this. And setting the table, suddenly it comes in a wave: why Mamcia and Baba Kacia never seemed perturbed by the interminable washing and cleaning and cooking. Years passing by pretty much all the same. It wasn't because they found life so meaningful in repetition. It was because they hadn't been tempted by anything else: no china or catalogues of pretty house wares, no bigger houses down the street, no flashier cars or fancier holidays. One set of hideous spotted red tea cups – communism, that awful but great leveller – a kind of poverty that kept people sane. In the end the system didn't work, couldn't have worked, because every person has aspirations and must be able to command his own reward. If you twisted that, discouraged it, people lost the will to work. Selfishness went underground, took a seedier turn.

But at the same time there *had* been a limit to desire, and that limit, whether external or self-imposed, kept order in their lives. Under the communists, there were things one simply never dreamed of, things you'd never do, like visit tropical islands or fly in supersonic jets. Such things were out of reach permanently, one had a better chance of meeting a cosmonaut or even being one. And there were things they never thought they'd own: like convertibles or big houses with driveways, fancy clothes or the newest hat. But these things didn't matter because they had remained in the realm of fantasy, like the royal family, a lifestyle open to a select few who happened to be born that way, good fortune, or Hollywood stars who worked slavishly but with luck too, or TV lottery winners, pure luck with those windfalls, suddenly being able to access anything at all. But it was never a question of *everybody* having it all, of everyone being privy to anything and everything that they wanted. To this day, she couldn't convince Mamcia and Tato to fly away on holiday, not even to Venice, which they *had* dreamed of. Life just wasn't like that. Liberty was one thing, Venice another. They were actually happy in Cafe Fiore.

She folds the napkins, wedges them safely under each plate. Yet here, now – and what was more frightening, increasingly and everywhere – it never seemed to stop growing, this greed. Possibility itself had become reality, everything was sold as attainable: live like a rock star, dress like one, turn your face into one. Aspire, but if you can't get there, pretend! Surely that was what was making people miserable. Because the happiness of getting was never as big as the hole of wanting left behind. Life could never be about status or material goods or an unlined face staring back from the mirror. It had to be about how you viewed life essentially, and whether you were prepared to accept and be grateful for being here at all.

She stands back from the table set so properly. This is part of her job. And the essential problem was what to do about it every day. Because if a holiday can't make you happier, only energise you for a time, then what can? How to achieve the essence of *being*, daily, without wanting at all? An enormous balancing act of trying and succeeding, wanting and negating that want, of inevitably failing or at least suffering negative turns, but being satisfied in working at it – and for that to be its own satisfaction.

Not only attainment, but *acceptance*. A kind of letting go, not a taking – acceptance as a kind of negation. That beguiling and jewel-like thing so many want, but so few manage to turn away, for something even greater.

The children bang through the front door, Harry's voice telling them to go upstairs, get changed out of uniform. Familiar sounds. Shoes discarded, post slapped on the table, Katya and Christophe greeting Roobarb and Custard. Family life, a test of her time on earth. The children scoot upstairs, calling cats to follow, hopefully Harry will go up after them to supervise. But as she turns, he's in the doorway.

'Eva.'

She catches him in a freeze-frame, feeble smile as he glances at the cake.

'Eva, it's over. He's gone.'

∞

She takes a deep breath. There are a lot of people here. More than you'd expect.

But that's what happens when you know a person in only one way. In death, that person is suddenly transformed into a multiple of themselves: father, son, employer, old university friend. Neighbour, coach, gardener and champion swimmer. Former counsellor, volunteer, besides being handy with a hammer. All these facets coming out in death, as the entirety of a person's life is laid bare, and you have to sit and wonder, how did they manage it all, how did we not know? More importantly, how can the universe continue without this universe of a person in it? A person – the remnants of stars, chemicals for all time, the soul, a pocket of infinity within itself – how can infinity continue with a chunk taken out of it? Not only emotionally, but logically, mathematically, it's impossible.

You should have known.

But what? What could anyone have known about this particular death?

She'd been suspicious of Jenny's overly optimistic reports, a kind of internal rallying born of desperation, leaking out in a way fit for public consumption. But Harry, like David, had clung to his optimism to the end. Now she must keep watch on him, he's showing no emotion and that's more worrying than any outburst. She leans on him, cheek to shoulder, to remind him she is there, for the small warmth they might share through the stiffness of his suit.

She watches the room fill with David's colleagues, her stomach tightening and releasing, the only relief in having been able to leave Katya and Christophe at home with a babysitter. What can Sophie and James, who must be here, possibly be making of this show called a funeral? No one's making any noise except sniffling Jenny, sedated in the front row, the children between her and David's father, grey and bewildered and alone, as David's mother, long gone, has been spared the agony of an only son's premature death.

What has Jenny told her children? Not of death, but afterwards? Christophe and Katya had questions that couldn't be answered but which had to be addressed. So it turned into a discourse on angels. *You mean like the angels we pray to at night,* Christophe asked, and Katya argued, *no there are other ones, ours are guardian angels, but people who die become angels, right, Mama?*

So she made up a story. Just another story. Like so many in the Bible and like the fairy tales on their bookshelf, to explain some of the frightful things that happen in life and how circumstances might be changed. Or if not changed, how they can be accepted. But Christophe had cried and Katya too, so she reminded them that when people die they make room for new babies. *Is that really true, Mama,* and she said, *yes, it's true, it's sad but true,* though that may have only addressed the scientific demographics of it, a positive knock-on effect of death, not a reason for it. Christophe had kept crying, *but I don't want new babies, Mama, I don't want you to die, not Daddy either,* so eventually, they all got into bed together, the four of them, the whole Holden family and held each other for dear life, because what other kind of defence is there?

Then days moving in a blur, but slowly, a contradiction. Like walking through a bog in dense fog but every day recently has been ridiculously sunny. Now everyone here, numb with grief and fear and nerves, the whole place covered in riotous bouquets but shrouded in reverent black silence, the observance of the decor of death. She gives herself over completely.

Why couldn't you have waited?

Yes, you, God, what a cruel joker you've turned out to be.

Eva, you can't make deals on death. This isn't a TV show where participants set their price – what's your limit, what do you think you can get?

Anyway what would it have mattered? What's the significance of a few days or weeks? A life is lived. The time – your life span too – is short anyway. Why count the last days?

Okay, no counting. But surely, a few months, even years, until Sophie and James were older. That would have been kinder, more fair and just. Fathered until they were able to stand on their own feet, take care of themselves. Why them?

Why anyone? Age doesn't lessen pain. Unless you are very old, then you are tired perhaps, you might want to rest. But for everyone else, it always comes too soon. Even for the old, Baba Kasia, Miss Miriam.

We all feel the shortness of breath – in the end.

For the tears falling, her sobs and those of others, she only half hears the speeches, even the words Harry stands up to say. So futile, words. She catches bits of readings, abysmal, inadequate, not anyone's fault, words just don't convey anything, not at this point. The feeling of being disembodied is taking over, because it's strangely distant, this process of death, cremation. Even Adam's, the perfect negation of his creation, ashes to ashes. Of course they call it celebration of life nowadays instead of a funeral. More euphemism. But really without the sliding down, the final drop of the coffin, earth shovelled on top, without *burial*, it almost seems surreal. Practical, environmentally less wasteful, yes, and hardly any room taken up, but still some space must be allocated for death, so instead you have this cold sterile room adjacent to the crematorium, itself barely brightened by funereal arrangements, flowers themselves cut off in the prime of life. And then the symbolism must be inserted, a curtain closing before them, because finality must be conveyed. David, the body, being transported to another room to be charred, until nothing is left. But what of David, the soul?

Her head spins in the clouds of unknowing. She puts her hand on Harry's lap to ensure she's physically here. Burial, cremation, what difference does it make what happens to a body if you don't believe it will literally rise up? Maybe the disturbing thing is how cremation plays out later, as a private matter. Not in the East where you're called to witness vast burning pyres, but in the West, where the final moments are obscured, the ashes remain in one person's possession, hidden in an urn, no grave to visit. No public place of mourning, only a small vial and the memory of a life, or a vast place where particles were scattered. The nothingness after that.

Trapped in the pew, she feels her anger surfacing. Not for Jenny's choice, because no one will mourn David like Jenny and it is her choice to make, but against obliteration itself as an ending. And her anger's directed at Jana too, someone she doesn't even know, because until this moment she hadn't realised that she'd never forgiven Jana for whisking the rest of Adam away so completely. For turning him into a wisp of smoke and a lump of ashes that only she, Jana, could be privy to. For controlling what was left of Adam, shutting everyone else out.

But then didn't Adam defy his end anyway? Visiting her in dreams all those months, appearing to her in church at Easter? Embodied in a real person, it wasn't Adam, but surely it was him all the same. Not an apparition – she did have that conversation – but an embodiment of him who came before. Yes, the whole human chain, stretching back in births and deaths, to the very first man and woman, a connection of dead and living, speaking, words, those who were, as those who are, and those who will yet be.

The people are singing a last hymn. She can't focus on the lyrics for the word in her head.

Accept.

'Amen.'

The curtain retracts again.

David is gone, hidden forever. And soon he'll be gone in the form that they've known him.

New music begins, the guests rise. She tries to focus on the positive aspects of this cremation, the comforting words Tim might provide later in church, but it's too much. Rising revulsion at this thing called death, the thought of a burning body. That it's David, right now, Jenny's pillar and her strength, all these years, gone up in smoke, and Adam gone, all these people going down in their prime, the great loss for the young living left behind.

'Harry, please, excuse me.'

'You okay?' he whispers.

No time to answer.

Moving out of the end of the pew quickly, to the outside, to the open sky, where the air is fresher but clouds are moving in, fast, better walk, better run, gulp as much oxygen as possible. The area beyond the first trees, fine, never mind the clouds, the rain that's starting, right at the old oak, where no one can see.

The retching begins.

∞

'Where shall I move this?' she asks over her shoulder, but there is no answer.

She turns around. Jenny's on the floor staring at a box as if it were an abstract thing. She doesn't seem to know what to do with it.

'Jen?'

Jenny looks up, doesn't seem to register, shakes her head.

'Sorry, you were saying?'

'I'm sorry, let me,' she sets her own box aside, reaches over. 'Where do you want this?'

A box, another box and another box, the going pile, the staying pile, the most important mementoes to be moved, everything else will wait, for later. Later: a time when it all becomes clear.

'You know,' Jenny starts, 'not everyone thinks this is a good idea. Stay in your house at least a year, they say. Don't make any rash decisions.'

'Who's they?'

'They, you know, people,' she sighs but it's a flat sigh managed by pills she's taking to keep her steady for this, the long aftermath.

'The secretary at school, for instance.'

'The *secretary*?'

'I overheard her talking.'

'Jen, you're joking.'

'No, she was telling someone on the phone, oh, those poor children, to be uprooted, and...' Jenny trails off.

'Jenny, how dare she, what does she know!'

Jenny looks up at her perplexed. 'Well, she may have a point you know, they say...'

She interrupts. 'Jenny, it doesn't matter what anyone says. This is your life to manage. And if you think you should go stay with your mum and dad for the summer, leave right now in the middle of term, then it's no one's business but your own.'

Jenny sighs. 'Maybe you're right.'

'That secretary is such,' she pauses. 'A royal bitch.'

Jenny whoops a laugh. 'Eva!'

'Well, it's true,' she smiles, pleased she got Jenny to smile. It's been weeks.

'Smug bureaucratic snooty-nose, I should imagine she sends a voluntary contribution notice home to her own husband. I wouldn't worry what she says to anyone.'

Jenny's smile fades and falls back to serious, eyes welling. 'I thought people would be kind, but they *are* talking.'

'Yes, they will. What do you expect from some of them? It's all they can do – be negative, criticise – but I will defend you and how you've dealt with everything. No one has the right to judge. No one will say an ill word as long as I'm around.'

'Oh Eva,' Jenny holds out her arms like a small child.

She rushes to her, holds her friend, trying to squeeze out the hurt.

449

'I don't know how I'll manage without you,' Jenny mumbles, tears rolling from her eyes. 'You've been so good.'

'No, Jen, I'm not good. I only try. And really I don't know how I'll manage without *you*. You've done far more for me than the other way around.'

'We can say we're even,' Jenny wipes her cheek. 'We'll stay in touch.'

'As if there would be any doubt.'

'It might only be for the summer,' Jenny pauses again.

'I know, it's all up in the air,' she stands up again, not wanting to mention Harry's idea. She returns to the packing. 'Take your time, Jen, there's no hurry.'

'It's just that life,' she starts, voice quivering, 'without David, it doesn't make sense any more.' She tries to hold back tears.

'No, it doesn't – it can't make any sense – none of it. But it's early days, and for the children at least, we carry on.' Then adding quickly, 'and for yourself. For yourself, you have to, Jen. But in time you will also want to.'

Jenny looks up through watery eyes. 'I'll be okay,' but she sounds less than confident.

'Knowing you, how much is in your hands, your strengths, I know you will be okay. You'll find a way to make a new start.'

'But if I stay there, in Cornwall, I'll have lost you, my friends, my clients here, the garden centre will have to be sold, so many decisions, I feel like I'm running away.'

'You are and you're not. Think of it as hibernation, like a good sleep. Everyone needs to recharge now and then. You can do anything you like, but later. Not now.'

Jenny yawns.

'Why don't you take a nap? I'll finish up. Just this stacking here, isn't it? And that pile upstairs, the kids' clothes?'

'Yes,' Jenny replies, already on the sofa, resting her back, closing her eyes. 'I'm sorry, I'm just so tired…'

'Don't worry and please don't apologise. I can deal with this, I'm an expert in tidying up.'

She's been trying to stay as positive as she can, hiding her own frailties. Jenny seems to have drifted off already, sedatives not her thing but a necessity for now. She stands over her friend, strokes her hair for a minute, then turns and heads up the stairs, to the work that needs to be done.

∞

'What do you mean, it's *over*. So quickly?'

Harry laughs. 'This has all gone on long enough, wouldn't you say? If you ask me, it's been a long slog, and a total wipe-out.'

'I don't know…'

'Like the election a few weeks ago,' he continues. 'Though of course, with a new coalition government, all we can do is hope. For once I actually disagree with the cynics. You have to hope.'

He sighs but he doesn't seem aggravated or upset. After David, he doesn't seem upset by much.

'Anyway, it was all decided for us. They had too much evidence, nothing to negotiate even. They won. It would be risky for us to even challenge.'

'You mean Miss Miriam was crazy?' She hands him his tea.

'Not necessarily. But a nurse and doctor team made statements about seeing early signs of Alzheimer's. Worse, one of the witnesses couldn't definitively remember signing the will. Apparently, she too was losing it. So the weight of evidence was on their side.'

Harry takes his cup, rests himself next to her. 'Besides, they had their father's will, which legally stood up to within a month of Miriam's death, when she apparently tried to alter it. Charlie was adamant about the children getting the house, her last minute move looked peculiar.'

He's drinking his tea slowly, savouring it, sets the cup down half full.

'And it's not like you were up for a protracted battle, or me, frankly. Months and a lot of money for the possibility of a win but more likely a loss.'

'So we've stepped out of a contest that we were likely to lose anyway.'

'Something like,' Harry pauses. 'Or we can look at it the way you did. You were right, you know. You can't lose something that isn't really yours.'

He signals for her to come over and she does. She sits on his lap like she used to, so very long ago.

'So what you mean is,' she smiles, 'sometimes you get more than you put in, sometimes less. Sometimes you get something in return that seems free but isn't, it's something you earned or were owed anyway. And sometimes it doesn't really matter.'

She's about to add – and to see all that you have to get past greed – but Harry laughs, a new kind of laugh, tentative but earnest.

'Something like,' he turns serious, stops caressing her legs. 'But I do have something to ask you,' he pauses. 'About Tilly.'

She looks him in the eye, nervous.

'Eva, did you actually try to give Tilly your engagement ring?'

She clears her throat, instinctively moving to his cup. Seeing it's done, she gets up to set it in the sink.

'No, don't run away, look at me. I'm not angry,' he looks incredulous. 'Just really confused.' He coughs, and she can hear it in his mind, *as usual.*

'I thought it belonged to her. A family heirloom. That she always wanted it.'

'But did it make no difference that I gave it to you?' He's more bemused now.

'Yes, but I was trying to let go, you know, in that moment when I felt we could be free, especially of anything that might be holding me – or us – back, from happiness. I suppose it doesn't make sense now. But I thought it would make her happy, and she seemed more interested in…'

'Yes, she would have been, though in this case, thank god she had the sense to refuse it. Eva, you don't know everything about Tilly,' he breathes a deep sigh.

'I never told you this before because it was way before us, but Tilly incurred quite a few debts even as a teenager. She sold some of Mummy's things. That's why the ring was never willed to her.'

She sucks in her breath. 'Oh,' pausing, 'What kind of debts?'

'The tens-of-thousands kind, and later, a kind of compulsive spending after Mummy and Daddy died, right on into marriage with Steve. That's partly why I worked so bloody hard, not just the house for a while or my parents' debts or wanting the best for us, but Tilly. I guess I thought family unity. She'd gotten herself into a real mess and Steve refused to help.'

'But why didn't you tell me?' She looks down at her half-drunk tea, wondering if she even has the right to ask that question.

'Eva,' Harry says insistently. 'Look at me. I didn't tell you because I thought it was my problem, or really, Tilly's. And that it was in the past. I stopped helping her a while ago, when Nathan came on the scene. Now I'm telling you because I don't want you to think I minded your generosity, even if it is,' he smiles, 'apt to take strange forms. But I certainly don't want Tilly pawning any more heirlooms, and I don't want you to fall afoul of – if she falls back into her ways.'

'You mean worse than she is now?' It slips out before she can stop it.

Harry laughs. 'Yes. I've washed my hands of her troubles mostly. She's my sister, but she is an adult, and I feel we have enough on our plates.'

He pauses. 'You know it's back to Poland for me, for a little while longer, I have to keep my job. But in a few weeks you'll come out, we'll have the summer together, and then we'll need to decide where we will live. Here or there.'

'I know. There's a lot we still need to resolve.'

She looks at her drink again, spills it away. Nothing seems to sit well these days, not Assam, not green, not even bland chamomile.

'Whatever we decide, it'll be okay,' Harry says, more with hope than certainty.

'Yes, it will be okay,' she echoes, then more firmly, 'it will be okay.'

Having heard it before from him, she never paid the phrase much attention. But now she repeats it *okay, okay, okay* in her mind. That one word seems to have taken on a whole new meaning.

∞

At this point she'd really rather lie down, but the children are waiting for their story, so she makes her way upstairs. Exhaustion like a fixture these days, persistent churning, everything crowded out by the sadness for Jenny. But there will always be the sadness of Jenny, in the same way there will always be a sadness for Adam and his little Eva and even their unborn baby. The baby that for years didn't exist except as a figment of imagination, but which now appears more and more in dream, not as a recrimination from Adam, but out of the blue, a deep, cloudless blue, a form of hope and purity in the sky. She reaches their room, knows exactly what they'll read.

'Come here you two, you've been so patient waiting. A new story for tonight, I'm sure you'll like this one.'

They huddle together on the bed, and she opens the one about Lulu – oh, it's all about Lulu – a stroppy toddler who's having a very bad day. And it's a very, very bad day. No one can make it better when you're feeling that foul. Even Daddy's suggestion to go round a museum can't cheer Lulu, she baulks as soon as they arrive. So Daddy takes baby brother Willy and walks off with Mummy, leaving her sulking on a sofa in the first gallery. But there isn't time to pout for very long, because suddenly Lulu's told off quite sternly by some cherubs hovering in a painting above her head. It's astonishing, being told off by angels, but Lulu's enchanted as she's whisked away on a flying adventure through Brueghels and Rousseaus and Dutch still-lifes. She flies all around the museum with these mischievous two angels, through landscapes of every kind, until they realise they're all quite lost. Luckily an elderly museum attendant takes the time to listen to their stories and helps look after them while waiting for her missing parents to turn up. The attendant shakes his head knowingly as Lulu's daddy appears: Lulu's still in the grip of her great adventure, recounting tales of flying babies. Her father nods, because it's just a figment of her imagination, this whole adventure. But actually it *isn't*, you see? It really isn't! Because after Lulu and her family leave, the attendant winks and escorts the cherubs back to their paintings. And in earnest he listens to their stories too.

'Mama! I wish I could go with flying babies! Could we go to a museum like that?' asks Christophe.

'Don't you think it was only her imagination?'

'No,' Christophe says sagely, 'even the museum man could see the babies with wings.'

'But was it real? Or is it about being open to the chance of something fantastic happening?'

'Real,' Christophe says.

'But it was fantastic,' Katya says.

'But you mustn't go about in cross patch moods all the time,' Christophe adds.

'She was quite naughty at the start, wasn't she,' Katya grins.

'Then she saw the flying babies and they cheered her right up!' Christophe jumps in.

'Probably, they were guardian angels,' Katya says, then yawns.

'Yes, yes, they probably were,' she yawns too. 'But now, it's time to go to sleep. Come on, let's tuck you in.'

She comes to them each in turn, Christophe first, then Katya, saying the angel prayer as reverently as she can ever remember saying it:

> Angel of mine, protector of mine,
> In the morning, noon and night,
> Be there to assist me.
> With a candle show the light,
> And envelop with your wings
> Guide me from all evil things
> Lead me to a life divine.

'Okay, I'm sleepy now,' Katya says.

'That's good, I am too. I don't know why I'm so tired all the time.'

'Because you're a mama.'

'I suppose that's it. Being a mama is tiring,' she smiles and gives her another hug.

Walking down the corridor towards her room, the thought comes quickly – well, they *do* recognise her, appreciate her. And another day has come to its fantastic conclusion, peacefully, uneventfully, the way so many people in the world must wish for. She is truly lucky. How did she ever not see it? Hopefully they'll all dream of cherubs tonight.

∞

Straight from school to the park, a week of bright days, a change of clothes and snacks packed, lots of lemonade, which they all seem to be craving, the children already racing ahead. She's hiding behind big sunglasses, not for sun but to cover the tears that seem to come and go uncontrollably these days. She doesn't want to have to explain that actually she's like glass, transparent and breakable, but sturdy too, in a way you can build on.

She takes a place on an empty bench, grateful there are friends for Christophe and Katya to play with but no one she has to engage in conversation. Sitting very still, she wills every ray of June sun on to her skin. Jenny, now gone with Sophie and James, a leave of absence, as she called it, because normal life here wasn't possible. Jenny was right, because sadly she too overheard mothers tsking, *not good, children need school as a distraction, you need stability after death.* But really, who knows what other people need? So she'd marched over and said: *never mind what you think others need. Maybe standing at the edge of the Cornish coast staring into the sea is as good a way as any to deal with death.* She too had no business prying, could or should have said nothing. But she defended Jenny, as promised, then walked away.

And walking away, or saying nothing is another option to fighting. Today she's choosing to sit alone. A kind of letting go, not a giving up, but a way of going around: finding peace without words. The sandpit's full, and the paddling pool too, as some bright spark at the local council took it upon himself to open the pool early. Unbelievable, responding to weather instead of regulations – bureaucrats letting go! – it's as though the whole world's filled with possibility.

She leans into the baby bag, the one that used to carry bottles and nappies but now swimsuits and snacks, and lays out their picnic blanket nearby. Christophe and Katya are playing on the climbing frame. Soon they'll come racing back to change into swimsuits or beg for money, the ice cream truck tinkling in the background. She watches the park, mothers and young children, a world of its own. Everyone seems happy. Though they also seem less happy than they used to be, as if while her back was turned, their lives had been transposed, and their responsibilities and households had taken a toll on them. But maybe that's why they're all in the park. Maybe their boredoms have to be spiced with temporary excitements, maybe they too claim secret Xaviers. Or maybe she'd always exaggerated their happiness. Maybe all of them had always been together, locked in a dance of pretence, false flatteries exchanged as a way of lifting spirits, because none of them – none of them – were really soaring. But then, they were part pillars of their families. What could bring more satisfaction than taking a break from holding it up, going for a sit in the sun, children healthy and carefree?

She shuts her eyes behind her glasses, hoping for a rest, but the phone rings.

'So, how are you today, love?' Harry says tenderly.

'Fine, a beautiful day, we're in the park. They've even opened the pool. What more could you ask for?' She smiles though he won't see it. But maybe he'll feel it.

'Sounds marvellous, and here I am, stuck in windy Berlin. Listen, I want to check a couple of things with you. First, tickets to Warsaw, done, you're out two weeks on Friday. Which is also your birthday, so is there anything special you want to do? Any wishes? You know I'm rubbish at conjuring up gifts.'

'No you're not,' she retorts. 'The earrings!'

'Okay, but I can't do those every time,' Harry protests.

'No, I didn't mean that,' she says, 'I mean, you have good taste.'

'Of course, I picked you.'

She laughs.

'Well?'

'No, nothing.'

'Really? Nothing special for that Friday?'

'No, I want nothing.'

'I have to do or get you something.'

'No, absolutely nothing! I don't want a thing. Don't you even dare!'

'How about dinner? It'll have to be with the kids though, I can't see them wanting to stay with a babysitter the minute they arrive.'

'Dinner's fine, we'll all celebrate. Though to be honest, I don't know what's wrong with me lately, nothing seems to sit well and this unease seems to have been going on for ages.'

'David,' Harry's voice drops.

'No, well, maybe stress is having an effect,' she pauses. 'But I promise you, no mystery pains, more of an overwhelming fatigue. I'm tired, Harry, sometimes I feel upset too, other times strangely serene. Anyway, I'm glad the school year's coming to an end, probably more than the kids.'

'Make sure you eat and keep up your weight,' Harry says.

'I don't know why I'm so apprehensive. We still have the big decision looming, and usually I do get reflective around my birthday, but I can't put my finger on it. I mean, who cares about forty-two?'

'There's a school of thought that says forty-two is all there is.'

'What do you mean?'

Harry chuckles. 'It's only a book. Cult English fiction from the last century, you wouldn't have read it back in Poland, I suppose. There's this giant computer called Deep Thought and it's supposed to calculate the definitive answer to life, the universe, everything. And it comes up with forty-two.'

'Forty-two? I don't understand.'

'I didn't think you would.'

'But you do?'

'No, it's just fiction. The point is that humans were created to wonder. Who knows what the answer is. When we come across it we probably won't accept it anyway. Or we won't understand it. It's beyond us. Anyway, that's the book's take on it, or my take on the book, but I don't spend nearly as much time as you pondering it. I accept life for what it is. Absurd.'

'I think that too, with some caveats.'

'Like what?'

'Like life's also beautiful and fun and incredibly difficult.'

Harry laughs. 'A contradiction. I'll give you that, but forget the hardships, enjoy the afternoon. I have to go. Remember – only a couple weeks.'

'Until forty-two or being together? Or until perfect satisfaction, the meaning of life, or something else?'

'Until everything!' And he says it with such glee she can't help but feel happy, even if it is the start of another countdown.

Satisfaction fleeting, Harry hurrying to hang up, she feels the sun beating down, the park absorbing every ray. The daffodils are long gone but in their place is dense grass, the breath of trees. How instead of *everything* did Sartre conclude *nothing* at all this? Life isn't at all a revulsion but a premonition, a recognition of being. And it could be that Harry's right again – more right than he's ever been in his life – what if the meaning of life is simply forty-two? Or forty-three? Or simply being and accepting absurdity while trying to make a go of it anyway? Not nothing, but everything. Every number and infinity, not even as a number but a symbol. An idea hidden behind a word, forever obscured but always worth fighting for.

Funny, these English. They always seem to have a book or fact or statistic to back up what they're talking about. And yet, if you started from scratch, you'd be none the wiser. All knowledge brings us back to the principal recognition: that we don't know very much.

∞

She'd like to think it was her imagination but the symptoms have been too real. She knows before she's told anyway. The little stick reveals the double line: pregnant!

Pregnant, and a few days short of forty-two! How long has it been? Quick, calculations – life's full of countdowns, not all bad. She must count back the days to when Harry was home. How many days since her last period? His leave of absence, the waiting for David, all the nights they held each other tight, sometime in that waiting for death, new life was created. Even at the funeral, the extreme nausea may have been it. Yes, then the tiredness, the crying jags, nothing settling since. With real stress to make a period late, no wonder she didn't notice. But honestly, how could anyone miss such a thing?

You should have known.

No way. She stares at the blue stick, no longer startled by the reality as surprised at how long it may have been already. Her hand moves to her belly instinctively. My god, more than a seed now, on the way to another child!

A miracle, Eva, a miracle!

Miracle? More like mistake! What the hell are you thinking? Imagine the age difference, starting over, are you nuts?

Oh yes, Noisette, absolutely bonkers. A third one!

Something must've gone wrong with the coil. Oh god, the coil!

Gone, you threw off your mortal coil and now you have it – another infinity inside you.

Wait, hold on, you've got to get to a doctor, they must check for the coil, check on the baby.

A baby, better hope one, not two…

Twins? No, no! Anyway Mamcia says you're not likely to have twins if you're craving fruit, lemonade and eating grapes like they're going out of fashion…

Never mind grapes, your diet! You have to start with folic acid!

Wait, think of the risks. Remember Magda? When you told her you'd like a baby sooner or later, and she said, Eva, you are later. You were in your thirties then, what can happen at forty-two?

Come on, this is fate. And such luck! So many women trying for their first, but here you are on your third! An old hand, you'll be fine.

You'll be old, alright. That's the only certainty. You didn't choose, it might not be fine. Don't fool yourself with silly trends having children so late. Enormous risks to the baby.

The baby. Oh, the sleepless nights. The fatigue. Those endless black days. Are you really ready for another round?

Oh god, what if there is post partum again?

Do you even want this? Really? What if Harry can't help? What if he doesn't want another child?

Oh god, Harry. What will he say?

∞

She rifles through the washing basket, separating lights from darks. Incredible that four people generate so much washing, never mind a fifth on the way. But of course Harry's away, so it's only three at home now, but once they're altogether with Harry and onesies changed two, three, four times a day…

No, no counting. Or only if Harry concedes. Though really she's begun to make peace with it already. Because numbers may not be set in stone but they offer a kind of reassuring permanence. Due date: January 14, the old Orthodox New Year. Falling right between the disputed dates of Epiphany: January 6 for Western churches, the celebrated presentation of Christ to the Magi, and January 19, for Eastern churches, Christ's baptism in the Jordan. Of course it's silliness and superstition, all this counting, but even without Harry's knowledge, there's that persistent feeling – *accept what cannot be changed.* If you let it, acceptance becomes peace. It breaks through fear like a laser clear light.

All set, doctors said. Although they looked at her strangely and she could tell what they were thinking because it's what she was thinking too – at this age? After your ordeals? But *you're lucky*, they said. *Lucky* – not unlucky. Lucky to have survived meningitis with no lasting scars, lucky to be having a baby instead of residual infection from a malfunctioning coil. But what's luckier, having an infection that would go away or a child you weren't planning to have? Because when the giddiness subsides, the fear is immense. A baby was definitely *not* in the Plan, and it's frightening to think of starting over, creating again. Then the spectre of post-partum, the dark nights, the crying, the many more years until a single day can be reclaimed. Oh god, no – not starting over.

She carries on sorting. Then again, what's so *unlucky* about an unplanned baby at this stage? She might have had more free time, gone back to work, but now she won't. That won't be possible, she'll have to adjust. She stands still for a moment, trying to drive the nausea away. The sickness seems to recede around lunchtime only to seize her whole being in the evening.

Still it's exciting having this secret, because she's waiting to tell Harry in person, face to face. So there will be no mistake about what he wants, what they should do, how they'll build a new life together. After all that's happened, no more running away. We accept. Then together they can battle the blackness.

She picks up the basket to carry it to the washing machine, sees the children's uniforms are missing. They must've been left on the floor in the bedroom. They don't see or hear her approaching so she lingers for a moment behind the half-open door, catching them in make-believe. Another moment to be savoured, a snapshot, a precious gift, but then she hears Katya.

'The cream-ation will be tomorrow.'

'But then Pookie will come to life,' Christophe's voice questioning, hopeful.

'No, he doesn't,' Katya replies firmly. 'It's like Sophie and James's daddy, he's going forever.'

'I don't want to play this game!' Christophe says angrily.

She wants to interject but has no idea what to say. Is it right to offer solace?

Then Katya. 'He has to die to make room for all the new babies.'

'But I don't want any new babies!'

From behind the door, she sucks in her breath noiselessly, holds it. Her heart's stopped, waiting for a response.

'Oh you'll see, it'll be okay,' Katya continues soothingly. 'The new baby will be cute, and it'll keep us very busy, being naughty and poopy and hungry, like Lottie's sister, and we'll keep remembering Pookie because he'll be an angel, flying over here. You'll see. It'll be okay.'

A sudden change in his voice, Christophe says, 'Pookie will be lucky because he can fly!'

'Yes and here's the baby,' Katya says solemnly, producing a long forgotten little bear. 'See?' she hugs the bear, 'Now what do we call him?'

'Baby Pooks!' Christophe shouts.

She grips the door frame, hiding, face streaming with tears. She had all but forgotten, keeping the secret from Harry, what about them?

∞

She rolls the last T-shirt into the bag. Packing for the next experiment, but what to take with you? Especially when soon her belly will push against every waistband. All of her pregnancies seem to be less of a gradual blossoming than an overnight determination to get as large as possible. A few loose dresses will do, some wedge sandals, she folds the things neatly, shuts the cases, heaves them downstairs.

Last glance at the family room, at least until they're back in August. Though who knows what decision will be made by then. This could be the beginning of a permanent moving on. She draws the curtains half-closed, the way you're supposed to when you leave. Signal to the outside world you're neither in nor out.

She shuts the door and straps Katya and Christophe into their seats. The driver's the same one who takes Harry but it's impossible to make conversation when every bump and twist in the road threatens to make you vomit. They drive down the road, developers already at Miss Miriam's house. Tearing it down, smashing foundations, nothing will ever be the same. But it never is. In their family too, Christophe will become the middle child. A wayward middle child like her? Or can she keep him close even if he must be reshuffled in the revised order of things? Surely it's how you manage the transition that makes all the difference.

She chews gum furiously to keep the churning at bay, like she's had to do with every pregnancy. Arriving at the terminal, a day of motion, everything pressing forward, another day that's a blur, this last day of her secret, through passport queues and security, setting up camp by enormous windows to wait and watch the planes, she and her tidy experienced team of small travellers. Soon that will fall apart. Or rather, it'll begin again, the messy expanse of the newborn: the pushchair and nappies, bottles and spare clothes and snacks. All the weighty paraphernalia for the fragility of one little life, which will shout uncooperatively and make every day a challenge but also pure joy.

The unborn variable, and yes, all that responsibility. But first a name, David, if it's a boy. But if it's a girl, it will have to be hope: Nadia. Because that's all we have in a world of madness and absurdity, and hope can be faith too, if you hold on long enough to get there. That's what she'll tell all of them, as her giddiness returns, the incredulity, appreciation, thankfulness, in the vision of nearly getting there. Soft round toes, tufts of newborn black hair, little fingers wrapped around a bigger one. First steps and words, another life. It's almost enough to banish the darkness. If you can just hold on long enough.

Yes, soon Harry's face and the reaction of her family, Mamcia who'll undoubtedly say, *see we told you good comes in threes.* But of course, that's true of any number, maybe even forty-two, and Piotr will be pleased, saying *I knew you'd catch me up,* and Magda will be concerned for her age, but Tato will wink and say, *never mind, there's technology these days.* Or maybe, suspecting it was an accident, like the existence of our own universe amid so many others, that multiverse system that so fascinates him now, he'll say, *what else could you do but accept, Eva. Even the multiverse theory, in the end, requires you just believe.* Then she'll go visit Baba Kacia and tell her the good news too. But only if Harry's pleased first.

She hasn't seen the flat since he moved in so many months ago. Maybe he's done something to it, though probably not. He told her he put up blinds instead of curtains, joking *I'd rather not go through all that again.*

Planes taking off one by one, and now the call for their destination: Warsaw. No more time to worry, she grabs their stuff, presses forward. Children running down the tunnel, a short flight anyway, three hours, but it helps to get on first when you're tired. Excitement and exhaustion give way quickly to the drone of engines, the white sifting past. No panic this time, only children's chatter, then quiet as they fall asleep.

She must have slept too. Her eyes still feel heavy as she opens them, the plane's already tilting downwards, the funny pull on the tummy, a jolt of wheels as they touch down. Stiff joints, the mayhem and crush of disembarking. They mustn't forget Baby Pooks or anyone, searching for bags on the carousel, emerging to the waiting area.

Harry is there.

Clearly just in from somewhere himself, he's in his travelling outfit, his favourite wrinkled jacket, his broken Churches. The shoes she used to scold him for, *don't partners dress better when they travel?* But he shrugged it off. *Who's more comfortable, me or them? The journey is for you only.*

'Hey there!' he practically shouts, obviously excited too.

'Daddy, Daddy, Daddy!' The children launch themselves at him.

'Look, Daddy, Pookie's come and Baby Pooks! It's his first time on an aeroplane, but he really liked it!' Christophe gets in first.

She smiles. Maybe she won't have to worry about him after all.

'And see, I brought Snowy,' Katya says.

'And you brought Mama too, well done!' Harry says cheerfully. *Yes, and someone else, but you'll find out soon.*

'Happy birthday, love. Oh, happy birthday! Yes, happy birthday, Mama!' They're all talking at once, moving to get to the driver who's waiting outside. She slips in another piece of gum.

The children keep up the chatter in the car, vying for Harry's attention as she sits quietly, chewing determinedly the whole way to the flat. Then the thrill of the lift, the children shouting, *weeeee*, bags carried in and Christophe and Katya scampering off to explore.

She looks at Harry. He can sense something's up. He's hovering, and she's like a cat ready to spring.

'What's with the gum chewing?' he teases.

But before she can answer, he says, 'You're not,' then pauses, 'Are you?'

'I am.'

His face crumples and for a moment, oh god, not anger please, not disappointment, please don't say abort. But his eyes well with tears, his lip quivers, then he swallows, reasserts himself. He doesn't say anything, just comes to her, embraces her.

'I was afraid you'd be upset,' she says, burying her face. 'It wasn't part of the plan.'

'Not the Plan or any plan, but we can make a new one can't we?' he clears his throat. 'I mean, no plan, just living.'

She looks him in the eye. 'So you're okay with it?'

'More than okay,' he says. 'Maybe it's what we need.'

'Not want, but need?'

'Maybe, who knows. Wow. Literally a birthday surprise. Life's a real experiment isn't it? Trial and error, sometimes a great success,' he pauses. 'I promise, Eva, this time it will be okay.'

When he says that, she can't help crying. The tears roll fast and hard. Because if there's one thing Harry does well, it's stick to his word. But that's when he's in control, and they both know they're not. There's no such thing as a promise to succeed.

But maybe it won't be like before, all the dark nights and solitude, all the times he never knew. Maybe it will be okay. Not ideal, but okay.

'The great and glorious masterpiece of man
is how to live with a purpose.'

Montaigne

SELECT BIBLIOGRAPHY
AND FURTHER READING

Although novels rarely conclude with a bibliography, some do provide further reading lists, so I decided to share with readers the books that influenced me as I wrote *Forty One*. Some of these works I read many times, while others I drew from only scantily for details, references or research. In a few instances, I discovered the books long after I'd conceived and written *Forty One*, even as I was making final changes. However big or small the contribution, I included those writings which I think are most worthy of an interested reader's time:

Adult Non-Fiction:

Applebaum, Anne, *Iron Curtain, The Crushing of Eastern Europe, 1944–56* (London, 2013)

Armstrong, Karen, *The Case for God*, (London, 2010)

Foley, Michael, *The Age of Absurdity, Why Modern Life Makes it Hard to be Happy*, (London, 2010)

James, Oliver, *Affluenza*, (London, 2007)

Lightman, Alan, *The Accidental Universe, The World You Thought You Knew*, (London, 2014)

Milosz, Czeslaw, *To Begin Where I Am*, (New York, 2001)

Pausch, Randy, *The Last Lecture*, (New York, 2008)

Perel, Esther, *Mating in Captivity, Unlocking Erotic Intelligence* (New York, 2006)

Peston, Robert, and Laurence Knight, *How Do We Fix This Mess? The Economic Price of Having it All and the Route to Lasting Prosperity*, (London, 2012)

Pirsig, Robert, *Lila, An Inquiry into Morals* (London, 1992)

Sartre, John Paul, *Being and Nothingness*, (New York, 1966)

Wilson, Edmund O., *The Meaning of Human Existence*, (New York, 2014)

Zamoyski, Adam, *Poland*, (London, 2009)

Adult Fiction:

Adams, Douglas, *The Restaurant at the End of the Universe*, sequel to *Hitch Hiker's Guide to the Galaxy*, (London, 1980)

Beard, Richard, *Lazarus is Dead*, (London, 2011)

Bradbury, Ray, 'A Sound of Thunder', *Colliers*, (USA, 1952)

Greene, Graham, *The End of the Affair*, (London, 1951)

Hesse, Hermann, *Steppenwolf*, (Frankfurt, 1929)

Lawrence, D. H. *Lady Chatterly's Lover*, (London, 1928) and *A Propos of Lady Chatterly's Lover*, (London, 1930), as found in the edition London, 2006

Sartre, John Paul, *Nausea*, (Paris, 1938 and London, 1963)

Sartre, John Paul, *The Reprieve*, (New York, 1972)

Tolstoy, Leo, *The Death of Ivan Ilyich & Confession*, translation by Peter Carson, (London, 2014)

Tolstoy, Leo, *Family Happiness*, a collection of stories, (New York, 2009)

Woolf, Virginia, *Mrs Dalloway*, (London, 1925)

Children's Fiction:

Burton, Virginia Lee, *The Little House*, (New York, 1942)

Flack, Marjorie and Wiese, Kurt, *The Story About Ping*, (New York, 1977)

Jeffers, Oliver, *How to Catch a Star*, (London, 2004)

Simmonds, Posy, *Lulu and the Flying Babies,* (London, 1991)

Poetry:

Szymborska, Wislawa, *View with a Grain of Sand*, (London, 1995)

For more information about *Forty One* please visit www.lesiadaria.com